Licked by the Flame

Licked by the Flame

A Forbidden Realm Novel

SERENA GILLEY

FOREVER
YOURS

New York Boston

Forever Yours
Hachette Book Group
1290 Avenue of the Americas
New York, NY 10104
www.hachettebookgroup.com
www.twitter.com/foreverromance

First published as an ebook and as a print on demand edition: July 2015

Forever Yours is an imprint of Grand Central Publishing.
The Forever Yours name and logo are trademarks of Hachette Book Group, Inc.

The publisher is not responsible for websites (or their content) that are not owned by the publisher.

The Hachette Speakers Bureau provides a wide range of authors for speaking events. To find out more, go to www.hachettespeakersbureau.com or call (866) 376-6591.

ISBN: 978-1-4555-8450-5 (ebook edition)
ISBN: 978-1-4555-8458-1 (print on demand edition)

Dedicated to the hottest, most magical group of writers I know. Thank you, my Sorry Wenches, for all the hours of support, brainstorming, and creative dragon taming.

Licked by the Flame

Chapter One

Nicolai Stefanya Vladik paced the length of the boardroom and wished in his very core there was a window in this damn place. It was not in his nature to be cooped up in these constructions, human boxes made of plastic and wood, substances that would wither and melt into a wisp of smoke at the very least hint of fire. It was a tenuous way to exist. No wonder humans were so short lived—they spent so much of their time in these fragile spaces.

It was a damned shame that Nicolai had so little opportunity to get back to his own familiar lair. He'd been here, on this jobsite, for months now. Several years before that he'd begun acting as one of them, studying, scheming, and manipulating them in this role he'd created. It was all to keep the humans in their place. To make very certain they never found what they searched for so diligently.

He'd done it all for the good of his kind, for the future of his clan. He was a warrior, after all, and this was his battle. It had been waging so long, however, that every now and then he worried he'd forgotten who he was. He feared he'd become too comfortable in this flimsy form.

Today was *not* one of those times. Today he itched to abandon it all. Clothing, technology, shallow entertainments…all of them were so frail, so meaningless. If he feared anything today, it was that he would discard the trappings of this human existence and give in to his nature. He longed for the heat of his lair.

For a year this team had been studying the thermal activities of the area, and Nic risked more than personal exposure if he abandoned his human form. Day after day, month after month, though, it was becoming harder to maintain. He craved…well, he craved something he could not have.

He needed to get his mind back on his work. This meeting today with a dozen so-called experts in their fields was a waste. None of these "learned" humans really knew anything. Of course he ought to be glad for that, but he was tired of the isolation and routine this situation required. He was exhausted from denying his needs.

And he did have needs. It was always this way if he let himself go too long without. He would have to do what must be done if he wanted to continue in his role.

The question, of course, was how. Even as the meeting droned on, as the men around him talked about projects and statistics and governmental regulations, he could wonder only how he would tend to his needs. This site inspection, after all, was scheduled to go on for another two weeks. In the middle of nowhere. Nic didn't dare leave at this critical time, but he also couldn't figure how to manage his problem.

He needed a woman. Badly. By the Fires, he thought he could almost smell one, feel her very real presence just beyond his carefully calm exterior. His skin tingled on alert. It was as if the air in the building crackled with the hot essence of woman. She smelled like heat and flesh and the promise of passion. Damn, but his situation must be worse than he'd thought; he knew only men had been assigned to this remote project site.

If he didn't sink himself into warm female flesh soon, he was likely to explode. And this was not just the wishful thinking of the usual frustrated human male. No, this was serious. If Nic thought he might be about to explode, everyone here had good reason to worry. Once his control was lost and he shed this human facade, the truth would be known. He would have to silence them all to keep his secret safe. Nic wasn't just any sex-crazed mortal man, after all.

Nicolai Vladik was a full-fledged dragon.

* * *

She was a woman and there was no way to hide it. Lianne McGowan didn't generally notice when she was the only female on a given project, or in a department, or perhaps even the only one assigned to any particular building. She was oddly aware, however, that as of her arrival at this jobsite today, she was the only female for a good hundred miles. Or more, maybe.

Iceland, as it turned out, was overflowing with volcanoes and geothermal hot spots. Not so much civilization. And certainly not privileged American women sent out to the frozen wastelands to represent their daddies' interests around a bunch of men with letters after their names.

She was getting used to making her way in a man's world, though. It meant she had to convey the point right away that she was confident in her role here and wasn't going to let anyone push her around. Also she wasn't going to let any of them think she wasn't just as tough and as determined as they were. Geo-Diagnostics had sent her here with one goal: the project had been lagging and she was supposed to get these guys back on the ball. The higher-ups needed to see some results if they were going to keep the investors happy.

Lianne was here to get those results. It was as simple as that. Her father had been grooming her for this job and she knew how to do it. Twelve men or a hundred men weren't going to distract her. She was ready for whatever attitude problems or temper tantrums they were going to throw at her. This little modular building on the side of the volcano they were studying wouldn't know what hit it.

She didn't bother to knock but pushed the boardroom door open and stood there for a minute, letting the group inside figure out that something in their little world had just changed. It gave her a minute to look them over, too. First impressions were important on both sides.

A few of the guys she recognized, having worked with them at other sites before. Mr. Casper she knew from way back, and Mr. Blanchard sitting at the head of the table with his usual smug expression made her want to roll her eyes. The other men looked like every geologist, engineer, and technical geek she'd gotten used to working with. No surprises here. Except…one guy was pacing at the back of the room.

Wow. He was not like the others. He paused in his pacing to stare at her, silver-blue eyes practically throwing sparks against exotic bronze skin. His gaze stalked her, wild and ferocious as a caged animal. No, he wasn't like the other ones. Not at all.

The smile he gave her wasn't like the usual patronizing smiles she got, either. His lips curled like he'd been starved for a week and was just handed a plate of lasagna. She'd never really wanted to be lasagna before, but for half a second she was ready to slather on some parmesan cheese and tell the man dinner was served.

The insanity lasted only a heartbeat, though. After a quick draw of breath and some rapid internal scolding, she grabbed control of herself and managed to take her eyes off him. It wasn't easy, but she knew better than to get carried away by a pretty face and a pair of ungodly wide shoulders. Any man who looked like that most likely knew he looked like that. Which meant he was probably an asshole.

She'd had enough assholes for a lifetime.

"Hello, gentlemen," she said, enjoying her moment of authority before they all started trying to assert their male dominance. "I'm not sure what you're up to right now, but I'm here to tell you vacation time is over."

She heard one of the computer techs mutter her name under his breath. That could be good, or that could be bad.

"For those of you who don't know me," *like the steaming-hot asshole with the silver eyes in the back of the room,* "I'm Lianne McGowan. I've been sent here to hold your little hands and dig through your procedures to figure out why we've got lots and lots of data here, but no usable information. Any questions?"

The men glanced back and forth between each other. She noted a couple of raised eyebrows. One of the computer geeks leaned in to his buddy and whispered something. They both snorted and tried to hide dopey schoolgirl giggles. Idiots.

This was where she either gained them or lost them, right here when these pubescent juveniles tested her. It happened at least once on every site. Sooner or later, they always wanted to see what she was made of.

So, she'd have to show them. They'd better not let her damn freckles or the fact that she wore a bra confuse them into thinking they could push her around. She knew exactly what she was doing and, whether it threatened their collective manhood or not, she was in charge. She nailed the giggling techs with an angry-schoolteacher glare.

"You two have a question?"

They shook their heads frantically. She was not about to let them off so easily.

"It sounded to me like you had a question. Did anyone else happen to hear what these two boys were mumbling about?"

Peer pressure was a wonderful thing. She loved to use it to evoke cooperation whenever possible. The men would band together, united in submissive silence as no one wanted to be the rat who threw the pimple-faced kids under the bus. It would establish her role as leader instantly. Men were so wonderfully predictable at times.

The asshole, however, surprised her. He cleared his throat and stepped forward.

"I believe the first young man wondered if you left your leather whip in your suitcase," he said. "And the other asked if we ought to call you Lianne, or if you prefer something more formal, like Mistress."

The horror on the faces of the young techs proved that the asshole had, indeed, heard their whispered conversation. They probably thought they were being clever to insinuate she was some kind of wet-dream dominatrix rather than a business-minded professional. They didn't look so clever now. One looked like he was almost going to cry, in fact.

The asshole, though…now, he concerned her.

She shifted her glare to him. "And who are you? I don't recall running across you in the personnel files."

"I'm a consultant," he said, and she detected the dark tones of a slight Russian accent. "Nicolai Stefanya Vladik. You can call me Nic."

"All right, Nic. And since you're so eager to help us answer the young tech's question, what do you suppose I like to be called?"

He narrowed his silver eyes and contemplated her. "Here on the job, no doubt you expect to be called Ms. McGowan. In your private time, though, I suspect you prefer something else."

Yep, he was an asshole. His voice was steady but his eyes were already undressing her; she could feel it. Hopefully he had a good imagination, since that was the closest he was *ever* getting to the goods.

"Well, nobody here is going to find out about that," she said sweetly. "From this point on, there is no private time, gentlemen. You're on the job, twenty-four/seven, whether you're in the office, in the lunchroom, or collapsing into your beds. Got it?"

The men who had worked with her before rolled their eyes and nodded. The others grumbled. The asshole smiled.

"I'm always on the job," he said. "In the office, in the lunchroom, or…wherever I happen to be applying myself."

An uninvited little thrill coursed up then down her spine. Damn, but those silver eyes of his…did things to her she really did not need right now. At all. And was that the jagged hint of a dagger-shaped tattoo she saw peeking out from the man's collar at the broad, bronze nape of his neck? What kind of consultant was this, anyway?

Hell. She flew halfway across the world to this frigid, rocky wasteland for the sake of dear Dad and *this* is what she was stuck with. It would figure.

Assholes with tattoos just happened to be her weakness. This was going to be a long, frustrating assignment.

Chapter Two

The sky was a dramatic wash of wispy blue clouds and the cold yellow glow of early morning. Raea fluttered her wings, Fairy Dust glittering around her as she stretched out the stiffness in her limbs. Not that they hadn't been getting a workout.

For the past three days, she and Kyne had been hiding here in this cabin, high on a densely forested hilltop, hidden by special magic she still did not quite understand. They'd been safe from anyone who might happen to be out hunting them, and no doubt someone was, considering she'd helped break Kyne out of his interrogation cell at the Fairy Council meeting hall. It had been all too easy to forget about that, though, and make the best of their time together here.

By the Skies, they certainly had made the best of it. Passion had ruled them night and day, and Raea's body still hummed from the pleasure she found over and over again in Kyne's arms. A lifetime of giving in to these forbidden wonders could never fully satisfy her. Still, she knew they couldn't hide here forever. Kyne would wake soon and they'd have to discuss their future.

And perhaps elements of his past he'd not yet been willing to talk about.

A sound in the doorway behind her alerted her to the fact that this time had come. Kyne was up, strolling out onto the wraparound porch of the cabin to join her in the dewy morning air. She smiled at him and his wings unfurled, barely clearing the door frame.

The Sizing Dust they had used still lingered over him, his fairy body holding to this human size longer than Raea's did when she was influenced by the dust. She was tiny in comparison to him now. Her toes wriggled as she dangled her legs, sitting on the porch rail in her usual fairy form.

"I can never get over what a giant you are," she said. "Too bad the dust wears off on me so quickly."

"It's all right," he said, breathing deeply and yawning. "We've still got a week's worth in that little pouch my father gave us."

A week. They could continue this way for a week, avoiding their lives and loving each other. But then what? Without the precious dust, their activities would be cut short. Literally. Kyne's half-fairy body was unique; when he reached his climax in the heat of their passion, he grew to human proportions. Huge, massive proportions that still took her breath away every time. Without their supply of the Sizing Dust, Raea would be too small to give him his full pleasure. She'd no longer be able to be with him that way.

"We can't wait that long to go back," she said. "It's been wonderful, staying here with you like this, pretending we don't have a care in the world, but you know we can't go on like this, Kyne. We have to go back."

"No, *I* have to go back. You need to stay here, where it's safe."

"I will go where you go, Kyne."

"No, Raea, you can't. When I leave here, I need to go alone."

"But—"

"No, it's the way it must be."

She hated what he was saying. Her soul ached at the very thought of being without him for as much as a day. How could she even consider existing without Kyne after the days they'd spent here, together?

"Do you mean you'll leave me forever?" she asked, struggling to keep her voice even.

"No, of course not. Just until…"

"Until what? We don't even know what we're really hiding from."

He was silent at that, so she continued.

"Besides, the Sizing Dust will run out. Whatever we do and wherever we go, we need to find more."

Now he smiled. "You mean you're not done with me yet?"

"Not by any means."

He leaned against the railing beside her, and she realized his body was changing. He was finally reverting back to his usual form. She smiled, watching him shudder as if with a chill and then shrink with a puff of golden mist. He plopped down to sit on the railing beside her.

"And now we are equals again. Are you certain you still have no regrets, Raea? I should have never involved you in this."

"I'm not involved in anything I didn't run into willingly," she assured him. "But don't you think it's time we try to find out just exactly what it is that we did run into?"

He sighed. She knew he would not welcome this discussion, but it couldn't be avoided. Strange things were happening, and the only way to get to the bottom of them would involve dredging up the history Kyne would much rather ignore.

"You want me to go find my father again, don't you?"

"I think we're going to have to. I don't know what the Fairy Council has been plotting, or really what that strange machine we found at the base of the mountain is for, but it seems that your father is involved in all of it. I'm afraid if we want to learn anything, we have to start there."

"You keep saying 'we.'"

"That's because we're in this together, Kyne."

"No. *I'm* in this. It has nothing to do with you."

"Nothing to do with me? I'm sorry, did I miss something? Who were you with when the council sent Swift to take you into custody? And then who came sneaking into the Meeting Hall to break you out of confinement? I had to seduce you while I was invisible, if you recall! And who has been climbing all over you like a raging wild animal ever since? Me, Kyne. It's me. You're not alone anymore, and neither am I."

His amber eyes searched hers, and she could see the concern that filled him. She loved that he worried for her, but she worried for him, too. Someone back in their Fairyrealm had been plotting against him, and she wanted to know why. Fairies and humans were in league and that could only spell trouble. Somehow she and Kyne had to uncover the truth.

"Please, Raea," he said, laying his hand over hers. "Don't make me drag you into more danger. Let me keep you safe. I don't know what I'd do if something happened to you. I need you to be safe."

"You think I'd feel the least bit safe if you went off and left me here alone?"

"I'd rather have you alone than dead," he declared.

The words rattled inside her. Did he really think things were quite that serious? Of course certain members of the council had been behaving mysteriously, and those two fairies they'd seen in the forest several days ago had clearly been up to no good…but was this truly a matter of life and death?

"You think it might come to that?" she asked softly, stroking his cheek and letting the warmth of his skin seep into her fingertips.

"I won't take any chances, Raea. I have to go look into this alone. I just couldn't live if I let something happen to you."

"Then you know exactly how I feel. I can't let you go, Kyne, not now. Whatever you do, I'm doing it with you."

"I can see we're going to have an argument over this," he said, clutching her hand to his lips and kissing it gently.

"I'll win it, of course. You know I have my ways."

"Don't be so sure of yourself. I've got a few persuasive tricks of my own."

"Then I guess I'll have to be especially convincing, won't I?"

"I'm not going down without a fight," he said with a crooked little smile that assured her they weren't talking about investigating the council right now.

"You're not going down?" she asked, flashing him her own wicked grin and letting the glittery aura emanating from her speak for itself. "Then you know I will."

She fluttered up off the railing and hovered before him, raking her fingertips over his solid form and slowly sinking lower, lower until her lips were perfectly positioned. Oh yes, he was going down, all right. And she was going to take him there.

Their argument might be on hold for right now, but one thing was certain. They were going to need more Sizing Dust again very soon.

* * *

Fairy Dust glittered in the air around them, and Kyne ran his hand over the soft, silky strands of Raea's tousled hair. Her pink aura glowed with satisfaction and a contented smile touched the corners of her lips. He touched those lips, tracing their contour and feeling the heat of reaction course through his veins. He wanted her again, already.

They'd spent the morning making love, as they'd done every day since they'd left their lives behind and come to hide here, safe in this strange, enchanted cottage on the top of a forested hill with the Great Lake barely visible to them off in the distance. The special magic here kept them protected from detection by the Fairy Council, as well as anyone else in the Forbidden Realm who might have reason to hunt them. And indeed, they had reason.

Initially he'd assumed the Fairy Council dragged him in for questioning because they'd become suspicious about his overly human behaviors. Passion was forbidden, after all, and he'd certainly given free rein to his. Worse, he'd drawn Raea into his shameful inclinations. He'd tempted her and she'd given in to the illicit thrill, despite the fact that it meant she faced the same censure and ruin that he did.

But it appeared that wasn't the only reason he'd been marked by the council. They'd not asked anything about his interaction with Raea, and in fact it seemed the council was not interested in her at all. She could have been free from the indictment that Kyne faced. But she'd shown up and used forbidden magic to help him escape. She was in just as deep as he was now, and he wished he was noble enough to regret that.

He couldn't, though. Raea was here, with him, and he loved her for it. They were fugitives now, but they were together. They'd discarded the rules, reveled in passion, and witnessed things no one had intended them to see.

But could he keep her safe? He was coming to realize the stakes were much higher than they'd ever imagined. These carnal infractions he and Raea engaged in paled in comparison to the things he'd learned his own kind were up to.

Fairies had conspired with humans to make a machine used in the collection and suppression of magic. Its ultimate purpose was still a mystery, but Kyne knew for a fact it did strange, horrible things when Veiled creatures were near it. He and Raea had learned that the hard way.

When they'd first encountered it, a machine had reduced Raea and Kyne to weak, helpless creatures controlled totally by their basest instinct. They'd become slaves to their passions. Sensors near the machine had somehow notified the council of their presence, too. They'd almost been captured.

For all the years Kyne had trained himself to deny his desires, being in the presence of that machine had sent his senses over the edge, pushed him beyond his ability to hold back. By the Skies, he and Raea had been so lost in each other that they nearly loved themselves into unconsciousness. Or worse.

The council came remarkably close to ridding themselves of two wanted fugitives that day. It had been mere luck that the side effect of Kyne and Raea's passion was an overload of the machine. When they reached their climax, the machinery reached its own climax and became disabled. Still, they had needed help to escape.

Baylor came along. Kyne's father. It had not been a happy reunion.

Baylor told them the machine was called a Regulator. It had been created by fairies and humans secretly working together to strengthen the Veil, and the machine required both magic and passion to work. He hadn't given much explanation beyond that, and Kyne wouldn't have trusted it if he did. Baylor was a human. Kyne had spent his life hating the man for siring him, making him a half-breed who didn't belong in either realm. Why should Kyne trust this man any more than he could trust the Fairy Council?

For Raea's sake, he needed to find out what was truly going on. They'd both been drawn into this confusing web and it was his fault. He was the one who introduced her to passion. He was the reason she couldn't dare show herself among their people again. She was innocent and shouldn't have to pay the price for his flaws, for his weaknesses.

She would argue with him, of course, but he knew what he had to do. He had to leave her. He just hoped that when it was time for him to go, he'd be strong enough to do the right thing.

The thought of it tore at his soul, and he instinctively slid his arm over her and pulled her tighter against himself. The Sizing Dust would be wearing off soon for her, so he'd just let her rest. As usual, she'd given herself fully; she'd loved him with all of her heart, every ounce of her passion. He soaked it up with abandon, leaving them both drained and exhausted. He would hold on to this moment as long as he could until—

A sound outside their bedroom jolted him. He jerked up, and his wings spread quickly to cover Raea and protect her as she slept. Someone was here! He could feel the presence, hear the light footsteps as they moved about the cabin. His senses went on high alert and he pushed back the covers, sliding into the pair of human shorts that he'd found in the closet and had been using during their stay here.

Raea stirred. "What is it?" she asked.

"Someone's here."

She was clearly startled, so he tried to be as calm as possible.

"It's okay. I'll take care of it," he assured her, moving toward the door. "Wait here."

She nodded, and he could see her body begin to shrink as fear canceled the effects of the Sizing Dust and she returned to her normal size. In a few moments she'd be small enough to fit in a man's hand, tiny and vulnerable to danger. Kyne would keep her safe no matter what. Whoever was out there, he sure as hell wouldn't let them anywhere near Raea.

He pulled the door open and peered into the main living area. He could clearly make out a figure—a man. Who was he and how had he found them inside their magical refuge? Obviously he was not trying to be stealthy, standing there in the open, his large, human form silhouetted before the window. Kyne's eyes adjusted to the bright sunlight streaming in and recognition swept over him before the man even spoke.

"I hope I'm not interrupting."

"What the hell are you doing here, Baylor?" Kyne demanded, pulling the door shut behind him as he stalked toward his father.

"I came to check on you. Obviously you took my advice to lie low for a while."

Baylor had been the one to direct them here, but Kyne wouldn't give him the satisfaction of a thank-you. The fact that Baylor had saved him from capture on this one single occasion did not even come close to making up for all the years Kyne had been abandoned and left to fend for himself and his heartbroken mother, struggling to hide his heritage and the shameful truth of his half-fairy, half-human existence. He owed Baylor no thank-yous, that was for certain.

On the other hand, the human owed him some answers.

"What is this place? How did you know about it?" Kyne questioned.

"I built it, of course," Baylor replied. "I didn't realize when I sent you here that you'd be making such excellent use of it, though. Who's the girl?"

"I'm alone here."

"No, you're not. You wouldn't still be here if you were alone. Is she a fairy? She must be. She was hiding with you in the forest, wasn't she? That's why you didn't stick around to beat the hell out of me the way you obviously want to. The council is after her, too."

"The council knows nothing of her yet, and neither do you. I didn't beat the hell out of you because, frankly, you're just not worth the effort. You *are* going to give me some answers, though. What have you gotten us involved in? Hybrid equipment? When did the Fairy Council start working with humans?"

"There's much more here than you know about, Kyne."

"And that's why you're going to tell me. Start by explaining this cabin."

"It's a cabin, protected by magic that only a certain formulation of Fairy Dust and a couple key human ingredients can penetrate."

More human and magical hybridization. Kyne didn't like that one bit. "Why?"

"We needed a safe place, somewhere beyond magic or human detection."

"*We?* You mean my mother. She lied to me, you know. All these years, she told me she had no idea where you were. But I found the photo; I know she's been here with you. Recently."

"She lied to protect you, Kyne. Like I said, there's a lot going on that you don't know about."

"Well, the Fairy Council seems to think I know all about it. They've been watching my every move for as long as I can remember. Just what do they think I know, Baylor? Just what were all these lies supposed to protect me from?"

"We were hoping they would keep you safe behind the Veil."

"By the Skies, Baylor. What is that supposed to mean? Of course I'm safe behind the Veil. That's what the Veil is for—protecting magical beings."

"Yes, but you're only half-magical, Kyne. There's a reason the council has watched you. Your human nature is strong, isn't it?"

Kyne refused to reply. The fact that he had any human nature at all was Baylor's damn fault. The fact that he'd battled that nature every moment of his life, only to finally fail magnificently and drag Raea into his human carnality, was proof just how strong it truly was. Hell, he was standing here six feet tall, eye to eye with Baylor right now, wasn't he? He'd not give him the pleasure of taking any credit for it, though.

"I'm a fairy," he announced. "There's nothing wrong with my magic."

"I never said that there was. But you're human, too. That part of your nature is what concerns the council. It might be stronger than the Veil, Kyne. Especially since they've found…"

"They've found what?"

Baylor glanced around the cabin, and Kyne watched him clench and unclench his fists. Whatever he'd been about to say, he'd caught himself and was wrestling now with whether to divulge his information or not. Kyne wasn't about to let *not* be an option for the man.

"What did they find, Baylor? You owe me the truth."

"All right, I'll tell you. The council has discovered some problems with the Veil."

Obviously Kyne was going to need more information than that. He glared until the older man continued.

"Holes. The Veil is developing holes, Kyne, though of course it's not public knowledge. There are areas where the Veil's power is weakening."

"I haven't heard anything about it."

"No, you wouldn't have. The council is keeping it quiet, but they've been monitoring weak spots for years now. In fact…well, that's how they found out about your mother and me."

"I can't believe I'm going to ask, but how'd they do that?"

"Think of passion and magic as balances on a scale. When they're equal, the barrier between worlds is strong; but when they're not, when passion invades the Forbidden Realm or magic gets into the mundane, the lack of balance weakens the Veil. The council claims your mother and I helped upset this balance, so they've forced us to either work with them or suffer punishment."

"You've been working with the council all this time?"

"Yes. They found out I have some skills they can exploit and they made me an offer I couldn't refuse. In exchange for giving you up and helping the council create the Regulators, they agreed not to punish your mother for our relationship."

"But you didn't give up my mother. Only me."

"It was years before I ever saw her again, Kyne. I swear to you, I tried to stay away, to keep my bargain with the council, but…"

"But you're only human, right?"

"I thought maybe you'd understand, but I guess not. Apparently that fairy in the other room there doesn't mean as much to you as I thought she might."

"Don't you dare bring her into this. Raea means more to me than my own life!"

Baylor smiled and Kyne felt just a bit foolish. The old man had been looking for a response and was obviously pleased with himself for getting one. Kyne promised himself never to let that happen again.

"Raea," Baylor mused. "It's a lovely name and I'm happy to make her acquaintance."

"You will *not* be doing that. I have no intentions of even letting you lay eyes on her."

"Too late," Baylor said with another damn smile. "She's standing right behind you."

Kyne whirled to find his father was correct. Raea had opened the bedroom door and stood there wrapped in a bedsheet, her wide lavender eyes blinking with a great number of questions. She'd obviously used Sizing Dust, choosing to show herself in human proportions, but every bit of her was pure fairy. Kyne wanted to shield her from whatever evil his father represented, but she stepped up to his side and faced Baylor unflinchingly.

"You are Kyne's father," she said.

"I am."

"Why are you here?" she asked. "You must have come for some purpose."

"I did. I came to see how you were doing."

Raea's eyes narrowed and she shook her head. "No, there's more. Why did you really come here?"

Kyne watched guilt flash over his father's face. Raea's instincts were right. Clearly Baylor had come for something more than just checking on the son he hadn't ever bothered to check on before. Whatever truly brought the man here today, Kyne knew he wasn't going to like it.

"I came to ask a favor," Baylor announced.

Well, that figured. "I'm not really in a favor-granting mood."

But Raea was at least curious. She hugged her sheet closely around herself, and her glossy wings fluttered nervously. "What do you need from us?"

Baylor's expression darkened. "There's something happening—something bad, and I think it involves my machinery. Someone may be tampering with it, misdirecting it, and using it for purposes we never intended."

"And what are we supposed to do about it?" Kyne questioned.

"I don't know, maybe there's nothing we can do. I need to know what is happening, and why. That's where you come in."

Kyne sneered at him. "You think we know what's going on? By the Skies, I barely know my own name right now."

"Of course you don't know what's going on, but you can find out."

"Why don't *you* find out? You're such close friends with the Fairy Council and all."

Baylor shook his head. "This doesn't involve the Fairy Council. At least, I don't believe it does."

"Really? So who does it involve?"

"Someone in Iceland."

Iceland? Kyne wasn't an expert at human geography—the Forbidden Realm did not rely on those imaginary lines of political boundaries that humans set for themselves—but he knew enough to understand Baylor was talking about a place half a world away. What on earth could be happening in Iceland that had Baylor so concerned? And how could it possibly have anything to do with his stupid hybrid equipment?

"The coalition that I'm working with is trying to preserve the Veil," Baylor explained. "We've kept our efforts secret so as not to upset the balance within the Forbidden Realm, but everything we do is to keep the Veil in place. Recently, though, some of our equipment has come up missing."

"You're telling us that some other secret organization is stealing from your secret organization. Why? What do they want the machinery for?" Kyne asked, hoping that the sarcasm was obvious in his tone.

"We don't know," Baylor replied. "But I found evidence that it's been shipped out to Iceland. To discover what they're doing with it, someone will have to go there."

"You'd better take a coat," Kyne suggested. He knew what the man was getting at. "I hear it's cold up there."

Baylor scowled at his tone. "I can't go, of course. They watch me almost constantly. I don't even want to think of what they might do to your mother if I run off to Iceland. No, it has to be someone they'd never suspect; someone they don't currently have eyes on."

"Then it has to be us," Raea announced boldly. "We'll go there and find out."

Kyne gaped at her. "No, we will not!"

"If your father felt it important enough to come here and confront you this way, then we need to look into it. Clearly there are things in the Realm we don't know about. We need to find out."

"If anyone is going, it's me. Not you," he said. "I won't risk you."

"And I won't risk you," she said, meeting his eyes. "We go together, Kyne. This argument is getting old."

She laid her hand on his arm, and his skin reacted with heat and electricity. By the Skies, what she could do to him without even trying. She really was ready to fight about this, he could tell. As much as he did not want to put her in harm's way by rushing off on Baylor's wild, paranoid quest, he sure as hell was looking forward to her trying to convince him.

"Maybe I'd better give you the specifics," Baylor suggested. "Then I'll let you two decide how to handle things."

Raea batted her eyes and lifted just one corner of her pink lips. "Good idea. Your son has become very adept at handling things."

Chapter Three

Somehow Nic made it through the morning's meetings without setting the building on fire. Or melting the glacier that wrapped around the base of the huge mountain beside them. Lianne McGowan was just too damn hot for her own good. The more she explained her plans for tweaking their procedures and reviewing their data, the more Nic realized she could pose a real threat. She could also be exactly what he needed to control the fires burning inside him. Lianne's energy and drive indicated a strong, passionate woman. His desire was stoked and he wanted to drag her out somewhere and convince her this energy and drive could be put to much better use.

He needed to bide his time, though. Even if he hadn't found the woman so scorchingly attractive, he knew he couldn't let his need race ahead of good sense. Before he could get into her pants, he had to get into her good graces. It would get him closer to his goal, plus slow her down a bit on hers.

The woman was smart, and her presentation today showed that she might actually get this project moving again after it had been more or less stalled for several months. The trouble with that, of course, was that Nic was the one who'd made sure it had stalled. These humans thought they were merely investigating the stability and reliability of thermal energy beneath the nearby dormant volcano. Nic had sworn his life to protecting the real cause of this energy and he'd taken great pains to falsify data and discourage this project. Now that Ms. McGowan showed up, all his hard work was in real jeopardy. He'd have to find some way to stall her now, too.

And hot, raging sex seemed like the perfect distraction. He'd simply have to convince her she wanted it as badly as he did. From the glare she gave him when he walked over to the table in the corner where she sat eating her lunch, it seemed that melting the glacier might be easier than melting Lianne.

Nic had never been one to back away from a challenge, though. He smiled and snapped open his soft drink.

"You give a good presentation, Ms. McGowan. You must be a real asset for Geo-Diagnostics."

"That's why I'm here," she replied. "To tell you guys how to do your jobs."

"Oh, I do my job just fine."

"Great. Then I won't be dealing with you very much, will I?"

"Maybe not. Or maybe yes. Maybe we'll find out I can be useful to you."

Obviously his charm and subtlety were slipping a bit these days. The glare she gave him said she knew exactly what he was up to and was in no mood to play along. That was perfectly fine with him. Her coy intelligence only served to make the game more stimulating for him. He smiled his most smoldering smile and simply sat back to watch the sparks fly.

And damn, but she did let them fly.

"Look, Nic, I know you've been stuck out here on a godforsaken tundra with a bunch of engineers and computer geeks," she said, her lips forming the words carefully, as if each one was an insult directly for him, "but you need to quit imagining I'm here for your personal entertainment. I'm not. I'm only here to get you guys off your asses and start making headway."

He darkened his smolder and sweetened his smile. "I like making headway."

Her lips and her eyes narrowed. He wondered if she might actually snarl at him, but in the end she did not. She took a deep, frustrated breath and scolded him soundly.

"I'm a professional, and a grown-up. You need to get right over this stupid notion that I can be flattered by childish jokes and tacky come-ons, Mr. Vladik."

"Well, I'm flattered you remember my name."

"Oh, you're memorable, all right. But don't think there's even the slightest chance you'll be making memories with me. I'm here to get the job done. The job we're all getting paid for. Unless you're here to talk about that, I suggest you go find another table and let me finish my lunch in peace."

Very clearly she meant it. He supposed he shouldn't be surprised. After all, she wasn't the one who'd been stuck here without companionship, burning up from the inside out every day and every night. He'd just have to be a little more patient, a little more careful in his dealings with her. If she wanted to concentrate on the job, he could do that. For a little while longer.

"Very well," he capitulated. "Let's discuss the job, then. You are here because Geo-Diagnostics is concerned that we've been testing things, probing things, monitoring things, and generally spending a great deal of money on things, yet we don't have a single reliable report to send back to your father, correct?"

"Yes. I'm glad you recognize this might be a bit of a problem for us."

"But of course you know that what we are doing here is unique, groundbreaking work. Delays and some level of uncertainty are to be expected."

"No, usable data and measurable progress are to be expected."

"Our team has provided you with all of our findings."

"Your team has been on-site for almost a year now and you've given us nothing. We're not one step closer to tapping into the resources of this mountain. We still don't even know what's causing the massive heat buildup half a mile below us. Lava flow? The usual superheated water? Is this activity indication that the volcano is growing unstable, or will it be feasible to invest in a thermal facility here?"

"This is delicate work we do, Ms. McGowan, and—"

"This is Iceland, for pity's sake. Geothermal technology is old hat around here. Why all the holdups now, at this site?"

"We've been carefully gathering all the information you need, trying to answer your questions."

"I've only got one question: Is it safe to start building, or is this site too dangerous?"

"If it was safe, wouldn't we know that by now?"

"That's what I'm asking, but all your data is inconsistent."

"The fact that our readings are inconsistent ought to answer your question," he said, clamping down the desire he felt, heated by her anger and her captivating will. "If you'd have looked at our reports, you'd see that—"

"I did look at the reports, and I agree that there are a lot of inconsistencies. However, to be honest, I'm not sure if the data was inconsistent, or the reports themselves."

His knuckles clenched white. Damn, but he had very much preferred when they were not discussing the job. He did not like being accused of incompetence, but he could hardly admit to intentionally submitting flawed reports. He'd have to deflect her questions before she either brought out his anger or dug down to the truth. Both were uncomfortably close to the surface just now and he needed to regain control.

But need was getting to be the hardest thing to control. Sitting here across from her, watching her moisten her plump lips as she prepared for a fight, meeting her flashing green eyes with his own, he was painfully aware just how strong his need had become. His body wanted her intensely and his ability to maintain human composure was wearing thinner by the minute. Instinct roiled and churned in his being. It required much more of a struggle than usual to hold them inside.

Even now he felt a wave of unbidden telepathy surge out from him. He had already touched Lianne's mind before he quickly drew his senses back. But he had touched her, his mind creeping inside hers just for a moment.

Had she noticed? Humans were unpredictable about such things. Most humans were fully unaware of such intimate contact with his kind, but some, unfortunately, detected it and reacted irrationally. They sometimes became agitated, anxious, or violent, even, without any idea why. It was generally a good idea to keep such contact to the barest minimum, and only when truly necessary. Consequences from prolonged mental contact could range anywhere from slight memory loss to complete cerebral deterioration. There was no telling yet how Lianne would react should he probe her mind with his.

He hadn't probed her, though. It had been merely a touch, and an accidental one, at that. She didn't seem to have noticed it. For him, though, it had been enough to convince him that he wanted more. Lianne McGowan's mind had felt nearly as heated as his own. Despite her cool exterior, this woman's mind had been a whirl of fire and raw emotion. It was just the fuel Nic's nature craved.

"Stop glowering at me," she ordered.

"I didn't realize I was," he lied.

"Well, you are. Did something I say offend you?"

He shook himself mentally, regaining his cool—on the outside, at least—and schooling his expression to show the proper disdain she obviously expected.

"As a matter of fact, yes," he responded. "It sounded to me as if you implied I don't know how to do my job, Ms. McGowan."

"Did I? Well, maybe it's a bit early for me to jump to that conclusion. How about if I just promise to keep my eye on you," she clarified, "and anyone else who is involved in the reporting process?"

He smiled. Damn, but she certainly did hide her emotion well. If not for his secret senses, he'd never guess at the tumult inside this woman. He would have expected her mind to be rigid and compartmentalized, very much the way she appeared. But no, inside she was a jumble of passions and desires, anger and fear, all tossed together as a huge pile of sharp, jagged bits that rattled and tore at each other. Touching her mind, even for that brief moment, had cut at him like he'd been plunged into broken glass.

It was tantalizing, to say the least. He'd never been one to shy away from pain. Perhaps he might just allow himself to reach into her mind again. If he became desperate enough, he knew he could use those jumbled passions for his own purposes. He could control her, if he had to.

He didn't want to, though. The way her mind cut him, seared into him, was a completely new sensation. Human minds usually did not hold this much power. Something about Lianne affected him in a way that went beyond usual need. Reaching into her mind left marks on him. It was not mere passion he craved from her now…he was left with some other type of want, something deeper.

He'd better take his time with her. There were other ways to feed his need beyond simple control. He would have her on *her* terms, in time. For now, he could wait. He met her glare with a deceptively steady one of his own.

"I think I will enjoy having you watch me, Ms. McGowan."

"Not the way I'm going to do it, Mr. Vladik. No, you're not going to like that one little bit."

He almost laughed at the cold, determined scowl on her face. She was wrong, of course. He would, indeed, very much like being watched by her. As if she could do anything to him that he might not like. Oh, but Lianne McGowan posed a delightful challenge that he was more than eager to take up.

"So the gauntlet is set," he announced with a grin. "Just know that as you watch with your eagle eyes, Ms. McGowan, I'll do my best to give you something interesting to look at."

He didn't give her the opportunity to shoot him down after that, though he could see that she wanted to. Her eyebrow arched and her lips parted. He really liked those lips, but he didn't let her use them. There'd be plenty of time for that later.

For now, he needed to make sure she understood he wasn't fooled by her. She could play her ball-busting games on all the other guys, and maybe they were intimidated by it, but things were different for him. Lianne McGowan had something he wanted—something he *needed*. He had felt inside her mind and realized she had her own needs, too. They roiled and strained inside her, threatening her tenuous control. He was used to wrestling that feeling, but he'd never encountered a human like this. What secrets did she hide? What tumult did she barely keep wrapped up deeply inside her?

He was determined to find out, to unleash all of it. Victory would be sweet. For both of them.

"Don't think for one minute that I won't be watching *you*," he added. "Now pass me the salt and tell me how you propose we issue a more consistent report about our inconsistent core readings."

* * *

Thank God she'd had her notebook with her. Lianne scribbled in it—nonsense, really—and flipped back and forth between pages at random times while the damn Russian rambled on about samples and readings and other things she ought to be making sense out of. She seemed to have no sense left, however. Nic with his bright, flashing eyes and that ever-present—and ever-sexy—smirk had thrown her off her game completely.

At least he'd stopped feeding her all the stupid come-on lines and seemed willing to get down to business. She took notes as he talked, glad for something to look at other than his dark, chiseled face and those sculpted lips as he formed words. The man was actually making some good points, too, discussing the various obstacles the team had come up against. What in the hell was making this particular mountain so much hotter than the others in the desolate Hornstrandir wasteland? Why was it taking so damned long to determine whether or not it was safe to establish facilities to harness that energy?

Well, she could half explain the extra heat in the mountain as Nic's swaggering presence. God knew sitting at the table with him now, she certainly felt a hell of a lot hotter than usual. And there was nothing wrong with the heating and cooling systems in this modular. Just listening to him be all technical and businesslike had her about to boil over in her chair. Damn it, but she needed to keep her mind on her work.

"So you're saying the mountain is unstable," she said, dragging her mind off his broad shoulders and that damn tattoo teasing her from just under his collar.

"It is. Yes," he replied, catching her eyes with his and holding them half a second too long.

She went back to her notebook, turning pages to find where she'd recorded the highlights of the last set of data sent to them while she was still in the States. That report had come in while she was…well, while she'd been temporarily out of commission. She'd lost a week last month and was still trying to put everything from that time in order, trying to regain herself after she'd crumbled.

Thank God no one knew about that episode. Well, almost no one. The guy she'd been dating turned out to be just another *asshole du jour* when she'd confided in him, but she found out she didn't care nearly as much about him as she'd thought she did. Obviously he hadn't cared much about her, either.

It was just as well. A relationship would have weighed her down. She had too much to do and not nearly enough time to do it in. Her father's idea of sending her to Iceland came at the perfect moment and she'd been happy to dive in. Geo-Diagnostics had a vision for a world built on renewable resources and clean energy. *This* is what she did, *this* is who she was, and *this* would make her life meaningful.

She'd come here to fix things and leave some kind of mark. Nicolai Vladik was an egotistical chimpanzee if he thought he could stand in the way of that.

"The numbers just don't match up with your recommendations," she announced, pulling a dog-eared stack of pages out of the file folder she'd been carrying around. "Look, I've charted them all the way back to our start-up here and, to be honest, the variance is well within usual tolerances."

"You've not charted the spikes, though, have you?" he asked.

"Spikes?"

"They occur randomly, and our instrumentation has found it difficult to adequately record them."

"Our instrumentation is state of the art."

"Then you should be able to chart the spikes."

"What spikes? How can I chart something that my reports tell me isn't happening?"

"They are happening. All the time."

"Based on what? A few unsupported readings from a few malfunctioning sensors?"

"They aren't malfunctioning," he said. "I've been trying to tell everyone. The readings are inconsistent because the mountain is unstable."

"The mountain could be sitting on top of the most powerful cache of geothermal energy ever located to date," she insisted. "You think our company should just walk away because of some inconsistencies? I'm not leaving until I know for certain the mountain is unstable."

"If you want to know if this mountain is unstable—and I assure you that it is—you need to stop looking at reports."

"What, and just take your word for things?"

"No. Take the mountain's word for things."

Oh good God. He was one of *those* people? How could she not have picked up on that? Every jobsite seemed to have one of them, some closeted new-age earth lover claiming Mother Nature spoke to him and begging them all to form a drum circle, or whatever. She'd never in a million years pegged Nic to be that guy, though.

"So the mountain talks to you, does it?" she asked.

He frowned at her. "You believe mountains speak, Ms. McGowan? Well, I suppose that makes as much sense as relying on a bunch of outdated, irrelevant data to tell you what's going on out there."

"You have a better way to gather reliable information?"

"Yeah, I do. I study the mountain—the *whole* mountain."

"And what exactly does that mean?"

"It means I don't sit here with charts and lopsided numbers. I've gone out there."

"You went out there, onto the mountain?"

"Yes."

"But we don't have permits for that."

"I know."

"Damn it, Nic! You mean to tell me you've gone out there, onto that so-called unstable mountain with no permit or authorization? That can jeopardize our whole operation here!"

"The mountain *is* what's jeopardizing your operation. Your data is incomplete because your view of the mountain is incomplete."

"Look, we had to pull every string we could get our hands on just to be allowed as much access as we got. Maybe you haven't noticed, but there's a huge, untouched glacier rolling along right next to our mountain. It represents years and years of pristine and uninterrupted climate study. We aren't allowed to go anywhere near it. We can't touch it or even breathe on it while we're here. That's why we set up our jobsite and our instruments way the hell over here on this side of the mountain, and not on the freaking glacier."

"And that's why you can't pick up on the instabilities. I'm telling you, if

Geo-Diagnostics gets the okay for more-intrusive exploration in this area, you're going to regret it."

"Is that some kind of a threat?"

"No. It's a statement of fact."

"Well, my data doesn't support your so-called fact, Mr. Vladik. Drilling a few holes and installing subterranean sensors won't cause a dormant volcano to erupt, if that's what you're implying. The fault lines here are just not that extensive. Now until you've got some hard, solid figures that you can give me, I'm going to have to proceed with what I know. And what I know is that reporting at this site has been sloppy and inconsistent. If I hear you've been outside the permit zone, you will be off this job and most likely you'll never work in the industry again. Got it?"

She could tell that he wasn't the least bit intimidated by her, but he did have the good sense not to laugh in her face. He merely sat back in his chair, folded his arms, and smiled.

"I understand completely, Ms. McGowan."

"Do you?"

"Yes. Clearly you are going to need some convincing."

"And just what, exactly, do you need to convince me of, Mr. Vladik?"

For half a heartbeat she thought she knew exactly what he was going to say. It was written all over his face, blatant in his smirk and the smoldering stare. However, he surprised her when he spoke.

"I will convince you that your concerns about this jobsite are every bit as valid as you believe, deep down, that they are. That's why you came here, after all. You could have sent anyone else; your father has lots of henchmen who could have come, twisted a few arms, and gotten these guys off their asses. But you didn't send them. You came yourself."

He was appraising her openly now, and she had to admit she liked that she saw approval in his eyes. The smart thing to do would have been to shut him up and tell him to get the hell back to work, but instead she cocked an eyebrow at him and let him continue.

"You had reasons for traveling halfway around the world, didn't you?" he asked. "You know there's something different about this site, that unlocking the secrets here is more than just business as usual. This job is special to you, isn't it?"

"All you need to know about me or my job here is that I'm highly motivated to get to the truth."

"Are you? Even if the truth isn't what your father wants you to find?"

"My father won't proceed with a project if it's dangerous. But he won't be bullied into backing away from a safe, lucrative opportunity, either."

"And what about you? What opportunity are you really after?"

"I'm doing my job, Mr. Vladik. Which is what you ought to be doing, too."

"I am, as a matter of fact. But how can I convince you, I wonder?"

"Straight answers and numbers that make sense would be a great start."

"Very well, then. You will have them. Despite what your father expects of you, Ms. McGowan, I believe you are eager to think for yourself."

"Are you suggesting my father sent me here as his little puppet?" she asked sharply. "You believe you know me pretty well, don't you?"

"Not yet. But I will."

Presumption and arrogance. Total asshole. Damn his smoldering eyes and sexy tattoo.

"I'm not so easy to figure out as you seem to presume," she assured him.

"Women who use their brains rarely are," he replied, not even slightly derailed. "But I think for myself, too, Ms. McGowan, and you will find my way of thinking can be very, very persuasive."

"Your way of thinking might just get you kicked off this job."

He merely shrugged at her words and laid his fork down next to his half-finished lunch. "Perhaps. But it also just might save your life. Now if you'll excuse me, I have work to be doing."

With that he stood, bowed ever so slightly like he was some kind of diplomat, then took his tray and left. No one else in the modular building

that housed the kitchen and dining area seemed to notice anything unusual, but Lianne could have sworn the air around Nic shimmered the way
a hot tar road did in the middle of August. She was glad she'd been sitting
down, because her insides felt weak—and hot. Damn, but she was hot.

Unfortunately, so was he. This was going to be a problem. Lianne had
spent the whole ten-hour flight into Reykjavik psyching herself up for the
challenge, forcing herself to pretend to be everything people said that she
was: unstoppable, a ballbuster, a steamroller. She gave herself the usual
speech, ordering herself to ignore the butterflies inside, to put on her big-
girl panties and *want* to accomplish this job. She *wanted* to fix the problems
here, she *wanted* to show these guys who was boss, she *wanted* to leave a
legacy for herself.

Right now, unfortunately, all she *wanted* was Nicolai Vladik. And to get
the hell out of these scalding-hot big-girl panties. For her whole life, no
matter how hard she tried, they just never seemed to fit her quite right.

Chapter Four

The square, impersonal workroom was silent. Lianne rubbed her eyes and wished she could rub away the throbbing behind them. The silence almost made the pain worse. It would have been nice to have some music or a radio or something, but no. There was nothing more than the sound of the tech she'd drafted to work with her tonight as he tapped endless streams of data into the computer and the constant *tick-tick-tick* of the battery-operated clock that hung on their beige wall.

Lianne frowned at both of them. Midnight. No wonder the poor tech had been yawning incessantly. Okay, so he had a right to be tired. They'd been going over the same data for nearly six hours now. No matter how she had him run the reports, the results were the same: incomplete.

Plain and simple, huge chunks of important data were missing. How no one had seen this before, she had no idea. All she knew was they had two weeks to figure out the problem and fill in the gaps or she'd be answering to her father.

Even worse, she'd be answering to herself. She'd never let failure be an option and she wasn't about to start allowing it now. She could sleep when she got back to the States. Hell, she'd be getting plenty of sleep once she got home. For the next two weeks here she could easily afford to go without.

The tech, however, did not appear able to do that. He'd been drifting on her for a while now, and she could see he had nothing left to give. She'd better let him go get some rest or he'd be useless to her tomorrow. There was a fine line between getting hard work out of the team members and draining them dry.

"All right, Davis, you can log out. I think we've exhausted all our options here tonight," she said and could see him practically rejoice at her words. "Head to your bunk and we'll hit it again in the morning."

"I don't know what other data you can pull from this," he said, pushing his chair back and stretching. "We've run it every way I can think of and still we're missing parts."

"I know. We've got to figure out why."

"Faulty equipment is my guess," he said, letting the machine power down as one by one the little blinking lights on printers, memory banks, and related equipment faded out. "Sandstrom Industries guarantees performance even in harsh environments, but I don't know. They've had a lot of trouble on the westward side of that mountain."

She puzzled over that. "The westward side? Isn't that the glaciated side?"

"Our permits let us get right up next to the glacier in that area," the tech explained. "We can't get out and check them very often, though, since we're only allowed limited access. I don't know, but I heard some of the guys talking that maybe there's a tolerance issue and we're taking readings too close together or something. You'd have to get one of the engineers to explain it."

"Thank you, I will. Now go turn in and get some rest."

She didn't have to tell him twice. He left and she stifled her own yawn but scanned the latest printout anyway. How could their numbers be so far off, the readings so inconsistent? Equipment failure could explain some of this, but not all of it. There was no pattern, no indication that any one network was acting up, one sensor group sending flawed data, or anything like that.

According to what she saw in front of her, all the sensors they'd placed around the mountain were working within expected parameters. The data stream appeared intact, no obvious holes or failures. Yet as they broke it down into specifics, clearly there were chunks missing. And yes, she did find one incident of an unusual spike, just as Nic had said, but she couldn't attribute it to anything specific or plot a pattern to try to estimate the occurrence of another.

It was as if the equipment simply did whatever it wanted, magically sending back data in no particular order or frequency. She could not get a handle on this, or guess what could possibly cause it. Had none of it been properly calibrated?

She swiveled her chair around to reach the filing cabinet. Someone must have kept records of installation for each piece of equipment out there. She had to rummage through two drawers of folders, but finally she found the section she wanted. Sure enough, the team had followed procedure and logged careful records of the personnel and procedures at play when things were initially set up on site. Oddly enough, one name kept jumping out at her.

Nicolai Vladik. He seemed to have been involved in this project from day one—no, even before day one. Before the team had arrived here to survey and install the various equipment, Nic was listed as being a consultant. It seemed he hadn't been in favor of the site study, either. She pored through the folders, scanning for his name and finding it everywhere.

He'd been involved in obtaining their initial permits—and that process had taken far longer than anyone had expected. And here was documentation that Nic had been instrumental in securing the contract with Sandstrom Industries, the firm that customized and manufactured all their detection equipment—the equipment that, so far, had proven to be practically useless.

And now Nic was still here, still on the site, and still acting like he called the shots. Clearly if she wanted to find out what was really going on, Nic was the key. She doubted he'd just come right out and explain everything to her, though.

She was going to confront him, of course, even if she knew he wouldn't give her a straight answer. Unless maybe he didn't realize that was what he was doing. Perhaps if the guy was distracted, he might let some information slip, might answer her questions without realizing it. She'd have to find just the right method of distraction.

It took about half a second to imagine what that might be.

* * *

He could feel her. She wasn't asleep, even though it was the middle of the night. Everyone else had gone to their rooms, shut down for some rest. But not Lianne. She was still working. He could sense her, sense the agitation and weariness in her. Something else, too…he could sense that some other emotion surged within her. What was it?

He would have to probe a bit deeper if he wanted to feel it with more clarity. Did he dare? He knew he shouldn't. His energy was already nearly depleted simply by maintaining his outward appearance, his human behaviors. He really shouldn't be wasting himself this way, useless mind scans and remote sensing.

But Lianne could help him reclaim his waning energy. One night with her and he'd feel like a new man. He needed her…badly. It would be a simple matter to reach his mind out to hers, to slide inside her thoughts and take control. He had already touched her mind to learn she was tired and vulnerable. She would be easy prey for him tonight.

He was alone, standing in the chilled moonlight just outside the small building that housed the bulk of their work space. Shutting his eyes to the barren landscape around him, he let his mind reach out, stretch itself until he was not only sensing Lianne, but he was with her. He could see her, smell her, feel the conflict that waged inside of her. Carefully, he touched her with his thoughts.

She startled. The feel of her jumbled emotions and the sheer force of her spirit was jarring. He pulled back, lingering just enough to sense her at a distance. She was not quite aware of his presence, yet he sensed that she glanced over her shoulder. Twice. He could feel her tension, her wariness.

Carefully, he probed just a bit deeper—what had she been thinking? Did tempting thoughts of sensual curiosity fill her mind as they did his? He tried to soothe her, keep her calm and submissive, all the while he explored her emotions.

Yes, her thoughts were warm, but not for the reasons he'd hoped. She'd been filled with questions regarding his involvement here on the jobsite, his actions throughout the project. He could feel suspicion—she distrusted him. But something more, too. Attraction was there; yes, he could feel it now, simmering just beyond reach. Her feminine need was very much aware of him, though obviously she was fighting against it.

Instinctively he retreated. She was not willing, even though the first embers of desire for him burned beneath her surface. Would he ignore her wishes? He could make her willing; he knew what to do. His mind was ancient and he'd long ago learned the ways of human passion. His very thoughts held the power to control her yearnings.

But he would not. He wanted Lianne, but she wanted something, too. He would find out what that was and then use it to redirect her efforts on the project, among other things. Gently he let his mind embrace hers, wrap her in his own energy and allow the heat of his desire to seep in and join hers. She would share her secrets.

He breathed in her emotions. So much of her was still hidden to him, but he touched enough of her soul to spark the embers smoldering there. He wanted her, and soon she would want him. His mind caressed hers and he felt her soften.

"What are you doing to me, Nicolai Vladik?"

She was speaking to him? His thoughts were frozen. How could a human know that he had invaded her mind? They did not communicate this way; they did not possess abilities to speak between minds. Yet he had felt her words just as clearly as if he stood next to her.

"I've got work to do and problems to solve," she went on. Her thoughts rambled and he could feel the turmoil inside her. "Why can't I keep my mind off of you?"

"Because you want me," he sent back a reply.

"Yeah. I guess I do."

"And you know I want you," he replied, keeping his touch gentle yet sending enough heat that she could not deny the truth.

Emotion churned inside her, making her mind hard to discern. He could make enough sense of her to understand what she felt, though. She *did* want him. Her thoughts, though, weren't directed to him. She had no idea he had strayed into the privacy of her mind. This internal dialogue Lianne carried on was meant for herself alone.

"Great," she said to herself. "Now I'm hearing his voice inside my head. Just what I need right now."

She might think he was not what she needed right now, but he knew for a fact *he* needed her. He simply had to convince her to feel the same way. Fortunately, she was making the task easier for him. As he caressed her mind, he could sense when her heart rate began to change. Yes, she was responding to him. He concentrated, pouring his desire over her, drenching her in his heat. It became easier and easier to reach just a little bit deeper into her mind.

Her thoughts were wide open to him. It was as if she spoke directly to him.

"You think you are so damn irresistible, don't you? I know all about guys like you. You expect women to fall at your feet. Hell, if it wasn't for this job I probably would."

"At my feet is not where I want you," he intimated.

He could feel her laughing response. "No, it's not your feet I'm interested in, either. Damn it, but why can't we have a little fun while I'm here? I know you want it, and I sure as hell don't have anything to lose."

Her thoughts and desire pounded inside him. He could feel her growing want and the empty abandon that went with it. His human form responded, his cock growing hard and his emotions becoming as tumultuous as hers. She was letting go of her resistance and he realized he was the one falling under her spell.

"I need you, Lianne. I need to fill you and make you cry out my name. I need to soak up your passion and burn with your heat."

He hadn't meant to share his thoughts so blatantly with her but they came tumbling out, spilling into her consciousness. Heat burned within him as her need mingled with his. He found himself struggling to breathe.

"I dare you, Vladik," she responded. "I dare you to get me into your bed and prove you're hotter than all those other assholes."

It was a challenge he wouldn't refuse. She invited his touch, invited his heat. He would show her just exactly how hot he could burn, then he'd take her into the flame with him. This mental connection was more than enough to get her stoked and ready for him. She'd thrown down the gauntlet and he took it up with eager fervor.

She was like no one he'd encountered before; the raw energy churning inside her intoxicated him. Having his way with Lianne would be a rare delight. In his mind he touched her skin, traced scorching lines over her shoulders and along the enticing length of her arms. Her nipples puckered when he focused on them. There was sweetness on her lips and temptation in her soul. He could feel how she enjoyed the fantasy. Soon he would make it reality for her.

* * *

Numbers and columns and statistics had been nearly swimming in front of her eyes. It was late and she ought to be in her bed. She had pushed herself to concentrate, to make sense of this data, but hadn't made much headway.

Nic. Why the hell couldn't she quit thinking of him? Because he was wild and sexy and she wanted to do nasty things with him, that's why. Damn it, but she hoped he'd give her the chance. After she got a few more answers from him, of course.

He was at the heart of all her questions as she'd gone over the readings and reports tonight. Everything always seemed to come back to him. She'd obviously have to confront him tomorrow. She would go to him…she would ask him about…about his shoulders, and that tattoo, and…no, damn it. That wasn't it. What would she ask him?

Hell, she could hardly think straight right now. She must be more exhausted than she realized, although her mind was far from shutting down. Her thoughts were a torrent of images, emotions. *Nic.* She couldn't concentrate on anything but Nic. His face, his arms, his perfectly cut clothing, everything he had under that clothing…for a moment she thought she even heard his voice.

She was clearly alone here, though. Of course she was thinking of Nic. He wasn't just uber-attractive, but he was involved in every questionable aspect of this disorganized project. To find any answers, she had to go through him. It only made sense that he should be on her mind. She just needed to quit thinking about how to get him naked and start thinking up how to get him to give her the truth.

It wasn't truth she wanted right now, though.

His lips. How would they feel pressed against her skin? Hot, demanding…she could practically feel them now. The skin at the back of her neck prickled. It was as if she'd been touched there, caressed by unseen hands that stroked gently over her shoulders, down her arms, warming her along the way. A tremor of excitement trilled through her.

Something sizzled inside—her blood boiling in her veins, perhaps. Her eyes drooped shut and she leaned back in her chair. Exhaustion, that must be the explanation. Her body must be desperate to stay awake, inventing these crazy sensations and the wild images to go along with them.

She could see Nic. He was with her—but he wasn't. She only saw him in her mind, and he loomed large, reaching for her and speaking her name softly, calling her to relax. How could she do anything else? Her limbs were beyond her control. A wave of scorching desire enveloped her and held her where she was, trembling in place as his touch roamed over her body.

The sensation was strong, almost as if he were right there in the room with her. She felt his demanding fingertips brush over her jawline, along her collarbone, and then slowly he was touching her breasts. She drew in a labored breath, begging him to continue but trying to remind herself this was not real.

Her arms moved of their own accord, her fingers moving to the pearl buttons on the thin blouse that she wore. Her shirt gaped open, her body begged for more of Nic's touch. She waited, panting for air, alone with her imaginings, yet very much not alone. She could feel him, sense him as clearly as if he had been standing there over her, reaching to take her into his arms.

For a moment the empty air nearly pulled her out of the fantasy, but then his hands were on her. He cupped her breasts, exploring them as if he'd found rare treasure. She gasped as searing desire shot to her core. She was hot and she was wet and she'd never wanted a man so badly in her life.

She reached for his hands, but found nothing. Her eyes opened and she shuddered, suddenly chilled, glancing nervously around. Empty. The room was vacant, except for her. The files she'd been studying were still laid out on the table in front of her. No one was here. No one had been touching her but herself.

How had it felt so very real, though? How could she have imagined Nic so distinctly? *Why* had she imagined him, of all people?

Because she'd never met anyone like him. And she wanted him.

"You should be in bed."

His voice. Had she imagined that, too? No. She hadn't. She whirled around to find him watching her from the doorway.

It took just a moment to catch her breath and begin fumbling with her blouse. "I'm working."

"No you aren't."

"I was, until…"

"Until what?"

"Until I started feeling…too tired. What are you doing here? Why are you still up?"

"Apparently I was feeling too tired, as well."

"Then you should go to bed."

"Exactly what I was thinking about you."

Instantly, bed was all she could think of. *Bed*, with him in it. Even with her eyes wide open and common sense screaming in her head, she still felt the heat of his touch and pictured herself ripping that shirt off his back. She wanted him as if she'd been starving for him all of her life. Thank God he had no idea she was feeling this way. Or did he? Hell. His smug smile and flashing eyes were just as cocky and annoying and damn tantalizing as she could have guessed they would be.

"I could tuck you in, if that's what you need," he offered.

Yes! Or rather, *No!* She had to concentrate on work before she could play.

"I need to finish going over these reports," she said, turning back to the pages laid out in front of her. "I've been looking over this data and comparing it to some of our start-up files."

"And what are you finding?" he asked, his voice closer behind her.

"I keep seeing your name pop up, as a matter of fact. I was wondering if—"

His hands were on her shoulders. His real hands! She wasn't just imagining his touch this time. He had come near to her and was now gently massaging her shoulders, his fingers kneading tenderly over her tight muscles. Her body responded immediately, her chest rising with a deep, halting breath and her tense shoulders sagging in welcome relief.

"You work harder than you should," he said softly into her ear. "It's time for you to rest now."

"I can't," she replied without any real conviction. "There's too much to do."

"And you'll be much better equipped to do it tomorrow, after you've gone to bed."

"No, I can't," she protested again. It was, of course, true. Her body was on fire right now and sleep was the last thing she could think of. "I'm not tired."

"You will be," he said.

He turned her chair around so she was facing him. Her skin still tingled from where he had touched her, but now he leaned in to take her hands. She let him and wondered when she'd lost control of her arms. It seemed her mind had gone numb, unaware of anything but the desire building inside her.

He loomed before her, the one crystal clear object in a world gone fuzzy and warm.

"Come, Lianne. Let me take you to your room and take care of you tonight."

Her room. That sounded good. His voice was so smooth, his words reassuring. He seemed to want to lull her into blindly trusting him, but he didn't need to do that. She knew who he was and just how far she could trust him. He was an asshole, but he wouldn't harm her. He might lie about the job, and he sure as hell wouldn't be someone to rely on for the future, but this had nothing to do with any of that.

She was smart enough to figure out the job with or without his help. And the future? Well, there was no way he would figure into that, so he was totally off the hook there. All she wanted right now was his hot body making her feel good. There was no doubt he could do that. She rose from her chair and he led her toward the door.

"Which one of these buildings are you staying in?" he asked as they stepped out into the chilled night air.

His touch was light as he helped her down the wooden steps onto the chipped gravel pathway that connected this modular to the others. It was late and the windows around them were dark. Aside from the wind, the only sound she could hear was the droning hum of generators and heating units.

And now their footsteps as she led him toward the boxlike building where she was staying. Would anyone see them? She hoped not. Maybe common sense would tell her to stop, to send Nic off and ignore the burning want in her core or the smoldering promise in his eyes.

She paused on the pathway and gave common sense about three seconds to chime in.

"What is it?" Nic asked. His voice was deep and hot and as intimate as if he breathed into her ear.

"Nothing," she replied. "Come on."

She reached the steps leading up to the main door of her modular. A porch had been constructed there to give the place a homey, welcoming feel. She took a heady breath and Nic's scent filled her senses. Her legs felt like jelly and she stumbled a bit on the stairs. He put his hands on her waist to steady her. She nearly melted under his touch.

"I'm okay, thanks," she said, steadying herself and realizing that she'd never before actually felt dizzy from pure desire. His hands practically burned through her clothes, yet she couldn't wait to get even closer to him.

She fumbled with the key card they'd assigned her. Finally the lock clicked and she pushed the door open. Nic was at her side, but he didn't follow as she stepped in. She held the door, confused by his hesitation.

"You coming in?" she asked.

"Are you sure that's what you want?" he asked.

Hell. Her heart pounded and her body threatened to burst into flame at any moment now. Yes, it was what she wanted! The fact that he asked made her remember how serious this was, though. She'd come to do an important job, not get herself tangled up with the resident bad boy. Would she be jeopardizing her ability to get things done? Would she lose the team's respect if they found out about this? Would she ever forgive herself if she sent him back to his room now?

She contemplated the answer. When she finally spoke, her reply hung like a mist in the crisp air between them. She couldn't take it back if she wanted to. Which she didn't.

"Yeah. It's what I want."

He smiled at her. Those damn eyes were black and fiery all at the same time. She fell into them, trapped by his intensity and aching for something to quench the heat burning inside her.

"I know what you need, Lianne," he said as he reached for her.

She pulled him into the homey modular and practically slammed the door behind him. "Good. Then you aren't going pretend this has anything to do with the job or any kind of relationship or fluffy rainbow dreams for the future, right?"

He gave her another of those boiling-hot grins just before he pulled her into his arms. "I was hoping it was about really hot sex."

Yeah, she was damn sure hoping that, too. She felt good, pressed up against him as his body literally sucked the cold night chill out of her. She'd left her sweater back in the computer room, but the way she was heating up now, she'd never need it again.

The man might be an ass, but he certainly knew how to give the right answers. From his cocky attitude to his smoldering eyes, broad shoulders, and tight, grabbable ass, he seemed to have everything that she wanted. At least for one night. She was getting really good at taking life one night at a time.

They were making out in the lounge area of the VIP guesthouse. There was a small kitchenette behind them, plus two bedroom suites, one at each end of the building. She was the only VIP staying here right now, so they'd have the whole place to themselves. Not that she expected they'd use much of it. The way he was touching her now, pressing his lips to her neck and murmuring in—she guessed—Russian, they might not even make it to the bedroom.

"Just be sure you're out of here long before anyone on-site wakes up and sees you," she admonished, knowing she'd better talk now before his kisses turned her brain to complete mush.

He scooped her up into his arms. "Which bedroom is yours?"

As if that really mattered. She'd settle for any place with a flat surface right now. But for the sake of propriety she pointed to the door at the east end of the modular, where she'd stowed her suitcase and freshened up after arriving. He marched forward like a man on a mission. Maybe she'd regret it in the morning, but right now she was perfectly content that *she* was his mission.

Chapter Five

He dropped her onto the bed. She was clinging to him so tightly that he followed her right down into the fresh linens and downy spread. He'd thought her persistent refusal of his attentions all day had made him more interested in her, but right now her overwhelming willingness was twice as tantalizing as her coy disdain had been. It was nearly enough to send him out of control. She was so open to his touch, so demanding with her desire, that he had to struggle to close off his mind. He needed to focus on the physical now, ignore the waves of sensation that assaulted him mentally.

The woman was a rampant torrent of emotion. He didn't want that—couldn't deal with that now. She claimed this was about nothing other than sex, yet her emotions whorled with much more.

Her raging mind and ragged passions were tantalizing. He wanted to reach deep inside her and discern what was at their core, what fueled such strong emotions. He wouldn't dare let himself, though. This was supposed to be about the physical, about him using her to feed into his need and to regain control over himself and his situation.

She was even hotter and more vigorous than he was right now. If he didn't slow her down just a bit, this wouldn't take any time at all. Although that would still certainly suit his purpose, it wouldn't be nearly as much fun. Lianne McGowan was the sort of woman a man wanted to take his time with.

And he sure as hell wanted her to take some time with him. He had plans for them tonight and they definitely involved more than just a few minutes of panting and sweating. He was counting on a few *hours* of panting and sweating.

She was clearly going for minutes though, the way she tore at his clothes and started fumbling with his belt buckle. Feeling her hands working him there certainly did put him in the mood for being agreeable to her accelerated pace. His cock was as hard as a boulder and straining at his clothing. He could hardly wait to get it inside her, feel the heat of her tender opening, the wet muscles tensing around him as he stroked her over and over again.

She suddenly went rigid underneath him, her hands clutching at the fabric of his shirt, and she moaned, arching up to grind herself against him. He ached with need, but he tried to push himself away from her, to get control of himself long enough to think straight. Hell, he realized he'd been so distracted that he'd allowed his mind to slip back inside hers. She'd felt his thoughts, felt him planning his onslaught, and she'd begun to climax already.

"Slow down," he soothed, shifting to lie next to her and stroke her wild, vibrant hair. "There's no reason to hurry."

"I want to hurry," she said, not meeting his eyes but instead turning her focus onto the buttons of his shirt. "Before I change my mind here."

"I promise I won't give you any reason to do that."

"Good. Then take off your damn shirt."

He had to laugh at her tone, not that it made his raging hard-on any less raging. No, in fact it made him all the more eager to get out of his shirt and strip her out of every scrap of her clothing. With that red hair, he was imagining a sprinkling of freckles over her shoulders and lily-white skin where the sun never shone. He loved the feel, the look of willing female flesh. He could hardly wait to have her laid out before him so he could take in every inch of her.

He leaned back on his elbow and slowly undid the top button of his shirt. He watched as she chewed her lip, mesmerized by his movements. Slowly, he moved on to the next button and then carefully to the next. Her eyes followed. The desire was so thick around them that he was careful not to breathe it in too deeply. He would maintain his control, stay in command of their actions here tonight. It was damn near impossible, though, to rein in his wandering thoughts.

He could feel her approval, the raw lust surging in her as he tantalized her one button at a time. By the Fires, he could feel his own flesh singeing where her eyes lingered on him. She was holding herself back from touching him, from running fingers over his chest or gliding over his skin, across his abdomen clenched tight. Her thoughts were having their way with him and he throbbed for the actual feel of her, for the hands he knew were just itching to get beyond his clothing and explore him in detail. He studied her lips and gave out a groan when the image of them moving over his flesh, devouring him, taking the full size of him into her mouth entered his mind. He'd never experienced this with a human before. Usually his was the mind that did the teasing, using his thoughts to increase the sensual need within his partner. This was the first time he'd encountered it working the other way around.

He liked it.

She startled him out of the fantasy, though, as she shoved him back down onto his back, brushing his hands away and taking over the buttons for herself.

"Hell, let me do it," she said.

She ripped his shirt open the rest of the way and yanked it out from his pants. She'd already gotten the belt undone and now immediately went for his zipper. The woman was nothing if not efficient, and before he could remind her to slow down, she had him exposed. His cock practically leaped out of its confinement, and she grabbed it as if she'd been stalking a wild animal.

He half expected her to exclaim, to make some randy comments about his size or the obvious state of his arousal—he was fairly used to those reactions—but she said nothing. She simply wrapped her hands around him and purred as if she'd won some sort of prize. He had to draw in a slow breath and remember why he was doing this or he would have been lost already. She was stroking him carefully now.

"So far I'm not changing my mind," she said softly.

"Good." He liked her mind the way it was, focused on him.

He needed to be a little bit more careful of his own mind, however. He kept forgetting to keep his dragon senses checked. This was a simple coupling, just another night of physical pleasure that his human body needed to engage in, but his very essence would not be a part of it. He could not let Lianne touch more than just his human body. She could never know about the parts of him that had gone untouched so long…no matter how much he might wish her to. He could not allow her into his soul. Slaking his desire with Lianne tonight would give him back some of the energy he used to maintain this human form, but he could not let it change who he truly was.

He was not a man, no matter how long he had lived in this form. He was from the Forbidden Realm; Lianne would never even have known he existed if he'd not chosen to appear as a human, to step through the Veil and reveal himself to her. His soul was not a part of her mundane world, despite his being ruled by the carnal desires this frail human form needed so often. He was a being of magic. He lived behind the Veil that separated humans from magic and kept him and all of his kind carefully hidden. And safe.

He couldn't allow himself to become involved here on any other level but the physical. He'd used his dragon senses to reach into Lianne's mind simply because it served his purpose. But now that he knew she was willing and eager for their joining, he could withdraw that part of him, give over to the physical and enjoy the purely human sensations they'd share together tonight. Human passions served a useful purpose. He took pleasure in them and drew energy from them, but he wouldn't involve his soul, despite how tempting it would be. That part of him must remain safely hidden, shuttered up behind the Veil.

Lianne's alluring little body, however, did not need to remain safely behind anything. He gritted his teeth as she stroked his cock and he went to unfasten the rest of the buttons on her delicate blouse. He was desperate for them to be skin-to-skin. Thankfully her cardigan had been left in the computer room when he'd seduced her out of that building. It was a simple matter of undoing her blouse and pulling her close as he reached around to unfasten her bra.

He had those perky breasts in his hands almost as quickly as she'd gotten into his pants. By the Fires, she was firm and full. Her nipples peaked for him as he brushed his thumbs over them. He toyed with them, loving the feel of her silky skin and the bounce of her tender flesh.

She liked it, too, cooing from his touch, and matching his vigor with her own as she played at pleasuring him. Her fist clenched around him, gliding up the full length of his cock while she watched him. He shifted uncomfortably. Damn, his body was eager to give in, but his sheer willpower would not yet allow it. He needed to benefit from her pleasure, not merely his own.

It seemed that would not be a problem, however. She was more than enjoying the moment. Pleasure came easily for Lianne, it would seem. Excellent. He could feel the passion radiating off her already. She was giving in and opening herself to the heat of their encounter. He was feeding from that energy already.

It would take hardly any effort at all to bring her to further climax. She sure as hell had thawed once she put her mind to it. He'd been prepared to use much more of his persuasive powers, but she'd not needed that. Having decided to pursue pleasure, her cast-iron persona had faded away to reveal a deeply passionate woman. The transition was captivating.

Nic was glad for the moonlight pouring in through the window—he was entranced by the pleasure and passion displayed in her features, her actions, the way she let her long auburn curls fall every which way around her. She was all about the physical right now and responding with full force to every caress, every brush of skin against skin. He cupped one of her velvety breasts and took the tantalizing nipple into his mouth.

Her eyes drooped shut and she let out a contented sigh. Yes, she would come so very easily for him. He would fill her, glide into her and share some of his heat. She'd climax in his arms and he'd watch her, experience the pleasure with her. He'd draw from her the energy he needed to continue in this human form. Then, if he'd done the thing well, she'd welcome him into her body again. And again. They had a very long night ahead and he was looking forward to every minute of it.

As he ran his hands over her flesh, pushing the light fabric of her blouse off her shoulders and breathing kisses on the delightful spatter of freckles he found there, he felt her body slightly tense. Was she beginning to regret her decision to invite him into her room? He hadn't pegged Lianne to be one of those women who let misplaced common sense creep in and douse the flames that wanted to burn inside them. No, she seemed far more sure of herself, confident and decisive. When she opened that door to let him inside, he'd known she meant it. He could feel that she needed this release nearly as much as he did.

"Just relax," he murmured into her ear. "I'll take care of you."

But her eyes were wide open now, and dark with an intensity he hadn't expected to find. Under his fingers, her muscles grew taut and she suddenly sat up. There was nothing he could do but fall back onto the bed and wait for some sort of explanation.

"No," she said defiantly. "You're not going to take care of me. *I'm* going to take care of *you*."

And she very nearly did. Her sudden shift in position, as well as demeanor, surprised him and he was caught off guard. She moved like a cat, practically pouncing so that she ended up straddling him, her blouse hanging off her and her luscious breasts taunting him. He had no choice but to lie back and let her do as she would.

His engorged cock rose valiantly before her and she smiled as she studied it. Her movements were fluid, but calculated as she positioned herself just right. He watched, eager for what she might choose to do to him. He wasn't disappointed.

She leaned in to press a hot, wet kiss right on the very tip of his throbbing cock. Then she arched her back as she slid up until she was sitting right atop him. He groaned from the pleasure of it as she ground herself against him, smiling as his length pressed against her sensitive area, even though the slacks she still wore prevented anything more dramatic from happening. She leaned toward him and must have known he would instinctively nip at her nipple. She rewarded him with a purr.

He grabbed her curvy little butt and pulled her more tightly against him. By the Fires, she was even more than he'd bargained for. Her hair fell over her shoulders, and the moonlight made her skin fairly glow. He rocked under her, watching her smile. The light abrasion from the fabric of her slacks was very likely making him smile, too.

"See, now isn't this better?" she asked.

* * *

She wanted him so badly her body practically ached. But she'd hold off just a bit longer. It wasn't as if the man was going anywhere. He was into this just as much as she was.

Lianne tossed her hair back and shifted position, bearing down on him so that he groaned under her. She'd purposely not taken her slacks off yet, even though she'd had him hard and ready and out in the open for some time now. God, but he was big. And solid like a rock.

It had seemed he'd been interested in some foreplay, too, but that was out of the question for her. None of that mushy, emotional snuggling. If she was going to do this—and she sure as hell intended to—she was going to be extra careful to leave her heart and any of her more vulnerable parts out of it. This was just about her body, nothing more.

Things would be better that way. For both of them. This would just be sex—really hot, spur-of-the-moment sex. That's what she wanted right now. The thought of giving in to such uninhibited passion was a little bit intoxicating, really. She'd never been the one-night-stand type in the past but now...well, this seemed to be just what the doctor ordered.

Of course, it was probably exactly the opposite of what her doctor really would order for her, given the circumstances, but she was going with a second opinion: her own. And her opinion was to prescribe a whole night of sweaty, steamy sex with the hottest man she'd met in a long time. Okay, the hottest man she'd *ever* met, actually. And she didn't have to care if he called her back or even liked her in the morning.

All he had to do was give her what she needed now, then show up to work tomorrow, which would be kind of hard for him *not* to do since they were pretty much stranded between a glacier and a big, barren mountain in Iceland. The helicopter that brought her out here had dropped off a week's worth of supplies and wasn't due back for another week. Until then, Nic was more or less stuck working with her. And making her nights a little more entertaining, if he lived up to expectations. Which it seemed like he would.

But she was for damn sure not going to let him get the stupid idea that she was looking for a relationship. She'd be in charge of this from start to finish. And by all indications, the finish would be well worth her effort. Even through her clothing she could feel her body growing closer to a climax.

Not that she wanted him to think he'd done anything special for her.

The man was full of himself enough. She needed to keep him in his place, especially since they still had plenty of work to do. She figured she knew just how to do that.

She slid slowly against him. He was cupping her breasts so he could get a good, long look at them in the light that came through the window overlooking the vast emptiness of the huge, forbidden mountain and the sprawling glacier at its foot. He was clearly a man who'd had his share of women, and she was just vain enough to feel a little bit giddy at the blatant appreciation she read in his expression now. He was drinking in his fill of her and he liked what he saw.

An involuntary sigh escaped as she filled her lungs. It would be so easy to just linger here, to let him bask in full view of her finest assets and wait for him to call the shots. The feel of his fingers over her nipples sent rivers of heat and desire surging through her extremities. Oh yes, he knew what he was doing, and he'd make sure she didn't have to fake anything tonight. It was tempting to take advantage of that and just enjoy the waves of pleasure.

But then it would be over. He'd leave—as she would want him to, of course—and she'd be left alone to come back to reality. She hated that part. Damn reality might get shoved under the rug for a while, but once this was over she'd have to face it again. If she was smart, she'd drag this wonderfully distracting event out as long as she could.

She ran her hands over Nic's chest, tracing his muscular contours and rubbing herself up against him. There was no use hiding how hot and ready for him she was, but as long as she kept her damn pants on she was the one running the show. She might prolong this fantasy.

He didn't seem overly concerned about who was in charge, though. He let her explore his body and merely smiled with approval when she shifted against him, the barrier of her clothing becoming more and more obvious as their need for each other increased. He put his large hands at her waist, holding her steady as he pressed up against her, adding to the fire inside her.

He shifted position and managed to find just the right spot to make her see stars.

Damn it, but he was going to make her come already and he still hadn't even actually touched her *there*! If she wanted to remain the one in control of this activity, she'd better let things move just a little faster.

"I'll take off my pants if you're ready to put on a condom," she said.

"I'm afraid you caught me off guard," he said. "I didn't bring any."

"Is that your way of saying you expect me to let you go on without one?"

"No, it's my way of saying you're welcome to keep your pants on while we do this. I don't need you naked to make your toes curl."

There was a little bit of a challenge behind his words. She was half tempted to let him prove what he said, but the other half of her didn't need proof. She knew he could do exactly what he said.

"That's okay," she said. "I plan to be the one making *your* toes curl, and I've got condoms in my bag."

That was just a happy accident. She still had a stash in her bag from the last trip she'd taken with the previous tattooed asshole who had occupied her time. The one who made her think he cared about her but then took off as soon as she needed something other than sex from him. It was a valuable lesson learned and she wasn't going to be making those same stupid mistakes ever again.

Even if she wanted to.

She shifted off him, enjoying the view as he lay there sprawled on her bed with his eyes dark and smoky and his cock rising up into the moonlight like a bronze pillar. She couldn't help but reach out and touch it again, stroking her fingers over the velvety sheath. He murmured in some unrecognized language and she gave in to the temptation to lean over and taste him. Not just a teasing kiss; she put her lips fully over him, letting her teeth graze him lightly as she sucked him deeper inside. Exotic. Tantalizing.

She wanted more. As her tongue flicked around him, tasting and tormenting, the heat coursing through her was almost too much. Was it possible she might climax this way, simply from pulling him into her mouth? As the familiar wave of electricity threatened to sweep over her, she knew it was entirely possible.

What kind of man was this? She didn't care. She wrapped her fingers around the base of his cock, marveling at the size of the thing as she continued to suck and glide her mouth over him, first slowly and then progressively faster. It was as if she could feel every spasm of pleasure that was building up inside him. It was building up inside her, too.

It was just a matter of who would succumb first. Damn, but she wanted to give in and focus on his hands that stroked over her body, toying with her breasts and leaving her marked by his heat. She wouldn't, though. She would prove to him she could handle whatever he had to give her. Even if he'd hardly given anything and she was the one doing the work.

Not that she minded. He tasted like fire, like raw, unfettered passion. She drew this passion from him, letting it swell inside her body as tangibly as if he had penetrated her and thrust over and over within her. Hell, just the thought of it made her quiver and go weak.

Not weak enough to stop her ministrations, of course. With just a bit more pressure, she dragged his cock through her lips. She could feel the pulsing begin as he moaned. Yes, she'd done what she wanted. He was helpless under his climax now. She drove her lips over him again, taking him into her mouth and holding him there until he could hold his control no longer.

He growled aloud, a deep, animal sound that made her thrill with excitement. Then he came. The waves rolled over him and she clung to him for dear life. She held him there, keeping him under her command until she knew he was finished.

She'd done it. She'd won. She'd dragged a raging climax from him despite the way he made her go weak with the slightest of actions. She'd proven that she was in charge. She'd wrangled her own body into submission even as she'd done the same to his.

That, in itself, was pretty damn orgasmic.

Chapter Six

Raea buzzed her wings and glanced over at Kyne. They'd been gathered around the rough-hewn dining table in the cabin's small kitchen area, listening to Baylor for some time now, and she could feel the tension building in the air around them. The taut muscles in Kyne's still-human-sized body were tight with his barely pent-up apprehension. She had long since shrunk back down to her natural size, but Kyne remained every bit as large as his father. His body held the effects of the Sizing Dust much longer than hers.

She watched him, studied his wary interaction with Baylor. Despite Kyne's obvious fairy features, the resemblance between the two men was uncanny. How had she not known right from the start how very human he was?

It seemed that his human characteristics were more pronounced the more he was around humans. His aura was just a bit dimmer and his body more angular, more rugged. She doubted that Kyne would appreciate if she pointed it out to him. She wished he could appreciate his more human attributes. Certainly she did.

Perhaps it was, in fact, his blatant humanity that had attracted her to him in the first place. He was wild, exotic, and absolutely irresistible to her. Of course forbidden passions and longings had come bursting to life inside her as she had been around him. Kyne was everything her deepest, most secret nature craved. Her initial battle against that had been futile from the start.

Now, however, it appeared they were being asked to help battle something else, something unknown. Whatever these forces were, they were actively compiling an arsenal to cause irreparable damage within the Forbidden Realm. The Veil itself seemed to be their target. Baylor had no idea whom he could trust and whom he could not, so he'd come here.

He needed Kyne to do what he couldn't, to travel swiftly and undetected to find out what he could about these strange happenings. And Kyne would go, she had no doubt of that. Despite his animosity toward his father, he would go. He loved the Forbidden Realm more than he hated the man who sired and then abandoned him.

And whether Kyne liked it or not, Raea would be going with him. She loved him more than she feared whatever they might find at the end of their journey. In the wild, uncivilized West Fjords of Iceland, of all places. There was no telling what sort of magic was running unchecked in a land such as that.

"It's here," Baylor said, pointing to a crude map he had drawn on a discarded paper. "I'd download more-specific coordinates for you, but I'm afraid none of my electronic technology works up here in this cabin."

"We don't work like that, anyway," Kyne said. "I'll be navigating by magic, so your human drawings are worthless to me."

"There's an awful lot of magic over there, I'm told. Really ancient things have been left undisturbed for centuries. You sure you can find the way?"

Kyne sneered his response, clearly insulted by Baylor's question.

Raea decided it was a good time for a question of her own. "You said your information indicated the equipment was being delivered to a remote location at a volcano. Is this the same sort of equipment we found here in the woods?"

"No, this machinery has been altered in some way. Instead of supporting the Veil, it seems to create further damage to it. All we know is it's highly dangerous and is being sent to the wilderness around the Drangajökull glacier. It's been shipped out of Sandstrom Industries in unusual quantities for some time now."

The named triggered a recollection for Raea. "Did you say Sandstrom?"

"Yeah," Baylor replied. "It's owned by some guy not too far from here. Not sure what his connection with the Forbidden Realm is, though."

Raea's heart thudded in her chest and she shot Kyne a quick glance. He frowned at her.

"Sandstrom? Is this name supposed to mean anything to me?"

"It's a fairly large corporation," Baylor said, not noticing Raea's panic. "It's owned by some genius recluse who spends most of his time out on his boat."

Kyne seemed to be digesting this. "Boat? Wait a minute, this isn't the same guy who—"

Raea interrupted him and sparkled for Baylor. "Do you know this Sandstrom person? Is that how you came by your information?"

"No, I've never met him," Baylor replied. "From what I hear though, Sandstrom's connection to the council was established by his wife, years ago. She's deceased now—died sometime back in a freak storm, I believe—but it seems she made some kind of deal. I don't know details, but Sandstrom Industries went from a little start-up in the guy's garage to a multimillion-dollar corporation practically overnight. They've got some pretty high-end technology there. I'm not even sure Devin Sandstrom himself knows what it is they're making and shipping all over the world."

"But Devin Sandstrom is the guy with the mermaid, isn't he?" Kyne asked, glaring at Raea.

"Mermaid?" Baylor exclaimed. "Now there are mermaids involved?"

Obviously they were going to have to explain this to him. Well, he already knew most of their secrets and hadn't betrayed them. One more couldn't possibly put them at any great risk, could it?

"Devin Sandstrom is a man we have dealt with before," she began. "And it isn't all mermaids who are involved, just one."

"I think *involved* is kind of an understatement," Kyne interjected.

Raea ignored him and continued. "She and Devin...well, they fell in love, and it was, more or less, my fault."

Baylor shook his head in dismay. "How is that even possible?"

"It's a long story," Kyne said quickly. "The point of it is that Raea found a way to work it out and now they can be together. Sandstrom has a nice new connection to the Forbidden Realm."

"I'm sure he would never do anything to cause harm to us, though," Raea added quickly. "He's a really nice man, for a human, I mean. No offense."

"He might be a nice man, but his company has been supplying equipment that is being used to destroy the Veil," Baylor said.

Kyne cursed under his breath. "And we helped the man possess more magic."

"I can't believe he would do anything that might put Aliya in danger. He loves her," Raea insisted. "There must be other forces involved, people or creatures we don't know about."

Kyne didn't seem convinced. "You really believe his company could manufacture this sort of machinery without Devin knowing it?"

"Well, if he knew about it, and if he had all this magic at his disposal, why did he need a Wish Fairy to help him find his true love?" Raea defended. "His company is very large, and you know he was completely distracted. Someone else must simply be using him."

Baylor surprised her by agreeing. "It's possible. You both know how things work. Your Fairy Council can make humans dance to their bidding if they choose to. I have no doubt that Sandstrom Industries has been in their pocket for years. Your man might truly be innocent."

"So you suggest Sandstrom Industries is being secretly operated by the Fairy Council?" Kyne asked.

"Fairies have a knack for hiding in plain sight," Baylor said. "They're using Sandstrom Industries to manufacture the equipment you found in the forest. Between magic and plain old deception, they've secretly put together a select group of humans and fairies to oversee the project. We all just manage our own little piece of the puzzle, and I don't even know who else is involved, beyond my immediate contacts. The trouble is, I don't think the Fairy Council is the only group doing this. I'm worried there is another faction operating around ours."

"You mean there is more than one magical coalition hiding inside Sandstrom Industries?" Raea asked.

"But how could something like that be hidden inside a human organization?" Kyne asked.

"My guess is they've set up their own division within the corporation," Baylor explained. "I believe the Fairy Council is managing the main one, yet someone else has infiltrated their organization and is siphoning some of the secret equipment, reengineering it and diverting it for their own use."

"Your mysterious person in Iceland," Raea said.

Baylor nodded. "Exactly."

Kyne shook his head, unconvinced. "So not only is the Fairy Council operating under Sandstrom's nose, but some entity in Iceland is sneaking around under theirs? Do we really believe this is possible?"

"That's what you need to find out," Baylor said.

"All the while being hunted by the Fairy Council ourselves." Kyne practically snarled the words.

Not that Raea could blame him. She'd certainly learned more about the workings of their Fairy Council in the last few days than she'd ever known in her whole life. Only a week ago she would have defended them, praised them for representing the needs of her kind. She would have called Baylor's claims about mysterious shipments and shadowy forces ludicrous. Today, though, she knew anything was possible.

"You want us to go find this equipment hidden somewhere in a faraway place called Iceland," Raea clarified.

"Near a semi-dormant volcano wrapped by a glacier, that's right. I really would go myself, if I thought I could get out from under the council's thumb."

"Pity you can't just ask my mother to look into this for you," Kyne said. "Or is she, perhaps, not as eager to do your bidding as you'd like to pretend?"

"She doesn't do my bidding. Hell, she's got her own tasks to be managing, plus…well, let's just say the council keeps their eye on her, too. Why do you think she never told you when we got back together? No one can know. The council constantly reminds me that anytime I step out of line, they'll find a way to make her life uncomfortable. As they will yours, I'm afraid."

"Is that the reason they dragged me into the Council Hall? You did something that upset them?"

"Kyne, this is so much bigger than us. Of course I would never want to do anything to make life difficult for you."

"Yet here I am," Kyne noted bitterly.

"Yes, here we all are. I can't protect you anymore, Kyne. Things have come too far. We don't have a choice. We have to take a stand and see this to its conclusion…whatever that will be."

"Will our going to Iceland bring on this conclusion more quickly?" Raea asked.

"I hope so," Baylor replied, shaking his head and looking as if he wasn't entirely certain he had any hope left.

"Then we'll go," Raea announced, fluttering over to alight on Kyne's arm. "Won't we?"

"Is there any way I can talk you out of it?" Kyne asked her.

"Not very likely," she replied with a smile. "But you're welcome to try."

Baylor chuckled. "I'd love for you two kids to have time to come to an agreement, but that's a luxury we don't have. We need to know *now* what this other group is up to, before it's too late. Let her go with you, Kyne. I have a feeling she's good for you."

For the first time, Kyne replied to his father without a scowl or a sneer. "Yes. She is."

She had to struggle to hide a satisfied grin. He was right, of course. She was good for him, but it ran both ways. They were good for each other.

Now she was going to find out how good they were for each other on another continent. Together. Near a volcano. And a glacier. With magical equipment that had the power to drain their magic and send them into a sexual frenzy.

If nothing else, this trip was going to prove to be interesting.

* * *

Baylor's words had proven true. Ancient magic did run wild in Iceland. Kyne could feel it from here, and they were still quite a distance offshore.

"So this is called Iceland?" Raea called to him as they zipped through wind gusts of salty spray and approached the dark, rocky land mass ahead.

"It is," he replied. "One of those peaks we see in the distance should be the mountain we are heading for."

They'd used magic to plot their course as well as to accelerate their pace, but he could tell Raea was becoming exhausted from the journey. He'd insisted they spend as much time over water as they could in order to avoid detection by any humans, but as he studied the land it was obvious there weren't many humans around. It shouldn't be too difficult to find a safe place to land and take stock of things.

Raea probably wasn't going to admit to him how tired she was, so he'd have to pretend he could use a rest. She was bravely matching his wing strokes and keeping up with him as they approached the jagged landscape of the huge, alien island. It was foolish and unnecessarily dangerous for her, but he was damn glad to have her at his side.

He pointed to one of the jutting mountains up ahead. His magical sense of navigation told him this was their destination. She probably recognized it, too, but he gestured toward it.

"Right there. That's where we're going."

"It's a very big mountain," she noted.

"It's a volcano," he corrected. "Dormant, supposedly."

"Semi-dormant," she corrected. "And your father said scientists are in the area, and many of those machines have been sent here to tamper with magic."

"Well, they haven't tampered too much. I can feel the magic from here, can't you?"

"Yes, actually, I can. There is strong magic here," Raea replied as they swooped over the waves below that crashed at the rocky shore.

They were both tossed by air currents every bit as ragged as the foaming sea waters.

"Ancient magic," he said. "Wild and untamed."

"Obviously we are in the right place."

"Getting tired, are you? Need a rest?" he asked as he twisted in air, watching her struggle to keep up with the frenetic pace of the wind.

"No. I can make it to the mountain."

"We should rest," he said. "Let's just get inland, away from the damp wind, and catch our breaths."

He could see how relieved she was at that suggestion. She had come all this way through the wind and some pretty unpleasant weather and hadn't complained once. He gave her a sizzling smile. The one that she sent back to him almost made up for the fact that they were flying straight on into danger.

This land that now greeted them was rutted with deep valleys and rifts, dark volcanic rock that had been cut over millennia by runoff from the nearby glacier as it advanced and receded. The low-lying areas were dotted with sparse patches of moss and scrubby tufts of coarse grass. Their kind were not often affected by weather and external temperatures, but even he could feel the cold begin seeping into his bones. Maybe he was more sensitive to it due to his human blood. Raea gave no sign that it caused her any discomfort. Apparently she was determined to prove herself more than up to whatever challenges faced them.

"How about there?" he asked, calling over the wind and pointing to the shadowy side of the mountain.

It was dark and desolate, and they could see for miles around them. Nothing but vast emptiness. If they were worried about being discovered by someone, they could lay those fears to rest right now. There was simply no one to do any discovering.

"It sure doesn't look like a hotbed of human and magical corruption," she commented.

"It doesn't look like a hotbed of anything," he agreed.

They had left the gusty shoreline behind them, and it was easier to talk now. The winds still blew with good force, but neither of them had to yell quite so loudly to be heard. Flight was easier in these conditions. He could spare a glance here and there to admire the way Raea's hair tossed in the breeze and how the strange colors in the arctic skyline reflected off her wings.

"Wait, look at that," she suddenly called out, pointing toward a shadowy area near the base of the mountain.

He studied the spot and a glint caught his eye. It wasn't large, but something metallic seemed to be reflecting. With so much nothingness around them, clearly this bit of something was worth investigation.

"Let's move closer, but be careful," he admonished. "We have no idea what to expect."

They swooped down, darting erratically just in case anyone should be trying to track them. When they were close enough, he could see that the object was indeed metallic—at least parts of it were—and clearly human in origin. It was some kind of scientific instrument, mounted on a stake that was driven into the rocky earth.

"It doesn't look like the machinery we found in the wood," Kyne pointed out.

"It's smaller, and no one went to any trouble to hide it. Do you think maybe it's one of the devices being used by that scientific team Baylor warned us about?" Raea proposed.

"It could be. I wonder what it does."

"This doesn't appear to do anything. It just pokes into the ground."

They moved in closer, approaching the object and circling it.

"Why would they monitor the ground?" Raea asked.

"This is on the edge of a volcano. Maybe they want to find out if it's going to become fully dormant, or if it's waking up."

She nodded. "Makes sense. Without magic, they'd have no way of knowing that sort of thing."

"I think it's safe. I don't feel any of the effects we've experienced before near the hybrid machines."

He touched down carefully on the rough, rocky ground. She landed softly beside him and brushed him ever so slightly with her wings. When he looked at her she was smiling.

"You don't feel *anything* like that?" she asked.

"When you're around, I *always* feel some of that," he replied with his own sly grin. "What I don't feel is the presence of the kind of equipment we came here to locate."

He studied this device. To a human, it would have stood up as high as a knee. To fairies, though, it towered over them, twice their height. About the size of an average fairy dwelling, it was rectangular in shape and rather ungainly in appearance as it hovered there on its thin stake. Raea fluttered upward, studying the pinpoint lights blinking on the front of it. Kyne walked around the base, investigating it from below.

A strange little box had been affixed onto the side of it, he noted. Somehow that didn't seem to belong, with odd wires protruding from a roughly cut hole in the side of the device. The humans who had constructed this clearly did not care for aesthetics.

He wondered how deeply this stake was imbedded into the ground. Most likely a hole had been initially bored into the rocky earth so the stake could be wedged in tightly. Curious, he kicked the stake. To his surprise, the odd box with the wires suddenly began humming.

"What did you do?" Raea called. "The lights on this thing just started blinking like crazy."

"I don't know. I kicked it, and now it started making noise."

He put his hand out to touch the stake. He shouldn't have. A jolt of magic suddenly coursed through him. He jumped, then swore.

"What is it?" Raea asked, dipping low to check on him.

"I don't think it's good," he said, reaching to touch it again.

Sure enough, there *was* magic around this device. It must not have been functioning when they first arrived, but somehow he'd triggered it. By the Skies, he could feel the effects already. Raea moved closer to him.

"So Baylor was right," she noted. "The humans *are* using magic here."

The worry and effort of their travel must have been taking a toll on her. He could see fear wash over her expression and she leaned on him for support. Her body trembled, so he put his arms around her. She felt immeasurably good up against him, so he pulled her close.

"Don't worry," he assured her, pressing a tender kiss on her head. "We'll figure out what to do about this."

"But what if..." She gazed up with huge eyes. The heat he saw burning there wiped every bit of chill from his body and kindled his desire.

"The machine is affecting me already," he said.

"Didn't Baylor mention once that the effects are more powerful when the machinery first starts up?"

"Yeah, something like that."

She was holding him now just as tightly as he was holding her. "And we are standing very, very close to that little box."

"We're closer to each other."

"I think we could get closer, even."

"I know that we can," he said, just before he kissed her.

* * *

Raea would never grow tired of his kisses. Her lips gave in to his easily, eagerly begging for more. Her skin celebrated his touch, energy flowing into her body despite the exhaustion she'd felt just moments ago. Desire burst into life inside her and she held on to him tightly.

"I almost wish we'd stayed back in the cabin," he said as he trailed kisses along her neck and over her shoulders. "This hardly seems the perfect place to give in to passion."

"It feels perfect to me," she said and encouraged him by running her hands over his chest and down between them to the heat of his thighs.

She was careful to simply tease him with touch, not let instinct take over fully and explore the hardening shaft she could feel pressing against her already. Kyne's lovemaking was so generous, so wonderful, she would hate to hurry things along. Although, there was a lot to be said for hurrying, too.

"I can't believe that I want you so badly right now," he whispered into her ear.

"We probably shouldn't let ourselves be so distracted," she agreed, but made no effort to slow anything down.

"It doesn't seem like we're hurting anything, though," he said. "We can get all the information we need on this damned equipment afterward."

"Yes. This is what I want right now, Kyne. Can you feel how much I want you?"

And she did want him, madly and desperately. There was no logic to this—one moment she'd been cold and afraid, the next minute she'd been in his arms begging him to take her. Everything that he did made her nearly insane with desire. It was wonderful.

"I want you, too," he agreed, his hands sliding down to clutch her butt and thrill her with a healthy squeeze.

She wriggled, making sure her feathery skirt hoisted up just enough that she could feel skin against skin. He seemed to appreciate her effort, his hands rubbing and stroking, sliding from the back toward the front. She practically purred from the blissful torture, shifting so that he could make contact with her burning cleft.

"By the Skies, you are so ready for me," he murmured.

She pressed herself against him. He rubbed the tender nub at her core. One finger dipped inside her. She thrust herself against him and instantly came.

Pressed up against the human device, she climaxed effortlessly without so much as even trying. The urgency and immediacy surprised her, as did the sudden shower of sparks that rained over them. Kyne pulled her away, shielding her as the smell of burning equipment filled the air around them and ruined the mood completely.

"By the Skies! What happened?" she gasped.

"The device," he panted. "We forgot what happens to this sort of equipment when we get so carried away."

Her brain was clearing now and she pushed away from Kyne, glancing wildly. How could she possibly have forgotten? The first time they'd encountered this type of technology, it drew out the passion in them, made them helpless slaves to it, in fact. They were left vulnerable and weak, easy targets for humans.

She took a deep breath and embraced the cold air. "Luckily, this thing seems to be out of commission now."

The little box on the side of the device smoldered and sputtered, a puff of acidic smoke wafted away from it, and the unsightly wires were burned and unsalvageable. As they'd experienced before, the act of passion in the vicinity of these machines sent them into overload. Clearly this was a design flaw that perhaps the humans had not yet discovered. It was going to be exhausting, however, if this turned out to be the only way to defeat them.

"It looks like only part of it is shut down, though," Kyne said. "The main box seems to still be working."

He was right. The little lights on the front blinked into the northern half-night. The cadence appeared somewhat more frantic than before.

"You don't supposed this is transmitting to the humans, do you?" she asked.

"I have no doubt of it. Whoever put this here did it for a reason, and they're going to be keeping track of it. Come on. Are you strong enough to fly?"

She shook out her wings. A little unsteady, yes, but she could fly. "I am. And you?"

One quick glance down at the front of him, and she could see he wasn't entirely back to normal. She'd been the one to get lucky this time. Poor Kyne was left with a little bit of a problem.

"Yeah, I'm okay," he said, sounding slightly pained. "Let's go."

Chapter Seven

Lianne slid away to go hunt for those condoms. Her pride in her accomplishment lasted only as long as it had taken Nic to compose himself and then shoot her a wicked grin. He'd appreciated what she'd done, but he assured her there was plenty more where that had come from. And she wanted it. *All* of it.

Her bag was sitting on a chair next to the dresser. She hadn't taken the time to unpack yet, so she unzipped the side pocket and started feeling around inside. Wouldn't it be tragic now if she realized she hadn't actually left the condoms in there all those months ago?

Her fingers had just brushed against the familiar packaging when a sudden alarm blared outside her room and startled her. She jumped, blinking wildly for a moment and glaring at Nic.

"What is that?" she asked.

He sat upright. "Seismic activity. Beyond the usual levels."

"An earthquake?"

"Yes."

"I didn't feel an earthquake."

He gave her another grin. "Liar."

"Don't flatter yourself. How far out of the usual parameters would this earthquake have to be to trigger that alarm?"

He had already swung his legs off the bed and was tucking himself back into his pants. "Enough to be of concern. This alarm means there is seismic activity below the mountain."

"And what does *that* mean?"

She took his cue and began putting her own clothing back in order. Clearly whatever was going on, their interlude here was over. Nic was preparing to leave her and she had every intention of following him.

"It means something is changing. The mountain is changing."

"Changing? You mean, like some kind of eruption?"

"I don't know. We'll have to see what the data says."

"What data? The so-called data I've been trying to make sense out of all day? We can't trust any of those instruments if that's the sort of information they're giving us."

"Those are the only instruments we have," he said. "Come on. Let's go see what they're giving us."

He sure was taking this awfully seriously. She was less inclined to give much credence to anything their sensors might indicate. From what she'd seen studying reports all day long, the data being streamed in from their on-site instruments was less than reliable. Who was to say this alarm wasn't just some additional malfunction?

Then again, the way Nic was putting himself back together and swiping his hair into place, she had to wonder if maybe there wasn't something to it. After all, he was the one telling her the mountain was unstable. There'd been no actual reports of volcanic activity here in at least the last few hundred years, but the guy must have some reason for getting up out of that bed when he had been pretty damn contented in it thirty seconds ago.

"You really think there's something going on under that mountain?" she asked. The damn alarm still blared from the horn attached to the outside of the building that housed the computer lab.

"Yeah," he replied. "And it picked a hell of a time to start up now."

Good. The way his eyes roved over her just before he pulled the bedroom door open to leave was enough to assure her he was none too happy about this interruption. She wasn't the only one feeling frustrated and grumpy just now. But at least she didn't have half an enormous boner jamming up against the front of her pants the way he did.

She smiled and nodded toward his very obvious problem. "You'd better get that under control before we go sauntering into that computer lab. Everyone on the jobsite must be awake by now and headed there."

"You should go on before me, then," he said. "I have a feeling it would be better for all of us if no one noticed me walking out of your quarters in the middle of the night."

She couldn't agree more. She wasn't above a little extra sway in her hips as she walked past him, though. His knuckles clenched white on the doorknob, and his breathing sounded just slightly like an irritated growl.

"You owe me some curled toes, Vladik," she said, meeting his sizzling eyes.

His smoky voice held a combination of promise and threat. "I always fulfill my debts, Ms. McGowan. You'll soon be paid, I assure you—in full."

* * *

Nic waited for Lianne to leave the guesthouse and dash across the open area between buildings. He let himself out but instead of following her, he slipped around the back of the guesthouse. The moon was bright and the sky glowed around it. He could see the vast, barren landscape around them plainly.

He could also see what the others could not. He opened his dragon senses once again and let his eyes readjust. Not only did he have powers of the mind that humans lacked, but his physical sight was far better than theirs, too. He could detect colors, heat signatures they couldn't see. These were the telltale evidences of magic and his fellow creatures who lived be-hind the Veil of the Forbidden Realm.

One of them glowed faintly in the shadows behind this building right now.

"You've been spying on me again, Eubryd," he called out in the low, rumbling tones of the language his kind had used for millennia.

"It is my duty to keep watch over you, master," Eubryd said, her quivering voice trilling through the icy air around them.

Eubryd was a wyvern, a tiny, ancient creature devoted to serving his kind. They were similar in their properties, wyverns and dragons. They used the same language, possessed similar skills and abilities. Wyverns were dependent, though. Tiny, vulnerable, skittish. They served dragons in exchange for protection. Eubryd had been attached to Nic and his clan for centuries.

That did not give her leave to take liberties and pry into his activities, however. By hovering so close to the buildings, she risked detection by the humans. That was the last thing he needed right now.

"Hush," he admonished as her trilling voice rose and she began her usual litany of worrying for his safety in this frail human form, as she called it. "Take care, Eubryd. You cannot let them hear you."

"How could they hear me over that terrible sound? What is it, Master?"

"An alarm. Something is happening out at the mountain. It has set off the alarm and the humans are on high alert just now. They'll all be roused in a very short time, I'm afraid."

"I know, and they will want to investigate. That's bad, Master. Not good for us."

"Not good? Why is that? Have you been out on the mountain?" he asked, and then glanced over his shoulder to make sure no one was nearby. "Our clutch is well hidden there, isn't it?"

"Yes, or so I thought, sir. But…there is magic!"

"What sort of magic? What have you seen?"

"Fairies! I saw fairies snooping about the mountain."

"Fairies? What sort of fairies?"

"I don't know. I couldn't tell. They were…they were trying to be hidden. You know their ways. Secretive, calculating creatures when they wish to be. Please, Master, can't you do something about that alarm?"

The silence was still being shattered by that damn noise. He knew the tiny wyvern's ears were every bit as sensitive as his own, yet of course she lacked the more rugged dragon abilities to block out such things. She did not have hands, either, to cover her ears. Wyverns were simple creatures, dragon in nature but possessing only wings and one pair of clawed feet. Helpless little beasts, really. They couldn't even shift into human form when needed. The most skilled of their members sometimes managed to pass themselves off as chickens, but that was the extent of their shifting abilities. No wonder they had indentured themselves to their larger, more self-sufficient cousins all those eons ago.

"I'm sorry about the alarm," he said, sending out a wave of localized heat that functioned as a slight dampener for the sound. It would not shield the delicate creature for long. "You should go, Eubryd. Just tell me, where did you see the fairies? I'll meet you there soon."

She flapped her leathery wings nervously, her glowing eyes flicking around and her voice even more trilling than usual. "I…I'm not sure. They were moving quite a bit and, as I said, they were trying to be invisible."

Nic knew his own senses would have picked up on even invisible fairies if he'd been close enough, but of course he could not expect Eubryd to do the same. "Where would you guess they might be?"

"Guess? Oh, well I think they might have been on the far side of the mountain, near the…near the auxiliary vent."

Damn. If they located that shaft, they'd very likely know where to start looking for the way in. By the Fires, what could fairies possibly be doing poking around a dragon clutch? Nothing they ought to be doing, obviously.

"Go," he ordered. "Wait for me there. Keep your eyes and your ears open."

Eubryd cringed and he had to chuckle at her discomfort. She gave him a weak smile. "I'll keep my eyes open, at least."

"Do your best," he said, waving her off. "I'll go to the humans and make some excuse. Then we'll get to the bottom of this."

She nodded and gave multiple assurances of her loyalty and dedication until he finally had to remind her time was of the essence. With a puff of steam in the cold night air, she huffed off to do his bidding. If there were fairies on their mountain tonight, she would hunt them with full diligence. He could trust her for that task.

As for himself, his task might be a bit more difficult. If there were fairies lurking about, the last thing he needed was humans getting inquisitive. His plans had to change.

Instead of claiming the alarm warned of earthquake or impending doom, he'd better convince the humans this alarm really meant nothing. While earthquakes might eventually convince the humans to abandon their project here, they would only do so after prolonged investigation. With magical creatures stalking his mountain, he could never allow that. He had to make the humans believe this alarm was nothing more than faulty equipment that hardly merited attention.

This was going to be a problem. He'd already convinced Lianne this was a legitimate concern, and now she'd gone off to rile up the rest of the group. They were being dragged from their beds by a frantic alarm. Redirecting their thought patterns and influencing their perceptions of this new data wasn't going to be easy for him, especially since his powers of manipulation were not as fully recharged as he had expected to be at this point in the night.

By the Fires, he'd been eager for Lianne and had planned to pleasure her and get what he needed. How had he let her take control? He'd been counting on her submission, the energy of her release, to give him his full satisfaction. He found it impressive as hell that she'd gotten him off before he'd been ready. Impressive and unbelievably sexy. He could hardly wait to get her alone and do all those things he expected to already have done.

But was his mind reenergized enough to take control of the rest of his coworkers? It would likely drain him completely. What if he encountered some unforeseen trouble with these damn fairies that Eubryd was stalking? He wasn't sure he should risk enthralling a whole group.

Then again, he might not have much of a choice. He needed to take charge of this situation before a team of frightened engineers and science geeks went rushing out to the mountain and started finding things he'd worked too damn hard to keep hidden. That would certainly cause troubles he was in no position to solve.

He'd just have to do what he could and hope it would be enough, at least for now. If he could keep everyone calm, perhaps he stood a chance of staying in command. It might help him buy a little time, too—time he could use for more interaction with Lianne. He hoped what had passed between them left her as hungry for more as it had left him. He'd need a full meal of her passion once this current confusion was under control.

* * *

Sure enough, Lianne had been only moments ahead of Dan Casper and Sid Blanchard when she left Nic behind in the guesthouse and let herself into the computer lab. She'd still been flipping on lights and turning on monitors when the two senior members of the team showed up, clothing hastily thrown on and grumpy from being pulled out of bed. If Nic had been here with her, things definitely would have been awkward. Sid was already looking at her funny when he came marching through the door, obviously wondering why she was fully dressed and in here so quickly at one o'clock in the morning. He probably thought she'd done something to trip the alarms.

Sid Blanchard never gave anyone the benefit of the doubt. She'd do well to remember that. She might allow herself to go back and screw the Russian like a woman gone wild, but she'd better be cool, calm, and completely sane on the job. The last thing she needed was for anyone to have reason to doubt her abilities here. She had one shot to get this thing done, and she wasn't about to mess it up. She wasn't even going to so much as look at Nic Vladik when he finally did show up in here tonight.

"What the hell is going on?" Sid demanded.

"What triggered that alarm?" Dan Casper asked.

She didn't bother looking up as she scanned the multiple printouts and seismograms on various machines around the room. "Some sort of readings from one of our sensors on the mountain, it looks like."

"Probably just another glitch," Sid grumbled.

"We've never had an alarm from a glitch," Lianne noted.

"Can you verify the readings?" Dan asked.

"How about if we shut off the damn alarm first?" Sid snapped.

"I can't figure out how," Lianne announced. "Either the control code is messed up, or it's continually retriggering. Get in here and help me."

They did. She wished she could believe it was because they respected her as the authority on-site now, or because she was compelling or commanding, but really she knew they just wanted the alarm to stop blaring every bit as much as she did. Her body was still not quite over the adrenaline surge from her time alone with Nic, so this grating, pulsating alarm was not helping. She needed to relax, to think straight and make sense of these readings.

Was it an earthquake? Right now she couldn't quite tell. It seemed that what triggered the alarm was the reading from one piece of equipment—a single Remote Ground Sensor that should have been just one of several to detect the harmonic oscillation that set it off. She sat at a computer and typed in the locater number for that unit. A display popped up, showing a topographic map of the area where that specific RGS was located. She hunted down the locators of other sensors in that general area.

"Is that where the event triggered?" Dan asked, leaning over her shoulder to view the monitor. "What readings did we get off other RGSs in that vicinity?"

"I'm checking right now," she replied.

Reports started scrolling down her screen. Each unit was listed by its locater, followed by the most current readings. Nothing out of the ordinary showed up.

"All of them are within normal parameters?" Sid asked, peering over her other shoulder. "How can that be?"

Additional members of the team had started to show up, filing into the computer lab and grumbling about the hour and the earsplitting alarm. There was no sign of Nic yet, but Lianne was glad to snag one of their techs.

"Here, you make sense of this," she called to the bleary-eyed geek and gave over her seat at the computer to him.

He plopped into the chair and set his fingers to work over the keyboard. Basically he was redoing what she'd already done, calling up the map, retrieving specific data from the sensors in that general area. His results appeared identical to hers: all sensors except that one were giving out normal readings for the past six hours.

"Check the MT probes," she directed.

The Remote Ground Sensors measured localized movement within the earth. Their Magnetotellurics probes could gauge the swell of hydrothermal fluids in the various fractures and faults within the ground itself. If something was going on inside this mountain that they needed to know about, it would show in the increased conductivity caused by a buildup of those superheated waters. If this event did signal a resurgence of activity in this nearly dead volcano, she wanted to know about it. Now.

"I'm not finding anything," the tech announced.

She watched as he ran the same set of data twice. Nothing triggered. That damned alarm still screeched in the night, but the reports continued to give them nothing to look at. How could it be that every other sensor out there said nothing happened within miles of this damned mountain?

"It's got to be another glitch," Sid declared.

"Can you get the alarm to turn off?" Dan requested.

The tech nodded and brought up a new screen. "Yeah, I can override if we authorize it."

"Do it," Sid ordered.

"What if it isn't just another glitch?" Lianne asked.

"It is."

She knew the voice and turned to see Nic stroll through the doorway. He seemed perfectly composed and as annoyingly confident as ever. He leered over the tech's shoulder and gave the information on the screen a dismissive nod.

"This data is clearly just a sensor malfunction," he announced. "It's nothing to worry about."

She glared at him. Earlier today he was acting like her reams of flawed data represented a major catastrophe waiting to happen. A few minutes ago he was diving back into his pants telling her there was an earthquake going on. Now, however, he waltzed in and claimed it was all nothing? She didn't believe him. What sort of game was this damn frustrating Russian playing at?

"You are completely sure of this, are you?" she asked him.

"Of course. I never say things I am not sure of."

"Good. Then we can all go back to our beds," Sid announced, barely stifling a yawn.

"But what if there *is* something going on out there?" Lianne persisted.

Nic just gave a dismissive shrug. "There is nothing."

Damn him, he knew she wouldn't call him on his inconsistency. She couldn't very well claim that he'd said the exact opposite when the alarm went off while they were alone in her room getting sweaty. He was hiding something right now, though; she could tell. The man had some kind of game going on, and she wasn't going to let him play it through. There *was* something strange happening and she wouldn't let him sidetrack her again.

"We've had faulty readings before," she reminded them all. "But nothing like this—nothing so extreme, and I've seen no reports of alarms. What if this is another one of those spikes you've been so worried about, Mr. Vladik? Can we be certain we don't have a superheated pocket building up pressure down there?"

Nic paused only a moment before giving a too-smooth reply. "You're right. There could be something building up down there."

Hopefully no one else noticed the superheated smirk he gave her. Luckily, they all seemed to be too busy staring at the readings and cringing from the alarm.

"You're saying you believe the validity of his over-reactive worries?" Sid grumbled.

"I'm saying this could be something we need to look into," Lianne said.

"Or it could be a glitch," Nic added with way too much conviction.

Why was he suddenly so determined to contradict himself? Every instinct she had told her Nic was hiding something, and she didn't like it.

"We can't simply assume that!" she fumed.

"Well, how do we know when we can't get corresponding data?" Dan asked.

"I will go out to look at the equipment on-site," Nic offered.

That wasn't what she expected him to say. "You'll do what? But it's the middle of the night."

"And everyone can either trust my word that this is nothing more than a glitch, or you all can send someone out to take a look at the sensor. I am volunteering for that."

"But it's halfway to the other side of the mountain."

"Then I should get started now, shouldn't I?"

"But the permits only allow—"

He cut her off. "The permits allow for us to access our equipment in the event of an emergency. The alarm went off, we all came running in here, there's a chance something might explode…I'd say that sounds like an emergency."

"So you'd go out there right now and find out what's going on?" Dan questioned.

"It needs to be done and I'm willing to do it."

"And we'd just have to take your word about whatever you reported, wouldn't we?" Sid grumbled. "What's your agenda on this, anyway, Vladik? You've been squirrely since the day I met you."

Lianne had to admit, for once she agreed with Sid.

"I've got no agenda," Nic assured them. "I want the safety and success of this project, just the same as all of you. Apparently I merely don't need as much sleep."

He added the last part as Dan and the head tech broke into contagious yawning.

"I thought you said this is just an equipment glitch," Lianne pointed out. "If you're so sure about that, why should anyone need to go out there?"

"But *you* aren't sure of it, Ms. McGowan," Nic replied, a slight tic in his jaw indicating he did not much care for her questioning his motives this way. "Why don't you come out there with me?"

"What? But I don't think…I'm not an engineer, Mr. Vladik, and I don't see how I could possibly—"

"You don't think you could know if I was lying to you about the equipment?" Nic asked. "Or are you afraid to go out in the dark?"

He was going way too far, putting her on the spot like this. Well, if he thought she'd crumble and cave, he was about to get a surprise. She was a woman with very little to lose. Calling his bluff wouldn't faze her in the least.

"Oh, I can smell lies, Mr. Vladik. And there's very little I'm afraid of. All right, if you need someone to hold your hand while you look at a little metal box out in the big scary world, I'll go with you."

The guys in the room were silent. She glanced at them, scanning their faces and expecting someone to raise up a protest or utter a modicum of concern. Oddly enough, though, the men's faces were blank. It must have been the late hour, but it seemed strange that with the alarm blaring and all the frantic questioning a few moments ago they could all be so sedate and almost trancelike now. Every one of them just stared at Nic, waiting for him to reply. He took his own sweet time about it, too. Finally he broke into a slow, wicked grin and nodded his dark head in her direction.

"Very well. You can come with me. I might need someone to hold on to my flashlight."

She knew he didn't mean *flashlight*. Damn it, but he had her sizzling inside again.

"Yes. Ms. McGowan should go with you," Sid said after another long, uncomfortable silence in the room. "We need someone there to keep track of you, Vladik."

Nic didn't seem the least bit insulted by Sid's implication. "You all trust Ms. McGowan to go with me and report back accurately what we have found?"

"That's what she's here for, isn't she?" Dan said, running his hand over his bald head. "I wouldn't have thought of it, but now that you mention it, I think it's a great idea to get her out there to monitor things firsthand."

The rest of the guys in the room all agreed. Nic was practically beaming with smugness at instigating this little plot. She shot him a look. How dare he drag her into this!

She had no desire whatsoever to go traipsing off into the frozen barrens, and the last thing she needed was for the other guys on the site to see her going off anywhere alone with Nic. No, he could sneak back into her bed, but he wasn't dragging her out into the wilderness.

"But I'm a manager. I manage people. One of the engineers should go. They know about equipment," she suggested, waiting for Sid or Dan to chime in and volunteer.

They didn't, though. Instead, the guys all looked at each other and Dan merely shrugged. Sid nodded, and then made a pronouncement as if he spoke for all of them.

"If anyone here needs management, it's Vladik. Ms. McGowan is the perfect choice," he announced. "We'll be here, eagerly awaiting your report."

Lianne was quick to protest, but no one seemed to hear her. They all seemed to be waiting for instruction from Nic. It was as if things were suddenly settled, as if this had been her idea right from the start. The tech started printing out some kind of codes Nic would need to locate the equipment in question, and Nic barked directions for a couple of the guys to collect tools he claimed he would need. Lianne couldn't even get a word in edgewise; everyone was suddenly bustling about doing Nic's bidding. They were practically falling over themselves to follow his orders, like he had mind control over them or something.

All she could do was glare.

"What the hell are you doing?" she hissed at him when it was clear nobody was paying attention to her.

His eyes were sparking brighter than ever. They pinned on her with determination and some kind of force burning behind them she didn't quite recognize. He held her gaze with his own, but there was no seduction or playfulness in his expression this time. He was cold, nothing but raw confidence and resolve just now.

"I'm taking you out to see just exactly what I've been telling you all along. The mountain is unstable. You will see for yourself, Lianne."

"But you just said this was only a—" She tried to argue, to break her eyes away from his.

She could not. Her body was suddenly warm and Nic's gaze held her as firmly as if he'd wrapped her in his arms. Her argument faded and her words trailed to silence. Even the blood in her veins, the pounding of her pulse, seemed to slow down and adjust to his will.

All she could do was stand immobile as her being was flooded by an irresistible urge to agree with whatever he said, to drop her hands to her sides and accept his leading. Suddenly it seemed the most logical thing in the world to do anything he suggested. She *would* follow Nic, wherever he might take her. Out to the mountain? Yes. She would go there. Every other thought had gone faded and murky in her mind. She was only aware of Nic and those deep, blazing eyes. Nothing else mattered. Nic called her to follow and that's what she would do.

Come with me tonight, Lianne, he spoke softly into her ear. Or perhaps not into her ear…perhaps his wishes simply materialized inside her brain. *Don't question. Just come.*

"All right," she replied. "I'll come."

At least, she assumed she replied. She might not have, though. She might simply have thought the words. The smoldering approval behind his eyes and the slow curl of his lip indicated he received her message either way.

I will show you, he murmured seductively. *You will see all that you need to see.*

Chapter Eight

And now he had her. At least, he *would* have her once he got her away from this place and out onto the mountain. His mountain.

He wasn't entirely thrilled that he'd resorted to using nonhuman powers of persuasion to get her to agree to this little midnight jaunt with him, though. But if Eubryd had been right and there were fairies from the Forbidden Realm poking around out there, he couldn't waste time using logic and petty argument to convince her to go with him. He needed submission now, as well as once they got out to the site and encountered whatever it was they might find. He would need to keep her under his command, to keep her mind blurred so she wouldn't realize what was going on around her.

He'd reached out his mind and mesmerized her as well as the others. The fact that it was late and everyone was sleep deprived had helped; they all gave in to his sway almost immediately. The lingering desire still surging through Lianne's body had made her especially susceptible to his will. It was unfair to take advantage of that, yes, but he had little choice. Until he knew what was going on out there, he had to make certain Lianne didn't continue investigating. She was just tenacious enough to keep at it until she discovered things that were not to be known by humans. With magical creatures showing up on-site, he had to act now.

She followed him dutifully as they packed up the tools and equipment they'd need for a quick trip out to the remote sensor location. No one questioned him when he included a few extra necessities, like food and a few blankets. If things got dicey, he might need to prolong his visit, which might mean he'd need Lianne. Or at least, he'd need her passion to fuel him.

He could feel his energy waning as he kept everyone in his hold, his mind touching theirs, numbing their senses and keeping them quiet and malleable. If he hadn't just rejuvenated himself with that pleasant interval in Lianne's bed, he very likely wouldn't have been able to accomplish this. But his fulfillment had been incomplete. He still needed to replenish his energy. It was only a stroke of luck that everyone had come under his power so easily now. He was very glad there'd be no need to keep this up very long.

Once he and Lianne had set off, the others would simply go back to normal, yet in their minds whatever he'd bidden them to do would make perfect sense. They'd not question his motives and he could release his hold on them. It would be hours before they began to wonder what was really going on. Surely by then Nic would have an idea of what he was up against out on the mountain. Lianne would be there if he needed more of her at that time.

She was cooperating with everything, stowing their gear and slipping into the warmer clothing he provided her. He liked the feel of being inside her mind. It was wild and untamed, despite the orderly facade she presented. It drained his powers to use this control over her and the others, but there was nothing he could do about that now. Perhaps once they were gone, off toward the far side of the mountain with nothing but glacier and barren wilderness around them, she would be willing to finish what they'd started back in her room.

He'd felt the desire in her; he knew the simmering, roiling lust lurking just beneath her calm, cool exterior. Far from the coldhearted businessperson she tried to portray, Lianne McGowan was a hot, passionate woman. She had needs, and so did he.

His need, in fact, was nearly consuming him now. Being in her mind this way, so intimately connected to her, made the heat of desire flame in his veins. Her passions transferred to him, her want surged over his body. Just a little while longer—he needed to maintain control and then he would allow himself to let go. He merely had to wait until it was safe. But by the Fires, his reserves were on empty and he could barely contain himself. They were alone now, the two of them in a storeroom gathering extra batteries that he'd convinced her they might need for the short hours they were expected to be gone. He watched her bend over to search through some boxes, hunting for the exact items he'd asked her to find.

Damn, but she was a temptation. It would be so very easy to just take more of what he needed from her now, to have his way right here and enjoy every minute of it. His human form craved her, and his dragon senses begged for the replenishment a quick, heated coupling would give. He could feel his nature burning inside him. Like lava, it threatened to melt off this constraining human form and erupt into the open, becoming once again who and what he was and consuming everything around him in ravenous flame.

He *needed* her. Now.

And he must have let her know it. She stood up and turned to him, blinking those wide, bleary eyes at him as if awaiting his next command. It was all he could do not to give her one.

"What is it?" she asked.

"Did you find the right batteries?" he asked, using every last ounce of control. "We should hurry now."

"Yes…hurry…" she said, turning back to the batteries.

She was just the right size for this body he inhabited…her curves were perfectly formed and as she bent, moved, stooped, and then straightened herself, his eyes followed every movement as if he'd never seen a female before. He could taste her, feel her skin against his…the want and the need all-consuming. They had to be done now or he'd lose it completely.

The supplies were collected into a case, and they were ready to leave. But he could feel his control faltering, and for one moment his hold on her mind slipped. He felt her mentally pull away from him. She stopped in the doorway of the supply room and turned back to face him.

"You…you need something," she stated.

"I need us to go," he managed to reply.

But she blinked, reality creeping into her mind and his blood pounding out of control. He had lost his hold over her and he realized he was nearly completely drained. He'd been too depleted when he took on the task of controlling everyone on-site. Now he had nothing left to regain his grasp on Lianne's mind.

He was losing his grip on the other team members in the nearby buildings, too. He could feel their minds slipping away from him. They were clearing, coming back to their senses, and they'd soon wonder what they were doing. He had to collect them, put them under his spell once more…but it was too hard. His energy was too low and his hunger too great. Damn this rampant need that flooded him; it nearly washed him away.

"What is it, Nic?" she asked, facing him as her delicious, feminine curves were silhouetted in the narrow doorway. Something's wrong. You need something from me."

"I need *you*," he growled and reached out for her.

This time he reached with his body, not with his mind. His fingers dug into the soft flesh at her arms and he pulled her back into the supply room. He kicked the door shut, plunging them into darkness. Alone.

He wrapped her in a viselike embrace that she would have no hope of escaping. His lips sought for hers in the darkness and he was all human, all passion. He had no idea what she was thinking and he didn't care. He would have her any way that he could.

She didn't fight him, so he pressed her against the door. His cock was hot and throbbing. So was the rest of him. Her hands skimmed over his back, her fingernails rasping as she ended up clinging to him. He lifted her, raising her just enough that his cock could grind into her, if not for all their damn clothing. Still, she groaned at the sensation. He rubbed hard against her.

"Let's go back to my room," she sighed into his ear.

He was too far gone for that. He could barely form words, as a matter of fact. "We can't. It has to be here."

She accepted his reason without comment. The passion in her own mind, in her own body, made her every bit as desperate as he was. She pushed him slightly away, just enough that her hands could reach down to unfasten his trousers.

He lowered her so that her feet touched the floor again and reached his own hands for her pants. Damn, this would have been so much easier if they were back in her bed with plenty of room for ripping clothes off and privacy for making all sorts of animal noises. Somehow they were just going to have to make do.

She had her hot little hands on his cock already, gripping him as if she were happy to greet an old friend. He wished for enough dragon senses now to be able to see in the dark, but it was probably just as well. The sight of her fondling him would have sent him over the edge. He was nearly there already.

But with their limited space, their surplus of clothing, and his very particular need, there was only one thing he could do.

"Turn around," he said, taking her by the shoulders and encouraging her to do as he asked.

She did, hesitantly, and he was quick to make it worth her effort. His fingers worked their way into her blouse, finding her luscious breasts and liberating them from her bra. Her nipples puckered under his efforts and he stroked them lightly. She seemed to like this, and she pressed herself closer into him, her hot little ass rubbing him just right. He slid his hands down to her waist and then pushed her pants lower, taking the delicate lace panties with them.

She murmured encouragement for him when he pressed the burning skin of his bulging cock against her naked ass. He growled and hoped that she knew how hot she was making him. She must have, because she wiggled a bit. He reached around in front and took her heated mound in his hand. Yes, she was burning up and wet.

They were dealing with space issues and all sorts of other drawbacks here in this tight, dark closet, but he was as turned on as he ever had been. He pulled her tight, propping her up just enough so that his cock brushed that taut little ass while his fingers explored as they would. She moaned and shifted. He dipped two fingers inside her, his other hand going back up to enjoy the plump feel of her breast.

She was so hot, so ready to come for him, that there was no question he'd have her panting and gasping in a short matter of minutes. For himself, he pressed against her, dragging his cock over her soft skin, being pleasured just by the texture and heat and the soft, primal sounds she was making. His desire was so great that all he needed was contact, and the feel of her climax.

He held her up closer to him. She was breathing heavily now as he stroked her, finding the tender spot that made her arch against him and urge him for more. Her muscles were tense, so he pressed his cock between her thighs. Ah, it was hot and it was tight. He let instinct take over, sliding against her and feeling her body react, molding itself around him.

Her breathing was getting louder now, so he pressed his lips against her ear.

"Hush. The others could come by; they might hear you."

She nodded slightly, clearly straining to stay silent as he continued touching her, stroking her, rubbing his length against her but never quite filling her. He needed her to come for him completely, so even in his urgency he would take his time.

"I want you inside me," she moaned in a hoarse whisper. "All of you."

"Soon. Let me make this good for you," he said, teasing her with the heated tip of his cock.

She barely choked back a moan. Now she was as lost in their passion as he was, and clearly neither of them were thinking of anything but finding fulfillment. He could feel the climax rising within her.

"Let go for me," he begged her. "Show me how I make you feel."

"I feel like I could do this forever," she said, but then her voice caught and her body spasmed against his.

She was coming. He held her, breathed her, kissed her neck to taste the salt of her sweat. She rocked against him, rewarded him with moans and trembles and the promise of more. He drained her desire, soaked up the energy that she generated. Even as his own body responded, his cock pulsing against her, he felt himself fill with much-needed power. He clung to her for a few moments, taking in as much as he could, letting her body recover and her heart rate slow to normal again.

Then he reached out his mind. His strength was returning. She was weak and depleted while he was gaining his control once again. He held her mind with his and felt the warm glow of pleasure that fully engulfed her.

"God, that was good," she murmured. "Do you think anyone heard us?"

He was already touching the minds of the others on-site. They'd not yet fully realized that their actions preparing for his trip to the mountain were not entirely their own. Good. The longer he could keep them from questioning things, the better. Soon they'd be back in their beds and he would not have to worry about them for a few more hours, at least.

"No one heard," he assured her.

Her body felt so damn good against his that he hated to give up this hot, physical connection. But he had to. He'd gotten what he needed from her and now he had things to attend to. If he was smart, he'd take over her mind again to ensure that she cooperated and didn't ask too many questions. He was hesitant, though. He loved the feel of her mind, the way her unfettered thoughts mingled with his.

He couldn't give himself the luxury of enjoying that, though. His focus had to be on his task, not on this human female. No matter how fascinating she might be.

He wrapped her thoughts carefully and pushed them aside. He felt her mind giving way to his suggestion. She was exhausted and still warmed from his loving, so he merely urged her to remain in that state.

"It's time to go out to the mountain," he whispered. "I'll help you straighten your clothes."

She was silent but he felt the fog returning to her mind. She moved away from him, shuffling in the darkness and doing his bidding. He felt the rest of the humans on-site, each one easily obeying his prompts. His power had returned, thanks to Lianne's powerful release. He did not know how much more effort would be required to control all these minds for an extended time, but for now Lianne had given him what he needed to carry out this next phase of his mission.

Lianne had proven to be invaluable. He responded to her remarkably well. For so long he'd had to ration his powers to make certain he would have strength when he needed it. With Lianne such a willing partner now, there was hope that he could increase his efforts. Her brimming passion could be the source of constant renewal he needed to finally finish this job once and for all.

For now, he could allow her to rest. Once he got out to the mountain to investigate these readings, he would know better what further exertion would be needed. He'd keep Lianne close. With luck, next time desire took them over, neither of them would have to settle for some quick groping in the dark. He would see just how much passion she truly possessed.

Chapter Nine

There, what's that?" Kyne pointed off toward the distance.

They had left the strange little box that had affected them, and gone higher up on the mountain. Raea blinked against the wind and could make out dots of faint light clustered on the stretch of flat plain that spread out from the base of the mountain. It was not magical light—it was very obviously human-made. A settlement, out here in this uninviting wasteland? No, those lights were more than likely evidence of the scientific group Baylor had told them they'd find working here. Clearly, they would have to stay very far away from that area.

"Well, at least we know where not to go," she said.

"I don't know, maybe we should check it out."

Had she heard him correctly in the din of the wind? He couldn't possibly have suggested they go that direction, so far out of their way and so dangerously close to people. Once Kyne had triggered that sensor, there was no telling who might have been alerted. Anyone could be searching for them now. More than anything, they needed to avoid habitations.

"There could be dozens of humans there," she pointed out, although how he could possibly overlook that fact she had no idea.

"Exactly. Whatever is going on, anyone from our Realm will intentionally avoid that human jobsite. They'll be hunting for us here on the mountain, but they won't think to look for us there."

"But the humans—"

"We've been hiding ourselves from humans all our lives, Raea. We know how to do that. What we don't know is what some of our own kind are doing working with the humans. We should hide ourselves where they'd least expect us so we can plan our next actions."

She hated to admit that he made perfect sense. Baylor had been right; fairies knew how to hide in plain sight. The last place the Fairy Council—or anyone else—would think to search for them would be around humans. Perhaps this would give them time to learn a few things before ending up face-to-face with an enemy.

"All right. We'll go there," she agreed and shuddered at her own words.

Kyne grasped her hand. "We'll wait a little while, though. We both need to catch our breath."

She knew he was just fine. He was stronger and more resilient than she was, but she appreciated that he was careful not to make her feel frail. Kyne was proof positive that sometimes being half-human had its advantages.

She dropped her head on his shoulder as they scanned the landscape below. "Thanks. There's no telling who we'll run into down there. I just need a couple more minutes to be ready."

"Take your time. Those humans might be the least of our worries."

Well, that was a sobering thought. As if she had ever in her life imagined that she'd rather run into a human than another of her own kind! How disturbing.

The world had somehow flipped itself upside down lately. She'd accepted help from a human, come to distrust her own council, and now here she was being battered by winds over the rocky terrain of someplace called Iceland. Yet all it took was one quick glance at Kyne, one glimpse of his confident wing strokes and the determined set of his golden features, and she knew there was no other place on earth that she wanted to be.

She *had* to be here. For him, for herself, and perhaps for everyone else. If this unnatural union between the mundane and the Forbidden Realm was as dangerous as Baylor seemed to fear, then there was far more at stake here than Raea's own feelings of comfort or security. The very Veil itself depended on what they were able to accomplish here.

"We should go now," she said, taking a deep breath and pretending she wasn't afraid. "I feel better. We need to get this done."

"Are you sure you're ready?"

She took a step away from him in order to appear more confident. "Yes. Let's go. Maybe we should head down that way, following that deep, shadowy rift. That way there'd be less chance that anyone...Hey, what is that?"

She pointed toward a small construction way down at the very base of the mountain.

"It looks like a building of some sort," Kyne said.

"Do you suppose someone lives there?"

"Pretty odd place for a house. And there aren't any windows. It could be an equipment shed, a place where they store things or house machinery."

"Machinery is what we came to investigate," she noted.

"Let's go check it out."

"Just be careful," she reminded. "And don't kick it."

The wind whipped around them but the rift she had pointed out ended up being an excellent way to stay hidden and avoid some of the more buffeting gusts. The tiny lights of the scientists' dwellings they had seen in the distance were disappearing behind the rise of the landscape as they made their way lower and lower down the mountain.

There was no sign of life anywhere. It seemed they were totally alone out here. If circumstances were different and they weren't in mortal danger, it could actually be kind of romantic.

"Do you think this equipment shed belongs to the science group, or is it a part of whatever the Fairy Council is involved in?" she asked as they approached.

"Who's to say the two things aren't related? It seems like a pretty big coincidence that a research project would suddenly appear here, right beside the very mountain where Baylor says that mystery equipment is being shipped."

She had to agree. They were very close to the shed now, so she refrained from speaking. It was time to be cautious and keep a lookout for anything suspicious. Kyne was tense, his gaze darting around, clearly on high alert. They paused just a few yards away, listening for anything that might give them alarm. Nothing. The world around them was vacant and dim.

It was full of magic, too. She could feel it flow through the air, immersing her body like warm water. It was similar to the magic she felt in their own Fairyrealm, yet different. Whatever this Iceland place was, it was ancient and it was magical. Humans had not yet pushed the Veil away as they had in her homelands. This place was still free and wild, and her skin prickled with energy as she alighted beside Kyne, drawing in deep breaths of the air and the magic and the essence of her very being.

"Come on," he said softly.

She followed him closely. He led her to the little building. They flew silently, carefully, circling it once, then twice. There was no sign of danger, so she nodded to him. He circled once more, then found a safe place to settle.

There was a little nook at the base of the shed, protected from view and from the tearing winds of the landscape. They landed there, sheltering next to the building. It had been constructed at the juncture where the mossy rocks of the plain gave way to the bare, soaring rocks that rose up to form the foundation of the ancient mountain. A concrete slab had been constructed and the shed was built onto it. As they'd noted, there were no windows. The lone doorway was locked securely with a chain.

Raea stood on the lip of the foundation that protruded from beneath the shed. She pressed her ear to the wall, listening.

"Do you hear anything?" Kyne asked.

"I don't know. My ears are still ringing from all the wind we've been in. What do you think?"

He leaned in next to her and listened. "Some kind of machine, maybe. That doesn't tell us much, though."

"Humans certainly do like their tools and machinery. I guess that's because they don't have magic. I feel kind of sorry for them."

"Don't. They get by just fine."

Of course that was true. Their lack of magic never seemed to keep humans from doing whatever it was they wanted to do in their world. Often it was to the detriment of the beings who did have magic. So what was their involvement here on this huge, foreboding mountain?

She turned her back on the shed and focused instead on the wasteland of jagged rocks spread out before them, shadowed by the mountain. Even as enormous as it was, it still could not block out the vast expanse of stars. They were beautiful. It was an alien world to her, yet as she stood here, close beside Kyne, she felt more and more at home.

Her tired muscles began to relax, Kyne noticed, turning to lean against the building with her and look up at the stars. It felt so peaceful and safe that she allowed herself to sag against him. He put his arm around her, his lips brushing the top of her head and sending a thrill that coursed through her, top to bottom.

"I'm glad I'm here with you, Kyne," she said with a sigh.

It really didn't seem to matter whether she was with him in Iceland, or safely back in that little cottage where they had forgotten the world and spent days enjoying the passion they'd so long denied themselves. She would be happy anywhere she could be with him, where his skin could touch hers and stir the embers of desire.

She snuggled close to him. Magic kept their bodies warm, even in this frigid place, but Kyne made her warmer. She reached to touch him, skimming her hands over his muscular form. Vibrations from whatever was inside the building thrummed through her, Kyne's earthy scent filled her senses. There was no danger, no worry, no emptiness here. Kyne made her feel safe, and passion made her feel daring.

She moved his light clothing aside to feel the breadth of his chest. He pulled her closer, lifting her and then lowering her as he found a comfortable place to sit. She curled onto his lap and she raised her face toward his. Her lips fairly begged for his kiss, and he'd never yet disappointed her. He took her mouth with enthusiasm, his kiss ardent and long. She responded by wrapping herself around him, straddling him where he sat. She could feel him pressing against her, ready to give in to their passion again.

And her body was equally eager. It crossed her mind that she should probably be a little more focused on their reason for being here, that she ought to catch her breath from their travels before she engaged in wild carnality, but the heat was growing stronger within her, and Kyne tasted so very, very good…she had to have him. This longing was rapidly taking over her conscious thought, her reasoning ability. The familiar abandon of lust and longing had possession of her mind. It was almost as if…

"Raea…wait…" Kyne said, his voice raspy and tight. "Something's not right."

"We'll make it right," she assured him, raining kisses over his face and running her hand down between them to free that straining organ that could release the explosion inside her.

"No, I mean…we shouldn't be doing this."

She argued silently, grinding herself against him. His breathy groan only served to make her hotter. She threw back her wings and pressed her body against his.

"We've felt this before," he murmured as he nibbled her neck, cupped her breasts in his hands, and sent violent jolts of pleasure through her as he fingered her tender nipples.

She sighed. "Yes…over and over again."

"I'm talking about what we feel around the strange machinery, like back in the forest, or at that sensor we found."

What, could he be right? Was she falling prey to the strange equipment *again*? By the Skies, the human world was packed full of those insidious machines now. She and Kyne were helpless under their influence as the machines sucked up their magic and left raw instinct to take charge of them. Passion would overtake them completely, leaving them vulnerable and helpless against their enemies.

"Is that what this is?" she asked, not hesitating a moment in her exploration of his hard, throbbing maleness. "You believe we've found more of these machines and that's what's making me want you so badly?"

He made a weak-willed attempt to brush her hands aside. "You know when you touch me like that I can't think straight."

"Then I'll never stop touching you, Kyne. I need to feel more of you...all of you."

"Damn these machines! I can't control myself, Raea."

He gave up his defense and began working at her clothing, sliding her skirt up and feeling his way. She chewed his lip and sucked in a ragged breath when he penetrated her in hurried fervor. There was no need for games, no teasing or foreplay. She rocked into position, taking him fully inside. Her body welcomed him with greedy response. He groaned and she cried out in pained pleasure.

He grasped her backside, she clutched his shoulders. The feel of him possessing her, filling her as he did, made her dizzy. Waves of passion and sensation rose to carry her. She kissed him, nipped at him, felt his hands on her skin and his body writhing with hers, tumbling toward that blissful edge where her climax would send them both into momentary oblivion. She shifted, riding him with all her might, determined to drain every ounce of sensation, every heated groan of passion from this fiery union.

Even after their days of eager lovemaking back in the cabin, she found herself nearly frantic for more. He was huge and she moaned with utter bliss as he chafed his body against hers, his solid shaft sliding deeper, then pulling away to torment the throbbing void he left behind. Over and over in increasing abandon, the motion ignited flames of need that burned to her very core.

"The machines, Raea…" He panted as his fingertips dug into her flesh. "I can't contain myself anymore. The passion is too strong. I can't stop."

"I don't want you to stop," she rasped in reply, grinding herself against him and shuddering as the first floods of climax washed over her senses. "By the Skies, I can't let it end. I only want more and more of you, Kyne."

"You can't bear more of me, Raea. You know what will happen. We have to stop now."

"I can't. I need this too much. I have to have all of you."

She wrapped herself more tightly around him. The sound he made was pure agony and she thrilled with an animal energy at it. She could feel how he struggled to maintain some shred of control while she gave in to every instinct, sliding herself over him again and again.

She knew what would happen when he lost the battle—of course she did, but she no longer cared. His climax would overwhelm him, and his body would take on his human form. He would cease being a fairy and become fully human, in every way. Her tiny body could never accommodate a human. She knew this, yet desire was her master and there was no reasoning left in her. She could only cry out to the stars, calling Kyne's name as the passion raged through her, and her muscles worked him in a fury of desperation.

It was no longer a tender act of lovemaking. Their joining had become a matter of life and death. So caught up in the whirl of sensation, she barely even detected when he shifted beneath her.

The world around her exploded in light. Sparks of magic swirled against the darkness of the sky. Raea's entire body was awash in glitter and sensation. It felt as if she were falling, tumbling into an endless abyss, yet clinging to Kyne's hard, damp body for rescue. He held her tight.

She could feel him throbbing inside her, his hot breath on her skin as he growled his release. She had brought him to climax and now he was doing the same for her. It would likely be the last climax she felt—he was becoming larger and more powerful with every heartbeat. The feel of him was nearly unbearable, yet she still rode the crest of her climax, clinging and crying his name.

Apparently they really had been falling, she realized. Suddenly she was on her back, pressed into the moss-covered ground beside the building. Her skin sizzled from sensation, her head spinning with color and light and a million erotic images of what Kyne was doing to her. He was driving himself into her, making her climax go on and on in a rolling sea of desire and pleasure. The constellations above them were whirling and she could feel the very life draining from her with every blissful moan.

She shut her eyes to try to regain her senses. Had she survived? Her body was limp and sated. Kyne's weight pressed against her, yet he was not crushing her. He shifted to the side and she dragged in much-needed air.

"Raea?" He spoke her name gently.

Her heart skipped a beat at the tenderness and concern in his voice. "That was amazing."

"Did I hurt you?"

Her body ached and she was dizzy from lack of breath, but no, he hadn't hurt her. In fact, somehow he'd managed to save her when she'd lost all of her senses. He'd used magic to change her to human form just as they'd experienced their climax together. She'd been too far gone at the time to notice, but somehow he'd had the presence of mind.

"You used Sizing Dust just in time."

"I very nearly didn't," he said, dropping onto his back beside her on the cold ground beside the little building. "The passion was so strong—I really couldn't think straight."

"I know. It was…unreal."

"It was the damned machinery. Are you still feeling affected by it?"

"No, all I feel is exhausted. I think you drained every drop of energy from me," she said.

"And you draw everything out of me," he replied. "That's what Baylor said the machinery does—it collects magic, draining us. The side effect, I guess, is that then passion takes over and we can't fight that off without magic. But listen. Can you hear the thing working?"

She listened. The building had been humming before, giving off a low sound with faint vibration from the equipment running inside. Now, however, she heard nothing. Just the silence of the barren landscape and the slowing beats of her own heart.

"No. I don't hear it."

"That's because it shut down," he said. "Just like before. The machinery affected us, heightened our desire, but our passion was too much for it. I think we broke it, Raea. It's not working now."

"Good. Maybe I'll be able to think straight for a while."

"And maybe we'd better get out of here. The humans will come here soon, no doubt, to see what happened. We need to pull ourselves together and leave. Again."

She sighed. Her body still tingled from all the passion. The last thing she wanted was to get back to reality, to find strength to go off into the night. But of course, that's just what she would do. They came here for a purpose, and this interlude—although wonderful—had distracted them from it.

"All right," she agreed. "Do we head back up the mountain?"

"Yes. It all comes back to this mountain, doesn't it?"

She pushed up onto her elbow and managed to give him a smile. "All right, then. With luck, maybe we'll find more of these machines up there."

He grinned back at her. "And just what do you think we might do about that if—wait, look over there! A vehicle is heading this way!"

He was right. A vehicle was moving toward them from the direction of the small compound of dwellings. Twin beams of pale light shot from it into the darkness, waving and bouncing over the uneven landscape. As feared, someone had been notified of their presence.

"We'd better go!" she said quickly, adrenaline pumping energy back into her body.

But Kyne hesitated. "No, look. It's not coming this way. It's veering off, going that way."

She thought for a moment to get her bearings. "Isn't that sort of where we started?"

"That's the direction where we found the sensor staked into the ground."

"And you kicked it."

"And then *we* broke it," he said. "This could be a really good opportunity for us to find out who is responsible for this equipment, what's really going on here. We should follow them."

The thought of encountering whoever set up these terrible machines practically terrorized her. Of course she couldn't admit this to him, though. This is why they were here. He was right. They should follow that vehicle. But how could they?

"Kyne, we're too big. They'd see us for sure, and it's too soon for Sizing Dust again."

He thought for a moment. "Well, we could always make ourselves invisible."

"Did you bring enough dust for that? I don't think I did."

"Yes. Let's do this, Raea. We'll have information to report back to Baylor, and if we do happen to find any more of this machinery out here, we'll be immune to the effects for a while. Until the Sizing Dust wears off of us, at least."

She had to admit, being able to control their actions would be a good thing, but she truly couldn't regret all of what the machines did to them. By the Skies, Kyne was a master at lovemaking. More than anything she wanted to survive this ordeal, just so she could look forward to many more years submitting to his efforts. She hoped to the Clouds that a frenzied coupling in the wilds of Iceland was not the final act of her life.

Chapter Ten

Lianne was aware of tension in her neck, a queasy feeling, and a slight headache. Slowly a fog lifted and she cracked open her eyes. Where on earth was she? At first glance, it didn't seem like she was on earth at all.

A deep indigo sky formed a huge dome, dotted with glittery stars and smears of otherworldly color. Finger paints from some galactic titan? No, the sky hummed and swirled with a brilliant aurora borealis. Beautiful, actually. Black crags reached up into this sky, cutting off some of her view. The rocky silhouette of mountain. But it was closer than usual, wasn't it? She blinked to clear her vision, clear her mind. She hugged her coat around her and was slowly aware of the chill that seeped all the way into her bones.

She was in a vehicle, parked in some desolate spot surrounded by rugged terrain. No wonder it was all so very confusing. How had she gotten here? She'd been back at the jobsite…in the trailer with that damned alarm, and then Nic…

Oh hell. *Nic.* Where was he? She must have been with him…she recalled that he'd been taking her somewhere. The driver's seat was empty, though. She glanced out into the night, searching for some sign of him. What were they doing out here, and why couldn't she remember?

The landscape around her was dark, but not too dark to make out the random angles of the rocky terrain. What was this place? Why would Nic bring her out to the base of the mountain?

But then he appeared in the near distance and she momentarily forgot her concerns. His face was in shadow but the sight of his muscular body moving with unexpected ease over the rough ground captivated her. The ambient light from the sky display illuminated his solid form, bouncing off him like a halo and causing his silhouette to practically glow. Memories of their bodies writhing against each other in the confined space of the storage room flooded her, bringing heat with them.

She had to forcibly hold her hands in her lap to keep from reaching for him when he moved toward the vehicle, opening the door and sliding in silently.

"Where are we?" she asked, her voice cracking as if it had been a while since she'd used it.

He seemed slightly startled by her question. "I was programming my GPS."

"Oh," she said, then realized that didn't answer her question at all. "Why? Where are we going?"

"There was an anomalous signal from one of the sensors. We came here to investigate."

"Yeah...that's right."

She chewed her lip. Yes, she remembered that now. The alarm system was set off by some unusual readings at the mountain. An RGS was sending impossible data, so Nic had said they needed to come look at it. He seemed to think it was important she come out here with him...for some reason. And she'd agreed.

Why on earth had she done that? It was cold and dark and she wasn't an engineer. How the hell did Nic talk her into this? And why was everything still so damn fuzzy in her brain right now?

He started the engine and put the car into gear. The mountain was dead ahead of them, and Nic was picking up speed. He seemed even more surly and gruff than usual.

"Why did you have to get out of the car to program your GPS?" she asked.

"Bad connection in here."

"We're behind a mountain in Iceland. Moving ten feet away from the car gets you a better connection?"

"I needed to get a feel for the air out here."

"The *air*?"

"Look, you said you were tired. Maybe you should go back to sleep."

"I don't remember falling asleep in the first place."

"Well, you did. Fall asleep again."

"I thought I was supposed to come out here and look at that RGS."

"You are."

"Then why should I go to sleep?"

"I'm not sure how long it'll take me to find what we're looking for."

"Use your GPS."

"I didn't bring it."

"You just said you were programming it. Hell, you keep contradicting yourself, Nic. What's really going on? Why did you drag me out here?"

"Because I…you need to see the mountain."

She did see the mountain. It was looming huge, directly ahead of them. It blocked the stars, blanked out the northern lights she'd been admiring, and no matter how jostled and tossed their rugged vehicle was, the mountain continued to monopolize her view. Nic glared at it like a man heading to war.

Or perhaps he was returning home. The way he clutched the steering wheel with a steely grip and laid on that accelerator, it seemed he wasn't just driving toward the mountain, but aiming for it. They'd hit it, too, judging by the look on his face and the speed of their SUV.

"Slow down, Nic. My teeth are going to fall out. Jeez, are we checking out an RGS or flying over enemy territory?"

"I told you; the mountain is dangerous."

"Then why are we here?"

"You need to see for yourself."

So he'd already said. "I won't be able to see very much if I'm knocked unconscious. Damn it, slow down. I think the back bumper just rattled itself loose."

It really hadn't, but she twisted to stare out the rear window anyway. Nothing but darkness behind them. There was no sign of the jobsite, no lights from their facilities, not anything comforting. There was nothing around but the black shapes of rock, swatches of sky, and the huge, looming mountain.

It appeared they were on the back side of it, all the way to the northernmost edge of their permit area. Nic must have skirted around the rugged east side of the off-limits mountain since the valley along the western side was filled with equally off-limits glacier. They were traveling up the fingerlike gorge carved out from glacial runoff as it made its way around the mountain and down toward the frigid North Atlantic to their south. Their campus lay somewhere back there, far to the west of what she presumed was their present location. The mountain was between them.

How long had they been out here, and how could she have slept through it all, especially if Nic had been driving like this? Maybe it was the jet lag. Hell, she couldn't even remember getting into the vehicle with him. She felt…strange.

Her mind was so foggy and her limbs felt so numb. It was a little bit like waking up after a night of too much partying, except that there had been no party. There was nothing to explain her odd grogginess and memory loss. Nothing except the one thing she was determined not to think about.

Maybe her doctor had been right. He'd told her to cancel this trip, to stay home and put things in order. To make preparations. Hell, how did anyone do that? How was she supposed to sit home and prepare to die?

She was supposed to accomplish something with her time on the earth, that's what she was supposed to do. Lianne McGowan was supposed to make a difference, to tackle life head-on. Instead, life had tackled her. A brain tumor. How in the hell did she get one of those?

The first diagnosis came while she was still in college. She never once considered that this damn thing would win. No, she was Crandall McGowan's daughter, after all. She had plans for her life. No mere tumor was going to get in the way of her forward momentum.

She fought it with all that she had, and she beat it, too. At least, they told her she did. After a year of chemicals and poisons, scans showed it was nearly gone. She had taken her life back, bought herself some time to finally do something important. Between Daddy's jobs and her unfortunate string of assholes, she just sort of never got around to doing that important thing.

And now her time was up. A routine screening came back positive. Additional tests confirmed the worst-case scenario: the tumor was back, growing twice as fast as it had before. And this time, it had nasty little tendrils wrapped around all sorts of sensitive parts of her brain. She asked the doctor how soon she needed to start treatments again. He'd just looked at her with pity.

Inoperable. Untreatable. Terminal. He looked her in the eye and used those words. It took a while for them to sink in.

"If you've got unfinished business in your life, Lianne, now's the time to get out there and finish it," he'd told her.

Unfinished? Hell, she wasn't even thirty years old. What exactly was she supposed to have finished already? Only one thing came to mind, so she'd gone home to Marcus and cracked open a bottle of wine. She'd wasted that damn expensive wine on *Marcus.*

They'd been together six months, at that point. He'd moved in with her after the first three. She liked him. He was funny, he let her do things her way, and he had some damn sexy tattoos. He also had a crappy job, a motorcycle that she bought for him, and two ongoing paternity suits. But she overlooked that. Those were awesome tattoos.

She told him what the doctor said and he seemed really concerned for her. The doctors said she had months. Months! How was she supposed to accomplish everything she needed to do with her life in just a few months? Marcus apparently didn't have an answer for that.

He was gone when she woke up the next morning. He took the motorcycle, all her credit cards, and his awesome tattoos. She didn't even bother to cancel the cards. Let him have some fun. What would it matter to her? It might be interesting to see what got maxed out first: her stolen credit cards, or her.

And now here she was, still desperate to make a legacy for herself, one month later. She hadn't seen Marcus or her doctor since then. She hadn't really missed either of them, though, until now.

The way her mind was so blurry and her memory fuzzy, she wished she'd kept those last few doctor's appointments. She'd known this would be a challenging job, and right now she needed all of her faculties. Maybe the doctor could have prescribed something to keep the tumor from having so much effect on her so rapidly. It really sucked that already she was starting to lose it.

"Are we getting closer to that RGS we need to check out?" she asked Nic as the vehicle rocked over the chunks of ancient, glacier-ravaged volcanic debris and she realized she was desperate to escape her own thoughts.

"It's just up ahead."

"Aha. No GPS needed, apparently. Did we bring all the equipment we'll need to make an adequate assessment?"

"Yes. You oversaw the packing yourself."

Yeah, she must have. No way she would have let him bring her all the way out here and not have been completely convinced they had everything they needed. She was just pissed off that she couldn't remember it.

Why would *that* be the sort of thing her brain would block out? It would be so much handier to forget she'd just been groaning and panting in a closet with a guy she barely knew. Remembering the feel of Nic's hands on her and the waves of climax he brought her to was more than a little distracting right now. She should be focusing on the job, not the tingling heat in all her sensitive places. It didn't help her mood any to glance over at Nic and realize he seemed perfectly happy to continue ignoring her. By all appearances, he was having no trouble focusing on the job and not her.

"There, just around that boulder," he said, pointing toward a spot on the moonlit landscape ahead of them that looked very much like all the other boulder-strewn spots out here. "Our sensor should be right about there."

"Awesome." She didn't even bother faking sincerity.

He continued happily ignoring her and maneuvered the vehicle into a near-enough position, then dropped it into park. The engine shut off and he slipped out of his seat belt.

She began removing hers, too, but he stopped her.

"No. You need to wait here."

"The whole point is for me to see this equipment, right?"

"Let me look at it first. I'll make sure it's safe."

She wanted to argue, but the bleary fog that had been hovering over her seemed to descend just a bit and engulf her in a warm, fuzzy feeling. Why did she need to get out of the car? It seemed important...but maybe not. She was comfortable here, and Nic asked her to stay. She would do anything Nic asked her to do.

"Wait for me," he said, his voice the only thing she was aware of. "And keep your coat on. It's cold tonight."

Of course she would do as he said. She was so tired, after all. It was cold out, just as he said, but she was warm here in their vehicle, waiting for him. Maybe she'd just close her eyes for a little while and take a rest. She could barely hold them open. Yes, she'd rest a while. Nic would be back soon and he'd explain everything.

She snuggled into her coat and gave in to the weariness.

* * *

Nic left Lianne in the vehicle. She seemed confused and his conscience pricked. He didn't like controlling her this way, but it was necessary. There was no telling what he would find out here, and he couldn't risk disclosing any of it to her. Strong minds like hers didn't give up memories easily—it would be much better to keep her at least partially under his sway so he could deter unwanted memories from etching themselves into her mind in the first place.

Just what those unwanted memories might be, he still couldn't be certain. All he knew was that he'd been sensing very strong magic out here. Fairy magic? Possibly, but more. He sensed a strange, sensual magic, too.

He'd redirected his course to follow it, feeling something rising then cresting in the way the magic pulsated from multiple locations. First he sensed it near the RGS they were heading for, then he sensed it a kilometer away, halfway around the mountain in an equipment shed he didn't know anything about.

Reaching into the darkness to examine the sensations had been more than a little…arousing. He'd stopped a couple of times while they were driving out here and took a few minutes to mentally scan the area. It used a lot of his mental resources to remain aware of such a vast area, but he could see no way around it. Strange magic was at work here and he didn't like it. He'd been so intent on studying it that at one point he'd lost his hold over Lianne and she'd woken and questioned him. She'd been too smart to fall for his lame excuse about programming his GPS, but hopefully her sheer exhaustion would work in his favor. He'd lulled her back to sleep and she had no idea he was searching for anything other than a defective RGS.

But what *was* he searching for? He'd known all along there were forces working against him here. But he'd thought those were human. Now Eubryd said she'd seen fairies? When had fairies ever been a threat? Yet he'd felt danger permeating the air, twinging in his senses. He couldn't quite put his finger on it, but the threat was real. It was his duty to neutralize it.

He had been posted here as Guardian, after all. The clutch of dragon eggs incubating inside this mountain must remain secret and protected, at all costs. Nothing could matter to him outside of this goal, not fairies, not dark magic, not greedy human entrepreneurs. He had to destroy every obstacle that got in his way. Preferably, Lianne would not be one of them. He knew better than to let himself care for a human, but he could not deny that he would do what would be needed to keep her safe.

The ground crunched under his feet as he approached the RGS. His own breathing echoed into the night. The ground was too rugged here for the SUV, so he'd had to leave Lianne and clamber down into a narrow crag, a gash carved into the volcanic rock by years of harsh weathering.

Magic still lingered in the air here, but it felt alien and unfamiliar. He didn't quite know what to make of it. Residual, no doubt. The magic was not active now and he could sense no other creature beyond Lianne. He would know if they were not alone. Aside from this strange magic, there was little else to interfere with his senses out here.

This specific location had been carefully selected because of that very thing—it was remote, uninhabited, and the land was full of ancient magic. There were no humans to interfere within hundreds of miles. When Nic began guarding the clutch, he had been totally alone. He'd reveled in the loneliness, in the great honor of serving his kind.

For the first time in a millennium, dragons had elected to propagate themselves. Queens were selected from every clan across the globe, and great care was taken to produce the very best offspring who would carry on their lines. This location had been selected and the clutch was gathered, placed in this hallowed nursery and assigned a Guardian. For nearly a hundred years, Nic had watched over the clutch, cared for the future of his kind with his very life. The time for hatching was growing near, and he would not fail at his task now.

If not for these damn humans and their constant curiosity! Five years ago, Geo-Diagnostics selected this place as a potential source for geothermal energy development. Crandall McGowan and his group had felt that due to the distinctive nature of readings at this location, they had possibly found an entirely new, unexploited type of energy that might revolutionize an already revolutionary industry.

Indeed they had found something new. Dragon magic was entirely unknown to humans, and the rarity of an incubating clutch would surely confuse their sciences and technologies. It was not something humans should tamper with. They might think this mountain held something revolutionary and useful, but they were merely endangering themselves.

Nic had used every subtle method possible to dissuade them. He'd instigated social dissent, fabricated environmental concerns, delayed government permits, even resorted to sabotaging their equipment, yet McGowan's outfit had been persistent. They'd been on-site nearly a year now and were inching forward every day, growing closer to their goal of tapping into the heart of the mountain to harness the energy burning below.

Movement in the shadows alerted him. He turned, ready for attack, but the creature made its presence known and he relaxed. *Eubryd.*

"I found you," his scaly friend said as she appeared nearby, dropping low to see what he was up to. Her tiny eyes glittered as they glanced here and there. "Where is your female?"

"She's back in the vehicle. How did I not feel you approaching?" he questioned.

"I don't know. Perhaps your energies are being spent on more-human activities?"

"More likely it's this damn strange magic in the air. Follow me. There is a sensor giving off unusual readings, right over here. But stay out of sight—there may be more at play here than we know."

Eubryd did not seem as frightened as she probably should have. She rose up higher, peering over the crag in the earth and craning her neck to spot the SUV he'd left parked just out of view.

"So you brought her out with you," she commented. "You're not worried she'll see things she shouldn't?"

"I'm tending to that, but keep your head down. Those would be difficult memories to erase if she should happen to see you."

"What, your sway is not weakening, is it?" Her leathery wings made a coy flutter as she hovered in front of him, meeting him at eye level. "I thought you were going to take care of yourself…*that* way."

"I'm taking care of myself just fine. What have you found out here, Eubryd? Did you find the fairies?"

"You feel their magic, don't you?"

"Too much of it, as a matter of fact. It's the strangest fairy magic I've ever felt," he said.

"Perhaps they are strange fairies."

"No, it has to be something more."

Yes, his senses could sort through the magic lingering in this place, and he did, indeed, recognize fairy magic. And Eubryd's magic, of course. And the hot, fiery magic from the clutch brooding inside the mountain…all of that was here, yet still he felt something more. Layered in behind all of it, he could sense a dark, dangerous magic that he'd not encountered before. It was old—nearly as ancient as dragon magic.

"Is this the sensor you were talking about?" Eubryd asked, flapping her way over to the spot where the sensor stuck up out of the ground, a small box jammed into place on a stake.

"It is," he said and knelt by it. "The humans placed these RGSs a year ago, but something is wrong."

Sure enough, the malfunction was easy to detect. This sensor had been modified. A strange component had been added, wired into it in an almost haphazard fashion. It was not the work of McGowan's careful technicians. No, this was something that had been added here, in the field. The wires, however, were blackened and charred. Clearly this little module had shorted itself out. And something more: it had the distinct feel of magic.

"This RGS has been tampered with," he said. "Someone added a component, and it carries magic."

Eubryd nodded. "I've seen that before. Most of these sensors have that little thing wired onto it. This is the only one that looks burned up, though."

"You have been inspecting the RGSs and never told me about that?"

"I only just discovered it! And really, Nic, you have to admit you've been a little preoccupied. This woman has distracted you."

"No, I've got her under control. Damn it, Eubryd, you should have informed me about all of this. Do you know what this module does?"

"Haven't the slightest idea."

"The humans use these sensors to detect seismic activity inside the mountain," he explained. "I've been carefully doctoring the readouts from them so the humans believe this mountain is unsuitable to their purpose and finally give up on the project. Plus, I have been using the undoctored data to monitor the clutch inside the mountain. This amateurishly added device, however, seems to be designed to further confuse the original sensor's readings."

"That's good, then, isn't it?" Eubryd asked. "Someone is working with you to disrupt the humans."

"No! Someone is working against me. I'm already disrupting the humans. This added device only serves to disrupt me. I'm afraid, Eubryd, that someone is deliberately trying to hide something inside the mountain."

"What would be the point of that?"

A very good question. He could come up with only one answer.

"By the Flames, Eubryd, someone has gotten into the clutch!"

She appeared as shocked by that notion as he was. "No, no. That can't have happened. The clutch is fine. Surely we'd know if it was not."

"But these sensors have been modified specifically to prevent me from knowing when there is activity inside the mountain. Someone intended to go in."

"They can't. You set up your safeguards, right? Only you and I know how to get inside the mountain."

"Safeguards can be broken. I need to go to the clutch."

"No! Not now, not with so many strange things happening, Nic. Fairies have been here—you know you can sense them. They're the ones who tampered with this sensor. They're deceitful little creatures. They must be trying to trick you into giving away your secrets. If you go into the mountain now, they'll watch and they *will* know how it's done."

His instinct was to run to the clutch, to defend it and make certain it hadn't been compromised. But Eubryd made sense. Fairies were notoriously scheming, always looking for ways to promote their agenda, to assume more power among magical beings and have a greater say in governing the Forbidden Realm. His own kind had joked for ages that fairies sometimes acted as if they ruled the Realm, as if fairy law covered everyone.

Perhaps Eubryd was right. Perhaps this was some misguided fairy scheme. Did they think they could hold the clutch hostage? Make some sort of power play against the dragons? It was ridiculous, of course, and could never work, but fairies were ridiculous creatures. Nic would do well to have a better idea of what was going on before he rushed into something and divulged the secret entrance to his mountain.

"Where are these fairies now?" he asked.

"I don't know. They're using their sparkling dust to keep out of sight, and the strange magic in the air seems to be obscuring them."

Nic closed his eyes and drew in a deep, demanding breath. He let the air fill his lungs; he held it there and examined it, searching through each molecule with his dragon senses. Fairy magic still crackled around them. The distinctive texture and scent was unmistakable. He reached out into the vastness, sensing the rocks, the breeze, the chill in the air. He forced his mind to reach past the temptation of Lianne. He had to keep focus…yes, there they were. Fairies were nearby.

"I feel them," he said.

"You do?"

"Yes. Not too far, I believe, and…"

Suddenly he felt their panic. They knew he detected them. Like a breath of air, instantly they were gone. They must have been watching him, using their Fairy Dust to make themselves invisible. Now they seemed to have simply dissipated in the wind.

"They flew off," he announced. "Whatever they were up to, those fairies are gone."

"What should we do?" Eubryd asked.

"Go to the clan and tell them what you've seen. I will stay here. One way or another, the clutch must be kept safe. I'll hunt down our enemies and get rid of them. Whatever it takes."

"Whatever it takes, Nicolai? Can you do that?"

"Of course I can."

"But what if our enemy is…human?"

"Do you doubt me, Eubryd?"

"You've been away from your own kind for so long. Nic. You've walked in that frail human body so many years…I wonder if you haven't developed an affection for them."

"Watch what you imply there, my friend. You might soon learn I have very little affection for anything these days. Go to my clan and tell them I will soon have this mountain free from any encroachment, human or otherwise."

"Very well. But I'll stay on my watch, just in case," Eubryd replied. "You might find you require my help."

"I won't. I can handle things here."

"Even the female?"

He snarled at his friend's insinuation. "Especially the female. Now go."

Eubryd shook her reptilian head and clenched her clawed feet. Clearly she had some misgivings about leaving him to deal with things entirely on his own, but he found her hesitation somehow endearing. Wyverns were tiny little things, yet they were fierce. She'd sworn an oath to serve his Dragonrealm, and she was deadly serious in her determination to fulfill that oath.

"I will return to complete this mission, Nicolai," she vowed.

He doubted he'd need her, but appreciated the sentiment. "Thank you, Eubryd. Take care on your travels."

She unfurled her wings—tipped with little hooks that she used as her fingers—and took off into the night. Her snakelike form undulated through the cool air and disappeared into the enormity of the sky in a matter of moments. Her wyvern senses would keep her safe, as would the security of the Veil. She would travel to their homeland in a matter of a few hours, magic assisting her the whole way.

Meanwhile, Nic had a few things here to deal with. He would start by resetting this sensor and doctoring the readouts. Then he would alter Lianne's memories of the night—she'd believe his so-called findings regarding their equipment were accurate. Now that he had his strength back, he no longer had to keep everyone calm by convincing them this was nothing more than a glitch. He could finally insinuate himself deep enough into their minds to actually control their perceptions. He would convince them that there had, indeed, been an earthquake, and that the other sensors recorded the same thing. The mountain was unstable and the humans would believe they were in danger the longer they stayed here. He could finally accomplish his goal of being rid of them once and for all.

Just in time to deal with this new threat from, apparently, fairies.

He stooped to examine the sensor with its odd little add-on. Fairies may have been responsible for altering the RGS, but they certainly had not manufactured the added device. That was clearly crafted by humans—humans who knew enough about magic to incorporate it into their technology.

They would have to be working with the fairies to accomplish such a thing. Could this really be so? What would be the point of such an alliance? And how did the magic pass so freely through the Veil that was made specifically to prevent such a thing?

If the Veil could be penetrated this way, then his protections over the mountain might be as well. How could he know, without giving away any secrets? The clutch could be in mortal danger even as he stood here.

He concentrated his energy once again, reaching with his mind into the darkness. He could feel Lianne, waiting for him in the vehicle. He could feel a storm gathering in the distance, too. Foaming black clouds were beginning to form over the waters and were moving this way. He could feel the magic of the mountain, and the strange, sinister sensation that lingered around him. Had his security been breached? Was his enemy still nearby, watching to follow him into the mountain? He wished he could be certain that was not the case.

He couldn't let fear cloud his senses. He would single out any anomaly and trace it to its source, or its destination. The equipment shed…he sensed this magic would lead him that way. Yes, something had happened there. Magic left footprints, and he was an indomitable tracker.

Chapter Eleven

Kyne kept Raea safely behind him as he peered through the darkness. As they'd guessed, the man they had seen left that broken sensor and was driving toward the equipment shed they'd also broken. He was tracing their actions—somehow he knew where they'd been. If only they'd been able to get close enough to him to really see what he was up to. Raea had sworn he'd been talking to someone, but even with invisibility, Kyne had insisted they observe him only from a safe distance.

Now, however, it was obvious they needed to know more. This man had magic. They had felt it all over him. When he used that magic to reach into the darkness and detect them, they'd taken off in a hurry. He hadn't followed them, though. He'd gotten back into his vehicle and gone straight for the equipment shed.

"Here he comes," Raea said, pressing her body closer to Kyne's as they hid in a shadow in the rocky face of the mountain overlooking the shed.

"Just stay calm," Kyne advised. "He can't see us, and he couldn't track us, so we will be safe. We will watch what he does and learn what we can, then leave before he detects us again."

"Okay. He has strange magic, though, Kyne. How can a human possess that?"

"I don't know. That's what we need to understand."

The approaching vehicle slowed, then came to a stop very near the small building. Raea trembled beside him, but she made no sound. Their invisibility was still strong and he assured himself they were safe here. The human would not find them.

He got out of his vehicle. The man was tall, and everything about him exuded confidence and power. Even Kyne had to admit this human commanded respect. In fact…he was not quite human, was he?

He could feel that strange, ancient magic that tainted the air. The man wore it like a dark cloak. He was imposing, even by human standards—broad, solid, and dangerous—but he was *not* human. Kyne understood why his magic felt strange.

It wasn't like fairy magic, a light, airy magic of the skies. No, the magic that radiated like heat from the man they were watching was more fundamental. This creature carried the same magic that had built the foundations of the earth, that forged the very rocks of the ground all around them. This was a magic that sprang from fire, from the very flames of creation.

The Veil contained only one source for magic like this. Kyne had never actually encountered it before, but it made perfect sense that he should encounter it here, stalking the terrain of a weathered volcano. There could be no better place for a creature like this than such a volatile wilderness. Kyne had no doubt what he truly was.

Raea must have suspected it, too. He heard her catch her breath as the feel of ancient magic flowed over them. He wished he could pull her tight and reassure her that they would be fine, that there was nothing to fear, but he could not lie to her. His kind may exist behind the Veil just the same as fairies did, but no one knew or understood their mysterious ways. By all rights, this fellow Veiled creature should be considered an ally, but no one knew better than Kyne that things weren't quite right.

"He's not human," Raea breathed behind him. "He's trying to appear so, but he isn't."

"No. He's not human."

"But I don't understand. He can't be a...?"

"He is."

"But we haven't seen his kind in centuries."

"No, we haven't. They've closed themselves off and gone dormant in the deepest recesses of the earth."

"But you're sure he's a *real* one?"

"I'm sure. He's a dragon."

He felt the shudder that ran through her, and she pressed herself against him.

"A *dragon*," she murmured. "But what's he doing here? Do you think he's involved in whatever has been going on?"

"He must be. Why else would he be here right now?"

There wasn't any sort of answer for that, so they were both silent. The foreboding creature was closer to them now, inspecting the little equipment shed that they'd taken shelter behind. Kyne could only hope the dragon didn't detect them. A strangely magical human would be one thing to escape from, but a *dragon*? There was no telling whether or not the Invisibility Wish they'd made with Raea's Fairy Dust was strong enough to hide them from dragon magic.

All they could do was duck deeper into the shadows and hope for the best. Fortunately, the dragon seemed content to concentrate on the building. The sound of keys rattling against a lock chained to the door around the front was more than reassuring. Despite possessing magic of epic proportions, this creature was fumbling at a lock as any mundane human might. He cursed like a human, too, when the lock appeared to hamper his progress.

Human curses turned rapidly to a more dragon-like rage. From their position they could not see exactly what was going on, but the dragon made no effort to keep quiet. He must have abandoned his key and resorted to ripping the lock fully off the door. There was a furious wrenching sound and the shed violently shook. The door banged against the building as the dragon obviously threw it open and gained entrance.

"This might be a really good time to leave," Raea whispered.

"You should go. Get somewhere safe and I'll follow."

He hadn't really expected her to agree. She didn't.

"Of course I'm not leaving without you."

"I have to stay. We need to know what he's up to."

"He's fixing the machinery," she whispered in his ear. "You know what will happen to us if we're still here and it starts running again."

"We're fine as long as our invisibility holds out."

"But what if—"

More angry cursing from inside the shed interrupted them. Had they been careless? Did the dragon hear their whispers, sense them hiding in the rocks? Kyne held his breath, mentally devising a plan to distract the damn dragon if he came charging around the side of the building. Kyne would attack, fend him off long enough to let Raea get away.

He was tensing his muscles, getting into position when they heard the door on the other side of the shed slam shut. The furious dragon did indeed storm back into view, but he was not moving their way. He went straight for his vehicle, curses still trailing from him and scorching the cold air around them.

"Thank the Clouds. He's leaving." Raea sighed.

"It looks that way."

The vehicle ground into gear and its tires spit bits of rock and earth up into the empty night. Beams from the headlights swept over the landscape as the dragon set his course toward the other side of the mountain. Whatever he planned to do now, he intended to do it without delay.

"I guess he couldn't fix the machinery," Raea said. "That must be what made him so upset."

That certainly did seem to be the case. It was obvious all the banging around they'd heard inside the shed hadn't accomplished anything. There was no humming drone of equipment, no lust-inducing side effects fogging Kyne's mind. It appeared the machines were still inoperative and he and Raea were safe—for the moment.

The red glow of taillights faded in the distance as Kyne inched his way out of their hiding spot and down toward the shed. They were still invisible, and there was no indication of anyone nearby to discover them, but it couldn't hurt to be extra cautious. He held Raea's hand to keep her close to him, and peered around the corner of the small building. The dragon had left the shed door hanging open.

He'd practically ripped the door completely off its hinges, as a matter of fact. Fortunately for them, this meant they'd have access to the equipment inside. Baylor would want a detailed description, no doubt, and the dragon had just made that easy for them.

Until Kyne slipped past the skewed door and into the near darkness of the shed's interior. Raea padded softly up behind him, then uttered a hushed expletive that was far milder than the one Kyne would have used.

"He destroyed the machine!" she exclaimed after taking in the scene before them.

The moonlight outside spilled through the open doorway. There was no doubt what they were looking at. Whatever this equipment had been created to do, it would never serve that purpose again. It was broken, smashed and dismantled beyond what could have possibly happened when it overloaded due to their passion.

"Maybe he knew we would find it," she suggested. "Maybe he trashed it all so we couldn't figure out what it did, how it was supposed to work."

"No, if he wanted to hide it entirely, he could have simply incinerated it. I think he just wanted to make sure no one could set it up running again."

"But why? If he is working with them, wouldn't he want the machine to work properly?"

"I don't know. I can't make any sense of it."

"Unless…maybe he isn't working with them. He certainly did sound angry when he came in here," Raea noted. "Maybe he didn't realize this was here."

"He drove right to this spot," Kyne pointed out. "He must have known it was here."

"He probably sensed the magic." She squeezed his hand. "Or maybe he senses us! We should leave, go back to your father now and tell him about this."

"We still don't have a clue what's going on. We found a dragon beside a volcano with some broken equipment, but all that gives us is more questions."

He could feel the fear clutching Raea. Even without seeing her, he knew how she felt. By the Skies, he should probably listen to her. It was time they went back to that cabin where she would be safe. Unfortunately, he'd already made his case for staying.

"You're right," she said. "We need to find more information. Where do you think the dragon is going next?"

Kyne peeked out of the shed and squinted into the distance. He could just barely make out the slight glow of taillights still jouncing over the terrain. "Looks like he's going around to the far side of the mountain."

"And…I think I noticed something," Raea said slowly.

"What was it?"

"I'm pretty sure he's not alone."

If he could have shown her his expression, she would have seen he was frowning. "Someone was with him?"

"I think so," Raea replied. "I got a glimpse of someone in the vehicle as he was driving away."

"Another dragon?"

"No. A human. He had a human woman in the vehicle with him. She wasn't moving, either."

"You didn't mention this to me?"

"I was afraid if I did, you'd go tearing off after him on some kind of rescue mission."

"So a raging dragon is carting an unconscious woman off to his lair. That sounds a little medieval, don't you think?"

"Yes, and from what I recall from history lessons, the last time things like that went on, humans tried to exterminate magical creatures."

"Maybe that's what's happening again. It would actually explain things, if humans found a way to harness our magic and use it against us."

"Unless it's the opposite, and dragons are trying to take over humanity, using their dark magic to control them."

"Yeah, I guess it could be something like that, too."

"What do we do? Should we try to go save that woman?"

"It's probably too late for her, sorry to say," he had to admit. "If a dragon has her in his sway, there's not much we can do. Besides, look at those clouds in the distance. There's a storm blowing in. We'd probably be better off to get back to Baylor. The more we're finding out, the worse this is getting."

"I know…but I wish we could help her."

She pulled her hand away from his, and the air beside him slowly began to sparkle. He could see her pink aura forming, large and nebulous at first, then shrinking and concentrating in density. A moment later, Raea was fully visible, her body returned to its tiny form and her wings fluttering to keep her aloft.

"Sorry. I didn't use much dust since I don't know how much we'll need to get home," she said with a sheepish smile.

"It's okay. I'll be visible in a little while, too. Why don't we look over this machine and figure out a few key components to take back to Baylor? He might be able to understand it then. If you still have some Sizing Dust, we can shrink the parts and carry them with us."

"That's a really good idea, Kyne. I just wish…" she said, hovering near the doorway and glancing out after the disappearing vehicle. "I just wish we understood what he was up to."

He let go of his physical form, shaking off the lingering effects of their

Fairy Dust. Soon his body was shrinking, shimmering into view, much as hers had moments ago. He smiled and moved toward her, pulling her into his arms. No secret machinery directed him now, only his sheer passion for Raea.

"He is a dragon," he said. "They do as they please. I doubt anyone understands them."

"The poor woman. I wish we could help her. I hate to think what that dragon might do to her."

"Be careful, my dear. You're starting to sound like quite the lover of humans."

She gave up her worry and melted into his kiss.

"No," she replied. "I'm simply a lover of one very specific half human."

Chapter Twelve

Lianne realized she'd been sleeping again. What was wrong with her? She hadn't known she was this tired, yet here she was, blinking into the dark and trying to shake the fog from her brain.

Where were they? Still out on the mountain, by the looks of things. Once more, the vehicle was parked and Nic was nowhere to be seen. How long had she dozed off this time? Where was he? The dark sky was still dotted with a myriad of stars; clearly, dawn was a couple of hours away. She must not have been asleep long. That meant Nic was, no doubt, somewhere nearby.

She unfastened her seat belt and opened the door. Cold wind rushed in immediately, helping to chase the fog from her brain. Good. She needed the wake-up. She pulled her coat more tightly around her and stepped out into the wide-open wasteland.

The mountain rose up on one side; jagged rocks surrounded the narrow valley that had served as their road. The huge glacier reflected moonlight in the distance as it wrapped its way around the mountain and scraped and gouged its way through the valley on the far side. Overhead, the stars crowded the dark canvas, glittering against the glow of northern lights and distant, gathering clouds.

It was like standing on an alien planet. She spun around and scanned for Nic, but there was no sign of him. Where could he be? He came out here to show her the remote sensors, yet he kept going off without her. What was he really up to?

Surely when the equipment had been placed here it had been somewhere accessible. It wasn't as if there were many hiding places, just crags and corners of rock, and who would put a sensor in such an out-of-the-way place? Nic had just vanished. Why couldn't she see him?

Her coat was secure, and she'd bought it specifically for her trip here, but still the wind cut right through it. No, not the wind…something else. Cold reached inside of her and wrapped itself around her bones, making her shiver. It was an unfamiliar cold, though. It didn't seem to come from the wind, but from something in the wind. It was a cold that felt…dark.

She shuddered. Maybe she was just imagining things; maybe little bits of sleep still clung to her mind. Maybe it was the tumor. Or maybe it was nothing more than being alone in such a strange, foreign landscape. She'd never truly been this alone in her life, this close to the endless breadth of forever.

She would find Nic. As cold and conceited as he was, she'd no doubt feel considerably warmer if he were here. And not just because of the heat he generated within her body at the thought of his touch, either. She simply needed to know she was not the only human on this mountain. At least, that's what she decided to tell herself.

The black, ominous form loomed over her. Beyond, the stretch of wasteland was empty and unwelcoming. She glanced up at the stars, hoping the sight of familiar constellations might make her feel as if somehow she belonged here, but the friendly stars were beginning to disappear. The clouds were shifting, evolving. Right before her eyes a bank of dark, roiling cumulonimbus flowed toward her, blocking the sky.

Lightning flashed in the distance, making the clouds flicker and glow as if they were alive. How on earth had a storm come up so suddenly? And where was Nic with this thing bearing down on them?

She opened her lips to call out his name, but a gust of glacial wind took her breath away. No word came out. A low moan sounded all around her, the echo of the wind whisking over the rocks, humming with force and with fury. Thunder rolled overhead, surrounding her.

Where was Nic? He was going to be caught in this. They both were. Instinctively she turned back for the vehicle, put her hand to open the door and find shelter from the increasing wind, but she paused. What if something was wrong?

What if Nic had fallen into one of the many cracks and fissures? He could have slipped on the rugged terrain, could have knocked himself unconscious. He could be out there now, dying. She had to go find him.

Again she tried to call out, but the wind howled and drowned out any sound she could make. She had no idea where the RGS was that they'd come to investigate, but it seemed logical that it wouldn't be too far from the vehicle. Nic had driven them to the edge of a flat plane, boulders and rocks jutted up from here, creating the base of the mountain. They were probably right at the edge of the area allowed by their permit, so the equipment could not have been placed too far away.

Unless Nic hadn't been entirely in compliance with their permits. He'd already admitted to coming out here without proper authorization. Nothing about him led her to believe he was much of a rule follower. Hell, there were probably sensors placed all over this mountain, beyond their official zone. No wonder her official data was so confusing. Damn him, he was probably up there, in the shadows on the mountain itself, just out of sight. She had to go look.

Bracing herself, she picked her way over the bumpy ground. The clouds were rapidly obscuring the moon, making things even darker and more terrifying than before. She just couldn't rid her mind of that image of Nic lying helpless and broken, trapped in some volcanic crevasse. Damn it, she knew her time on earth was getting more limited as every hour ticked by, but she never expected she'd freeze to death in some freak storm on a mountain in Iceland.

"Nic! Where the hell are you?" she called out, useless in the rumble and shriek of the storm.

He didn't answer, of course, so she moved farther upward, heading for the darkest, most forbidding area she could see. It was probably well out of their permit zone, but to hell with that. If something bad had happened out here, the shadowy, rocky cleft appeared to be the prime place for it. She'd start hunting him there.

* * *

Fairies. He knew there were fairies around here…somewhere. Eubryd had been right. Nic could feel them, feel their glittery, cheerful magic filtering through the air, even in the dead chill of the night. A breeze was whipping up, but he could still feel the magic. Damn, but he couldn't quite locate the source of it.

Where were they? Perhaps an even better question might be, what in the hell were they doing out here? Obviously tonight wasn't the first time they'd been here. The modifications on the RGSs showed signs of weathering, though he still didn't know what had caused the readings that set off the alarm. Obviously the little schemers had something to do with it. Nic just had to find out what that was.

He thought he'd found them when he sensed something odd at that equipment shed. By the Fires, he hadn't found fairies inside that, though. The shed had not been built by the team from Geo-Diagnostics. It had been put in more recently, and the machinery he'd found inside it infuriated him.

Human technology coupled with magic. Who was responsible for such a thing? The machinery he found inside that shed could have easily controlled a myriad of those small devices like the one he'd seen attached to that broken sensor. It was not a part of the Geo-Diagnostics network, yet it was clearly hacked into that system. Someone would have to have intimate knowledge of the network to make that happen. Clearly someone on their jobsite was not who they pretended to be.

Even more than this unexpected scheme, though, what really caused Nic's blood to boil was the power source for that machinery. The equipment was built to draw magic directly from its surroundings, in this case the mountain, and use that magic to power itself as well as the small add-on devices attached to the RGSs he'd found. Technology like this could be immeasurably dangerous, and he was seriously pissed that he had never even heard of such a thing.

Now here it was, trying to take over *his* mountain.

The equipment was not functioning when he'd found it, which was strange considering that he'd been drawn to it by a powerful surge of magic. He'd been quick to destroy it once he found it, of course, but until he knew how to find his enemy, that would barely slow them down. He had to find out if the clutch was in danger. If, as Eubryd seemed to worry, fairies were out here watching him, entering the mountain would be risky. He could lead his adversaries right to their goal. If they hadn't already breached his safeguards and gotten inside.

From all appearances, the rocks around him looked as dark and as dead as ever. He knew fairies possessed magic enough for simple tricks to hide them from view, but his ancient dragon senses ought to be more than adequate to penetrate that. If these fairies were hidden from him tonight, he was going to find them. If he could not, that could only mean something darker and more ancient than fairy magic was at play. And *that* meant he could be facing his equal out here.

The wind was getting increasingly stronger, catching him off guard. His hair blew into his face and he stumbled over a loose rock. The mountain was jagged and steep. He was forced to claw at it with his hands to keep his footing. Damn, but where had this storm come from? He glared at the clouds as they encroached on the sky.

It wasn't an ordinary storm. He paused, shutting his eyes to reach out into the wind with his senses. He'd been so focused on hunting those fairies that he hadn't paid attention to the weather. How had he not noticed the change in air pressure, the bone-jarring cold that came blowing in from the fjords? He should have felt it approaching, recognized the heavy feel of magic inside it.

It prickled inside him with malice and danger. He was instantly on high alert. No, this wasn't just any ordinary storm. This storm was being used for a purpose—a purpose that targeted him. And Lianne.

By the Fires, he'd left her alone! And now he'd become so distracted that he'd let his mind lose his hold over her. He had to send his senses back out into the night to search for her—but she was not where he'd left her. Damn! This storm was bearing down on them and he had no idea where Lianne was. He ignored everything else but the need to find her. Immediately.

Thunder rolled and lightning flashed, lighting up the clouds from the inside out. Still, they brought thick, impenetrable darkness as they roiled closer and closer. Nic cursed his clumsy human feet. He needed to move, to cover more ground, but this fragile form was unable.

It was forbidden, of course. He must never reveal his true form in the presence of a human, but he didn't care. Lianne was in danger. He had to get to her *now* or it would be too late. He could feel the storm building in strength, focusing energy on the mountain, on the area where Lianne had been. There was only one thing he could do.

A crack of lightning ripped through the sky above him. His body responded to the surge of electrified air. With a deep breath and a roar that erupted from deep within him, Nic let go the last of his ragged restraint and gave rein to parts of himself that had been tethered for so very long. The storm hit with full force, blasting him with gusts that literally blew him off the rocks he'd been clinging to. He embraced the wind, welcoming it and sucking it into his lungs.

His body unfurled as his nature burst forth with all the power and urgency he contained. His muscles, his limbs, his sinews…every part of him extended and expanded. The creature inside him lurched into being, the feel of it after all of these years incredible. He spread his wings wide in the wind, catching it and commanding it as he soared up into the night, using the storm to propel him almost instantly toward the spot on the other side of the mountain where he had left Lianne.

He could feel her now. Yes, she was awake, thinking of him and worrying in the storm. There was so much magic in the air, no wonder he hadn't been able to feel her before. He felt her now, though. She was nearby.

He swung around the mountain, his huge dragon wings beating through the pelting rain, and the fresh scales on his back enjoying the feel of it all. For so long he'd been pent up in that tiny human form, it had almost begun to feel normal. But now…now he was back. This is what he was bred to be: huge, powerful, all dragon.

His clothing had shredded off him in the change, but the weather did not bother him. It would take more than a few gusts of wind and some raindrops to penetrate the steel-like skin of a dragon. He would find Lianne and protect her.

But the storm did have some effect on him, after all. Not the wind or the elements, but something else. The darkness, the evil he'd felt inside it…that was clouding his senses, blocking him from finding her. He could feel her fear, he knew she was close, but where? He had to find her quickly.

The vehicle. There, he could see it now. He'd left her sleeping in it; safe, he had thought, from the chill of the night and securely under his influence. He reached with his senses for her; yes, she was very near. Probably inside the vehicle, in fact. Surely she'd taken shelter there when this storm came up. He would go to her, get her off this mountain and away from whatever darkness was targeting them.

But the fury inside the storm churned itself up. The force of the wind increased, throwing him off course and slamming him into the side of the mountain. He regained his course, but not before thunder cracked with a deafening boom and lightning shot past him. For a moment he felt a smug satisfaction that the fury had missed its mark, jolted past him to strike harmlessly on the vacant landscape below. In an instant, though, his gut contracted and another furious roar escaped him. The lightning did *not* strike harmlessly.

The bolt hit its mark, slicing into the vehicle parked down there in the open. It exploded with a shower of sparks that rained over the mountainside. The pungent smell of burnt air and melted plastic filled the icy wind as the glow of flame licked at the underside of the vehicle. Lianne would be trapped in the inferno!

He swooped low, barely dodging another sizzling bolt as it shot past. He reached the vehicle and covered it, his huge scaly body offering protection from the onslaught above, but he could do little to douse the fire that already burned. He clawed at the door handle, finding it fused. The heat and electricity from the lightning had melted the latch! He'd have to rip the vehicle apart to get Lianne to safety.

But as the storm flashed around him, he could see inside the vehicle. Lianne was not there. Thank the Creator, she was not burning to death, not trapped in there, breathing the poisonous vapors released from the flames. If not inside the vehicle, though, where was she?

He whirled around to begin searching. With another earsplitting crack, a bolt shot toward him and he surged up into the sky just in time to avoid being struck. He could not avoid the next one, though. It anticipated his movement and blasted directly for him, slamming him with enough force to plunge him back toward the earth. He could feel the powerful heat penetrate even his tough scales.

He struggled to regain control, even as another bolt pierced him like a knife, cutting him deep. He deflected it with his wing, but his body was shaken. The explosion of power battered him against the rough rocks of the mountainside, pain nearly blinding him. All he could think was how Lianne could never withstand such onslaught. He had to find her, to shelter her.

More lightning crackled toward him, but he was able to shift out of the way just in time. Pebbles sprayed around him where the bolt struck rock, shattering it into glowing, scalding-hot bits. Nic scanned his surroundings for any sign of Lianne.

A tiny pink glow caught his attention. He blinked through the particles pelting him in the wind. What was that? He could barely make out a tiny form moving toward him. Was it…yes, it was a fairy. A tiny, misplaced fairy fluttering in the fierce gusts here on this mountain.

Glaring, now he could see two of them. One glowed pink and one gave off a rich, summertime-gold aura. Were they causing this storm? He rumbled in the back of his throat, feeling the heat building up with fury and determination. With one halfhearted breath he could turn those damn fairies into char, let them blow away as nothing but ash in their malicious wind.

He'd never known these little creatures to be so violent, though. They continued moving toward him at a remarkable pace, considering how they were clearly struggling in this weather. He could do away with them in a heartbeat, yet he held off. Something was not right…he simply couldn't credit these fairies for such a grand display as this storm. Nothing made sense.

Thunder roared and another bolt cracked out of the sky and shot toward him. He dodged, slamming his wing against a boulder as he struggled to get out of the way. Suddenly a mass of multicolored glitter surrounded him, billowing like a cloud but clinging to him even as the wind threatened to tear it away. He could feel the magic in this wispy mass. *Fairy Dust*. It had been years since he'd been touched by it, but he recognized it well. Instead of intending to harm him, the dust added an extra layer of protection as another flashing bolt slammed into him.

The fairies were not targeting him. No, they were *aiding* him. He could make no more sense out of that than he could the rest of this bizarre event, but at least this was a welcome development.

"The human female," he shouted toward the fluttering creatures. "Where is she?"

He could see the fairies better now. The pink one—a female—seemed especially terrified, but she pointed upward. The golden one with her nodded and called back to Nic over the crash of the storm.

"Higher on the mountain. She went that way." He gestured, pointing the same direction as the female.

Nic glanced upward toward...*oh, hell*. When he craned his neck around a splintered outcropping, he could barely make out Lianne's form. She was on the mountain, sure enough, clinging to whatever she could, pressed tightly against the cold rocks, looking small and helpless.

It was obvious where she had been headed, too. What had she been thinking? Clearly she'd been inching her way toward the one and only place on this mountain that was completely forbidden to her. She was mere feet away from the dark void that Nic had specifically constructed to keep humans out. If she reached that spot...well, he'd created security features that would make certain no human who ever went there lived to tell about it.

* * *

It really wasn't surprising that Lianne wasn't literally screaming for her life. Oh sure, she was terrified enough, clinging to the brittle rocks of this barren volcanic mountainside. But screaming was entirely out of the question. The wind sucked up all of her breath and she barely had enough to remain conscious, nothing at all left for screaming.

Not that her screams would have done any good. There was no one around to hear her if she had been able to make more than a rasping gasp every now and then. The storm was so loud, anyone who might have been nearby would have been made deaf by it. All in all, she decided the best thing to do was to use the little energy she had left to hang on to her spot here, to keep from tumbling to her death.

As miserable and frightened as she felt, and with her head pounding with stabbing pains, a small part of her wondered if maybe tumbling wasn't actually the better option. At least then all this would be over. Although, she figured it would be her luck not to die from the fall, just end up horribly mangled and maimed. That thought kept her clutching the crumbling rocks and praying for a miracle.

What she got instead were damn hallucinations. She cursed the tumor inside her head and blinked into the wind, amazed that no amount of blinking could chase away what her eyes thought they saw. Among all the wind and the lightning and the bits of dust blowing around her, two distinct glowing lights fluttered like butterflies along the base of the mountain, darting in and out of the shadows.

One light was pink, the other a reddish-gold color. What on earth were they? Clearly they were not actually on the mountain, but hovering in midair. They were flying, or floating, but not in tempo with the course of the wind. UFOs? No, way too small for that. All the pseudo-documentaries on television portrayed them as much larger than these. What Lianne was watching appeared more like…intelligent insects.

Of course they weren't, though. Hell, no intelligent insect would turn up in the Icelandic wastelands in the middle of a freak storm, so obviously that couldn't be it. But there they were, flitting below her and seeming very intentional about it. Clearly they had some sort of intelligence, whatever they were.

She battled the wind and the loose rocks at her feet to push hair from her face. Lightning slashed through the air, more than once exploding into the rocks. Lianne's footing slipped as a rock beneath her toe shifted, but she held on somehow and readjusted her hold. It wasn't easy, staying up here while everything around her seemed to wage war.

Another crash of lightning and she realized her vehicle had been struck. Damn it! She gazed down the mountain face and watched as glittering sparks flew out in all directions, the vehicle erupting in smoke and the glow of fire in its undercarriage. It only took a few moments for the acrid smell of burning plastic to waft up to her on the violent gusts that pounded and pelted her body. Hell. Now how was she getting back to the jobsite if she ever did find Nic's lifeless body out here?

She figured he had to be dead. There was no other excuse for the fact that even in the midst of this storm he still hadn't appeared. She'd been moving toward the darkest, most unseeable area on this rock face to look for him, and the closer she'd come the more foreboding it felt. Just glancing over at it now, only a few yards away, sent chills up and down her back. As close as she was, even with the frequent lightning strikes, her eyes still couldn't penetrate the thick shadows there. It was almost as if the mountain just simply quit being at that point, that some great void of nothingness was fastened onto the side of the cliff, and the shadow opened into oblivion.

Maybe that was where the UFOs came from. Oh God, she was messed up. She shook herself and started plotting her descent. She hadn't thought much about that as she inched her way up here, which was probably a mistake. With all this lightning, she'd be fried here any minute if she didn't find some way down.

But how about that dark void? She'd been heading there; maybe she ought to continue. If that little crag in the rocks was so shadowy, maybe that meant it cut deep into the mountain. A cave, maybe. She could tuck herself in there and get out of this wind, not be such a target for every lightning bolt that flashed out of the clouds. At the very least, she'd get there long before she could make it to the ground. And even if she did get there, it wasn't as if their smoldering vehicle would offer her any protection.

She reached her numb, bleeding fingers outward toward what seemed the next promising chunk of rock that would move her slightly closer to that void. Bits of the ledge she stood on shifted again, but she quickly found a new foothold. The designer boots she'd worn for this trip didn't provide nearly enough warmth. She laughed at herself. Yeah, she had been heading to Iceland to work with a bunch of engineers and nerds, so of course she put style ahead of functionality. Well, at least when they finally found her frozen body out here someday, she'd look good.

Another adjustment and she had moved a good ten inches closer to the darkness. It was no small feat, considering that she shuddered and twitched at every crash of thunder, every jolt from the nearby lightning. The wind was not getting any easier to ignore, either. What kind of crazy storm was this? If she didn't know for a fact the very notion of it was ludicrous, she'd think it was targeting her specifically.

Suddenly her whole body was enveloped in darkness. That was weird, considering her peripheral vision could still see flashes of lightning all around. Right where she was, though, it felt as if some huge form suddenly blocked her from view, shielding her from the storm and even canceling out the wind. She blinked through her tangled hair and could see that, as crazy as it seemed, this was indeed the case.

Something huge was swooping directly toward her! Giant wings flapped against the storm and a body came into view. What grabbed her attention—aside from the giant wings and overall hugeness of it—were the eyes. Hot, fiery eyes glowed behind an impossible face. A dragon!

Hallucinations, of course. That had to be the explanation. Still, she huddled tight up against the mountain, and an involuntary whimper escaped her. Her head knew this couldn't be real, but the whole rest of her believed it sincerely. She was being preyed upon by an enormous red-glowing dragon.

She couldn't take her eyes off it. Its wings blocked the sky, its eyes nearly burned through her, and its sharp claws gleamed as it reached its powerful arms toward her. She screamed and fought it off as best she could, but the action was stupid and futile.

Her footing gave out and she fell from her perch. The dragon—or whatever it was—scooped her up and clutched her tightly against its hard, heated body. She could see that it was covered in scales. Layer upon layer of them, shiny and nearly as hard as metal but somehow warm and flexible, too. She struggled against this incomprehensible monster but it held her fast. Escape was out of the question.

She forced herself to look at it, to make whatever sense she could out of this. This couldn't be a dragon, but what the hell was it? She was pressed so tightly against its body she could see very little of it now. The wings flapped, she could hear them, and she felt the muscles of the creature's broad chest flex and labor with the action. It felt…alive. Real. It couldn't be, of course. There was no such thing as dragons, after all.

It sure as hell looked like a dragon, though. Above the chest was a long neck that reached up above her, putting the creature's angular face out of clear view. She shifted her focus to its arms. Ripped, powerful, and oddly humanlike, except for the knife-sharp claws and the rows of spade-shaped scales.

As the creature shifted these muscular arms, she could see between the scales. Instead of flesh, it appeared the monster was made of molten steel, bursting with occasional flares. The bright glow of heat and fire matched what she'd seen in his eyes.

His eyes? No, *its* eyes. This was not a human; it was a *thing*. A horrible, terrible, impossible thing, and she'd rather fall to her death now than let it carry her off to feed its young or do whatever it was it might be planning on doing with her at this point. She pried at its claws and kicked against it. Apparently her new boots weren't very good for this, either.

She could have sworn the creature merely chuckled at her feeble attempts. The steady whoosh of his wings against the air, though, did seem to be slowing down. They were losing altitude, too. At first the creature had swooped her high into the air, but now they were descending again. Maybe she could get away after all!

"Put me down!" she railed at him, kicking and clawing for all she was worth.

"Not until I've got you someplace safe," the horrific beast replied.

What was that? The creature *spoke* to her? And his voice had been…oddly gentle and soothing. In fact, he had sounded a lot like Nic. Well, clearly that could only mean one thing.

This really *was* just another hallucination and she had nothing to worry about. In fact, this whole mountain fiasco with freak storms and fluttering UFOs was probably nothing more than a bad dream. Yeah, she was probably back in her bed safe and sound and warm. Well, maybe not warm. Maybe she'd kicked her blankets off and that was what sent her into this frigid nightmare to begin with.

Okay, then, she guessed she could just relax until something finally woke her up. She gave up the kicking and fighting and let her body slump against the warm form of the dragon. It did feel oddly secure here, as a matter of fact.

"That's better," he rumbled into her ear. "You should rest now."

And then, with one more flap of his wings, he whooshed her toward that terrifying, dark void in the side of the mountain. The tiny colorful glows she had seen earlier suddenly showed up next to them, accompanying them on their flight. The void appeared darker and larger than ever. No wonder that spot had seemed so foreboding when she'd first seen it. Clearly it was an alien dragon's lair and she was about to be held captive there.

Okay, whatever. This hallucination or nightmare or tumor-induced delusion kept getting weirder by the minute. She kind of wanted to know where it would go from here, actually. At some point she was bound to wake up and laugh at it all, wasn't she?

Chapter Thirteen

Nic did his best to shelter Lianne as they passed into his safeguarded entrance. He reached out with his mind to disarm the security measures made of ancient magic he had placed as enchantment here, but to his surprise he could not find any. His securities had been stripped.

Carefully depositing Lianne on the smooth floor of the fire-worn cavern, he whirled to find the two fairies trailing him. They had no trouble passing his security, either.

"What have you done?" he demanded.

The male fairy glared at him defiantly, but the female was more intent on Lianne.

"Is she all right?" she asked, pointing at Lianne's limp, silent figure.

"Yes. I've put her into a sleep. She'll be fine."

It had actually been very easy to overcome the woman's jumbled thoughts. She was fully overwhelmed; her mind had welcomed his suggestion of sleep. She'd struggled only briefly, then gone limp in his arms as he carried her in here. He'd expected to need to shield her from the securities he'd placed here to keep humans out, but obviously not.

"Now tell me how you disabled my magic," he asked the fairies. He allowed the fire within him to show close to the surface, a clear threat for these tiny creatures just in case they had any ideas of lying to him.

"We did nothing," the male fairy said. "We were sent here to find out what's going on."

"Who sent you?" Nic asked, twisting his huge form in the narrow passage so that he was able to keep himself between Lianne and these two fairies.

"That doesn't matter. What we need to know is, what were you doing on the mountain with a human?" the fairy asked sharply.

Nic had to give him credit for bravery, fluttering into his secret abode and facing him boldly. The only reason he hadn't fried the little insects already was because they had tried to help him. Now he needed to know why. If he wasn't happy with their answers, their fluttering days would be over.

"You're a little out of your element, I think," Nic stated. "This is dragon territory. How did you disable my safeguards?"

The fairies simply shrugged, glitter spilling off them with even the slightest movement. Their colorful glow combined with the heat emanating from Nic's own body, causing shadows to dance over the walls of his carefully constructed entryway. Stray gusts from outside penetrated occasionally, making Fairy Dust and raindrops filter through the air.

"I didn't see any safeguards," the gold-colored fairy said, his small voice surprisingly strong as it echoed off the cold rocks. "What is this place, dragon?"

"I am Nicolai Stefanya Vladik and I will ask the questions here. Why have you come to this mountain?"

"We've come here to find out what you and the humans are working on," the female fairy declared. "We know about the machines the Fairy Council is secretly using, and that someone has been redirecting them here. We want to know why."

She spoke with conviction, her tiny finger wagging in his face. So the Fairy Council was somehow involved in this scheme? That was most interesting. Everyone knew elves held primary jurisdiction in Iceland, and *they* certainly had enough sense to stay away from this mountain. What would fairies be doing here?

"You must be confused," he said. "Human scientists are here studying the viability of using this mountain as a power source for their cities. I am here to prevent that. Now explain why you believe your Fairy Council is here."

The male fairy sneered at him. "They're involved with the machines. We know about them, dragon."

"Do you mean the sensors the humans have placed here to monitor geo-thermal and seismic activity?"

"No," the female answered. "We mean the hybrid machines, the ones that gather magic."

They certainly seemed earnestly troubled by these machines, as anyone with half a brain ought to. Could he really trust them? He still wasn't sure.

"No such thing exists. The Veil prevents that."

"You saw them yourself," the female declared. "We watched you. You were so angry that you destroyed the machine in that little building."

"And did that disrupt your plans?" he asked.

The male fairy was getting downright belligerent. "We don't have any plans. We weren't the ones who set up those machines, but we're for damn sure planning to find out who did."

The female watched Nic's reaction carefully. "If you didn't do it, then it seems like we're on the same side."

"If that is the case, then perhaps you wouldn't mind allowing me to know your thoughts," Nic suggested. "Just so we can all be assured."

"I don't see how you reading our minds will make us any more comfort-able," the male grumbled.

Nic shrugged his enormous wings. "It might make me less inclined to turn you to cinders."

The female's eyes grew large and terrified. "Well, that does make for a compelling argument."

"Very well," the male assented. "Read mine, but leave hers alone. She's only here because I brought her. If you need to know what we're up to, you wouldn't get anything from her that you can't get from me."

Nic was almost impressed. "How chivalrous of you. Very well, you first."

His first impression was that the fairy did indeed possess some secret information about the machinery in question. Upon deeper probing, however, he came to understand what that was. Indeed, no wonder he'd felt such interesting, arousing sensations as he'd tracked the movements of magic on the mountain. This equipment had some unique side effects on these fairies.

Just as the male fairy had said, it seemed these two had only recently come here, interested in finding the source of this new technology, just as Nic was. They did not trust their own Fairy Council, but the reasons for that were not entirely clear. Nic had to search the fairy's mind for more details. They were getting increasingly difficult to come by, for some reason.

"I sense deception in you," he announced. "You are hiding something from me."

The gold fairy glared at him. "It's nothing that involves you. Surely you keep a few secrets yourself, dragon? Things that you'd rather not let everyone know?"

"Like what you are doing hauling a human female up here to your lair?" the pink fairy interjected.

"My personal affairs are my own," Nic informed her. "But you are correct. I find no reason to suspect you two are a danger to me or to my plans."

"Then perhaps you might share those plans with us," the gold fairy said.

"No, I don't think so," Nic replied.

"Tell me what you intend for the woman," the male fairy said and locked his tiny amber eyes with Nic's.

He certainly was bold, for a fairy. There was something different about him, too. He had a depth that Nic had never encountered within a fairy before. A quick probe of the creature's mind ought to give Nic any details that he lacked.

The wind howled outside the cave entrance, yet the silence inside was almost deafening. Nic tried to reach into the fairy's mind to find out why he was unlike countless other fairies he'd encountered over the years. He was surprised to find so much resistance.

"Stay out of my mind, dragon," the fairy snarled at him.

"Why? What are you hiding?"

"Nothing that you need to know."

"Oh, just tell him already," the pink fairy admonished her friend. "He's going to find out."

The male fairy continued to resist. Finally the female huffed and turned her attention to Nic.

"He's half-human," she announced. "And we have been carrying on a forbidden relationship, and I don't regret it even a little bit."

"Damn it, Raea, stop implicating yourself," the male said. "I wasn't going to let him find out about that."

Nic decided it would be rude to laugh at their paltry concerns. "Sorry, but I knew about the affair. That much was easy to read the moment I saw you two."

"You did?" the female asked.

"I did. You've both been thinking about it pretty loudly."

She blushed, but her partner kept his angry frustration focused on Nic. "That is none of your business. If you turn us over to the Fairy Council, they'll take away our magic and then no one will stop them from whatever it is they're planning to do with these machines."

"No worries," Nic said at last. "Kyne, is it? Yes, I know your names now, Raea and Kyne. So that's what you were so intent on hiding from me; he's half-human and you two can't keep your glittering little hands off of each other. By the Flame, who knew fairies were capable of such...stamina?"

"What goes on in our private lives is our business alone," Kyne declared. "Can we count on you not to give us over to the council?"

"I have no dealings with the Fairy Council," Nic assured them. "And you're right, I don't really care how often you do whatever you do in your private lives. What I *do* care about is this hybrid machinery we've discovered."

"We know nothing about any of this—" Kyne began.

"Don't waste my time with lies," Nic interrupted him. "I've been inside your mind. I know what you've been told about these devices, and I know you came to Iceland to learn more."

"I *will* learn more," Kyne replied. "The Fairy Council has one agenda, whoever stole the machinery has another, and obviously you have your own. How many more factions will turn up? We could be dealing with a dozen plots, not simply one or two."

"Well, at least we discovered how to disable the machines," Raea said, then timidly tried to explain. "I mean, at least temporarily. You see, apparently the machines shut off when you—"

"I am aware of what it takes," Nic said before she glowed fuchsia from her embarrassment. "You discovered that passion overloads their systems and shuts them down."

"It has to be in very close proximity, though," Raea added hesitantly. "We found it out by accident."

Nic snorted. "I'll bet you did. Very well, I'm convinced you have told me everything you know and are not here to threaten the clutch."

Raea squealed and gave off a puff of sparkles. "The dragons are incubating a clutch? After all of these years, more dragons are to be hatched?"

Damn, he should have more carefully governed his tongue. These two were not his enemies, but his enemy could use them against him. It would be child's play to retrieve this knowledge from them should they fall under someone else's control. Even now, here he was with his defenses down and this entrance lying open. The clutch could be in grave danger and he had just informed two strangers of its existence. He'd not incur further risk by being careless with his words.

"The Dragonrealm does share our plans," he announced. "If you wish to prove yourself my friends, then you'll leave and go directly back to your Fairyrealm, never mentioning my presence here. The storm is dying down now; you should be safe to travel. You suspect you know the manufacturer, correct? Focus your efforts there, and stop the supply, if you can."

"This thing is so much larger than we bargained for," Kyne argued. "And our own people are working against us. You must want to end this as much as we do. Why not assist us?"

"My duty is to my own kind," Nic reminded them. "You tend to your people, and I will tend to mine."

"Fair enough," Kyne consented. "We'll see what we can do, if anything. But be careful, Nicolai. We might be on our own in this, but it appears you are, too. Unless your woman there is going to support you."

"She will never remember any of this," Nic assured them. "I will keep her safe. You need not concern yourself with her."

"I hope we can trust you about that," Raea said. "Do you promise to take care of her?"

"She'll be fine. Now go. I will keep your secrets if you will keep mine."

Kyne grumbled. "That's easy for us, since you haven't exactly shared much."

The female fairy gave Lianne a long, careful look to reassure herself that everything was as Nic said. They seemed like noble creatures, and he was relieved not to have been forced to blast them into oblivion.

The mysterious storm had lost much of its lethal force. Apparently whatever had been behind that threat had given up. Nic ushered the fairies out and peered into the night after them. Lightning flashed with a muted glow now and the thunder no longer shook the whole mountain. Wind still whipped at the rock face, but it was nothing like it had been. If the fairies had negotiated that, they would certainly be able to move around freely in this.

He watched them flutter off into the dark, then he turned back to Lianne. She slept soundly, propped up against the glazed wall of this passageway. Heat had formed this tunnel, heat from the dragons who had built it and made the place ready for the clutch. Their blasts had melted through the solid mountain, polishing the rough volcanic stone as they went. The rock walls were cold now, but not as cold as the outside of the mountain. Here, even at this distance from the core, the clutch gave off a slight warmth. Lianne would be fine. He hated to leave her, but he needed to go check on things below, and, for her own safety, he was not about to take her down there.

Other than the safeguards being down, there was no indication of intruders. He could sense no one lurking about, but he needed to make certain. This clutch was his utmost priority—nothing could deter him from that, not needy fairies and not even Lianne. His body ached from his battle with the storm, and his energy was rapidly being depleted by all of his efforts, but he drew in a deep breath and headed for the darkened passageway that led deep, deep into the mountain.

There was no need to heat up his scales or blow up a flame to light his way as he went. He knew it well. He may have presented himself as a human for many years now, but this was his home and he had forsaken it too long. He had no right to be comfortable anywhere else, or *with* anyone. Especially not a human.

Chapter Fourteen

Raea followed Kyne as he cut his way through gathering wind. The storm clouds were dark and furious over the horizon, overtaking the sky. Flashes of lightning ignited the air, and thunder growled low. Raea shuddered as the rumble rolled through her body. This was an alien place and she could not wait until they might leave it.

What sort of storm was this? She could have sworn those lightning strikes earlier had been specifically targeting the dragon. He'd barely gotten himself and the woman to safety. Would they encounter trouble out here? Even the dragon seemed concerned by it. Who could be controlling something so vast as the weather?

"Have you seen anything out here that might have been used to create this storm?"

"All we've found is that equipment in that shed and then several of those small sensor things. Wouldn't any machinery powerful enough to control weather have to be much bigger than that?"

"I would think so," Kyne replied. "I don't know where you could hide something like that, especially if there's been a dragon prowling around."

"If there was equipment like that nearby, you'd think he would have found it," Raea agreed. "Maybe we should go back to your father and show him what we did find."

They'd resized some of the parts from that machinery in the shed and were carrying them tucked in their pouches. She hoped Baylor could answer some of their questions. Those machines were powerful, but nothing they'd encountered so far appeared capable of manipulating the weather. If this wasn't just a natural storm, then they'd probably be smart to get as far away from here as possible. Soon.

Fluttering against the wind, she brushed her windblown hair out of her eyes and scanned the hulking silhouette of the mountain. It was as dark and deserted as before. No sign of anyone, magical or otherwise.

"I just don't see anything," Kyne said, calling to her over his shoulder. "Maybe we should do what the dragon said and head back."

"Do you think he knows more about what the machines do than he told us?"

"Who knows? I'm getting used to being lied to."

"I would never lie to you, Kyne. And I think maybe the dragon was telling us the truth. I got the idea that he even cared a little bit about that woman."

"He sure put himself through hell to get her to safety. And he could have burnt us to a crisp, but he didn't. Raea, watch out!"

She jolted as another burst of lightning flashed a bit too close for comfort. "He could have let us wait in his nice safe cave for a little while, though. This storm is getting worse again. I really don't think this is just a random weather pattern we're seeing."

Kyne was tempted to agree, but he knew too much about weather to even begin to guess how anyone could control it. "Not even fairy magic could create a storm like this. Magic and nature work together; one never controls the other."

Raea struggled against another gust. "Unless maybe someone figured out how. Baylor said the machines collect all the magic, but then they must do something with it, right?"

"They're supposed to put the magic back into the Veil, but...Hey, what's that out there?"

He pointed off toward the dark line of horizon, past the mountain and beyond the craggy cliffs overlooking the fjord. A narrow sliver of ocean could be seen, and as Raea hovered in place to peer into the night, she realized what he was indicating. A bright light blinked on the water.

"Is it a low airplane?" she asked.

"I think it's a ship."

"It's coming into one of the fjords. In this weather, that could be dangerous, couldn't it?"

"It could. Either that ship is drifting out of control, or it is intentionally approaching the rocks."

"Do you think someone is coming after us?"

"Or after the dragon."

He caught her gaze with his. She'd never seen him so dark and serious.

"The storm seemed to be targeting the dragon, too," she commented.

"It did. You really don't think it's possible that..."

He didn't finish his sentence, so she did it for him. "Whoever is controlling the weather might be out there on that ship?"

It was farfetched, but there wasn't anyone else around right now. It looked like a pretty big ship...like a warship, maybe. And those lightning bolts had acted like weapons, targeting the dragon and his female companion. Maybe a ship was just the place for someone with a magical machine that could control the weather. They could create all sorts of havoc here, then simply sail off to their next target.

It was a horrible possibility and definitely ought to be checked out.

"We should go take a look," she announced.

Kyne swore. "You've been in enough danger already."

"Kyne, we have to."

"I know. All right, we'll go a little bit closer to see if this is just an average, ordinary ship about to crash on the rocks, or if it's part of the plot."

"Whatever the plot really is."

"If it involves controlling the weather, it's a plot everyone needs to know about, I'm afraid."

"Then we should totally get as close to that ship as possible and look it over."

He shook his head. "You know what being around one of those smaller machines does to us. Imagine being close to a whole ship full of machinery powerful enough to control weather."

She realized what he was saying. It probably shouldn't make her grin like she was. Yes, imagine, indeed!

"We *need* to go check out that ship, Kyne."

Chapter Fifteen

Holy hell. She was alone in the dark…again. She wasn't in their vehicle, though. This time she was sitting on a hard, glassy floor. It was slightly warm, and not quite flat. The floor actually curved upward behind her. Was she in a room? No, it seemed more like a tunnel.

She felt along the walls, getting her feet under her and standing. Yes, this was a tunnel, and some sort of breeze tossed her hair and brushed over her face. Hmm…that felt familiar.

Oh, that's right. A breeze had come up, and it turned into a storm…a storm with horrible wind and lightning. She remembered now…she'd been on that damn mountain! So how did she get here? Unless maybe this was still the mountain.

She must have made it into that void, that dark cleft she had seen. Ah, that would make sense. She'd been trying to get to the opening in the rock face, to get out of the storm, when…

And now she was laughing at herself. A dragon. Yeah, dragons and UFOs. What kind of crazy hallucinations was she having? Man, but she must be so much worse off than she knew. Thankfully she'd somehow gotten herself into here and she must have passed out. How long had it been?

Her head still ached a little, but not like before. She could tell from the direction of the breeze where the opening of this cave was, so she felt her way toward it. The cave was incredibly smooth and level inside, but she figured that was probably because at one time it had been a lava tube. She'd never seen one like this, but she wasn't really much of a geologist.

How had she gotten herself inside? That storm was so fierce…and those damned hallucinations. Well, at least her imaginary dragon was gone now and she could think straight again. She'd find her way out of this cave and back down from the mountain. Maybe Nic was out there somewhere, hunting for her. Or maybe not.

Either way, the guys back at the jobsite would realize something was wrong and come looking for them. She needed to get herself out into the open so that at first light, she could be found. Then they'd discover Nic's fate. God, but she hoped he was okay.

The first glow of early morning moonlight crept into the cave. She could see the opening ahead, the sky still a spread of roiling clouds. The storm was not nearly as violent as it had been, though. Thank heavens things were calmer, and it was still before dawn. She'd not been unconscious too long. Perhaps Nic had simply found someplace on the mountain to wait out the storm. There was still hope for him.

She scooted to the edge of the opening and peered out. *Steep!* How had she managed to drag herself in here, half-insensible and fighting against that horrible storm? Good thing that she had, though. Already she could feel a huge difference in air temperature, just from the spot where she'd been inside the cave and here, at the opening. She pulled her coat tighter and shuddered. Her toes tingled from numbness. She'd be useless if she tried to go after Nic now.

Maybe she'd wait until daylight to venture back out there. Surely no one was looking for them yet, and she'd stand a much better chance of getting herself down from this mountain safely and locating him if she had a little more light and whatever heat the Icelandic sunrise could bring. For now, she really ought to just wait here and clear the fog from her brain.

She moved back toward the interior, out of the cold air blowing in, but not quite all the way back into the darkness. The smooth walls made it easy to navigate, and she found a comfortable spot to sit down. Her feet ached in these damn new boots, so she slipped them off. It would be good to get some blood flowing into her toes again, so she sat cross-legged on the cave floor and rubbed them. Ah, that felt better already.

Her brain was running over all the possible scenarios for what might have happened to Nic last night, and none of them were good. Unfortunately, some of them included such ridiculousness as dragons and space aliens. Damn, but those hallucinations had been so real! If she hadn't sworn off her doomsaying doctor, she might be tempted to call him and see what he said about them.

She leaned back against the cave wall, wriggling her toes. Was it wise to abandon medical science and ignore what was happening to her body? No, probably not. But she knew as well as the doctors did that nothing would change the inevitable outcome of this tumor. It was her choice to make and she'd made it. She would live out her life on her terms, even if it meant there'd be slightly less of it to live.

It was funny, actually, and she had to laugh at herself. If she'd stayed home for another round of useless treatments, she'd have totally missed out on this. All in all, she guessed she'd much rather be taken out by a freak storm on a mountain in Iceland than to die hairless and suffering in some hospital bed with her friends and family feeling sorry for her. It was kind of invigorating, actually, to realize she'd cheated that storm, despite all its best efforts.

She stared out the opening of the cave, at the swirls of galaxies and stars glowing in the midnight of the sky. Yeah, she'd beat that damn storm and sent it back wherever it came from. She decided to take credit for that, and she smiled.

Her smile faded when she realized that a tiny dot she had noticed in the sky through the cave opening was not one lone star peeking through the clouds, but something heading directly toward her. Whatever the odd little light was, it was clearly getting brighter and brighter. An airplane? Helicopter? No, given the way her night was going, it was probably nothing that innocuous. With her luck, this was a meteor with her name carved right on it. Hell, it would just about figure, wouldn't it?

She grabbed up her boots and scrambled to her feet. Her eyes never lost sight of the glowing dot. Thankfully it seemed too small and too close to actually be a meteor. But it was definitely not an airplane, or even a helicopter that might be searching for them, either. It was very much like…those orbs she had hallucinated last night on the mountainside.

Crap! She was doing it again. Unless…maybe she wasn't. Maybe this was something real. But how could it be? She couldn't even tell fact from fiction anymore. She felt panic rising inside and she instinctively pressed up against the side of the cave wall. She found a slight ridge to tuck herself behind, where she could peer out and watch the oncoming glow-ball, but not let it see her.

If glow-balls had eyes. What the hell was happening to her? She had to struggle not to hyperventilate.

Just as she had almost convinced herself with repeated internal chanting that this was not real, this was not real, the object began to take form. It was in the opening of the cave now, about half a foot in diameter, hovering there until it slowly descended to the cave floor. Silver and blue glitter seemed to emanate from it, sparkling against the smooth cave walls, and she could make out a tiny form there inside of the glow.

A fairy. She held her breath and stared. She was looking at a fairy, a tiny blue-glowing fairy. And not some pretty little princess thing, either. No, this was a guy fairy and he did not look very friendly. Even from where she hid in the darkness, she could see a sneer on his face.

But then he held up some kind of device. Was that a tiny cell phone? No, it couldn't be. What would a fairy need with a cell phone? But then he spoke into it and she had to admit that maybe her first guess was accurate.

"I'm in," the tiny creature said. "The safeguards are off. No sign of Vladik or any of the others. We can go ahead and send the next shipment down."

A voice crackled back on the tiny device, but it was too small and too far away for Lianne to make any sense of it. Not to mention that she couldn't make sense out of anything right now.

"All right," the fairy continued. "Contact me when they're close by. I'll wait here for the signal."

He must have finished his conversation, because he tucked the device into a little bag that he carried at his side. Lianne stared, but then he took a few steps into the cave and his gaze shifted her way. She sucked in a breath when he spotted her and they made eye contact.

"Who are you?" he demanded. "Explain yourself, human!"

She was suddenly struck by the absurdity of it all. A six-inch fairy fluttered up to her and was demanding she explain herself? She didn't have time for this. She needed to get out of here, find Nic—or whatever was left of him—and get back to the jobsite. These hallucinations were starting to suck.

Without thinking, she swung her boot around and nailed the snippy little fairy right on the side of his tiny, glittering head.

"I've got fucking cancer," she told him as he went sailing senseless into the wall. "I don't need to explain *anything*."

* * *

He had no explanation. *Something was wrong.* Nic could feel it, but he could not determine what it was. His mind was tiring, growing weak. His body, too. The closer he came to the clutch hidden deep inside the mountain, the more his power drained.

He pressed on, concentrating on keeping his movements silent, stealthy. The labyrinth of passageways was intentionally complex and he purposely did not take the most direct route. His dragon senses—dulled, though they were—told him caution should be his first priority. There was a reason his safeguards were gone from the entrance, and he did not like to think of what it could be.

Someone *had* come through. It was not anyone of his kind, either. He would have felt them, known they were here. Whoever it was that had penetrated his defenses, they were not here on friendly business, and they must have gone to great lengths to keep themselves hidden from him. His instinct pounded with worry for the young, curled inside their iridescent eggs below, growing and incubating in the clutch. It was an effort to keep himself calm as he moved steadily through the passages, reaching with his senses for anyone who might be waiting to surprise him.

He'd been forced to release his mental hold on Lianne. As he'd grown weaker, it was impossible to keep his connection to her and search through the myriad of hiding places down here. He hoped to the Depths that she was still sleeping above, oblivious to anything going on around her. It grated at him to have to leave her alone, but his first duty was to the clutch. He had to get there, to see that it was safe.

The clutch was his future, the hope of his kind. Nothing could be allowed to endanger that. When he did find whoever—or whatever—was down here draining his power, it would be his life or theirs.

And he had no intention of dying today.

Something caught his attention. He froze, his huge body tensing as he put all of his effort into his thoughts. Yes, he could feel someone nearby…several someones, actually. Human. By the Fires, there were humans in the clutch!

He made himself drain all his fury. He must stay cool, keep his temper low and his fire doused; it was the only way to keep hidden. He breathed slowly, methodically, reaching ever so carefully with his mind. No one must feel him. No one must know he was here.

He found the first mind easy to penetrate. This was a human, someone simply doing a job without much passion or drive. He searched carefully but could learn very little. This human was a mere technician, someone simply hired to install machinery, but that was all that he knew about it. He'd likely been kept ignorant for this very purpose, so that no one could learn valuable details from him.

This meant Nic was expected. Whoever was in charge of this operation knew telepathic searches could be a possibility. They'd likely taken precautions. It might not be so very easy to get information out of the others whom Nic could feel moving around just one passage over, working at the very mouth to the cavern his kind had crafted especially to harbor the clutch.

He had to try, though. Gingerly, slowly, his mind touched the next human he found, and then the next. So very empty—how could their minds be so blank? He reached into a fourth—the final human in this group. Ah, here was the leader. Nic could feel that immediately.

But there was something more. He felt something inside the man, something that shouldn't be there. He sensed magic! This human possessed magic within his mind? How could that be?

He probed deeper to understand what he'd found, but suddenly an alarm began blaring loudly, echoing through the passages and alerting anyone within earshot. Damn it all, but the magic inside the human had reacted to Nic's presence. Now all four of the humans knew he was here, and Nic could feel their desperate thoughts loud and clear. They were prepared for him.

The leader ordered his men to attack the clutch—to destroy it! They possessed weapons to do so and Nic could feel their vicious intent as they began their onslaught. He gave up stealth and caution, charging ahead, letting the full fury inside him boil over. His weariness threatened to slow him, but sheer force of will allowed him to ignore that. The walls of the passageway glowed with his flame, although he had to notice the intensity was not nearly what it should have been. Still, he pushed himself forward.

Sparks shot from his claws as he tore at the rock with all four legs, covering distance in labored strides.

He rounded the final turn in his route toward the clutch and burst into the nursery cavern only to come to a screeching halt. All four humans stood there, some sort of weapons in their fleshy hands. The weapons weren't aimed at the helpless young in the clutch, though. No, each human stood at the ready, his weapon trained on Nic as if he had been fully expected.

Obviously he had been, at least by the leader of their group. That man Nic recognized immediately by the smug sneer on his face. The other three men seemed somewhat less prepared to find a huge, fiery red dragon raging over them. They each took a step back and held their weapons just a bit higher. They did not fire, Nic noted.

"Nicolai Vladik, I presume?" the group leader said confidently.

"You should not be here," Nic roared, not bothering to acknowledge the man's question. "This is not your place. You will die for being here."

"I think not," the man continued. "As you no doubt have already noticed, you're lacking a little steam right now, aren't you? Yes, I can see it in your eyes. You know something's wrong, don't you, Nic?"

"I have more than enough steam, as you say, to make short work of vermin."

"Is that so?" the man asked with a shrug, then gestured toward one of the others. "I guess we'd better do something about that."

Before Nic even had time to react, one of the weapons exploded with a shot. Immediately Nic felt a burning in his side—he'd been hit. Damn, he should have been ready for that. He should have known what was in the man's mind long before he had time to use one of those weapons. And by the Fires below, he ought not feel so much searing pain from one simple human weapon. He staggered back, unprepared for the whirling sensation inside his head.

The humans waited, as if they expected Nic to lash out and defend himself. Hell, *he* expected to lash out and defend himself. He could not, though. His legs felt weak and the cavern was losing focus before him. The boldest of the humans laughed at him, then the others followed suit.

"What's the matter, dragon? Can't find it in you to breathe fire or do any of your scary dragon things to us? Aw, so sorry."

Nic craned his long neck to see that he had indeed been shot, but not by any ordinary projectile. Whatever had come out of that weapon had punctured his scales as if they were paper, then clamped onto his side. He could see it there, a metal device with a small blinking light. What was this, an incendiary of some sort? Was that their plan? But what could be making Nic feel so totally weak, so drained of his very essence?

"You're curious, aren't you?" the man asked. "Very well, I'll explain. We've just attached one of our dampeners. Oh yes, they look harmless enough, but as you can see, that little device can suck magic right out of you and transmit it to something more useful, like this, for instance."

As he spoke, the man shifted so that Nic could see an equipment case next to him. He could hear its low, steady humming, but could feel nothing from it. Usually human devices emitted energy, electrical static…something. This gave off nothing. It was as if the air all around it was turned into a vacuum, but of course it was not. Nic was simply noting the complete, impossible absence of magic.

Whatever this human machinery did, it was as the man said. Magic was being pulled from him and transmitted away. He was being drained of everything that made him who he was. His legs gave out and he collapsed onto his chest. Damn these humans! He could not let them get away with this.

With every ounce of strength he had left, he swung his head at them. Two of the men were easily out of his reach, but the others were not. One man fell down, his weapon skittering helplessly across the smooth cavern floor. The other man was standing closest to the lip overlooking the clutch. He dropped to his knees, then lunged for his weapon as it slipped from his hands. Nic took advantage of this and swung again, knocking the man completely off balance. The man and his weapon were easily swiped right over the lip.

He screamed as he fell into the superheated lava pool that acted as a nest for the clutch. His scream did not last long. Of course, this infuriated the other men.

The double crack of weapon fire reverberated around them. Nic jolted as two more of those devices imbedded themselves into his body. The effect was instantaneous and suddenly even his own head was too heavy to lift. He crashed onto the floor, his bony jaw sounding against the rocks every bit as loud as the crack of the weapons.

They hadn't counted on the intensity of his rage, though. One stupid human made the mistake of overestimating their weapons. He did not move away once he regained his footing. Nic summoned the heat from deep within his core and lunged out with all that he had. Flames shot from his roar, singeing the air and filling the immediate area with acrid smoke. The human never knew what hit him; he was instantly charred.

The leader of these spineless humans kept his distance, but his last remaining companion whipped out a lethal-looking knife and dove for Nic, digging the knife into his body between the scales at a sensitive spot under his arm. The additional pain ripped a groan from him, but it served to shoot a burst of adrenaline into his system that allowed him to swing his injured arm, catching the man with his own lethal blades.

Four steely-sharp talons raked over the man's midsection. His innards spilled out in a heated pile. Falling to the ground, the human writhed in agony. Unfortunately for him, he was not merely writhing in a pool of his own vital fluids, but of Nic's sizzling blood as well. The man was burned instantly. Dragon blood was fatal for humans. The fool.

Now only one lone man remained. Nic glared at him. The man glanced at his watch. Was he waiting for something? Checking to make sure the devices had enough time to be fully effective? Nic focused inwardly, testing his body for any parts of him that were not yet drained by this strange human invention.

He was weak everywhere. Even though the three devices had been shot into the heaviest part of his torso, they seemed capable of draining his limbs, his mental abilities, and his core. He could feel himself cooling rapidly. That was not good. In his dragon form, he needed to maintain heat to remain fluid inside. If he cooled too much, his body would become solid as stone. He would be little more than a dragon-shaped mineral here in the center of this mountain.

The clutch would, no doubt, suffer the same fate. Without the magic that gave all of them life, they would be nothing more than cold, dead rock. The future of Nic's people would be in jeopardy. He simply couldn't let it end like this. He had to find a way…somehow.

"Not so badass without your special powers, are you?" the human snarled at him.

The weapon, apparently, was only useful once. The man tossed it aside now that he'd fired his implement. He was not without defenses, though. A huge knife was tucked into his waistband and he reached for it now.

"I'm told after a while you'll cool down enough that your body will turn into rock," he said, eyeing Nic with a covetous leer. "Kind of a pitiful end for something so glorious."

"You should never have come here," Nic grumbled. "You don't know what forces you've awakened."

"Forces? Really now, dragon, there's no need for lies. I see no *forces*. No, look around. All I see is a field of helpless little eggs, just sitting there waiting for us to suck the life out of them. Do you have any idea how much magic we can pull out of those things before they shrivel and die? Very resilient creatures, you dragons. Well, the young ones, anyway. You, Nicolai Vladik, don't seem to be doing so well."

"There are a hundred who will come after me. You will die here, human. I promise you that."

The man was unimpressed by his pledge. He held his knife up to the glow from the nursery area and studied it. When he spoke, his mocking tone proved he had no idea what he was truly dealing with.

"First lies and now promises you can't keep. Really, I'm kind of disappointed. I thought we might get a little more fight out of you. Oh well. I've got a shipment of ten more dampeners and a fresh crew coming in once that storm is done in about an hour, I'd guess. You'll be long dead by then, though. We'll shove you out of the way and forget all about you, Vladik. But first, I think I'll just get myself a little souvenir before you've completely solidified."

He ran his eyes over the full twenty-foot length of Nic's body. His gaze settled on Nic's tail. It didn't take dragon sense to recognize what the bastard had planned. Nic rumbled a snarl.

"If you think to dismember any part of me, I'd advise you to rethink that plan," he warned.

The man simply laughed. "You're not exactly in the position to be telling me what to do, Vladik. I know how these devices work. I've seen grander ones of your kind laid low by this technology. Sorry, Puff, but you've got three of those in you. There's not much you can do. I'm afraid you're rather at my mercy just now and, to be honest, I don't really have any."

Holding his knife out ahead of him, the man took a few steps, then watched for a reaction. Nic was still. The man took a few more steps, reaching the tip of Nic's tail and picking it up. Nic held back his rage. He could feel the human's touch on his scales, sense the warm blade of the knife as it was pressed to his tail. Yes, he could feel it, but he gave no sign whatsoever that he could feel other things as well.

He still had heat in his core, enough to demand one more effort from himself. The devices still drained him, but because of such close proximity to the heat from the nursery, he suspected the technology was not functioning quite to its full capacity. The human clearly expected him to be nearly drained of all energy by now, and he was careful to let him go on thinking he was correct.

He had one last chance, but he'd have to be cautious. He would wait until just the right moment. It meant remaining completely still as the human studied the sensitive tip of his tail, tracing over the small spade-shaped fin and lifting scales one at a time to find the opportune spot for a cut. It seemed he wanted to be able to include some of the tattoos that marked Nic as a protector for his clan. If the fool had any idea just what the barbed symbols that had been ritually dyed into his scales truly meant, he'd have gone running from the cavern.

He didn't, though. He thought Nic was just some dumb beast, cowed by unfamiliar technology and waiting to die. The human had magic implanted into him through some extraordinary means, yet he didn't think to use it now to ascertain the true state of Nic's powers. The fool did not even deserve to die in this sacred place.

But die he would, Nic would make certain of that. He held perfectly still as the man's knife dug into his tail. So the asshole thought he was taking a souvenir, did he? Nic was going to make this a memorable moment, all right.

He felt the pain, the sawing motion as blade collided with bone. He waited just enough to feel the blood flow and the fury rise up within him. One last burst, that's all he could muster. But it would be enough.

He roared. An insufficient blast of fire shot from him, but he did not intend to use flame to dispatch his assailant. No, he knew he did not have enough for that. He needed to rely on the man's own vanity and greed if he intended to kill him.

He channeled all his remaining energy into his tail. It was a wonderful appendage, his tail, and this paltry human could not even guess what power was contained there. With a flick, he swatted the knife out of the man's hand, then wrapped his bloodied limb around the man's neck. He squeezed just enough to hear the man gasp.

"You underestimated me, human," Nic growled. "Tell me who has orchestrated all this, what purpose it will all serve."

But the human merely struggled against him, grasping in vain at Nic's tail and gurgling for breath. The blood from Nic's wound was eating into the man's flesh, burning away at his neck. The smell was unpleasant, but the sight of the man going limp brought some measure of satisfaction. All four of them were gone now. The clutch was out of immediate danger.

Nic dropped the body and slumped back onto the floor. What of this fresh crew that the man said would be arriving here soon? How could Nic fend them off? How could he protect his clutch? There was little he could do, so drained of his power. In ordinary circumstances he could simply rest here, drawing power from the heated bed of the clutch, replenishing his exhausted being. But with these damned devices plunged into his body, he seemed to be losing power faster than he could absorb it.

If he were back at the jobsite, in his human form, he knew exactly what he could do to revive himself. But he was not there, not in that form, and not with Lianne. Once again he'd been forced to leave her alone and unprotected. This time she'd been right in the very entrance to these caverns! If that other crew did arrive, they'd find her immediately.

He had to get word to her, tell her to hide. Could he do it? There was no choice—he had to find a way. He shut out everything else, his exhaustion, his pain, his concerns for the clutch. If he could just reach out far enough to touch her, he could send a warning. He could tell her to go, to find someplace to hide until the humans could find her.

He wished he could see her again, to be certain she was safe. He shouldn't have brought her out here. It was selfish of him. He should have found enough strength in himself without using her the way he had, the way he would have used her again if they'd been given the chance. Regret was not an emotion he was often familiar with, but he understood it now. He regretted that he'd never feel her body beneath his again, hear her soft sighs and see the glow of passion on her face, but mostly he regretted that he'd put her in danger. She might never again feel any passion or pleasure with anyone—and it would be his fault.

Unless he could make her hear him. He reached out with his mind and groped through the cold, empty spaces. She felt so far away from him now. Could his weakened mind penetrate the distance? He would use the last of his life force to try.

Lianne…you're in danger!

Chapter Sixteen

Lianne was staring at the faint, throbbing glow of the…thing…laid out on the floor of the cave. Why was she still seeing it? Surely once she slammed the "fairy" with her boot, that should have vanquished it from her imagination, right? It didn't. The little wings simply crumpled and the unconscious body sprawled where it had fallen.

At least, she hoped it was merely unconscious. She would hate to have hallucinated killing the thing, even if it was scheming something against Nic and had been rather rude toward her. But why on earth would her mind fabricate this sort of thing? Why not something sensible like a warm, cozy fireplace or some practical footwear that actually kept her toes from being frostbit? No, her stupid tumor brain had gone and invented a tiny blue jackass with wings. It figured.

She blew a deep breath into her boot to warm it up inside, then stuck it back on her foot. Well, it was better than standing on the cold rock in her socks. She did the same with the second boot, stamping to make sure they were secure. The fairy didn't flinch. He didn't look too good. She thought about going over to see if she could help him, but something stopped her.

Lianne…

A voice was calling her name. No, not calling, actually. It was not an audible voice. It was inside her head! Oh, hell. The tumor must be getting worse.

It called again, clearer and with added information this time. *Lianne…you're in danger!*

Danger? She glared at the fairy to make sure he wasn't messing with her. He was clearly not capable of conversation right now, and she knew what she'd heard hadn't been a fairy voice. It wasn't some alien from a UFO, either. It was Nic's voice. And it seemed so real! She stood still and held her breath, listening as closely as she could.

They're coming, Lianne. You have to go. Get out of here. Hide.

The fairy had mentioned something about a shipment on its way. A dangerous shipment, maybe? It made sense that Nic's disembodied voice would know about what the fairy had said, since it was all just some weird fabrication of her own mind, anyway. But why *this*? Was her subconscious trying to tell her something? Could it be that she really was in some kind of danger?

She didn't know what was real and what was hallucination at this point. She did know that Nic was missing. What if that really was his voice and he was calling for her? The cave did seem to go deep into the mountain, much deeper than she had considered investigating in the darkness. And with the glassy-smooth walls, sound would echo and carry in odd ways…What if she hadn't imagined Nic's voice?

"Nic!" she called out. "Are you here somewhere, inside this mountain?"

Yes, I'm here, Lianne.

Thank heavens! He didn't sound very good, though. Just as she'd been afraid, he was in trouble. She had to help him.

"I'm coming, Nic. Where are you?"

No, you can't come to me. They'll find…

"What is it? Are you injured, Nic? Keep talking and I'll follow your voice."

But his voice was very quiet now, nearly imperceptible. He was fading in and out and not making much sense. She caught bits of babbling about danger and hiding, and she was pretty sure he apologized at some point for something. Then he mentioned eggs, but she guessed that part actually made sense. The poor guy was probably hungry, maybe a little delirious from the cold. She needed to find him and get him out of here as soon as possible.

But he wasn't being very helpful. How was she going to find him in the dark? One quick glance back at her wounded hallucination and she had an answer.

She scooped the little fairy up and held him in front of her, toward the darkness at the back of the cave. Sure enough, his blue glow was just enough to light up the nearest ten to fifteen feet. All right, then. She could proceed. Probably when her head was clear and things were making sense again she'd find out this was just a flashlight or something, but for now it sure as hell looked and felt like a fairy.

She dangled him by his wings and let him light the way as she moved deeper into the cave. After several yards she came to a fork. One passageway went off to the left, and one went to the right. The one on the right seemed to be larger and more heavily used, so she started toward that one.

No, take the other.

Ah, so Nic must hear her footsteps. He must be close by. She adjusted her route and followed his lead, moving carefully in the direction his voice indicated. The glowing fairy twitched in her fingers, but made no effort to escape.

Again she came to a fork, but this time there were three possible options. Nic directed her to the one on the right. She was hesitant to follow his lead this time because the passageway took an obvious downward angle and she worried about losing her footing, but she realized that could very well be what got Nic into trouble. Maybe he was just down the slope of this narrowing passage. She moved carefully along, holding her fairy out like a lantern and steadying herself by clinging to the smooth walls.

Turn to the left. Then a quick right.

She did as he said. Sure enough, after she made a sharp left into a passage that seemed to come from nowhere, there was an almost immediate intersection. She turned right. This passageway continued a gradual downward slope, but it was somewhat more twisting than the others she had been on so far. It also had quite a few other passageways leading off it, but Nic was silent, so she continued onward.

What a strange place this was! And getting warmer, too. At first she hadn't been sure of it, assuming that maybe she simply felt warmer due to all her activity, but now she was certain. The air was definitely warm.

She also had to admit that there was no way Nic had been directing her by hearing her footsteps. It was entirely possible that he'd not been talking to her at all, that this was just more of her hallucinations and she'd led herself down into this dark, unwelcoming place. She had no idea how she was going to get herself out of here, either.

"Nic? Are you down here?" she called out just in case maybe there was some small hope she wasn't as crazy as she worried she might be.

Stay where you are, Lianne. You'll be safe there. Well hidden.

Hidden? What the hell was he doing, bringing her down here only to keep her hidden? No, she came down here to find him and that's what she intended to do.

She could feel him. She knew where he was. She hadn't felt him before, but now she did. He was close by, and he was in pain.

Her footsteps sped up as she moved through the passageway, instinctively making two more turns before she could see the warm glow of what appeared to be fire ahead of her. The air brushing her skin was hot, and very dry. She no longer needed the fairy to light up her way, but she held him carefully in her hand, just the same.

Nic was just through the next opening. She knew he was there, could sense him even though he hadn't spoken to her for several minutes now. She burst from her passageway into a huge, bright cavern, lit by the glow of what could only be a lava pool. So this was the source of energy they had been trying to tap into—the ancient volcano was not dormant at all. No wonder their readings had been inconsistent. It was just as Nic had warned.

But how had their team not discovered this? Surely they could have detected this even without a permit to come onto—or into—the mountain. And what were those oddly round boulders doing in the center of this lava pool? It struck her as very strange that they could appear to be floating there, not sinking and not being consumed by the molten rock that they rested on.

And then she noticed another strange thing in this cavern: a dragon.

At least, that's what the giant thing looked like, stretched out on the cavern floor near the edge of the lava pool. Was it alive? No, of course not. Dragons weren't real, so this one couldn't possibly be alive. But then again, this wasn't exactly Disney World, either. Who would have built a life-sized dragon in the middle of a volcano?

And this one looked an awful lot like the one she imagined in the storm, the one that had protected her from the wind and the lightning, then carried her into the cave. The one whose voice sounded just like Nic. Oddly enough, this rocky mound of incomprehensible dragon was lying exactly where her instinct had told her to find Nic.

Oh my God. Did the dragon eat Nic? No, her mind was telling her what it all meant, but she was ignoring it. No way would she even admit to herself such crazy imaginings. There were no such things as dragons, and Nic sure as hell wasn't one of them. She had *not* made out with a reptile.

But she did know that whatever the thing was, it needed her. Clenching her still-groggy fairy, she hurried across the distance between them. By God, it sure as hell did look like a dragon when she reached it.

Huge, steely scales covered its long, thick body. It was hard to determine what color the beast actually was. The scales were iridescent, their color appearing bright red in some areas to accentuate his huge, muscular frame, and darkening to a deep, deep burgundy in others. Orange flickers from the burning lava pool reflected off the creature, making him appear to radiate heat. Between the scales here and there she caught sight of a deep red glow that came from inside him. It pulsated like a heartbeat, slow and labored. The body expanded and retracted with pained, shallow breathing.

Leathery bat-like wings sprouted from its back, but now they were furled helplessly against the creature's side. It appeared to have four legs ending in digits with knife-sharp claws, those on the forelegs appearing more like hands than feet. She walked along the length of it, terrified yet fascinated.

Above the wings, a long, serpentine neck extended. It was lined with the same metallic scales that covered the rest of his large, rugged body, but these were smaller and more intricately aligned. She noticed there were black markings adorning his sides, wrapping around his muscular limbs, twining with thorny points, barbs, and symbols she could only wonder the meaning of. The markings culminated in the shape of a stylized dagger running the length of his neck. No, not a dagger. A sword—long, razor-sharp, and deadly.

It was a dragon-sized version of the tattoo she'd seen on Nic. She could no longer pretend to doubt. This truly was Nic. *A dragon*.

She was suddenly filled with dread. What could possibly have happened to bring him to this state? He was so weak, so helpless…there was so much pain in his body and she could do nothing to ease it. She didn't even truly know if she could make herself face him like this.

What would she find when she looked him in the eye? And what would he find in her eyes? She hated to let him know that she feared him, this place…her own sanity.

But sanity wasn't the issue. She reached her hand out to touch him. Warm. Moving. Alive. Yes, this was very real and she wanted to understand how.

She followed the neck until she came to the huge, arrow-shaped head. Her steps faltered. His face was angled away from her so she couldn't see his eyes. A crest of glinting spikes lined his jaw, while his skull seemed to be formed of impenetrable plates. His appearance was something like the dragons she'd seen depicted in art and in movies, but the reality of standing next to such a creature, feeling heat radiate off his body and hearing the rush of air through his lungs, was so much more than she could have ever imagined.

Yes, she had to admit even her wildest fantasies could never have produced something like this, with or without the help of a brain tumor. He was the embodiment of danger, of power, and yet...he was beautiful.

You shouldn't be here, Lianne. It isn't safe.

"I think I need to be here," she replied, moving around so she could meet his gaze. "You need me, Nic."

His huge head shifted, his scales scraping over the rock like flint sharpening steel. She found his eyes. Nic's eyes, dark but fiery, piercing into her soul as if he could read her very thoughts. Maybe he could.

You need to hide. Some others will be here and...What is that in your hand?

"Oh, this?" She held up the fairy. He had moved once or twice, so she knew he wasn't dead, but for some reason he wasn't coming around very well. Had she really nailed him that hard with her boot? She felt kind of bad for the snotty little guy.

"I found him in the mouth of the cave. He was talking to someone on a device of some sort, something about a shipment arriving soon. Then he found me and he looked like he was going to start trouble so I...well, I slammed him with my boot. He's still alive, though. Sort of."

The dampeners. They must be affecting him, too.

"Dampeners? What are you...Hey, you've got something jammed into your back. Oh my God, there are three of them!"

That's why you have to leave. I can't help you, Lianne. You've got to go before they get here.

"These weapon things are the reason you're just kind of lying here? Will it help if I pull them out?"

There's no time. It's too late for me. You have to go.

"It's *not* too late, damn it! What are these things doing to you, anyway? They've got blinking lights on them. Are they bombs or something? Are you going to explode?"

No, they're dampeners. It's complicated, Lianne. You won't believe me even if I do explain.

"I'm holding a half-dead fairy in my hand and having a conversation with a giant dragon. Try me, Nic."

The fairy is half-dead because these devices that were shot into me are dampeners. They collect magic and store it in that large console over there. I need magic to exist, Lianne, and so does that fairy. And so do the eggs incubating in the clutch here in this mountain.

She looked around. As he said, there was a large equipment console sitting nearby. The blinking lights on it roughly matched the lights on the devices wedged between Nic's metallic scales. But *eggs*? Her gaze shifted to the rounded boulders cradled in the heat of the lava pool. Obviously not boulders, after all. They were dragon eggs! No wonder nothing about this project had made sense. This whole mountain was just one big nest for little dragons waiting to hatch.

Wait, did that mean Nic had kids? A whole lot of them, by the looks of things. Damn, he should have probably mentioned that at some point.

But now his body rumbled. She brought her focus back onto him—the pain he must be in. He wasn't groaning from pain right now, though. He was laughing.

They're not mine.

"What?"

The eggs. They're not mine. I'm just the Guardian. Hatching takes a long time, by human standards, and a Guardian is appointed to watch over the clutch. It is unfortunate that your people decided to target this mountain so close to the time when the eggs will be ready to hatch.

"So, you don't have forty-seven kids I need to know about?"

No, and with these damn devices, I'm worried there won't be any hatchings at all.

"Then we have to do something! I'll unplug them, or turn them off, or something."

Now the fairy wriggled in her hand and she jumped. One glance at his limp form and she realized he was awake, although clearly not very energetic. Somehow he found enough strength to laugh at her, too.

"You can't turn them off," he warbled in a funny little voice. "They're powered by magic, stupid human bitch."

She pinched his crumpled wings and held him up so she could glare at him. "What did you just call me? And to think I was feeling bad about whacking you with my boot! I ought to just go ahead and stomp on you with it."

No, don't. We can use him.

She didn't bother to tell Nic that she really had no intention of stomping a fairy. For one, it seemed a pretty cruel thing to do. For another, it would make a huge mess of her boot. Also, the fact that Nic seemed to think there was some measure of hope by keeping him alive made her extra glad she hadn't killed the damn thing. She was sure to hold it a little bit tighter just in case it thought about limping away.

"We can use it?" she asked. "Can we make it shut off the devices?"

"I won't do anything to help you!" the fairy snarled, sounding an awful lot like an angry Chihuahua. "My companions will be here soon and you'll both be sorry."

"So there *is* something you could do to help us, isn't there? Well, I'm about fifty times your size, so I figure anything you can do, I can do better," Lianne announced. "Nic, have you got enough strength to hold him under your…paw? claw? hand?…while I work on these things stuck into you?"

He rumbled another deep, steamy chuckle. *I think I can manage that.*

The fairy was kicking and screaming, but he was so weak it hardly counted for anything. Pitiful, really. Lianne picked up one of Nic's huge, bony, terrifying hands and shoved the fairy under. The glinting claws flexed and the fairy was trapped. He wheezed his displeasure, but it was hardly more than the buzzing of a gnat, and Lianne easily ignored it.

The deadly projectiles poking out of Nic's damaged body were more than enough to take up her full attention. She had no idea how much of the device was actually wedged inside. Clearly they had been shot into him with some force. Had they opened up inside with a hook to hold them in place? How on earth would she get around that? She eyed them cautiously, watching as thin trickles of dark, steaming blood traced patterns around the spade-shaped scales.

Slowly she reached for one of the devices.

No! Don't touch it!

She jolted back. "Why? Is it booby-trapped or something?"

It's my blood. Don't touch it, Lianne.

"I'm not freaked out by blood, don't worry."

No! It's toxic for you. Stay back.

"Toxic? Well, shit, Nic. How am I supposed to get these things off of you?"

You're not. You're supposed to get the hell out of here.

"I'm not doing that. I can tell you're not doing so well, and this fairy dude already told his friends out there that the coast is clear, so they're on the way. When they arrive and can't find him, they'll probably come down here with guns and bad attitudes. I won't leave you here for that, Nic, so you'd better tell me what the hell I can do to help!"

* * *

So she thought she wanted to help him, did she? Nic felt the heat rumble inside him as he watched her study him, a frantic expression of worry and determination taking over her pleasant features. She surprised him in her reaction to what must be quite a shock for her system. She hadn't run from him or fainted in terror despite the fact that he could feel the turmoil inside her. Oddly enough, she accepted what her eyes saw in front of her and she wanted to help. It was almost endearing.

But endearments were not any way of life for him. He did not need help from a human, and he sure as hell didn't want it from her, especially not when helping him would almost certainly get her killed. She was just another human female, of course, but he still didn't want that for her. She had a lot of life in her. He wanted her to go on long after this, living that life and sharing her passion with anyone worthy of it. It was a damn shame that he would not be the one to share it with her.

He adjusted his hold on the struggling fairy and turned his head to watch Lianne. She muttered about the heat in the cavern and slipped out of her coat. The light blouse that she'd been wearing was damp from her sweat and it clung to her body, highlighting her delicious curves. The glow from the molten rock incubating the clutch made her shine.

It was a good look for her and he roved his eyes over the rest of her form. Even in his dragon body he couldn't help but appreciate the tautness of her skin and the swell of her breasts. He usually did not notice humans this way when he was in his natural dragon state, but their recent encounter still lingered in his mind. He could still taste her, feel the stroke of her hand over his flesh, smell the fresh, floral scent of her hair.

He wanted her. If he could take back his other form, he would show her the only help he needed from her. And she would take everything he offered, and more.

By the Fires, where was he finding strength to even contemplate such a thing?

His tail flicked, causing Lianne to jump nervously. He flexed the muscles in his limbs, his neck, his heavy jaw. Damn, but how was it possible he was feeling noticeably stronger?

"You're moving," she noted. "What's going on?"

"I don't know…" he said, and then realized he spoke aloud rather than simply sending the thought out with his mind. "Something is making me stronger."

"That's terrific! Then come on, let's get you out of here. Can you stand?"

"No, not yet, I don't think—"

He made the mistake of shifting himself and testing his legs. Unfortunately, this gave the fairy just the slightest moment of opportunity. He must have been feeling stronger as well, and very nearly fluttered himself right out of Nic's grasp. But sharp dragon claws were too quick, too powerful for him, and he remained captive.

"No you don't, damn insect," Nic growled at him. "I've got a few questions for you."

"Well you won't get any answers!" the little creature shouted.

"As if you have a choice in it," Nic assured him.

He'd ask his questions, and he didn't need his voice to do it. His mind was stronger, clearer now and he could focus on more than just keeping his contact with Lianne. He probed the fairy's tiny mind and didn't like what he found.

A conspiracy. Just as the fairies earlier had indicated, there was some sort of alliance between magical creatures and a contingent of humans. This insignificant fairy didn't know many details, but Nic was able to read enough from him to know that primary leadership came from rogue members of the Fairy Council. No wait…there was more. The fairy had no personal knowledge of more intricate details, but he held suspicions. Nic searched them, pillaged the little traitor's fears and emotions as he moaned in his struggle to keep his thoughts away from the dragon.

Darkness. Oh hell. It was worse than expected. This fairy was just a flunky in the great scheme of things, but in the back of his mind he had misgivings. He believed there was more than he knew, and that spoke volumes, as far as Nic was concerned.

This fairy played a small part, but there was much more going on than simply draining a little magic from the eggs in this clutch. Somehow this was just one cog in a giant wheel—a part of a complex design the fairy did not understand. He did have some ideas, though, and Nic had to pry them forcibly from the creature's mind. The great instigator behind all of this—behind the schemes of the Fairy Council, the involvement of humans, the creation of machines to gather up magic—was Darkness.

Someone ancient and dark was pulling the strings, and they were a tangled mesh that interwove deeply within the Forbidden Realm. The fairy had seen nothing to give proof of this, but Nic knew his suspicions must come from something. If ancient Darkness was involved, this would be powerful magic, indeed. Obviously the plot ranged far beyond what was going on in this mountain right now.

The clutch was in much greater danger than Nic had even imagined.

"We have to stop them," Nic announced.

The fairy whimpered under his grip.

"How? What can I do?" Lianne asked, sounding as frustrated and helpless as Nic felt.

"I don't know. I'm feeling slightly stronger, but still I can't—"

His complaints were cut off as a sudden bolt of pain ran through him. His muscles spasmed out of control as some great electrical current ran from one device in his side to the next. He could hear his blood sizzle and smell the scent of seared dragon. But then suddenly it was done. The pain was over and his muscles slowly relaxed. He coughed and realized the low, droning vibration that had been running through his body since he'd been shot was now gone.

"The lights have gone out!" Lianne exclaimed. "Look, the console is shut down. I think it shorted out, Nic. Those devices in your skin have turned off."

She was right. He could feel magic flowing back into his body again. Somehow the dampening effect was suddenly gone, the equipment shorted out with a surge of some external power from somewhere. Had the fairy's companions arrived and shut their equipment down? Or had some other force acted on it? Whatever it was, Nic knew he needed to take advantage of it—now.

The trouble was, this renewed energy affected the fairy, too. As Nic struggled to regain his faculties, the fairy squeezed from his grasp and made it into the open. Nic swiped at him with his claws, but he was still too weak, too slow.

Lianne noticed the escape and called out as she lunged for the creature, but the fairy merely laughed at their efforts and fluttered up into the air. He thought he was safe, so he had a few insulting things to say about both of them. That was a mistake.

Nic let out a bellow. Superheated air blasted with flame. The obnoxious fairy never knew what hit him. There was not even ash left to flutter back down to the floor of the cavern.

"Damn, Nic," Lianne murmured, blinking into the charred air where the fairy had just been. "That's kind of terrifying."

"You should see me at my best," he said, wincing as he reached around to claw at the devices still stuck into his body.

He knew Lianne hated that she was so helpless, useless to him in this. He could tell his connection to her mind had not been fully broken. She felt a portion of his pain as he tore at his scales, ripping them wide so the devices could be removed. They were anchored tightly, having expanded once they'd entered his body and gripping from the inside. The first one finally clattered onto the floor, and his blood was flowing freely.

"Keep back," he warned Lianne as she gaped in horrified wonder. "I'm serious—you cannot let my blood touch you."

"How are you doing that?" she asked, but did take several steps back. "That must hurt like hell."

"I'll take pain over helpless incapacity any day," he assured her. "Don't worry, I can take a little pain."

He had the second device removed and was digging at the third. It was in more deeply than the others and he rumbled with fury as he slashed at himself, determined to get the damn thing as far away from himself as possible. There was no telling when the next threat would present itself. He needed to be ready.

"So much blood…" Lianne mumbled.

"I'm fine. Just stand back."

Then the third one was out. They lay in a pile before him. What hideous, horrible inventions. How many others of his kind had been subjected to this? And to what purpose? The Darkness could only have something huge, something heinous in mind to go to so much effort.

He roared with his anger, shooting a ball of fire that would permanently disable the devices. They were resilient, but his fire was more than enough to render them useless. He was left with three melted, distorted chunks of metal. They were easily swept into the void, burned in the lava surrounding the eggs. He glared into the white-hot pool and watched as they were fully consumed. Good riddance.

When he was strong enough, he went to the console and gave that a solid crunch with his powerful arms. He chose not to toss it into the pool. It might be useful to get a good look at it when the more pressing danger had passed. He would love to understand what made this technology work.

A wonderful wave of power suddenly washed over him. It surged through his body and gave him strength to rejuvenate and heal. Magic that had been trapped in the console, apparently. It was released and his famished body soaked it up readily. He breathed in deeply, relishing the flood of unexpected magic throughout his system.

"Now that's better!" he said. "Come on. Let's get you somewhere safe. I can fly you back to the jobsite."

"Nic…your injuries look pretty bad. You can't exert yourself like that. Maybe there's some kind of first aid kit around here or something."

He had to laugh at her. "I'm afraid this place isn't set up for maximum comfort. I'll be fine, Lianne. Look."

Stretching the soreness and kinks out of his body, he rose to full height and swung his neck around. It was hardly any effort at all to do what needed to be done. With three well-aimed huffs, he cauterized his wounds, burning off any residue of his blood. If he did need to carry Lianne out of this place and somewhere to safety, he could do so without worry that he'd cause her injury...or worse.

And if such close, physical contact with her just happened to lead to something more...well, he'd need to be fit for that as well. Of course, there wasn't enough room for flying in the various caves they'd need to travel through to get out, so perhaps this form wasn't the most efficient right now. She might be more comfortable if he appeared as she was used to seeing him, too. Now that his strength had returned, he could assume human form again, feeling more healthy and virile by the minute.

Plenty virile enough, as a matter of fact.

"What is it?" she asked nervously. "Why are you looking at me like that?"

He curled one spiky corner of his wide, dragon mouth. Yes, he could well understand why she might sound a bit insecure. He must have been leering at her as if he could gobble her up.

"Sorry. I was just thinking maybe getting through these passages here would be easier if I took on my human form."

Clearly, she was relieved. "Yes, that would most definitely be easier, if you think you're up to it."

He puffed two perfect rings that drifted through the hot cavern air, twisting and twining themselves around Lianne before they dissipated and floated away.

"Oh yes, I'm most certainly up to it."

Chapter Seventeen

Right before her eyes, Nic transformed from enormous, terrifying dragon to the same enormous, terrifying man she'd made out with just hours ago. He looked even better to her now, oddly enough. Her body reacted instantly when his fiery eyes latched onto hers.

"Come," he said, reaching his hand toward her. "I'll lead you out of here."

"What if they are here already?" she asked. "What if that next shipment of whatever is on its way down? Won't we run into them along the way?"

"I will sense when they are here," he said and seemed to know what he was talking about. "Now that I have my strength back, I can sense the entire mountain. No one has arrived; we are still alone."

"And all those eggs?"

"Safe. Healthy. The mountain gives them their strength, so now that the device is inactive, they will regain anything they have lost. They will hatch on time, just as planned."

"You can feel that? Just standing here, you can feel all this stuff with your mind?"

God, but the grin he gave her nearly set her toes on fire. "I can feel a great many things with my mind, Lianne. But come, I want you to be safe."

She had to admit, she did like the idea of being safe. If Nic thought he could get them out of here and back to their jobsite, she was all for it. She took the hand he extended. His fingers were warm and they wrapped tightly around her hers. With her coat slung over her shoulder, she followed him toward one of the passageways.

"That isn't the one you brought me here through," she pointed out.

"There are many ways into this cavern. Trust me, Lianne."

Trust him? Now there was a thought that made her chuckle a bit. But of course she would trust him. Her brain had been whirling in circles since…well, since the Geo-Diagnostics helicopter dropped her off on the jobsite and left her there. She couldn't think straight enough not to trust him.

Besides, dragons apparently didn't wear clothes. When Nic changed back, there hadn't been anything for him to change into, so he was standing here now completely, beautifully naked. God, but she did like the tattoos. And everything else.

She let him lead her into the relative darkness of the passageway. This one was wider than the one she had come through before. It had the feel of frequent use, too. In fact, there was more than enough light spilling into it from the glowing cavern beyond that she could see evidence that humans had been here.

Boxes of supplies and unused equipment parts lined one wall. They must have been using this as a staging area. One box caught her attention and she tugged at Nic's hand.

"Not that I'm in any hurry to cover up the view," she said and gestured for Nic to notice a pile of folded clothing. "But it's going to be cold when we get away from all this lava. Do you need some clothes to put on until you decide to go all dragon again?"

"You'd rather I put clothes on?"

"Absolutely not. I just don't want you getting pneumonia."

He laughed at her, but took a moment to grab a jumpsuit and a coat as they went by. She snagged the largest pair of boots she saw in the line of boots waiting there. If Nic did have to go around in human form out there in the Icelandic wasteland, he could do it at least fully covered.

They moved into the passageway and Nic took a moment to pull the jumpsuit on. Well, mostly on. He wore it up to the waist, then left the top part hanging down. The resulting bad-boy-cover-model effect was inspiring, to say the least. Damn, but she loved those tattoos.

He led her along this passage for a while, until the light behind them was distant enough that she could barely make out Nic's perfectly formed shape in the darkness. He was still holding her hand, though, so she was close enough to occasionally bump into him—accidentally, of course—and cop a cheap feel. He didn't seem to mind. After a few minutes of darkness, he slowed his pace.

"I don't sense anyone close by yet, but I think we should continue on in a less direct route just in case."

"All right. I can't see anything at all, so unless you can glow, or something, you'll need to guide me along."

"Sorry, no glowing in this form. But I promise to keep you close to me, Lianne."

That was a promise she could live with. She made sure he didn't have to work too hard to keep it. As the air temperature slowly grew cooler, they followed first one passage, then another. He was guiding her through the labyrinth, keeping his pace steady but slow enough that she had no trouble along the way. She had no idea how he could possibly know all these twisting, sloping passages, but he did. He assured her more than once that they were not lost, merely taking an obscure route to avoid any unexpected arrivals.

He became increasingly quiet and she started to wonder what that must mean. She could feel the tension building in his body and it sparked an anxious worry in hers. Did he sense something? What did he know that he wasn't telling her? She was just about to ask him, as a matter of fact, when he stopped short.

"What is it?" she whispered.

"They're here. Humans, with fairies. I can feel them nearing the entrance to the mountain," he replied.

"Shit. Do we have time to get out of here?"

He waited a moment before answering, probably using those crazy senses of his to feel around, or whatever. "No. They're coming in fast. They must be using human conveyance, of some sort."

"Then they'll find us!"

"No. Stay calm, Lianne. Their equipment is ruined—my magic is strong again and there are secret places I know. I can hide us."

She had to agree that these tunnels were a maze. Even with powerful lighting and a good map, they could likely stay hidden for hours. But did they have hours? What if these people set up more magical dampening equipment? Nic would be in danger, and she had no hope of ever finding her way out, especially if the only entrance was guarded by evil fairies, and humans who were involved in some sort of plot with them. They'd find the mess Nic made of their stuff—and their friends—in the cavern and they'd be understandably pissed.

Her only hope was to trust Nic. She gripped his hand tighter and let him practically drag her along an especially narrow downward-sloping passage. The walls were smooth like all the rest of the passages she'd been on, and she was glad for it. More than once her shoulder or elbow slammed against it as she hurried to stay beside Nic, clinging to his hand as her lifeline.

They turned another corner, then another, until finally they came to a halt. She felt the wall beside her and could tell that it curved just in front of them. They were not following the passage around this curve, though.

"Where do we go?" she asked.

"Up," he replied. "Sorry, there are no steps and no footholds for you. I'll have to hoist you up."

"Um, up where?"

"There's a crack in the rock ceiling just above us. I'll push you through, then you'll find yourself on a narrow ledge. Hang on, and move to the right. I'll follow you and guide you from there."

That did not sound like someplace she wanted to go, especially if she had to go first.

"But how will you get up there?" she asked. "You can't fly in here, it's too narrow. I can feel both sides of the passage when I put my arms out."

"Don't worry, I'll manage. Just trust me. You'll be safe up there."

"Um, okay…"

It sounded like a really bad idea. She couldn't see a blessed thing and he was going to shove her up through a crack in the ceiling and she was supposed to find her way along on some ledge? Well, if they were looking to hide someplace where no one would come looking for them, this was probably it. She felt Nic's hands at her waist so she took a deep breath and made a little hop as he hefted her up.

She was moving toward the ceiling as if she weighed nothing at all. Wow, Nic's awesome biceps must not be just for show. He held her high and steady so she could reach her arms up and feel around.

Sure enough, she felt a gap in the ceiling. It was not smooth as the rest of the walls, but this was rough and jagged. The rest of the caves felt as if they'd been formed by great heat, molded and polished as part of some great design. This was just as Nic said, a crack. She felt her hands over it as Nic pushed her through, grabbing at outcroppings and pulling herself upward.

When he'd lifted her as high as he could, he stooped to allow her feet to find purchase on his shoulders. It was just enough to give her the support she needed to find the base of the ledge he had mentioned. As he stood to full height below her, she was raised up just enough to get leverage to pull herself up. She twisted, sitting precariously on the ledge, just as blind as a bat and shaking with fear.

"I'm supposed to go to the right? Does that mean my right, or your right?" she called down to him.

"To your right," he answered.

She nodded, not that he could see it, and began scooting. On her second scoot she reached her hand to steady herself on the ledge and suddenly the ledge just was not there. She wobbled, flailing for something to grab onto. In the frantic movement, she knocked herself off balance and started to slip off the ledge. As she fell forward, her leg swung back and became wedged between two broken rocks. She cried out in pain, the full weight of her body suddenly supported by her leg, jammed at an odd angle.

Suddenly Nic was there. He was pressing against her with his shoulder, pushing her back up onto the ledge. Her leg came free and she was able to find something to hang on to again. He was slightly huffing, so he must have propelled himself up through the crack by sheer upper body strength. She sucked in a breath as his leg brushed against hers. Ouch! Whatever she'd done to herself, it hurt. Badly.

"You were sitting on the ledge, weren't you?" he asked softly. "I assumed you'd be standing, facing the wall."

"So I guess I should have moved left instead of right, huh?"

"Yeah. Sorry. Are you hurt?"

"A little bit." She gasped again as he ran a hand over her leg. "Okay, maybe more than that."

"Shit. You're bleeding."

He was right. She could feel the blood starting to trickle. In the darkness she had no idea how bad it might be, but obviously any sort of injury here, in this situation, was bad enough. He hoisted himself up to stand over her. She had no idea how much room there was, or how she was going to get off this ledge.

"It sure would be nice to have that fairy back again," she said. "He was a jerk, but he glowed and I could see at least a couple feet in front of me."

"Forgive me. I forget how dark everything must be for you."

"You mean you can see? You went back to your human body but you kept your dragon eyes?"

"I don't need my eyes. I have other senses to keep me aware of my surroundings. Right now I'm aware that we need to take care of this leg. Come on."

"But how can—"

She didn't get to finish her question. Somehow he had both of her hands in his and was helping her to stand, then supporting her as she limped off the ledge and onto what felt like solid cave floor again. They had come through that crack and were now…somewhere else. It was an open area of some sort, but still pitch dark. Nic seemed to have no difficulty standing beside her, helping her along, so clearly there was ample ceiling space and width.

When she brushed against the wall behind her, she found it was not smooth and polished as the other surfaces had felt in the passageways. Since Nic had her hands, she couldn't feel around to know how wide or how long this particular area was, but a slight draft of air brushed her face, so she had the impression it was more than just another narrow passage. What she could tell for certain was that they were heading upward.

"Will this take us back to the entrance of the mountain?" she asked, trying to ignore her pain.

"No, it is someplace safe."

He kept saying that. *Safe.* She had to admit she liked the sound of it, but obviously it was a little hard to believe. How would they be safe anywhere? There was a whole shipment of magical machines coming their way, orchestrated by homicidal fairies and humans with evil intent. Already she'd gone and injured herself, and in the ultimate darkness of this labyrinth of caves, she had no hope of ever finding her way out on her own. Still, Nic seemed to think there was someplace safe for them, so she followed him blindly, dragging her injured leg along as they went.

"In here," he said, turning her sharply to the left. "Careful, it gets a little tight through here."

She quickly found out that he wasn't kidding. She had to lean very close into him—which wasn't really a hardship, considering how much her leg hurt and the fact that, well, he was still half-naked. The walls of this passageway were jagged and rough, as in the last. It was getting chilly, too. She wished she'd pulled her coat back on, especially when she slammed her elbow into a rock jabbing out from the wall.

"Ouch. Damn it."

"Almost there," Nic said, pulling her around another tight corner into an even narrower passageway.

This time something was different. "I think I can see light!"

"Yes, you can," he said. "Around the next bend there will be enough light to get a good look at that wound."

That meant she'd be able to get a good look at him again, too. The thought of his hard body with those tempting tattoos definitely helped take her mind off the pain in her leg. She hobbled just a little bit faster.

Exactly as he said, when they came around the next turn, orange light spilled in from a slit running lengthwise on the wall. It appeared to be another crack, similar but much smaller than the one they had crawled through. She blinked in the light, loving it, but turning away from it after so long in the dark.

"Is it morning? Is that crack open to the outside?" she asked.

"No. Come up here and squeeze through the opening."

As she watched, he scrambled up onto a rock and pressed himself into that orange crack and disappeared. She followed and was instantly amazed. Out of the dark passageway, she had suddenly stepped into a warm, tidy apartment.

Light was filtering in through a horizontal slit in the wall, but heavy drapes were hung nearby to cover over the crevice they'd both just come through. If they had been closed, she never would have seen the orange light spilling into that rough, dark passage. Indeed, Nic's little hideaway here could be perfectly hidden. She stared in disbelief at the cozy dwelling.

The room itself appeared to have been carved, or rather molded, by fire. The walls were smoothly glazed, and whatever furnishings that might be needed had been hewn out of the rock. A slab was left jutting out from one wall and appeared to be a functional table. A squared-off rock next to it made an adequate chair.

Lining the wall opposite that, shelves had been carved. A few items of clothing were folded there, as well as a healthy assortment of books that that seemed especially out of place here. Who would go to all the trouble of hauling this many books up here?

"I like to read," he noted, unapologetically.

"Is this your place?" she asked.

"It is. The main chambers are fine when I'm in my natural form, but I found that I needed...well, my duties have kept me so very often presenting myself as human that I chose to create a space where I could be comfortable in this form as well."

"I don't believe it," she said, shaking her head. "You like being a human!"

"I don't."

"Yes, you do. Look, you've even got a fancy tapestry decorating the place. Hell, what is that, Nic, your sense of humor? Is that Saint George battling the dragon?"

"The actual historical event went somewhat differently than the legend."

"Yeah, I'll bet. Seriously, I'm seeing a whole new side of you. I mean, even more than the whole new side of you I just saw a little while ago."

"All right, all right. Now sit down so I can tend to your leg."

The man had crafted a bed. It would have been impossible to wrangle a mattress up here, of course, but the pallet he'd made for himself with blankets and a big, soft comforter didn't look entirely uncomfortable. She sat down on it and found it more than a little inviting.

He filled the space with a possessive air, not the least bit self-conscious as she gawked shamelessly at his naked torso. Bookshelves and rock chairs were not the only interesting items in the room. The man himself was a work of art.

"I might have some gauze or something in the other room," he said, disappearing around a corner.

"What's in there?" she asked.

"I tapped into the heated groundwater and found a way to run some up here," he replied.

"You've got a bathroom with hot running water?" she questioned. "Inside a volcano?"

He came back around the corner, carrying a damp cloth and a roll of white gauze. "If a man's got to look like a human, a man's got to live like a human. That glow coming in through that gap in the wall there? That is my window."

She twisted to see what he referred to. It was like a window, but it did not open to the outside world. The view he had from here would have been infinitely more important to him than an Icelandic landscape.

"You can watch over the clutch from up here, can't you?" she asked. "That gap looks down into the main chamber."

"Yes. Welcome to my home, Ms. McGowan. I'm sure you won't be surprised to know you're the very first guest I've ever had."

"I don't doubt that. I don't suppose you have a beer in the fridge, or...ouch!"

She had tried to scoot to a more comfortable position and managed to bang her leg against the rock that served as the man's box spring.

"You should hold still so I can take a look at your leg," he advised.

Obviously he was right. She propped her leg up so he could see it as he came to sit beside her.

"Let's get you out of these boots so I can take a look," he said and gently ran his hand over her leg.

His touch was incredibly tender, but she still winced as he pulled the boot off. That spot on her leg was pretty damn tender, too.

"Now take your pants off," he said.

She raised an eyebrow. "Seriously?"

"Unless you'd rather I rip them halfway up your leg."

"No, I'll take them off."

Now he raised his dark eyes to meet hers. She'd seen only concern in them until now, when a fire kindled behind his expression and he gave her a sly, half-quirking grin.

"And it's about time."

Chapter Eighteen

Nic was pleased that she let him tend to her injury. Not that he'd given her any choice. The woman was too damned independent for her own good. He'd tried to manipulate and control her for his own purposes, yet her will had proven too strong for him. He owed her his life because of it, too. Indeed, she was so much more than he had expected her to be.

How had he not seen right from the start that she was so very special? Even now, after all that he'd put her through, she met his eyes steadily and did not turn away from him. She trusted him to dab at her wound, a jagged cut that bled profusely but—thankfully—hadn't gone deep enough to cause immediate concern. When he was content that no bones were broken and that he'd cleaned the area adequately, he laid his hand over the wound and caught her gaze again.

"This might hurt a bit, but it will stop the bleeding."

She wrinkled her brow in confusion, but that was quickly replaced by a wince of sharp pain. Searing heat coursed through him, and he let a localized wave pass to her body. The wound was instantly cauterized. He pulled his hand away quickly, hoping to spare her from any more pain than was necessary.

"Crap, that hurt!" she exclaimed.

"It should protect you from infection," he explained, immediately wrapping it in clean gauze.

No matter what happened from here, this wound would not pose any further threat to her well-being. He wished he could say the same about himself. Being alone with her here, momentarily safe from the dangers they'd faced and feeling strong once again, that familiar craving was boiling up inside him.

His energy had been replenished when the stored magic was released from that console. He knew he was fully strong enough to defend this mountain and the precious clutch in it. He didn't need passion or heat. He didn't need to seduce Lianne for any purpose. He wanted her, though. He wanted steamy, hot sex right here and right now, with her.

Even more than that, though, he wanted to take care of Lianne. Sex was probably the last thing she wanted right now, especially now that she knew the truth about who he was. For her sake, he'd put his own desires aside.

Her long legs were naked before him, her pants crumpled on the floor where she'd left them as he tended her injury. His hands ached to touch her, so he let his fingers barely trail over her skin. So soft, so tender…so human.

"Are you sure no one else has arrived here?" she asked, tension still keeping her body tight, nervous.

"I will know when we are not alone."

He hoped it was true. With his safeguards dismantled and Darkness working against them, he could not quite be certain of anything. Well, anything aside from the fact that his body hummed with desire for Lianne. That was the one thing he knew absolutely. Not that he understood it, however. Desire was a tool he'd often made use of; it had never been connected to the sort of emotions he was feeling for Lianne just now. He wanted to protect her, pleasure her, and reach into her mind merely to know more of her. There was no purpose to these feelings, yet he felt as if he needed them to live.

"Why are you looking at me that way?" she asked after a few moments of silence.

He realized he must be making her nervous, so he took his hand off her leg and looked away. To his surprise, she reached for him and turned his face back toward hers. By the Fires, her eyes were so bright, so full of life and fervor and energy. There was no fear at all as she smiled at him.

"I'm not afraid of you, by the way," she said softly.

He hadn't been inside her mind. So much had happened to her in such a short time. He'd purposely been giving her space, allowing her time to come to grips with it all. There was no need to read her thoughts, though, to know she was telling the truth.

"I do not want you to fear me," he said. They were petty words to convey the vast depth of emotion he had for her right now.

"But you do want me, don't you?" she asked, offering him another one of her irresistible smiles.

"So very much, Lianne."

"Good."

She brought his face close to hers and gave his lips a light, feathery brush with her own. Energy and flame danced inside him at her touch. He wrapped her in his arms and their kiss grew in intensity. She responded eagerly, fueling his desire. He laid her back into the soft bedding as an encouraging murmur of enjoyment escaped her.

The air in this chamber was comfortable and warm, heated by the fires from the nearby incubating pit. The very walls around them radiated heat. He slid the fabric of her blouse aside to let his hands contact her skin, glide over her delectable body.

"I'm not distracting you from more important things right now, am I?" she asked, but shifted her body just slightly to let him have better access to the tiny buttons on her blouse.

He pressed his lips to her neck, just below her ear. "There is nothing in the world more important to me than you right now, Lianne."

"Oooh, good answer, but…Oh, wow. Your hands are like fire."

He'd gotten inside her blouse and moved her bra out of the way. Perhaps he'd been moving too quickly for her. He pulled back just a bit.

"Am I too hot for you?"

She smiled. "You're hotter than hell, all right. But I can take it."

An invitation. By the Flame, her words loosed his passion and he felt need taking control of him. She was hot and ready for him, and he would have her here for no other reason than that he wanted her. He'd make certain she wouldn't regret it, though. Tonight he would not take from her, only give. Because she deserved no less from him.

In the very back of his mind, the distant voice of reason reminded him that there was no wisdom in this. What was the point in passion without need? He did not *need* her; his strength was restored. He should not toy with her this way.

She was all human and he was all dragon. Now that he no longer needed her, he owed her nothing more than to keep her safe and return her to her life. His sole concern should be tending to the clutch, not dabbling in passion.

This yearning he felt for Lianne was not natural. Dragons *made* love, but they did *not* love. Humans were treated fairly, but even during such intimacy, dragons never crossed that line into caring. This was pure heat and unbridled passion, that was all. Why was he imagining so much more?

"What is it, Nic?" she asked, pulling him away from his thoughts. "Something *is* distracting you."

He was not reading her mind, yet she seemed to read his perfectly. How could she know him when he'd given her only lies and deceit? He brushed a wave of auburn hair back from her forehead and kissed her there.

"Nothing but you," he assured her. "Tell me what you need from me."

"I don't need anything from you. You fixed my leg, Nic. So I'm fine. But…I like what you're doing right now."

He ran his fingers through her long hair, brushing her earlobe and her neck and feeling desire sizzle off her skin.

"You like this?"

"I do."

"Good. Then I'll do more of it."

"And maybe we could...Oh, that's really nice, too."

He trailed kisses from her face down her neck and to the soft valley between her breasts. She moaned with pleasure when he took one puckered nipple between his lips—so sweet. She was still tense, tied up inside with knots, but he could undo them. He'd get her to let go so her passion could run free and they would both soak in release.

His body tingled with anticipation of the surge he'd receive when a full, searing climax raged over her. His soul hummed to know that for the first time their joining would be unhampered by lies and agendas and the fear of being found out. They could both give themselves fully.

That's what he needed. Perhaps this wasn't unnatural, after all. She was a fiery woman and he was a dragon. Their completion would be unfettered and hot beyond measure. All the pent-up emotion he felt inside her—a wild torrent of fury, courage, delight, and pure lust—would finally be free. He simply had to get past the careful walls she had built. Once inside that bastion, he'd unlock the doors and throw them open. Release would surge through them. Her passion and power would become his, magnified a hundredfold by his own.

If he was going to be called on to do battle to defend the clutch, he needed all the strength he could get. Joining with Lianne now was not about what he *wanted*, but what he *needed*. It was not feeling or emotion that made him ache to see her writhe with pleasure beneath him, it was pure need. There was nothing unnatural about that.

Her body was so taut, her quiet moans so tantalizing and erotic. He just had to keep focus—it would be easy to get lost in the sensations. He wouldn't, though. No matter how powerful their connection was growing, this was still just a means to an end. He could not lose sight of that, no matter what.

"You make me want to forget everything...all the crazy things going on around us..." She sighed against his skin.

He caressed her with his fingers, his tongue, his voice, and his mind, using every part of himself to give her pleasure. "Give in, Lianne. Forget all the horrible things you've seen and concentrate on what you're feeling right now."

She was melting under his attentions. He could feel those walls crumbling, the viselike grip over her senses weakening. His own carefully constructed battlements were fading, too. His body was becoming hers, and hers was becoming his. Passion engulfed them and they were free to do whatever they liked.

And he liked.

* * *

She loved what he was doing to her. It was insane, to give in to this right now, but it felt so damn good she ignored the little voice of reason niggling in the back of her mind. She was tired and aching and terrified. What Nic was doing to her now—stripping off her clothing and running his hands over the most sensitive parts of her—was exactly what she needed.

He said he would take care of her and for some reason she chose to believe him. She'd been with her share of assholes, and they'd never made her feel like this. Whatever his reasons for doing this now, she was happy to let him take control over her body.

"You are beautiful, Lianne," he said as he continued to trail kisses over her skin, lingering in just the right spots.

"And you're like some damned Russian sculpture," she said, sliding her hands over his arms and his shoulders, loving the feel of him. And those sizzling tattoos. "These letters look like they mean something. Is it Cyrillic?"

"Er, it's a very ancient form, much older than any Cyrillic script known today."

She traced over the outline of the word seared into his shoulder like a brand. It was tantalizing and she could almost imagine that her fingers tingled as they touched it. "I see. Are you into ancient languages or something?"

"Right now I'm into you," he said smoothly, taking her hand in his and bringing her fingers up to his lips.

Okay, so his body art was off-limits. Of course that really only made her more curious about them, but if he didn't want to go there she wouldn't push. Clearly they both had secrets they weren't ready to share. She would give up on figuring things out and just enjoy what he could do to her. There would be time for conversation later.

She hoped.

"Lie down for me, Lianne," he instructed. "I want to look at you."

Since she loved the way his dark eyes raked over her with greed and desire shining like hot embers in them, she happily complied. Her blouse and her bra were long gone. The man seemed to have superhuman abilities in the field of undressing women.

If she thought about it too much she might be a little bit jealous by all that implied. Instead, she simply relaxed and enjoyed the wonderful sensation of being in the hands of a master. His hands, in fact, slid over the length of her legs, teasing her when they lingered in places that made her tingle and squirm. She watched him intently, drinking in his bronzed skin and the hint of a pleased smile at his lips.

"If you're peeling me like a grape to just stare at me, the least you can do is return the favor," she said.

He shot her a burning look and the hint of smile broadened just a bit. That jumpsuit hung low at his hips, but still it covered too much. He rectified this, standing so she had an excellent view and slipping the suit off completely. He tossed the jumpsuit across the room, then stood there, presenting himself before her with invitation written all over his face. The warm fiery glow from the outside chamber fell like a halo over his skin. She reached to barely touch the sculpted form of his thigh with her fingertips.

He moved back onto the bed, rising up like a giant over her, and she felt dizzy with excitement. She could hardly contain the anticipation, as a matter of fact. Her body was trembling with it now. The man wasn't even touching her and she was nearly orgasmic just looking at him.

She couldn't have ripped her gaze away if she'd wanted to. He was beyond imagination. Huge, yes, but perfect in symmetry and tone. The ripped abs she'd admired above the waist certainly didn't stop there. Every muscle was clearly defined, rippling before her and just bursting with virility. His thighs were like granite, and when she craned her neck she could see around to his delectable backside.

It was a crime against humanity that he was forced to spend so much time wearing clothes. No one should have an ass that perfect. Even the artfully dispersed dark hairs that wisped over his body were absolute perfection.

She reached out and took his glorious cock in her hands.

"Don't you want to take this more slowly?" he asked.

She answered him honestly. "Oh, hell no. I want you now, Nic. I've wanted you since I saw you in the boardroom looking all dangerous and smug, and we've been interrupted too much already. I don't want to waste time playing around."

"Very well, then. I aim to please, and if serious action is what you want, then I will not disappoint."

"That is exactly the right answer," she said.

The man's cock still continued its triumphant rise. She was a little bit annoyed when he obstructed her view, leaning forward to kiss her on the lips. She forgave him, though, as electricity flowed between them and his mouth took charge of hers.

She kissed him back. These weren't the sweet kisses of discovery or the demanding kisses of lovers staking their claim; they were the hot, searing kisses of pure, unfettered desire. Two people equally determined to fully enjoy themselves with one another. It was beautiful in its simplicity and intoxicating in its sensuality.

She wrapped her arms around him, pulling him closer and testing his taut skin with her nails. He might appear solid and ungiving, but he was tender and soft when they connected. She skimmed her fingers over his back and took hold of that wonderful, muscular ass. He kissed her harder, drawing her tongue past his lips and sliding his burning cock against her.

Damn it, she hadn't taken off her panties. She shifted against him, trying to take him inside her, anyway. He deftly refused.

"You are not ready, my dear," he murmured, moving his kisses from her lips to her neck.

"You sure as hell are."

"I will make certain we are ready together."

He seemed determined to make good on his promise when, about ten seconds later, he put his hands on her hips and scooted her up so suddenly his kisses went from her upper body regions to the lower ones. And good grief, where did her panties go?

"You deserve proper attention," he whispered, running his finger over the inside of her thigh as his lips nibbled her there. "I want to see how you open for me, taste all that you are."

She could only watch long enough to see his head dip low over her. Then sensation took over and she shut her eyes, reveling in his touch. His tongue explored her, his hands kneaded her, and his kisses found the secret place that made reality fade away completely. She sagged into the soft bedding and let him have his way.

The rush of sensation washed over her again and again, each time nearly sending her over the edge. Yet somehow he continued his attentions without letting her fully succumb. He truly was an expert. Light and warmth filled her, and her body tensed and relaxed with an increasing pulse. She arched against him, groping for something to grasp to keep from spiraling out of control.

"What are you doing to me?" she moaned as another wave threatened to crush her, then harmlessly subsided.

"I am loving you, Lianne. Give in to it. Let me show you how you make me feel."

"I don't know if I can," she rasped. "It's too much."

"No, you have so much to give. Let it go and I will show you how."

And then he wasn't speaking, he was pressing his mouth against her again, drawing something from her. Her soul, maybe. She didn't know and she didn't care. It felt too good to worry about what might be happening to her. She would do as he asked.

She gave up her control, letting go of her tenuous hold over her body, her emotions. He was touching her whole body at once, engulfing her in heat and desire. She breathed it all in, filling herself with sensation and letting it flow out of her again. The climax was just waiting there, hovering over her until she could finally reach it.

With one little nip at the very peak of her arousal, Nic sent her soaring into an ocean of bliss. She cried out, gasping for air. No one had ever taken her so far with so little effort. She breathed in and out, waiting for her head to stop spinning.

"Ah, *now* you are ready," Nic said.

His voice was smoky and ragged. She didn't even realize he had let up on his kisses, but now he was above her, his lips close to her ear and his hot breath whispering her name.

"*Now* I'm ready?" she panted. "I think you've finished me."

She felt him press against her, softly, tenderly. Her body reacted like fire, raging and burning for him in a way she never imagined was possible. Apparently she was not finished yet. Not by a long shot.

"Now you will have what you need," he murmured for her. "We both will."

He was careful. Her body welcomed him eagerly as he thrust his cock into her. The heat, the electricity…it was blinding but oh, so very good. She wrapped her legs around him to take him all in.

"You are perfect for me," he said. "I will be perfect for you."

For a moment he let her get used to the feel of him, then slowly he began moving. Gently at first, with long deliberate strokes, he tormented her with his prowess. She wanted to climax again, to fall into that endless abyss of pleasure and ecstasy, but he held her back. He kept the waves at bay just enough that she was aware of what he was doing, but she was helpless to urge him along.

Her body was his, completely at his mercy as he pleasured them both. She could feel the warm flow of emotion that saturated them now; it went back and forth between them like the very oxygen that they breathed. Gradually his pace increased. He was thrusting with more power now, more urgency. She needed him more and more as he continued on. She held herself to him and rocked, again and again in desperate effort to survive the excruciating torrent of pleasure.

The waves of her furious release were not safely at bay now, they were swallowing her fully. She was drowning in a sea of sensation. Had she climaxed before? She had obviously thought so, but this was something much more than she'd ever felt. This went beyond pure physical pleasure. What Nic was doing had transferred her to another realm, another plane of existence.

She cried out his name, riding with him as he thrust against her over and over again. Her body seemed to become part of his, or perhaps he'd become part of her. The world was all Nic, his skin and his warmth and the way that he filled her.

She could take it no more and finally crumbled under that passion. He came over her at the same time, pouring himself into her and breathing her name as if it were a holy chant. She clung to him, shaking and gasping for air. He pulsated within her, tiny climaxes racing over her and carrying her slowly back up to the surface.

Her arms went limp and she could do nothing but wait for the tide of bliss to retreat. Nic dropped down beside her, bundling her into his arms and pulling her tight. She could do nothing but snuggle against him, warm and safe and exhausted beyond measure.

She'd never been so thoroughly happy in her life, though. Nic had made her feel things she'd never thought possible. And somehow, she knew she'd given him something, too. He had needed her and right here, right now, she had been enough for him.

That, she was pretty damn sure, was not something he could very often say.

* * *

Heat still whorled around them. Nic sheltered her with his body, but he knew she must feel the sting from some of it. His passion had filled the chamber with searing colors and light. The might of it had slammed into him with unexpected force, penetrating his skin, his will, and his soul.

Lianne had given more than he'd ever imagined, and he'd given in return. The flame in his core roared to full life. He was an inferno now, raging with every dragon power he had. He hoped he'd not been too much for her.

Years and years of denial, of hiding his true form and blending with humans, had cost him. Wearing their form and governing his thoughts and his actions day after day had drained him more than even he had been aware. Now, just now with this trembling, moaning woman in his arms, he was himself once again. She had filled him and revived even the parts of him he hadn't realized he'd let go dormant. He owed her everything, and he'd given her everything that he'd had. He cradled her carefully as the tumult within and without them slowly began to settle.

When she spoke, her words were languid and slurred. "Wow. If this is all just part of some brain-damaged delusion, I don't even care right now. That was amazing."

Her pleasure was beautiful. He was happy to have satisfied her. Aside from his own needs, there was a great sense of pride in knowing hers had been met as well. She was completely at ease in his arms and he liked that. Her mind was as open to him as her body had been. He could touch her mind and know her like no one he'd ever encountered before. The walls he had felt earlier were entirely gone.

Fully exposed to him in their place was the raw, aching realization that Lianne had protected her secrets for a reason. She'd been protecting *herself*. What she'd kept hidden was deeply personal to her, a vulnerability she'd never meant for anyone to discover. But Nic had, unintentional though it was now. He felt every part of her, even this harsh, shocking reality.

You are dying.

He hadn't spoken the words aloud, hadn't wanted to hear them, let alone acknowledge their validity. But his mind was meshed with Lianne's now and she knew what he knew.

"I am. How do you know that?"

"Your mind. I'm sorry, but I can enter your mind. You let me see inside of you, so I know."

"I let you see that, huh? Well, I guess it doesn't matter now. I didn't want anyone to find out, but it's a little late for that, I guess."

"You believe you don't have much time left."

"A few months, so they say. It's a tumor, inoperable and without any hope for a cure."

"And you knew that when you took this job?"

"It's why I took the job. I needed to do something, to prove my life wasn't completely a waste."

"So this project...it will give you that?"

"My father's company is searching for energy sources that can be tapped without damaging the world. Even magical creatures like dragons must realize that we can't go on the way we have been. I thought if I took over this project, then…"

"Then you'd be leaving a legacy of hope for your people."

"Something like that."

"Sadly, it was not to be. The energy in this mountain is not for humans to use."

"No, I get that now. But damn…I wish I could have done something to make things better. You understand that, right?"

"I do. But there is time. Perhaps another volcano will provide what you've been searching for."

"I thought you said you could read inside my mind? There's no more time for me. It's been getting worse. Hell, for the longest time I thought all this was just a hallucination."

"This is real, Lianne. You are here and you have given me more than you can ever know."

"Oh, I'll probably know about it as soon as I try to stand up and walk. You really don't hold anything back, do you?"

"Did I harm you?"

"No, you were amazing. Seriously, you're not like anyone I've ever known."

"Well, you probably haven't been with many dragons."

"No. That's pretty much a given. But…you still look human enough."

"I can maintain this form when I choose to."

"Thank you for choosing to, then. I really, really like this form."

"And I'm glad that you do. I've never been so drawn to a human female in all my years, I must admit."

She laughed at him and her voice made the chamber even warmer than it was. "I'll take that as high praise. For two people who don't really care much about each other, I'd say we've got some pretty intense chemistry."

"Intense, indeed, although I'm not sure it's fair to say we don't care about each other. As a matter of fact, I find I care a great deal for you,

Lianne. And go ahead and admit it; I do have some measure of importance for you, don't I?"

"Well, I guess you do have a few qualities I find kind of important."

She was smiling at him with the warm, tender smile of afterglow, and he could feel her emotions. They filled up his mind and permeated his skin. She loved what he had done to her, and she never would have let herself enjoy him so much if she didn't care just a little.

It was a surprise to discover that this mattered to him. He'd never found himself actually *wanting* his human companion to care. The very process of acknowledging this felt foreign. He wasn't supposed to feel this way after passion. The fact remained, though, that he did. He wanted Lianne to care. Very much.

Because he cared about her.

Panic suddenly washed over him as he realized just how much he did care. It was like a knife plunged into his heart when he thought of the danger she was in right now.

"I have to get you out of here," he said, forcing the warm fog of pleasure out of his mind to make room for a more rational plan. "You have to be safe."

"I am safe with you, Nic. True, I've got a bum leg, there are magical creatures ready to attack us, and I'm trapped in a volcano with a freaking dragon, but I've never felt so safe in my life." She laughed at herself. "Hell, and here I thought my brain tumor was a bad thing."

Her laughter was real, but so was the pain behind it. He touched her face and let his thoughts caress her wounded soul. So much he would do for her, if only he could.

But it was too late. He could feel them—fairies and the damn humans working with them—entering the mountain. It wouldn't be long before the fate of Nic's clutch, his very life, and the future of his kind, would be set.

"They are here now," he told her.

"The ones who want to steal all your magic?"

"Yes. There's no time to get you away from here, but if you remain in this room, you cannot be found. I will do all that I can to keep you safe."

"But you won't be in here with me?"

"No, I have to protect the clutch."

"Then I'll help you do that."

"Absolutely not. It's far too dangerous for you."

"And it's not exactly safe for you, either. I saw what they did to you."

"I'm better now. I have my strength back more than ever now, thanks to you."

"Thanks to me? What did I do?"

"You shared yourself with me. You gave me your passion."

"You mean…this? Sex gets you your strength back?"

"Yes, and I'm feeling more powerful now than I ever have before."

"*Seriously?* Is that what this was? You made love to me to get back your strength?"

"Yes, but…no, it was more than that, of course."

She shoved him away from her. The sudden space between them sent an odd chill through his bones. He wanted her back in his arms, wanted to drown out the cold with the heat from her soul. When he reached for her, though, she slapped his hand away. It stung all the way into his core.

"I can't believe it," she grumbled. "All those times back at the jobsite, the way I kept hearing your voice in my head and I couldn't keep my hands off of you…that wasn't cancer brain, was it? That was you using your weird dragon powers over me. Damn it, Nic, you've been using me all along!"

"Lianne, it isn't like that. I only—"

"You only made me want you so you could get back here and fight off these creepy little fairies, didn't you?"

"I never used my mental powers to control you for sex."

"Yeah, that's what they all say."

"Hell, Lianne, it's true! Yes, I'll admit to clouding your mind a few times to hide the truth from you, but I didn't—"

"Save it, Nic. I don't even know why I'm surprised about this. I knew from the start I should never trust you. Go on out there and make yourself all big and scary. Fry those damned fairies and whoever else you don't like very much. I'm going to stay here and put my clothes back on."

"Lianne, you must understand that—"

"No! I already understand more than enough. Hell, maybe there's really nothing to understand. Maybe this is all just some damn hallucination and none of this is real. Maybe I'm not even here, maybe I'm still back in a hospital bed waiting to die."

"You *are* here, and I *do* care what happens to you."

"Just go. I'll be fine."

He wanted to argue, to convince her that she was wrong about him, about his motives. What would be the point, though? She wasn't wrong. He had used her from the start—it's what he did. He was a dragon, after all.

Humans were supposed to mean nothing to him. Once she fulfilled her purpose he should have been ready to go and fulfill his. Why was this so damn hard for him now? He had to leave her, to tend to the clutch.

The clutch. He was sworn to protect it and nothing else should matter. He could sense the strange magic being brought into his mountain by his enemies. Even now, as he lingered here, still feeling the surge of passion through his veins and the hum of satisfaction in his skin, the danger was growing. He had to put Lianne from his mind and focus on his duty.

But he couldn't. His mind was still linked to hers. Perhaps it was the recent passion they'd shared, or because her illness had left her more vulnerable and open than others, but the link between them was strong. He knew that her harsh words and the cold disdain in her eyes were entirely an act. She was aching inside. It made him ache, too.

"I don't want to leave you," he admitted.

"Well you'd better," she snapped. "I don't want you here."

If he wasn't still buried deeply inside her mind, he would have likely believed her. The venom in her voice was convincing. The hurt in her eyes, however, ruined the effect.

"Stay hidden. I'll be back for you," he promised.

"I hope so. I don't have a lot of time left, and I'll be damned if I spend it trying to find my way out of this stupid volcano on my own."

The heat of passion and battle raging through him flared even hotter. He met her eyes and saw what he'd felt in her mind: she worried for him. An involuntary thrill coursed through him at the realization of her concern, and how much he liked it.

"I will come back to you, Lianne."

She must have felt the intimacy in his words and felt uncomfortable. She looked away, busying herself with the hunt for her clothes and the effort to keep herself hidden from him. As if he didn't know entirely too well every curve and contour of her body now. Each velvety inch of her was burned into his mind, his fingers still tingled with the warmth of her skin. Loving Lianne had left its mark on him, inside and out. He would forever see her, taste her, sense her no matter what barriers she put up between them.

For now, though, he'd let her have her privacy. He felt her inward struggle, the fear warring with other emotions she would rather not be dealing with right now. He understood completely.

At this very moment he'd like nothing more than to grab her back into his arms and kiss her until they both forgot duty and cancer and all their warring emotions. Of course he couldn't do that. The best he could do was leave her in peace and vow to return.

As much as his clan's future depended on him protecting the clutch, he sensed his own future required he do exactly the same for Lianne.

Chapter Nineteen

She had her back to him but she could feel when he left the room. He moved silently, yet she sensed him moving farther from her, deeper into the labyrinth of tunnels that honeycombed throughout the volcano. Still, she could feel his presence not entirely gone.

He must be using those stupid dragon powers again, holding her mind and bending her to his will. He could say what he wanted, but she'd never forgive him for taking advantage of her. There was no way she would have ever jumped into the sack so quickly with him if he hadn't been controlling her mind somehow.

He was an asshole. He was conceited. He was a freaking *dragon*, for God's sake—not even the same species. No, she would never have thrown herself at him if he hadn't made her do it. Now she didn't care if she ever saw him again.

But she did care. Damn it, why should she be worried about what might happen to him out there? She probably didn't even need him to get out of here. She could maybe just feel her way, retracing her steps. How hard could that be?

Too hard. Yes, she needed Nic. But only to escape this place and get back to the jobsite. Nothing more.

So why was he still stuck in her head? She could feel him, sense his heart pounding as he moved through the tunnels. She'd gotten used to hearing his voice in her mind, and apparently he'd been able to subliminally influence her actions, but this went beyond that. When had she started being able to actually feel what he felt, sense what he sensed?

Her skin prickled with the same tension she knew that he felt. She could sense the darkness around him, yet he was having no trouble finding his way. The walls, the crevices in the rock, it was as if she could trace them all with her fingertips, yet she hadn't left the warm living quarters. Her eyes could see only the same things she'd seen when he first led her here; the bed, the bookshelf, the table in the corner. How could she possibly feel as if she were looking at the dim passageways between here and the clutch?

Damn him for invading her mind! The tumor had done more than enough of that already. What space she had left in there, she'd rather keep it all for herself. Maybe if she just quit thinking about him, he'd lose his hold over her.

She grabbed up her clothes and fumbled with them. Her body was still weak and trembling from the amazing things he'd done to her. Why couldn't he have just been some regular guy? If she had to dive into meaningless sex, it would have at least been nice for the guy to be just an ordinary dickhead, someone she wouldn't feel too bad about if he never called her back. Now she had to spend the rest of her life pining for magic.

She had no delusions on that; magic was the only explanation for the way he'd made her feel. She'd never been with anyone like him and there was no way she'd ever be with somebody better. Not even if she did have a full life span ahead of her. Damn him and his creepy dragon powers! He'd flat out ruined her for anyone else.

And of course she'd meant nothing to him. He'd played with her like a toy, then used her for whatever it was that he got out of her. She could still barely catch her breath or stand on her unsteady legs, but he went off to do battle with a cheerful swagger and that damned cockeyed smile. He probably would come back here, just as he said. No doubt he'd need a little pick-me-up after slaying the magical bad guys.

Well, she wasn't going to fall into his bed so easily next time. She pulled on her pants, wincing at the pain in her injured leg. He'd done a fairly good job of distracting her from it, at least she was slightly thankful for that. She slipped on her boots and realized she'd be okay to walk out of here on her own. It would have been infuriating to need him to carry her.

The walls of their little room flickered, the warm light from the glowing chamber outside making it almost homey. She paced a bit, then found a book on the shelf that looked interesting. The only really comfortable place to curl up and read, however, was the bed and she couldn't quite bring herself to hop back in. It would make her remember Nic's hands and his lips and his crazy-hot abs and…well, she was trying not to think about all that stuff right now.

She dropped the book on the rock table and went closer to the narrow opening in the wall. Would she see him down there yet? He moved quickly; it probably had been long enough for him to wind his way through the dark tunnels and get to his clutch. She peered out, careful to keep herself hidden just in case anyone was down there looking this way.

The clutch seemed untouched. The fiery pool surrounding the eggs seemed hotter and stronger than before. There was no sign of Nic, but no sign of any fairies or other humans, either. Was that a good sign, or did that mean Nic had already found them? Was he okay?

Yes, she knew that he was. She could still feel him. The sensation was more vague, more distant now, but she knew he was not in any danger. He was waiting, prowling. Apparently the creatures he was after had not yet made it to the large chamber where his clutch lay. Obviously he wasn't planning to let them get there.

She hoped whatever ensued wouldn't play itself out in her mind. She didn't need any more craziness in there, that was for certain. She didn't want to know if anything bad happened to him, either. The thought of anyone harming him…she couldn't let her mind go there. It was too hard to forget how angry she was with him for using her.

Except that he hadn't used her. He'd taken care of her and kept her safe, and she was pretty damn sure when it came right down to it, she'd gotten a hell of a lot more out of their lovemaking than he had. She'd do it all over again, too, if they ever got the chance.

God, she hoped they got the chance.

Desperate to keep herself distracted, she went back to her wincing, hobbling version of nervous pacing. How long was this going to take? What was going on here, anyway? Maybe she ought to read that book, after all. She'd go nuts worrying if she didn't find some way to keep her mind occupied. Too bad her phone wouldn't work in this place, she could…

What was that sound?

She paused, holding her breath. Had she heard something? No, probably not. Nic wasn't anywhere nearby, she could feel that. She couldn't have heard anything. She took one step to start pacing again and then froze.

She *had* heard something. Way off in the distance, echoing around the narrow passages just out beyond the doorway…*voices*. Oh, hell. Nic wasn't around here, but somebody was. More than one somebody, by the sound of it.

She had to hide! If they found their way here, they probably weren't going to be happy to see her. Scanning the small room, her options seemed limited.

Under the bed? No, there was no "under the bed"; it was carved out of rock. Damn it. Table and chair? Same problem. Bathroom? She peeked around the corner. Whoa. Kind of primitive, and certainly no hiding place.

The tapestry on the wall! Yes, maybe that would work. She darted over to check it out. Miraculously, there was a little bit of a gap just behind it. The rock face was uneven and maybe that was why Nic hung the thing here in the first place. But it sure was lucky for her. She could tuck herself in there and not leave a bump or even her feet showing from the front.

It was a long shot, but not like she had other options. Gathering up the rest of her clothes and making sure there was nothing else to indicate she'd been here, she pulled up the tapestry and slid behind it. God, she hoped it stopped swaying before anyone might come in and wonder who'd disturbed things.

Mostly, though, she hoped no one would come in at all. Were they still out there? She wasn't close enough to the doorway to hear. Maybe they'd gone on, maybe they hadn't been able to find this place.

For a few seconds she dared breathe a bit, but then a new sound caught her ears. She tensed, but held perfectly still. From the doorway she could hear just the slightest whisper, the hint of a flutter, something light brushing the walls.

"This way," a hushed voice breathed almost inaudibly. "He's gone."

The voice was strange, clearly not anyone Lianne recognized. Not any*thing* she recognized, perhaps. She couldn't say that it even sounded human. Was this a fairy? Maybe. She didn't exactly know a lot about how fairies sounded. This one sounded like…well, like maybe a sneaky, evil, snakelike grandmother fairy. If there were such a thing.

Another voice replied. This one most definitely sounded human. It sounded a hell of a lot like Mr. Blanchard, one of the engineers she'd left back at that jobsite, as a matter of fact. What could he be doing here?

"Ouch! Damn it, how can you see anything in this place? Why'd you make me turn off the flashlight?"

"Shut up," the strange, hissing voice shushed. "You'll be able to see fine inside. Come on, slide through the opening."

"Walk here, climb this, slide through. What sort of place are you taking—"

Mr. Blanchard's voice broke off and was replaced by a low whistle. "He's got a regular apartment set up in here. No wonder he never seemed to be in his room at the site. He's been coming out here all along."

"I told you that," the other voice snapped. "Now stop talking and get the gear set up. We don't know how long the others can keep him distracted. He'll sense me if we don't hurry."

"Sense you, huh? He sure didn't sense us wandering into his damn living room."

"Of course he did. He knows we're here—he just doesn't know who poses the greatest danger. He'll figure out what we're up to soon enough, though."

"When we fry those goose eggs down there, huh?"

"We can't fry them, you idiot. They're *dragon* eggs."

"Okay, we'll blow them up. Whatever. Now where do you want me to set this up?"

"Over here," the other voice said, moving threateningly close to where Lianne was hiding.

"Ah, you can see right down into that steaming nest," the man said. "I can launch from here, no problem."

"Exactly. And we'll be safely out of the way."

"Not a bad plan, lizard girl."

"Stop calling me that! Hurry. Make sure you have the perfect vantage. We'll only get one shot at this."

There was much shuffling and the sound of metal clanging against itself. Lianne could only guess what they were doing, but she had a relatively fair idea. The man must be putting together some sort of weapon, a gun, maybe. A big gun if he was using words like "launch," actually.

Were they going to launch something down into the clutch to destroy the eggs? Damn, that was harsh. If Nic was anywhere down there near the clutch, it probably wouldn't go so well for him, either.

What could she do? How could she take on two people and a great big gun? Her leg throbbed even harder just thinking about it. Where was Nic when she needed him?

Wait a minute, Nic was in her head, wasn't he? Why couldn't she just let him know what was going on? It's not like she knew how to carry on deep telepathic conversation, but he'd given her directions for finding her way through the tunnels, hadn't he? Maybe she could get another message to him.

It seemed like that was just about all that she could do. Concentrating on all the sounds she was hearing and the fear thumping hard in her chest, she tried to focus her energy on Nic, wherever he was. It felt stupid, but she tried to overlook that. Pretending to be psychic was not half as stupid as jumping into bed with a dark, dangerous Russian the day after she met him.

But damn, she would never regret doing it, that was for sure. Getting caught here by some crazies with a rocket launcher, she might totally regret that, of course. Somehow she'd just have to make sure they didn't catch her.

She huddled behind the tapestry as they shuffled and moved about. Minutes ticked by and she kept trying to concentrate on contacting Nic, but there was no way to know if he detected her. Fortunately, it seemed like the two people in the room with her didn't either.

They seemed to be concentrating their actions near the narrow openings that overlooked the incubation chamber. Metal feet scraped across the floor; a tripod, maybe, being set up to support whatever weapon they were planning to use. Lianne's heart raced.

She still searched her mind for any real indication that Nic read her thoughts. They were such a jumble of emotion and what-ifs that she had no way of knowing whether or not Nic was aware, or if he could make any sense of it if he was. She needed to focus, to sort through the jumble to the most important thing he needed to know: someone was planning to kill him.

"Ah, there's the ugly bastard now," Blanchard announced.

"You see him? Nic is down there?" the woman questioned, her voice very near her companion's.

"Yeah, look through here. See? You can't miss him just on the other side, in the shadows. Damn, he's big and evil looking. You sure that's him? I only see him looking more humanlike."

So Nic was in his warrior mode. He was in his big, terrifying dragon form. Good. Maybe he wouldn't be so easy for these two to pick off.

"Yes, that's him. Take your aim and make it count."

"Hell, dragons sure are ugly sons of bitches."

"You have a problem with how dragons look?"

"I have a problem with how *that* dragon looks. He's been masquerading as human all this time and now I see this is what he really is. I find it insulting."

"Only because you didn't figure it out until I had to tell you."

"Well, now I know and he's going to pay for it. Trying to breed a whole army of scaly abominations to take over the world…we won't let that happen."

"That's right. We'll put an end to it right now. Go ahead, take the shot."

"Right now?"

"Shoot him, damn it. He's close enough to the clutch. Fire that thing into his heart. The explosion will be enough to destroy Nicolai Vladik and his whole precious hatchery."

"You sure? It'll take them all out and it won't be too much? I mean, we'll still be able to get out of here, right?"

"Yes, of course. Do it! Take the shot!"

"I don't know. What about the McGowan bitch? He brought her out here with him. Maybe she's still—"

"Do you see her anywhere? No. She's dead. He bewitched you all and took her for his own purposes."

"Maybe he's got her tied up somewhere or something."

The woman was clearly becoming frustrated. She obviously wanted Nic dead. If Mr. Blanchard didn't act soon, Lianne figured the woman would grab the gun out of his hands and take care of matters herself. She didn't sound like someone who would stop shooting until she hit her target.

"It's too late for her," she declared. "You want him and his dragon swarm going after all your women, or are you going to take him out now?"

"All right, back off. Let me get him in my sights."

"Right through the heart…there, a little more to the left."

"I got this, okay? Just shut up and let me concentrate."

"You have to get it right. We won't get a second chance."

"I get it; I know."

The voices faded to silence. It was deafening. She still felt nothing from Nic. He must not be aware of what was transpiring. He was down in the central chamber with the clutch, waiting for danger to appear there. He had no idea he was about to die!

Well, not if Lianne could do something about that. She shifted just a bit, turning her head so that with a slight pull on the tapestry she could peer out. The man was about ten feet away from her, leaning over a huge gun that he had propped up on a tripod and aiming out one of the narrow openings in the wall.

Where was the woman? Lianne would have to move the tapestry more to get a look at her, apparently. She could hear her, though, very near to the man. She shifted just a bit. Why couldn't she see the woman? She heard her breathing and it sounded to be right over the man's shoulder.

Wow, she was a seriously heavy breather, too. She actually caused the man's hair to ruffle. And the sound of her breath was rapid, almost like she would hyperventilate. Only…that wasn't exactly what it sounded like. Something was off.

Lianne risked leaning just a bit more and tugging the tapestry. Hopefully her unwelcome guests wouldn't notice. She was counting on their attention being fully focused on the chamber below. If she could just get a glimpse of the woman to know where she stood, maybe there was a chance Lianne could just…

Her own breathing caught in her chest. She saw the woman at last…only, it wasn't a woman. It was another dragon.

It was a tiny dragon, actually. Half the size of a human, snakelike with leathery wings that beat the air rapidly and one set of clawed legs ready to rip into anyone who might disagree with her. The glow of heat behind what appeared to be gills at the side of her head indicated that just like a full-sized dragon, this thing could get fiery.

And at this moment she was helping Mr. Blanchard aim some kind of military-grade launcher at Nic. Lianne had to do something. Her options were severely limited and it dawned on her that whatever she did, she'd probably regret it.

At least she probably wouldn't regret it for long. Between dragons and RGSs and volcanoes and brain cancer, she figured she really didn't have that much to lose. If somehow Nic made it out of this and managed to save his people's clutch, then maybe she hadn't wasted this trip to Iceland, after all.

One way to find out. She threw back the tapestry and lunged at the man with the gun.

* * *

Lianne was in danger! Nic had been sensing her, feeling her torrent of desperate emotion for some time now. He'd hidden himself in the shadows in one of the many tunnels leading off from the main chamber and he'd reached his mind out for her. In his full form now, his senses were much heightened. It had taken a few minutes before he could sort through the multiple stimuli in his mountain and focus on her.

They were not alone in this mountain. He could sense them, sense the danger they brought with them. Also, he could feel the strange darkness he'd felt when that human machinery was running. Someone was bringing more of this machinery into his mountain. It would soon be affecting his abilities. He couldn't yet tell where it was coming from, either.

He could feel Lianne, though. Was she reaching out to him? Yes, she sensed the danger and she was trying to warn him. Warn him of what? A gun? But how…

In his living quarters! He felt her clearly now. She was not alone, someone was with her. Someone familiar…and deadly.

He closed his eyes and tried to shut out everything but Lianne. He needed to feel what she felt, see what she saw. It was difficult; her senses were confused and her mind was in turmoil.

Mr. Blanchard. Nic could sense him now, see him near Lianne. How had he come into the mountain, found Nic's secret room? And what was he doing with…he had a weapon. A weapon he intended to use against Nic. He would destroy the clutch, all of them. And there was another…

He could see through Lianne's eyes now. She couldn't make sense of what she saw, but he understood. He'd been betrayed by the only one who could possibly know how to target him and get through his safeguards. *Eubryd.* She was working against him!

Everything happened at once. Nic sensed it all, but could do nothing. Lianne attacked Mr. Blanchard. The gun shifted. Eubryd screeched into action, her serpent body heating with rage. Flames shot out—Nic could feel them, see the glow in the tiny rock crevices high on the wall at the other side of the chamber. He could hear Lianne's cries as much as he could feel the terror within her.

Without warning, an explosion rocked the mountain. A huge fireball erupted through the far wall where Nic's living quarters had been. The gun must have gone off, turning the rock wall into a rain of shrapnel and ash. The sound was still reverberating through the mountain when Nic leaped out of his hiding place and unfurled his wings.

The explosion had, indeed, blasted an opening in the wall. He launched himself upward, soaring through the smoldering maw and blinking in the haze of smoke, heat, and dust. He barely fit in the space, feeling cumbersome and alien in what used to be his home. It was nothing more than charred rubble now. This was not his home and there was nothing human about him.

He clawed at a slab of rock that had sheared off the ceiling. By the Fires, there was a body below. A body that did not move. He swiped rubble and pages from books aside, relieved when he recognized Mr. Blanchard. Not Lianne.

Where was she? Could she possibly have survived the blast?

"Is this what you're looking for?"

Eubryd appeared, coming around the corner from the bathroom nook. Her eyes were fiery wild, her wings beat furiously, and in her talons she gripped a motionless Lianne.

"What have you done to her?" he demanded.

"I was actually going to fry her, but she ducked in here and I'm afraid I sizzled my friend Mr. Blanchard over there instead. Guess that set off the launcher and sort of took out your wall."

"Get your claws off her, Eubryd."

The wyvern shrugged, then dropped Lianne's limp, dusty form onto the floor.

"I never could understand what you see in these fragile little humans, anyway," Eubryd said, still hovering dangerously close to Lianne's body. "But you always have liked to pretend being one of them, haven't you?"

"Get away from her."

"If you move any closer, Nicolai, I'll turn her to ash."

"Don't. I swear, Eubryd, if you harm her any more I'll—"

"You'll what, shed a few tears? For a *human*?"

"It appears I'm not the only one keeping human company lately."

She didn't appear to appreciate being reminded of that. Her pointy tail flicked angrily and the heat within her was practically melting the paint off the broken chair crumpled beside her. He worried for Lianne.

Was she alive? It was hard to believe a human could survive that explosion, but if she had gone into the bathroom as Eubryd indicated, just maybe she'd been protected from the brunt of it. He watched her for any sign of life. A tiny throb at her neck reassured him her heart still beat, but for how much longer he couldn't know.

Damn Eubryd! He trusted her and this was how she repaid him? It was all he could do to keep from scorching her along with everything in sight.

"I guess you were right," she cooed, dropping low enough that her wings tossed Lianne's hair and stirred dust into choking, swirling eddies. "Humans do serve a purpose every now and then."

"And what purpose did *that* one serve for you?" Nic asked, whipping his tail to smack the rubble beside the body of Mr. Blanchard.

"He knew how to get his hands on that weapon there."

"A grenade launcher? Why, Eubryd? Why destroy the clutch this way? You've been sworn to our clan all these centuries. Why turn against us now?"

"Against *us*? I'm not turning against *us*. You already did that, Nicolai."

"What are you talking about? I've dedicated myself to the clutch, to our future."

"What future, Nicolai? All these years I've watched you with your human ways, your human books, your human females. You have made yourself one of them!"

He flared. Smoke billowed from his nostrils, glowing red then fading as it dispersed into the air. His tail thrashed and he spread his wings as much as he could in this confined space.

"Do I look like one of them, Eubryd? Look at me!"

"Look at yourself, my old friend," she continued, snaking through the dusky air and edging past him. "Your clutch is under attack out there, Nicolai, and yet you are in here with your human things, begging me not to harm your pitiful woman."

He craned his neck to see. By the Fires, she was right. Even now he could sense the dark absence of magic growing stronger in his mountain. The others had arrived. They were setting up more equipment to replace what he had destroyed. They were resuming their assault on the clutch and he had allowed it to happen.

"You and all the rest of the clan have forgotten what we are," Eubryd went on. "We are dragons. There is no power on earth to compare to us! We could rule everyone; none could stand against us, Nicolai. But what have you done? Nothing. You and the clan chose to brood a clutch, but what sort of dragons will these be? Cowering, fearful creatures taught to hide themselves in human bodies, denying their powers and living as slaves to the Veil and its protectors? Creatures not fit to call themselves dragon."

"And that's why you planned to destroy them, to partner with these humans and wipe out our kind?"

"No, to make our kind rise up and take their rightful place."

"But the humans bring machines, Eubryd. They are taking our magic, draining us of our very essence."

"They're only humans, Nicolai. When the rest of our clan see what they've done, when the humans have taken our lives and devastated the clutch…well, then they'll stop hiding. Dragons will rule once again, Nicolai. The foolish humans will tear down the Veil and nothing will stop dragons from taking their rightful place."

"You were doing this to instigate war?"

"It's for our future, Nicolai. You will be the first martyr. Our clan will avenge you and humans will stand no chance. You fear their machines? They will be ash when the clan rises against them."

"Eubryd, no…it can't be like that."

"No more hiding, Nicolai. No more dragons forced to deny their true nature."

"But they're destroying the clutch!"

"You've lost so much of yourself already, you can't even see this is the only way."

"It's not the only way. Get out of here, Eubryd. Don't ally yourself with my enemies."

"I'm your last true friend, Nicolai," the wyvern said. "That useless female is your enemy. All of them are."

She shot a scorching blast directly at Lianne. Nic barely had time to throw up his wing to shield her. His action, however, left the hole in the wall fully untended. Eubryd darted through it and out into the brood chamber. He had to decide, would he go after her to defend the clutch, or stay to try and save Lianne?

Damn it, maybe Eubryd was right. He *had* forgotten who he was. Instinct took over, and without hesitation, he pulled himself back into his human form and stumbled over the debris to reach Lianne.

Chapter Twenty

W hat's going on?" Raea whispered.

"Not a shipwreck, that's for sure," Kyne replied.

They hovered over the ship, high above it and oddly safe from the storm that raged all around them. The ship, it appeared, was actually at the very center of the storm. Whatever created this strange weather, it had created an eye just large enough for the ship to remain undisturbed while the waters and winds nearby went absolutely wild. They'd very nearly not made it through the storm to find rest now in this spot of calm.

Raea worried that they'd be detected, in fact. Without the raging weather to hide them, she felt dangerously exposed, even at this high altitude.

"It does seem like this ship is at the heart of the weather situation," she mused. "How do you suppose they are making it happen?"

"It's got to be magic," Kyne replied.

"I don't feel any magic. Do you?"

"No, and I don't think that's a good thing. There's no way the humans can do all of this without some sort of magic. The fact that we can't detect it must mean they've got it harnessed, pent up somehow."

"That's really strange."

"And dangerous."

"We've got to go tell your father," she said.

"We will. I just...have you got any more Fairy Dust? I need to be invisible so I can get down there and take a closer look."

"Don't be crazy."

"I'll be careful. Have you got any dust?"

"Not very much."

"All I need is enough to get closer for a little while, just to find out what's going on."

She felt for the little pouch she kept the precious stuff in. She'd been right, there was not very much left, and they were still a very long way from home. They'd need some for the journey. Did she dare risk giving a little bit to him here, where so much was at stake and so much could go wrong?

"I don't think you should go down there," she cautioned. "We don't have any idea what's going on."

"Exactly why we need to get closer. Look, what's that? See, someone is moving around on the deck."

She could see what he was pointing at. She could see why it caught his eye, too. It wasn't simply a form moving around below them, but the form had a glow. This huge vessel was built by humans for humans, and they'd seen humans apparently operating it, but this person they were watching right now wasn't human. And he wasn't the only one of his kind.

"Fairies," she breathed.

"Whatever they're using to manage the weather, it's based on fairy magic," Kyne said. "By the Skies, this is a lot bigger than we thought."

"You're right. Okay, let's use just a little bit of dust to drop down low enough to try to find out what they're up to. Then we'll go straight to your father, all right?"

"I'll use the dust and go in closer. You stay up here where it's safe."

"Safe? We're about ten feet away from lightning and hurricane forces up here. How will I know when they alter the little bubble they've set up around the ship? Hanging around up here, I might end up in the middle of the storm any second."

"We flew through it to get here; you'll be just fine. If something happens to me down there, I'd rather know that you can still get away and take that piece back to Baylor."

"We go *together*, Kyne. You agreed to that. We're partners now, connected to each other. What we do, we do *together*."

"I plan to be with you forever, Raea. We're partners in everything. But this...damn it, you never planned to be involved in anything like this."

"And you did? Come on, Kyne. This is a joint effort. We'll be okay as long as we stick together. Right?"

"All right. But just...be careful down there."

"We'll only go as close as we need to, and we'll stay out of sight. And away from any of those awful machines!"

"The good news is the machines must not be sucking up magic, if we can see a fairy moving around," he said, then frowned. "The bad news is if we can see fairy glow from here, then that fairy can see us."

"We'd better disappear quickly then, huh?"

She doled out the dust and they made their wishes. Instantly Kyne and his vibrant golden glow faded into obscurity. She could still feel his magic near her, so she knew they couldn't dare get too close to anyone on that ship. If the machine that depleted all their magic wasn't being used on board, then any magic creature nearby would sense them. An Invisibility Wish couldn't cover for that.

"Take my hand," he said.

"That would have been easier to do about two seconds ago."

"Hold your hand out and I'll take it," he said.

Even in the middle of this storm and the almost impossible things they'd been through tonight, his voice still warmed her and made her believe that things would somehow work out. She held up her hand. Somehow he took it, even despite the buffeting wind and the fact that they were invisible.

"Let's go," she said.

He led the way and she was happy to let him. The ship was huge. She couldn't even guess what humans needed to do with such an enormous vessel. Its size would work to their advantage, though. It was more than big enough for a couple of invisible fairies to dip down unseen toward the inhabited parts of it and hide among the towers and hoists and other unidentifiable ship elements.

"There he is," Kyne whispered.

She was glad he still held her hand. He'd been so quiet that if she did not feel the warmth of his body so close and his fingers laced tightly with hers, she would have thought he'd gone off somewhere without her.

Fortunately, he hadn't. The pale yellow glow of the fairy on the deck below their hiding place could not in any way be confused with Kyne. He was no one she could recognize, but at this distance she couldn't see him very clearly. She could, however, easily see that he was hovering near a pair of humans.

They worked near some crates. Raea and Kyne shifted position as needed to stay near enough to hear their words as they moved around, apparently checking the binding on first one stack of crates then another. There was no indication what was in the crates, but it was obvious they were important.

"Sure don't like being in the middle of all this," one of the humans was saying.

"Better here than out in all that mess. How long you suppose they'll keep it going?" his companion replied.

"Not sure." The human dropped the clipboard he held down to his side and turned to look up toward the yellow glow of the fairy with them. "What are they trying to do? That storm looks pretty rough over land there, but I don't see any kind of town or anything. Who are they going after with it?"

"If they wanted you to know the target, they might have told you," the fairy replied. He had a strange accent. Clearly he was not from their Fairyrealm, but one of the others scattered across the globe. Again, that indicated this was a much bigger problem than they'd suspected.

"Well how are we going to know if they hit the target? Outside the safe zone, our instruments don't tell us a hell of a lot in this mess."

"Just keep checking on these crates," the fairy instructed them. "We'll be headed out pretty soon and things need to be secure."

The information was tantalizing, but hardly enough for Raea to make any guess at all about what might really be going on. So the ship would be leaving this area soon? Where would it go? She wondered if maybe Kyne was making more sense of what they were hearing.

Another glow caught her attention and she squeezed Kyne's hand. He squeezed back and she was confident he saw what she did. Two more fairies were approaching the little group inspecting the crates. Raea instinctively held her breath and pulled back into the shadows where they had been eavesdropping. Kyne's tug at her hand and his soft whisper of her name reminded her that they were safe.

"You're heading to the mountain now," one of the new arrivals called, presumably to the yellow fairy.

"But it's still storming over there," the fairy complained.

The other fairy grunted, apparently insulted by this show of cowardice. The third fairy of the group moved forward, his green aura more intense than the others. It was a green that Raea thought she recognized. When he spoke she had no doubt. The harsh curse Kyne uttered under his breath further convinced her. He recognized the green fairy, too.

It was Swift, the same fairy who had hauled Kyne in for interrogation and nearly cost him his magic. Somehow Swift was here, and he was working with the enemy. That meant either he was a traitor to his own council, or the council was involved in this part of the conspiracy, too.

"You'll be with me," Swift announced. "Things should be well under control by now, and we can arrange for retrieval of our equipment."

"That's it?" the yellow fairy asked. "We go out there and pick up those collectors we placed? So why all the bother with this storm?"

"I didn't ask. Come on. You got dust?"

"Are we going to need it?"

"We need to be prepared. Let's go. The sooner we get this done, the sooner we sail out of this place."

"And on to Caribbean paradise, right?" one of the humans interjected.

"Hell, after this place, anywhere is going to feel like paradise," his partner remarked.

"I hear where we're going it *is* paradise."

The fairy with the accent seemed to be directing things, and he scolded the humans for wasting time. They grumbled and went back to looking over the crates and marking things on their clipboard. Swift gathered up his yellow fairy and hung around to get last instructions from his leader.

"I'll oversee things here. You go make sure things are all wrapped up in the mountain. Be quick about it."

Instead of fluttering off as instructed, though, Swift seemed to be unsure. "Wait, *in* the mountain? I thought the equipment we were retrieving was *on* the mountain."

"One of our associates will meet you there and explain. Just do as you're told, Swift. The coalition appreciates your work."

"So we have team members already on the mountain?" Swift asked. "I thought we left that equipment there to gather up surplus magic from a derelict dragon outpost. The place has been abandoned for centuries. We don't need a team on the ground for that, so what are they doing there?"

"It's not your place to ask. All will be explained once you get there. Go now. Eubryd will find you when you are near."

But Swift still did not leave. "Eubryd? That's not a fairy name I'm familiar with."

"Because she's not a fairy."

"And I'm supposed to meet up with her? Why don't you tell me what she is, then?"

"A wyvern. She's loyal to us and will tell you exactly what to do. Follow her instructions to the letter, Swift. No matter what."

That sounded almost ominous. So now a wyvern was in league with this coalition? Just how much of the Forbidden Realm was involved with this scheme, anyway? Raea did not like the sound of any of it.

Swift, however, seemed content with the answer and chastised the yellow fairy to stop slouching and prepare himself to leave. The fairy in charge gave them last-minute instructions and sent them off in the direction of the distant mountain. Immediately the storm began abating, almost as if someone directed it in order to make their travels easier.

It was the strangest thing and, again, left Raea feeling more than a little uneasy. Fairies were supposed to protect the natural order. Conspiring with humans and stealing magic to use for controlling the weather…well, there was nothing at all natural about that.

"This is not good," Kyne whispered beside her.

She breathed a timid agreement. But now the glow of Swift and his yellow partner rose up into the backdrop of the lessening storm. It was obvious what she and Kyne needed to do.

"Come on," he breathed, with another squeeze of her hand.

She didn't have to be asked twice. She left their hiding place immediately and flew after the two scheming fairies. There was no chance that she and Kyne could get to the mountain in time to warn the dragon that his wyvern companion was in league with the others, but at least they could be there to find out what other actions had been planned. Baylor would want to know.

To be honest, Raea had a sinking feeling that she would rather not.

Chapter Twenty-One

Nic felt Lianne stir in his arms. Thank the Flame, but she was still alive. He brushed the dust and soot from her beautiful face as her eyes slowly fluttered open. It was hard to contain himself when she gave him a weak smile full of warmth and recognition.

"You're alive!" she murmured.

"Of course I am. Things were a bit iffy for you, though."

She frowned, trying to remember. "That little dragon was here…and Mr. Blanchard, too. He was with her. They were going to blow up the clutch. Oh no…did they?"

"Shh, keep calm. The clutch is fine," he assured her, though of course Eubryd was out in the central chamber and at any minute now she might do something terrible and prove him a liar.

He couldn't think about that now, though. He had to protect Lianne.

"I need to get you out of here," he said.

"Why? What's happening?"

It would probably be better if he didn't answer that. "I'll have to take you back the way we came in here. Are you in much pain?"

She thought about it for a moment, winced when she tried to sit up, but shook her head. "No, I think I'm okay."

Of course she wasn't okay, but as she struggled to stand, he assisted her. Apparently nothing was broken, though she would be bruised from head to toe by tomorrow. If she hadn't made it into the other room before that blast went off…well, they wouldn't be having this conversation right now.

"I'll help you. There are some tight passages out there, but for most of the way I can carry you," he said.

"No, I can walk. You look like you've been through a lot already yourself," she said. "You lost your clothes again, as a matter of fact."

"Is that a problem?"

"You'll be the sexiest warrior out there, battling the forces of evil."

"Hmm, maybe I should slip into these," he said, digging through the rubble and pulling up a pair of sweat pants that at one time appeared to have been folded with some other clothing on a shelf just out of the blast zone.

He navigated the shards and debris covering the floor, digging out a pair of shoes to go with the pants. She let her eyes linger over his form as he bent, sliding one muscular leg at a time into the pants and then crouching to pull on the shoes.

"Kind of a shame to cover that up," she mumbled.

He grinned at her. "Let's just hope it's not too long before I can get out of them again. In the meantime, I guess I'm lucky they didn't get roasted."

"Well, not totally, at least. They've got a few holes burned into them."

"As do you, I'm afraid," he said, his grin fading to a concerned frown. "Come on now, before anything worse happens."

He was helping her pick her way through the rubble when her eyes must have caught on Mr. Blanchard. She knew what had happened, but still seeing him this way caught her off guard.

"Is he…dead?"

"Yes. I'll bet he never knew what hit him."

"He had a gun, a big one. It shot grenades or something. He was aiming it at you, Nic. He was going to kill you!"

"And somehow you stopped him, didn't you?"

"I heard them coming…ouch."

She stumbled a bit and bent to rub her injured leg. He held her so she didn't have to put weight on it, but urged her toward the doorway. There was no telling what Eubryd was up to, or if she had access to more weapons out there. The sooner he got Lianne out of this place, the better.

"We'll get you to a doctor," he told her. "You need that leg looked at."

She merely chuckled at his concern. "It's not broken, just sore. I'm pretty sure I won't die from it."

He wished he could be as lighthearted about this as she seemed to be, but he was glad she didn't realize how much danger they were actually in just now. Still, he needed to keep her moving.

"Come on, slide through the opening out into the passageway. I'm right behind you."

"Okay, okay. I just…it was a total shock finding Mr. Blanchard working with that little dragon person. Wait, where is she? What happened to her? Did she have stuff fall on her as well?"

"She's…she got away."

"Got away? Damn it, Nic, you need to go after her! She might still be trying to harm the clutch."

"First I need to get you somewhere safe."

"You mean…Hell no. I will not let you waste your time with me when you need to be somewhere else. That clutch is your responsibility, your legacy!"

"The clan will go on. I need to take care of you first, Lianne."

She wouldn't budge, even though he practically shoved her into the opening ahead of him. Instead, she held her ground and faced him with fiery eyes.

"That's the stupidest thing I've ever heard, Nic. You—more than any-one—know what's going to happen to me. If I don't die in the mountain, I will in a couple months in a hospital somewhere. You shouldn't be here with me, not when you can get out there and fry that scaly little bitch to save your batch of eggs. I'm not worth your effort."

On that last point she was wrong. Very, very wrong. He took hold of her shoulders so she couldn't avoid him.

"You *are* worth it, Lianne. You're worth every moment I've spent with you and every moment we have left together. I won't give up any more than I have to."

She merely stared at him as if she was trying to make sense of his words. They probably did sound senseless to her, as a matter of fact. How could she possibly believe him? He didn't even know what to make of it himself. Why would he turn his back on the clutch, on everything that was important to his kind, to his clan, in favor of some human female he'd only known a short time?

There was no sense to it. He only knew this was the way things had to be. He was choosing Lianne over everything else.

"Why?" she simply asked after an almost painful pause.

"Because I love you," he said.

And that made sense out of all of it.

* * *

Holy hell, he was serious, wasn't he? Lianne stared at him in the firelit glow of the room and waited for his words to truly sink in. He loved her!

It couldn't be possible. Hadn't she torn into him just a few minutes ago about how he used her and took advantage of her? He hadn't denied it, either. But now here he was, stripped down to his roughed-up human form wearing burnt pants and looking at her with eyes that almost made her want to cry.

He loved her! And damn it, she realized she loved him back. Right at this moment it almost didn't matter that they were both probably going to die, that his kind would end up extinct and that some crazy mixed-up human/magic scheme was going on around them. Whatever she was feeling for him right now, she'd never experienced it before. She liked it.

"You realize how insane this is, right?" she asked him.

He laughed. "Yeah. I do, actually."

"So why are we standing around here talking about our feelings when there's a bunch of dragon eggs to be saved?"

"*Our* feelings?"

"Yeah, *our* feelings. I'm not sure how this could possibly happen, but you aren't the only one feeling stuff, you know. I love you, too, Nic. So what in the hell are we going to do about this?"

"I suppose if there weren't several species of conspirators out to murder us, we could find a quiet corner and make love."

She knew he was only half kidding. She kind of wished it hadn't only been half. Forgetting about all this other crap and giving in to more of his hot kisses sounded like a really good idea right now.

Of course they couldn't, though. He had entirely too much at stake. If he wasn't going to do the right thing, she was just going to have to push him into it. She never really wanted to die from this damn tumor, anyway. Death by magical creature sounded so much more exciting.

"Well, I'm afraid all the quiet corners in this mountain have been used up," she said, moving half a step closer to him and gingerly running one finger over his rock-solid chest muscles. "Why don't we go find those evil conspirators out there and kick some ass?"

"But I have to keep you safe, and—"

She put her fingers over his lips. "You're not afraid of that lizard girl, are you?"

"Hell no! She betrayed me; she betrayed our clan."

"Then let's get down there and make sure that's the last stupid thing she ever does. What can I do to help you?"

"No, Lianne, I can't let you get involved."

"I am involved, damn it! And I'm dying, Nic, whether you like it or not.

I came here to make a difference. I don't want to leave this world never having meant anything, as just another rich girl who rode on her daddy's coattails. Let me help you."

She could tell he was going to refuse again, but then he stopped himself. His fingers gripped tighter on her shoulders and his eyes narrowed. It felt like they bored into her soul. She kept her mind open to him, let him feel the raw pain as well as the burning heat she felt for him.

"All right," he said at last. "I think I know what you can do. Help me find the case of explosives I keep under the bathroom sink."

* * *

He knew she was in more pain than she let on. He'd been inside her mind off and on now as they'd worked to set up his plan. It wasn't the best plan, but he hoped it would work.

Lianne set up the explosives in one of the tunnels leading off the main brood chamber. He'd appear from another, attacking Eubryd and pushing her toward the explosives. Lianne would get herself somewhere safe, and then Nic would trigger the explosion when Eubryd was in position.

Then he'd wait around to fry anybody who might show up looking for Eubryd. Somehow along the way, he was going to get Lianne back to her people. She insisted they make the clutch top priority now, but he wasn't ready to give up on finding help for Lianne. She might be determined to die for a cause, but he wasn't planning to let her.

What's she doing in there? he felt Lianne ask in his mind.

He glanced around the corner of the dark tunnel where he hid, and caught a glimpse of Eubryd, darting around, flitting over pieces from the console he'd crushed and toying with them.

Looks like she's getting all the bits of machinery into one pile, he replied. *Maybe she thinks she can fix it.*

Can she?

I doubt it. That's human technology. Wyverns are notoriously antihuman.

She seemed pretty buddy-buddy with Mr. Blanchard up in your little chamber there. Is she still alone?

Yes, but I sense she is expecting company very soon.

They won't try to get there through this tunnel where I am, will they? Lianne asked silently.

No. I didn't detect any residual magic in that tunnel. I don't believe it's been used. Anyone who is coming to help her will probably come a more regularly traveled route.

I hope so. Can you tell if anyone is close by, on the way here?

He felt out into the distance, his mind reaching through solid rock to try to feel the world outside. It was difficult. He'd been fully strengthened by their passion, but since then he'd been through a lot and could tell he was slightly depleted. It didn't help that he was unable to take his focus off Lianne. It was as if a part of him were permanently connected there. Even if he wanted to forget her or concentrate on other things, he couldn't.

Maybe if he wasn't pent up in this human form he could reach farther with his mind. But he wasn't ready to shift into his natural form yet. He didn't want to risk alerting Eubryd to his presence down here, and it was much easier to hide as a human.

I can't detect anyone yet, he told Lianne. *I'll let you know when… Wait, I sense magic. Growing nearer now.*

What kind of magic? Good magic or bad magic?

He had to smile. He wished they could have a lifetime together to learn all about each other's ways. *There is no good or bad magic, just magic. Some magic is darker or more ancient, and it is generally different depending on the element it is drawn from, but it is only good or bad depending on who uses it.*

Huh. Interesting. And to think I wasted a whole semester studying French in Paris when I should have been studying magic in Russia.

When we're all done with this, I'll let you study Russian to your heart's content.

It warmed him to feel her pleasure at his words. The magic surged within him as his passion for her boiled. He could feel someone approaching, entering the mountain. Several someones, actually. Light, airy magic. Fairies.

We have more fairies on the way, he told Lianne. *Get yourself to safety; go back the way I told you and wait for me there.*

But what if you need me?

I need you to be safe, Lianne. Once I've taken care of the threat, I'll meet you at the entrance to the mountain.

I don't like being separated from you, Nic.

You're not. You never will be. I'm only a thought away, Lianne. Trust me.

I'd rather be able to touch you.

Stop talking like that or you'll get me distracted.

Yeah? Well, maybe we don't need to actually be together then to…you know, be together. *Want to try?*

The thoughts she sent to him were positively indecent. His mind flamed and his blood raged at the images they conjured. By the Fires, he would love nothing better than to try a few things with her. Not now, though.

Behave yourself, woman, he chided softly. *The magic is moving closer now. Eubryd left them a trail; they are coming directly to the brood chamber. Two fairies.*

Only two? No humans?

Not yet. I don't dare try to search their minds to know what nonmagical assistance they expect. They're probably on guard for that. But there's no one else in the mountain yet, of that I am sure.

Good. You can take care of them in your sleep.

It did seem a little too easy. How could two fairies and a traitorous wyvern possibly hope to overpower him? They couldn't, of course. That must mean they knew something he did not. He'd better be extra careful and not be too sure of himself.

Lianne kept her thoughts quiet for a few moments while they waited. He could not see anymore what Eubryd was up to in the brood chamber, but he could see several eggs from his vantage point. They still appeared fine, and the cauldron of molten rock that they rested in boiled and heated the air of the cavern at the same scalding temperature he'd grown accustomed to. Nic had no reason to suspect she'd done anything to damage them yet. She must be waiting for her coconspirators.

I see them! Lianne exclaimed in his mind. *In one of the tunnels across from me, I can see a little bit of a glow. It's getting stronger. They should be coming into the chamber through a tunnel about thirty feet to the right of yours.*

My right or your right? he asked for clarification.

Um, yours. Can't you feel them?

Yes, I was teasing you. I know exactly where they are. He could feel her rolling her eyes at him. *Can you tell what color they are?*

I can see a greenish glow…okay, one green fairy and one yellow, she informed him.

He let his mind range farther, sensing for subtleties and any details that would give him the edge. He found two fairies, just as she'd described. What he needed now was to single them out, decide which one to target first.

One of them feels stronger than the other, he mentioned. *Which one is that? Describe him to me so I'll know him when I see him.*

She paused for a moment and he could feel her considering the question. He knew she wasn't used to communicating like this or using her senses the way that he did. She seemed to understand what he was asking, though. She studied the fairies, watching their body language and assessing their attitudes. At last she gave a confident reply.

The green one. Yes, definitely the green one.

He commended her. *Excellent. He's the leader, then.*

I could tell because he glowed brighter than the other, Lianne announced. *I wish people glowed like that. It's kind of pretty.*

Don't get too attached. They're going to be snuffed out very quickly.

Pity. But whatever. Burn the little bastards and let's get out of here.

Damn it, but he loved that woman.

He could feel the fairies entering the chamber. Eubryd must have felt them, too. She called out a greeting.

"It's about time! All was very nearly lost, but I think we can salvage things."

"These are dragon eggs," the green fairy noted.

"Best source of magic in all of the world," Eubryd announced. "We had equipment set up to collect here, but my larger hot-tempered friend sort of destroyed it."

"We've been collecting magic from incubating eggs?" the green fairy questioned.

"Brilliant, isn't it?"

"And the dragons are with us on this?"

"Er, not quite," Eubryd admitted. "That's why things are a little bit of a mess right now."

Nic could feel the fairy's indignant energy. Whoever he was, he'd had no idea what had been going on in here. What sort of conspiracy was this that didn't keep its members informed? He could feel anger building inside the green fairy. Likely Eubryd could feel it, too.

"Hey, don't get all righteous with me," she scolded the newcomer. "We're doing this for the good of all the Veiled creatures."

"Stealing magic from dragons without their consent? Where is the dragon that destroyed this equipment? What have you done with him?"

"He's gone off to side with the humans," Eubryd hissed. "That's what's been going on, that's why we have to do this. We're becoming pets, harmless caged animals, taking scraps from humans while they keep the best parts of the world for themselves! It's time we use magic for something more than just surviving. We're going to break out of our cage and show the humans what magic is for."

"I thought we were working to strengthen the Veil, to keep the humans farther away from our magic."

"We've been doing that for thousands of years and what has it gotten us?" Eubryd asked. "Now help me reconnect this part."

"You think you can fix this? You can't. The power supply is destroyed and the components are all crushed."

"The human components are all crushed. The magical components are just fine. The magic that was being processed in here all escaped, but see this containment box?"

Nic could hear some scuffling and some mumbling. Unfortunately, this green fairy knew a bit about hybrid machinery. That might be to his credit where this damned fairy conspiracy was concerned, but Nic counted it as a strike against him. That fairy would be the first one he fried, as a matter of fact.

"The containment box is good," the green fairy acknowledged. "But what can you do with it? There's no electrical impulse, no catalyst."

"I see your human associates have taught you not to think for yourself," Eubryd said. "What's your name?"

"I'm called Swift. I work for the council of the Great Lake Fairyrealm near—"

"I don't care about that," Eubryd interrupted. "You've lived behind the Veil for so long you think you belong there. You have at least part of a brain, though, unlike your dim little partner here."

"Er, I'm Lem, ma'am," the yellow fairy stammered.

Eubryd seemed unimpressed. "Well, flutter over here, Lem, and let me show you how this thing works."

There were a couple of moments of clanking metal, then a sudden shout. Nic could feel Lianne's shock as she watched on from the other side of the chamber. He peered down the tunnel where he'd remained concealed, moving just enough to see the action out in the open.

Eubryd had grabbed the yellow fairy and held him securely in her talons. She was just slightly more than twice his size, but her dragon reflexes were quick. She'd snapped him up before he had time to react and she held him, flapping her leathery wings and hovering over the pile of equipment she'd gathered up.

"What are you doing?" the green fairy demanded.

"I'm showing you that we don't need human components to create a perfectly good catalyst," she replied.

With that, she swiftly ripped the pale yellow fairy in half. The little creature barely had time to cry out before Nic felt his life force evaporate. Magic sparked from him, and Eubryd quickly shoved both halves of him into an oddly shaped box that rested atop the pile of equipment. The box suddenly glowed and the equipment started to hum.

Nic could feel its effects almost immediately. Yes, By the Flames, Eubryd had known something he did not. She knew she could get that damn machinery working again! How had he not known that's what she was planning? When did she become so accomplished at keeping her mind closed to him?

"You should come out here now, Nic," she called, as if the whole damn thing had been perfectly on cue. "Did you finally give up on your frail little human up there, or did she expire?"

"Damn you, Eubryd," he growled.

His already torn pants shredded as his body roared into its natural form. He burst, full, sizzling dragon, out of the tunnel where he'd been hiding. The green fairy zipped up toward the ceiling, uttering curses as he went.

"Aw, too bad. The scrawny human must not have made it," Eubryd said with a delighted smile. "So sorry for your loss."

Well, that was interesting. He might not be able to reach into Eubryd's mind right now, but clearly she could not read him, either. Apparently whatever bond they'd once had, her betrayal had broken it. He was sure he could read her if he tried—his mind was much more powerful than hers—but for now it was good to know his thoughts were a mystery to her.

"Whose side are you on, anyway?" Nic asked her. "That was one of our own kind, another Veiled creature that you just destroyed!"

"He gave his pitiful life for our cause," she said with a shrug of her wings, her beady eyes flashing and puffs of glowing smoke emitting from her tiny, pointed nostrils. "In the end, it will all be worth it, when magic controls the earth again and humans are put in their place."

She was delusional. She had the upper hand right now, though. He could feel his strength being slowly drained by that machine. It was not functioning at full capacity, but the fairy magic she jammed into that box had jump-started it, and he could feel the effects increasing. It was drawing in magic again, sucking it up from everything in proximity. The more magic it collected, the stronger it would get.

"You shouldn't have done that," the green fairy called down from where he hovered above, clearly trying to stay just out of blast range. "The Regulator on that equipment was destroyed. It will continue to gather up magic over capacity."

Nic had a fairly good idea what might happen at that point. Uncontrolled magic was a very dangerous substance. With the practically endless supply it could collect from the clutch, this equipment would overload at some point. The result would be catastrophic.

"Oh dear, will this make the mountain go boom?" Eubryd asked sweetly. "Too bad I'll be long gone by then. And what will you do, Nic? Stay to save your precious, useless clutch of weak little dragon pets? Or will you come with me and put your efforts toward a far more rewarding task?"

"You know I can't leave the clutch," he growled. "By the Flames, you won't either, Eubryd!"

He released a powerful blast, enough to leave the walls of the chamber burnt to a glassy sheen where the giant fireball hit. Eubryd dodged him easily, though. She was a dragon, however small and misguided. Fire was not her enemy.

It could harm Lianne, though. Nic would have to be careful where he aimed his flame. He could feel that Lianne had not done as she was told and fled the area. She was nearby, clearly in harm's way.

"What is that you are feeling, Nic?" Eubryd asked. "You've closed your mind to me, but I can detect…ah, so the female isn't expired. You brought her down here with you."

"She has nothing to do with this!" he commanded. "Face me Eubryd, if you have any honor left in you at all."

For a moment it seemed the wyvern would indeed face him with honor. But she was distracted.

"No, face *me*, you damn bat-winged chicken!"

Lianne. Damn her, she'd come out of the tunnel and stood there in the open, yelling at Eubryd and tossing stones, of all things, through the air at her. Nic couldn't dare blast Eubryd away for fear he'd char Lianne. The little fool! What was she thinking?

Whatever it was, Eubryd fell for it. She glowered at Lianne, and her scales glowed with molten fury. She had to get closer to do any damage to the woman, however, so she left her spot at the buzzing machine and flew toward Lianne's tunnel.

Lianne gave one quick glance at Nic and then took off running. He understood now and both loved her and hated her for it. She was going through with their plan, only right now it didn't seem she'd be out of the way in time for it to work.

"Now, Nic!" she ordered, yelling out loud.

Her voice sounded strong, but he could feel the pain in her body. It was excruciating. Still, she was running up that damned tunnel for all she was worth.

"Do it now!" she repeated. "I'll be okay, but you have to do it now!"

By the Fires, he hoped she was right. He'd hung the remote detonator around his neck. His scaly fingers grasped it, but he could not bring himself to press the button. She was still too close, still in that tunnel with the explosives, damn it. How could he do this thing, even to save his clutch?

"If you don't do it now, we'll all be toast," she said.

He could see through her eyes. She was in darkness, pressing her bruised, trembling body into the tiny cleft where he'd shown her to hide. Eubryd would find her there. Lianne was right, if he didn't set off the explosives now, Eubryd would burn her and then leave the chamber to explode when the machinery overloaded. This was his only chance.

"I love you, Lianne."

He said it aloud and sent the words with every ounce of mental energy he could, then pressed the little button on the detonator. The tunnel exploded with a boom and a whoosh of dusty, ashy air billowed out like furious storm clouds. It overwhelmed him in a second, knocking him backward and obscuring his vision. The entire chamber around him glowed red from the heat of the brooding pool. He was momentarily dazed.

The echo of the explosion reverberated through the chamber until finally the sound dissipated. He was aware of the green fairy flapping his tiny wings furiously, faltering and dropping lower as he choked on the hot, dusty air.

"By the Skies, what did you do?"

Nic wasn't sure how to answer. What *had* he done? Did he just kill the woman he loved? He reached out for her.

"Lianne…are you there?"

No answer, not audible or mental. He was still too disoriented to find her mind. The machine, though, still hummed away. He was very close to it and could feel it draining him, sucking at his very essence.

"Get away from the machine," he ordered the fairy. "Get out of here before it depletes your magic. Go find help—anyone who can help me get the woman out of the tunnel."

"You think she's still alive in there?" the fairy asked, clearly wondering if Nic had suffered some form of brain damage.

"I hope so. Are you with me, or do I need to get rid of you, too?"

"Hey, I was sent here to help our people shore up the Veil. I don't know anything about plotting to take over the world. If you want to save that human, I'll do what I can."

That was the right answer. Now if he could just feel Lianne, find her mind or her heartbeat or some sign of her life…It was reassuring, though, to know that he could not find Eubryd, either. Apparently his efforts had managed to get that part of the plan right.

He hoped the cost had not been entirely too high.

Chapter Twenty-Two

Lianne slowly became aware of Nic calling her name. She cracked open her eyes, but they stung so she shut them again. Dust—it was all around her, choking her and making her eyes burn. She reached up to swipe at them and found that, although she could open them, she still couldn't see. Everything was black all around her.

She groped in the darkness, trying to remember where she was. Oh yeah…she was in a tunnel. But why couldn't she see the bright red glow from the main chamber? It was blocked. She could feel huge chunks of rocks all around her.

Pain stabbed through her leg as she moved. She found a big chunk of rock on top of it. Pushing herself into a seated position, she shoved the rock over. It clattered and made sounds of little pebble slides where it landed. She must have just barely missed being crushed.

So Nic had set off the explosives, just like she told him. He trusted her. That warmed her a little, despite the fact that she hurt and felt completely alone here in this rapidly cooling cavern.

But was she alone? That overheated lizard bitch had been coming at her, blazes roaring. There was no sign of her now, though. Lianne supposed if the creature was anywhere to be found, she'd be making herself known right about now. The creature's absence probably meant the explosion had done its job.

But what about Nic? Where was he? She shut her burning eyes again and concentrated on finding him. She had heard his voice, hadn't she?

Yes, there it was. Through all the rocks and debris, she could feel his desperate thoughts. He was searching for her, begging her to reply.

"I'm here," she called out, and nearly gagged at the ragged condition of her throat.

Her head rang pretty good, too. It made her voice sound muffled and foggy. Maybe she did sound muffled and foggy; she couldn't really tell. She went ahead and swallowed back some of the grit and tried calling out to him again.

"I'm okay! I'm in here."

She waited, then suddenly he filled her mind. He was not as near as she wanted him, but they had found each other.

Thank the Flame, he said. *Are you injured?*

Not too much. More bruises and…ouch, a nice cut on my head, I think. It seems to be bleeding.

Put pressure on it, if you can.

Yeah, all right. I probably look like hell, just so you know.

Are you in any other immediate danger?

From your mini-dragon friend? I don't see her. I don't see anything, actually. Either I'm blind, or there are a hell of a lot of rocks fallen down in here.

The ceiling caved in, but I'll get to you, he assured her. *Just stay where you are.*

That was my plan. Damn it. My leg hurts pretty good, too.

I'm coming for you.

Good. I like it when you come.

She could feel his chuckle rumble through her brain. It wasn't hearty and rich, though, as she'd come to know it. In fact, his thoughts hadn't been sharp and clear. Did she really rattle her head so much that she wasn't receiving properly? She must have.

Just hold on, Lianne, he said, weaker than she would have expected. *I'll get to you.*

Hey, what's wrong with your voice? I mean, your thought voice. You sound like you're a hundred miles away. Are you okay, Nic?

I'm fine. I just... The equipment is collecting magic at an increasing rate.

And you're still in there with it? Get out of that chamber, Nic! It's draining you. Find some other way to get in here to me.

No, there isn't time. Just sit tight, Lianne. Let me concentrate.

There isn't time? Why? What's the next disaster I need to be worried about?

The equipment is collecting too much. It's going to overload itself soon.

Oh, hell. That can't be good.

It isn't. Now stay back while I try to clear out this debris.

And by that she figured he probably meant burn the shit out of it. Since she didn't really want a lap full of molten rock anytime soon, she scrambled back, crawling over broken hunks of rock face and finding her back against the far wall of the tunnel. She pulled herself up to stand, resting all her weight on one good leg and feeling her way along the wall. She moved farther into the tunnel, away from where the opening to the main chamber used to be.

At first she thought she was imagining it, but after blinking and rubbing her eyes again she couldn't deny there was a faint light. Some of the rocks at the opening were starting to glow, and she could feel the air warming up around her again. Nic would be breaking through to her anytime now.

And he'd be a dragon. The thought of seeing him again that way sent a jolt of electricity through her. She'd been a little bit afraid of him, not quite sure how to react. But then she'd looked into his eyes, felt his mind touching hers, and he'd treated her so tenderly. No, she wasn't afraid of him now. She wouldn't react with fear when he burst through the rubble to get to her.

Well, maybe just a little. He was a big-ass scary dragon!

She held her position as the light grew brighter and she began to make out shapes. Her eyes could pick out individual formations and bits of shattered ancient lava rock that glittered in the growing glow. She rubbed her arms to both calm her nerves and revel in the warmth Nic's blast created.

Lianne, can you see me yet? he called into her mind.

I see light, and the debris is starting to glow. It's getting warm in here.

Good. How are you doing?

My leg isn't much help to me, and that bump on my head is making me a little bit woozy, but overall I'm thrilled that you're coming to get me.

Me, too. I'm worried about hurting you, though. Do you think you can move farther from the tunnel entrance?

Sure. Now that I can see better, I can find my way. I can't move very fast, Nic.

Do what you can. Let me know if it starts to get too warm for you.

She agreed, and held on to the tunnel wall for support as she scooted back deeper into the tunnel. It began to turn to the left, so she was moving out of the nice warm light and farther into the darkness. She could hear the walls and ceiling of the tunnel creaking, popping as the fractured rock heated from Nic's blast. If it wasn't for the fact that she knew he was just a few yards away from her now, it would be terrifying.

Hold on. I have to work my way through this big chunk. Get back as far as you can, Lianne.

That sounded ominous, so she pressed on into the darkness around the bend in the tunnel. She couldn't see the bright glow where Nic worked, just a dusky beam of flickering red spreading across the tunnel floor and twisting up onto the opposing wall. It got brighter and all of a sudden, with a loud crack and the whoosh of more dust and debris, the beam shone bright and she knew the tunnel was open. He'd gotten through to her.

"Lianne! Are you all right?"

"I am." She coughed with her reply. "I'm back here."

The beam of light was quickly blocked by the huge shadow of something. Nic's giant form swiftly moved toward her, filling the tunnel and creating wicked patterns of dancing red light as he moved. His eyes glowed and the gaps between his scales were like rivers of fire. It was as if he himself were molten in his core and the dragon form was simply a suit of armor he wore to contain it all.

Terrifying, but hot as hell.

His fiery eyes searched for her and she met them boldly. Yes, he was a dragon through and through, but she knew the soul behind those eyes. That would never change. The emotion she saw in them when they caught on her was unmistakable, too.

She didn't have to say anything. Surely he could feel her thoughts for himself, know that everything he felt for her, all the love that was displayed in his eyes was echoed within her. She released her desperate grip on the wall and let her aching body fall into his arms.

* * *

He'd done it. He'd destroyed Eubryd and somehow managed to keep Lianne safe. Their stupid, hasty plan had worked, despite a few glitches along the way. She was the bravest, most determined human he had ever known. And she was *his*.

He held her tightly, pressing her against him and praying he could keep his body temperature cool enough not to burn her. He should have at least waited to turn into his human form before lunging for her this way. But he'd needed to touch her, to hold her and feel the life surge through her body and know that she was all right.

But she wasn't all right. He could feel it even now. The wound on her head had been bleeding profusely, and as she wheezed under his crushing embrace, he knew there were less visible wounds as well. The force of the explosion had likely thrown her hard against the tunnel wall. Her lungs were filling with fluid; he could hear the raspy sound that she made when she whispered his name.

"I've got to get you out of here," he said, stroking her hair and cradling her against him.

Even with his wings furled tightly against him, he barely had room inside the tunnel to maneuver. He managed, somehow. This tunnel would wind and meander through the depths of the mountain. He needed one that would take a more direct route to the surface, away from the churning machine that was draining his strength and would eventually destroy the mountain.

Already he was weary from the labor of searing his way through the debris that had blocked the tunnel. If he had his full strength, that should have been child's play. Obviously the machine was becoming more and more effective as the minutes ticked by.

Damn, but he hated to admit defeat. Eubryd would succeed in destroying the clutch, after all. He would be forced to abandon his duty. It made him so angry, he had to be extra cautious not to let his body flame up or hold Lianne too tight.

"What is it?" she murmured, pressing herself against him as they emerged into the main chamber. "You're upset about something."

"I have to get you out of here before that machine blows," he said. "We should go this way."

He began moving toward one of the tunnels, but he pulled up short. The little green fairy was still hovering listlessly nearby.

"What the hell are you still doing here?"

"I wanted to make sure the human got out of there all right," the fairy replied.

"She did. You should be gone while you still have any strength," Nic admonished him.

"I can feel its effects getting stronger," the fairy admitted. "What will you do with her?"

"I'll get her to her people. They can help."

"A dragon is just going to swoop down into a little village somewhere and get help for his injured human? No, let me help her."

Nic didn't trust this fairy one bit, but he did realize that the damn little creature was right. Their vehicle had been struck by lightning and Nic had left everyone back at the jobsite groggy and confused about what he was up to. There was no telling if or when anyone might realize they needed to come looking for Lianne, or where. If he took on his human form, they were both stranded here. And honestly, he wasn't certain how much energy he had left for a long overland flight, if Lianne even could survive such a thing in a freezing storm with her injuries.

"How can you help her?"

"I've got some dust with me. If we can get her away from that machine, there's probably still enough magic to heal her."

"You can do that?" This was the first glimmer of hope Nic could truly latch onto.

"I can try. It will depend how much magic I have left, and how bad her condition is."

It's bad.

He hadn't needed Lianne to confirm his worst fears, but she had. He craned his neck to peer down at her. Her eyes told him all he needed to know. Now that the initial surge of adrenaline was wearing off, she was beginning to realize the extent of her injuries.

"You're willing to let this fairy try his magic on you?"

She nodded. "There's something wrong in my chest, Nic. I mean, besides the other stuff. I think...I might be bleeding internally. I didn't notice it at first, but maybe one of my ribs is broken. It's getting harder to breathe."

Immediately he relaxed his hold on her. Damn it, but things were going from bad to worse. If this fairy thought he could help, then there was nothing they could do but let him attempt it.

"All right," Nic assented. "Let's go over there, into that tunnel. It is the most direct route up to the surface and away from the machine."

Before they could even enter the tunnel, however, the feel of new magic tingled through him. He barely had time to twist his body to shield Lianne from whatever this was when the glow of two more fairies appeared in the very tunnel they'd just been about to enter. Nic glared as a fiery golden fairy appeared with a more delicate pink fairy at his side.

"Friends of yours?" he asked the green fairy.

"Not exactly," Swift replied.

"What are you doing here?" the golden fairy grumbled at Swift.

"There's no time for an explanation," Swift answered. "This human is injured. Have you brought any dust with you?"

"Only a little bit," the pink fairy replied, eyeing Nic nervously. "What happened to her?"

"Long story," Nic rumbled. "Can you help her?"

"We can try, but—" the pink fairy said but faltered in midair. "Whoa. Is that…there's a machine running in here! We've got to get out."

"Damn it, Swift," the golden fairy snarled. "What are you up to? And where's your little partner?"

"He didn't quite make it," Swift replied. "Now come on, we've got to get back where we came from."

They were all about to head into the tunnel when a ball of fire slammed into the wall beside Nic's head. He whirled around to find a broken, hissing Eubryd crawling out from under the melted debris of the cave-in. By the Flame, how could she possibly still be alive?

He ducked, depositing Lianne just inside the entrance to the tunnel. She moaned in pain when she tried to cling to him.

"Stay here. I'll take care of Eubryd."

Lianne was afraid for him, he could feel that. "But you're weak, Nic, I can tell. She can't have much fight in her. Let's just get out of here."

"And have her attack us from behind? No, wait here."

He gave each of the fairies their own killing glare. "Tend her," he ordered. "Keep her safe. I'm going to end this once and for all."

Chapter Twenty-Three

Kyne did what he could to position himself between the injured human and whatever was going to transpire in the main chamber. The effects of the machine were already getting to him, though, and he could see that Swift and Raea were fading, too.

"What is your name?" Raea was asking the human as she looked over her wounds.

"I'm Lianne McGowan. And you?"

"Raea. You are a friend of the dragon's?"

"I guess you could say that. Ouch. Can you help me sit up? It's kind of hard to breathe lying down."

Raea and Swift looked kind of helpless, so Kyne stepped in to assist. Apparently their dust was in limited supply here and neither of them wanted to waste it on resizing. He didn't need dust for that. He took a deep breath and gave in to his half-human nature.

The woman made a slight gasp as he transformed from a six-inch fairy to a full-sized human man. With golden gossamer wings. He figured in her situation, he probably would have been kind of surprised, too.

Clearly Swift was. "By the Clouds in the Sky, you *do* become one of them."

"Don't mess with me, Swift," Kyne grumbled at him.

"So not all of you magical people go around shape-shifting, I take it," the woman said.

"I'm half-human," Kyne explained. "I can assume this form whenever I need to. These others, well, they need to use Fairy Dust if they want to change size."

"Ah. Of course that makes sense."

"Let me help you," Kyne said, stooping beside her and helping her shift position as he slid her deeper into the tunnel, away from the danger outside.

He could hear the raspy effort of her lungs. As the dragon had indicated, this woman needed help quickly. To be honest, Kyne wasn't sure they'd gotten to her in time. There might not be enough magic among them to help her even now. Whatever that machine was doing, it was doing it well.

He glanced over at Raea and knew her assessment was the same. He also knew she was feeling the same effects from the machines that they'd felt before. That familiar yearning was welling up inside him. He wanted to forget all about this human and get Raea alone in a dark corner somewhere.

They had to ignore those urges, however. Another flash of fire sizzled through the air in the chamber outside. He could hear the dragon curse at his smaller attacker.

"So the wyvern betrayed her dragon, did she?" Raea asked, almost as if simply trying to make small talk while she touched the woman's bruises, inspected the gaping wound on her brow, and mentally calculated how much magic was needed.

The woman winced, but nodded. "Yeah, she did. She showed up here with a man that I trusted. Who knew there was some huge magical conspiracy going on? They planned to kill Nic, then blow this place up."

"Why would she destroy the clutch?" Raea asked. "That is a dragon clutch, isn't it? I've heard of such a thing, but never known of one in my lifetime."

"That's what it is, and Nic is the sworn defender of it. Ouch! Damn, that hurts."

"Hush, I'm trying to clean out your wound. Who brought that machinery in here?"

Kyne moved back to the tunnel mouth so he could watch what unfolded. Raea had things under control with the human. She was being smart, tending the woman's injuries but asking a lot of questions, too. Not only was that keeping the woman calm, but it would also be useful information when they reported to Baylor. If they ever got out of here.

Another fire blast scalded the walls nearby them. The dragon was noticeably weakening and somehow that damned little wyvern, with her tail dislocated and dangling, one wing fractured and useless, had climbed up onto the humming machinery, clinging to it as if to protect it from Nic. No wait, what was she doing? She was clawing at it...trying to upend it, perhaps.

Oh. Damn it, she appeared to be trying to send the machine into the very pool where the clutch rested. There was no telling what devastating effect that might have.

Nic seemed hesitant to send his strongest blasts at her. He circled her, studying her actions and clearly considering his options. But by the Skies, he was a dragon! Why was he being so hesitant about this? It almost seemed as if he felt sorry for her. Or perhaps he was simply waiting for the right opportunity to end her in a final blaze of glory.

Dragons were odd sorts. Kyne decided not to even bother trying to understand this one's motives. Rescuing humans, battling against his own kind...this dragon seemed even odder than most. Kyne needed to get himself and Raea away from this place as soon as possible.

Raea, however, was deeply involved with trying to figure out how to heal the human. Knowing her, none of them would be going anywhere until that task had been accomplished. He loved her compassion as well as her dedication, but right now those two qualities might get them killed.

"I'm not sure the dragon is doing very well," he muttered over his shoulder, hoping to encourage Raea to hurry along.

All he succeeded in doing was upsetting the woman.

"What happened?" she cried, wheezing as she shifted and tried to peer around Kyne. "Is he all right?"

"He needs to get out of there. That equipment is getting stronger by the second, and he's right up there next to it. I'm not sure what he's trying to do. Why doesn't he just fry the wyvern and be done?"

"She was his friend." The woman sighed. "He's more kindhearted than he seems."

"Well, he's not going to be any kind of hearted at all if he doesn't speed things up," Kyne grumbled. In his human form the effects of the machinery were slightly diminished, but he needed to get them away from here while he still could. Too much longer and he'd be sapped of his energy, too.

Swift buzzed up beside him, his wings slower than usual. "What's the wyvern doing to that machine?"

"Trying to dump it into the pool, I believe." Kyne kept his voice quiet so as not to further upset the human.

"Well, that should make a pretty horrific explosion."

"Seems like that's what Nic is trying to avoid. What the hell is going on here, anyway, Swift? The council is in on all this insanity?"

"No," Swift said quickly, then seemed to reconsider. "I don't know. I thought we were simply partnering with a few trusted humans to subtly come up with a way to make the Veil stronger, for everyone's benefit. Now…I'm not so sure."

"I would say if it's come to controlling weather and exploiting dragons, there's something a lot more sinister going on, wouldn't you agree?"

"Yes, I know. I should have suspected long before now. I just…I didn't know how big this thing is."

"What do you know, Swift?"

"The ship. It's full of machinery that probably does a lot more than we were told. The council isn't as informed or as in charge of things as they think they are, I'm afraid."

"The ship is headed somewhere?"

"South. The Caribbean. There's some important person at a resort down there, and they're planning a meeting."

Kyne swore and shook his head. "Humans. Can't even plot to take over the world without figuring vacation time into it."

The woman cried out again and distracted their attention. One glance at Raea and Kyne knew things were bleak.

"I need your dust, Swift," Raea called. "All that you can spare."

"What can we do to help, Raea?" Swift asked, going back to hover over the woman.

Kyne kept his position near the tunnel opening, but shifted his gaze just enough to watch the devious green fairy. No matter what Swift said about his ignorance of evildoings, Kyne wasn't going to rest until he got Raea safely away from Swift *and* this ill-fated mountain.

"If you can get her strong enough to move, I can carry her out of here," he offered.

"I don't know," Raea said. "It's going to take all of our dust."

The woman protested. "Don't worry about me. How is Nic? You should use whatever magic you have to help him!"

"He told us to use our magic for *you*."

"I'm dying, you sparkly morons. Can't you see that? If he's having trouble out there, help *him*. Forget about me."

And answer to a lovesick dragon? Kyne didn't think so. "We're not going to forget about anybody. What can you do for her, Raea? A wish?"

"I don't know…healing usually requires more than a wish."

The woman was incredulous. "You guys want me to just *wish* myself better? Don't you dare tell me that all this magical stuff is nothing more than the power of positive thinking."

"I'm a Wish Fairy," Raea explained. "That's what I'm best at. I've solved some pretty big messes with wishes before, so don't disregard the idea."

Kyne chuckled. "Made a few messes with wishes, too." Raea shot him a scolding look, but it didn't help to wipe the smirk off his face.

"What about you, Swift?" Raea asked. "Any magic that you're especially good at? What is it that you really do for the council, anyway?"

Swift didn't seem all that eager to answer, and Kyne could guess why. He'd tried to present himself as some sort of aide, an administrator of sorts, but Kyne had him figured out. Swift wasn't the hapless underling he pretended to be.

"He's muscle for the council," Kyne offered. "He's the one they've got off doing their dirty work. Isn't that right, Swift? You're the Fairy Council's secret police, aren't you?"

"That's ridiculous," Raea said. "The council doesn't have secret police."

But Swift was notably silent on the matter. "We are all in increasing danger here. If there's anything we can do for the woman, we'd better do it and get out of here."

Kyne wasn't quite ready to drop the subject, but sounds of fire bursts out in the main chamber interrupted him. He should have been paying better attention. That wyvern could have crept up on him and gotten into the tunnel.

She didn't, though. She was clinging to the machinery, rocking it with all her might and hurling blast after blast of her hottest flame directly at Nic. He was enduring it, moving steadily toward her and shielding his face as best he could. Apparently one Dragon could burn another and the wyvern was compensating for her tiny size by throwing every ounce of fire and brimstone she had at him. Between that and the effect of the machine, he was definitely showing signs of distress.

Through the flame and his pain he glanced over at Kyne. "Get Lianne out of here!" he roared before his voice was choked off for lack of oxygen.

Clearly he refused to blow the thing while the woman was nearby. The fool, his face was being practically melted off by that little wyvern. Kyne needed to act.

"All right," he said, moving back to the woman and ignoring her protests. "Let's go."

She didn't have much strength left, but she used it to fight against him. "No! What about Nic?"

"He's going to blow that damn machine and he wants us to get you out of here," Kyne told her.

"No!" Lianne protested.

"It's the only way," Swift said, finally making himself useful. "There's no way to shut the equipment down."

"Um, that's not entirely true," Raea said, giving Kyne a knowing look. "We told the dragon how to disable those machines, didn't we?"

What? She couldn't seriously be suggesting he drag her out there into the presence of angry, murderous dragons and start making passionate love? Thank the Skies, that did not appear to be her plan.

"The woman clearly loves him," Raea said.

Kyne was inclined to believe her assumption was correct. But would it actually work?

"Wait, what are you talking about?" Lianne asked. "Of course I love him, but how can we shut down the machine?"

"You have to literally *love* him," Kyne explained, if somewhat indelicately. "Physically love him."

"Oh, you mean...so this is about sex building up magical power and stuff like that? This could have an effect on that machine?"

"Passion," Raea said. "It's passion that can override magic."

For the first time Lianne's eyes showed the signs of hope. "Well, all right, then. Leave me here with him. Go, get out of here and fly off to warn your people about what's going on. Maybe some good will come out of this yet."

"But we cannot be sure—" Raea cautioned, only to have the woman swat at her and shut her up.

"If there's even a slight chance it might work, we have to try."

"Your dragon will be angry at us," Raea noted.

"What's he going to do, come after you?" Lianne said with a bitter laugh. "This place is ready to combust any second now and we have one shot at shutting that machine down. Personally, I'd like to take it. If I can't go out there and save Nic, then I sure as hell want to die with him."

Kyne met Raea's eye and realized she saw as well as he did that they were fighting a losing battle. The woman was not long for the world anyway. Maybe she really ought to be allowed one last moment with her dragon.

"You don't have a lot of strength left," Raea pointed out to her.

"Then use some of that Fairy Dust. Let me have whatever you can. You don't need to heal me, just buy me a little more time."

"What is she talking about?" Swift finally asked.

Raea wisely ignored his question. "Swift, give me your dust. Here's what we can do."

Chapter Twenty-Four

Nic could hardly believe his eyes. Partially because, thanks to Eubryd, they weren't working very well at the moment, and partially because it was inconceivable that Lianne might come hobbling out of that tunnel right now. He risked glancing up just long enough to make sure he wasn't imagining things.

He wasn't. Lianne was limping toward him. Damn those useless fairies! He could barely defend himself out here; how was he going to protect Lianne?

Eubryd seemed to have exactly the same idea. She was hardly more than a little charred heap on top of that damned, overloading machinery right now, but he could see her head perk up just a bit and she paused in her last throes of fire. Damn it, but she was turning her aim away from him toward Lianne. Her weakening flames might be getting less and less effective, but with Nic's diminished strength and Lianne's total lack of defenses, the spiteful wyvern could still do lethal damage to her.

He drew in as much strength as he could and rose up, lunging forward in an attempt to get between Lianne and Eubryd's hateful breath. It was just enough movement to deflect the blast, but it had taken monumental effort. Fortunately, this put him finally in contact range with Eubryd, and she was apparently out of fire.

He swung his huge, heavy head and connected with her tiny body. She screeched as the force of his hit sent her careening off her perch and into the lava pool. The molten rock sizzled as it engulfed her, dragging her down in the space between two precious eggs. In her miserable state, she would never survive the consuming heat. Even a dragon could not survive that. Eubryd was truly gone this time. He felt one involuntary pang of loss, but it was short-lived. She had thrown away years and years of their friendship. He would not grieve for her now.

"Damn it, Lianne. What are you doing out here?" he grumbled, moving toward her as she kept up her steady—but slow—pace toward him.

"I'm coming to save your reptilian ass."

It was getting harder to breathe now. His battle was over and his body was already shutting down. He had failed in his duty to the clutch, as well as to Lianne.

"The fairies were supposed to get you out of here. This machine is going to take out the whole mountain."

"Not if we shut it down first."

"And how the hell are we going to do that? It's sucking up magic faster than ever. I haven't got anything left, but it's still draining the clutch. It can't go on much longer before it overloads."

"Then make love to me, Nic."

He raised up his head to meet her eyes. His body felt cumbersome, limp and too heavy to move. His heart was slowing and his lungs were seizing up. She didn't look like she felt much better, to be honest, yet here she was wanting to get kinky? He could only laugh at her.

"By the Fires, Lianne, I wish I could."

She reached up and pressed her cool hands against his face. "You're hot."

"I've been getting pummeled by fire for the past ten minutes or so."

"But you won. Let's celebrate, Nic. She's gone, there's nobody trying to kill you, and the fairies were kind enough to tell us how to shut off this machine."

He was going to argue, to say there was no way to shut it off now, but he recalled the fairies' words. *Passion.* Passion was the one thing that would disable the machine. Well, it was a nice thought, but he was fresh out of passion right now. Damn it.

"I can't even move, Lianne," he admitted. "I'm sorry, but it's too late. You've got to go, you've got to leave here right now."

She leaned in and pressed her sweet, wounded forehead against his. "Use your mind, Nic. Touch me with your mind. Our souls can make love even when our bodies can't."

He did love her mind. She was so open to him, no secrets hidden, nothing held back. Her mind was open and warm and loving.

It was not anything he was used to. What did he know of love? He was a dragon. Yet when his mind touched hers, he knew there was no doubt. He understood love and he felt it.

I love you too, she said silently.

I don't want to lose you, Lianne.

Then love me. Let me feel what you feel, Nic. You must be able to sense how much I want you.

He did. He could feel her desire as strongly as if it was his own. It *was* his own, actually. It was a thing they both shared equally.

There was no effort needed to touch her with his mind. So he did. His thoughts reached into her and held her, caressed her as if they had no cares in the world.

She touched him back. He felt her mind wrap itself around him, felt her cling to him the way she had done in his bed. The desire stirred deeper and he let her feel that.

He blocked their surroundings, shutting off every sense. If these were their last moments together, they were going to be good ones. He pulled all the energy left in his body and shared it with Lianne.

His mind became a vast, wide space. Nothing was there, only openness and warmth. And Lianne. He could see her, moving toward him, reaching to hold him.

He took her into his arms. Her skin was cool against him, her curves pressed against him in all the right places. He ran his hands over her back, cupping her round bottom and pulling her tighter. His cock was hard and eager for her already. She slid her body against him, the sensations making him grow hotter.

Yes, Nic, that's what I want, she was whispering. *I want you. Make love to me now. I need you, Nic.*

Her breasts bobbed before him, full and perky with pink nipples just begging for his attention. He bent to suckle at one, then the other. She moaned with pleasure, pressing her body tighter against his.

Now her delicate hand found his throbbing member. She grasped him, held his cock as if it were her lifeline for salvation. She stroked him tentatively, cautiously, her emerald eyes bright with expectation and wonder.

Do what you want. You won't harm me, he assured her.

His words seemed to encourage her, so her hold on him grew tighter. Now it was his turn to moan from the sensations. She pulled him closer, her body practically melting into his. He could feel the heat from her core. She was soft and radiating with want. He couldn't hold back anymore.

He hoisted her up and she wrapped her legs around him. They were floating in emptiness, supported by nothing more than their passion and the desire that drove them together. He thrust himself into her, growling with pleasure as her tight, wet body invited him deeper.

He held her there, pushing into her and reveling in the feel of her pushing back. The perfect dance of their union went on, each moment more blissful than the last as desire and love became one with their thoughts, their unspoken communion. She whispered his name over and over, and each time he plunged himself deeper and deeper into her. The passion filled him until it seemed he might burst from it. Still, she was begging for more so he gave it.

She was the one he had spent his life wanting. He'd never been fully empowered, never truly maintained his full strength. Always he'd needed to move on, from one partner to another. This time—finally—he'd found the one who could make him complete and give him what he'd never had.

The power surged within him. She threw her head back and cried out, venting her passion as she came in his arms. He watched her release with amazement and with gratitude. The sight of her so enthralled sent him beyond his own threshold, the climax taking him and carrying him with her to ecstasy.

There were no physical bounds to this passion. It rolled on and on, tossing them over and over as they held on to each other. He was inside her and she was inside him. They were one being, one mass of passion and sensation. He gave her everything that he had and waited for the end to arrive.

He would be content to stay just like this for the rest of their lives.

* * *

She clung to him, her body reacting to his thoughts every bit as much as it had to his physical touch. He was remarkable, and she loved him completely. She barely felt the rough edges of his heated scales, the searing moisture from his breath, or the jagged planes of his beautiful, alien features. She stroked his cheek, traced the long, steaming line of his jaw, and looped her arm over his neck to help hold herself upright. Her body thrilled and sang with the same satisfied electricity she'd felt last night in his bed.

She had to concentrate on breathing while her body regained control of itself. For those few moments, her pain was gone and it was as if she and Nic could go on this way forever. Now, sadly, the sights and sounds around her were starting to infiltrate her private place of bliss, and she would soon, she feared, be saying good-bye.

She didn't feel like dying quite yet and held herself closer to him. He shifted and swept her into his huge, heated embrace. His powerful arms encircled her and she marveled at how deadly they appeared, yet how gentle he was. She leaned her face against his warm chest and studied the metallic sheen of his talons as they rested against her arm. He was so huge that she felt nearly invisible nestled up against him this way. It was wonderful.

"It's no wonder I never felt like my life mattered to anyone," she murmured. "I never had you as a part of it."

"Well, I'm a part of it now, however much more of it you have," he replied.

"Can't be too much," she said, not really caring one way or another at this point. "At least I'll be with you when that machine blows."

"I can't think of anyone I'd rather meet my demise with," he said, almost with a laugh as if it weren't the saddest thing ever that they should finally find each other just when all hope was lost.

"Unless, of course," he added, "we might not be meeting our demise just yet."

She frowned, his words not making sense. What was he saying? She'd gotten used to the idea of dying in his arms here. But, obviously that hadn't happened yet. How much longer could that thing go on? It had been buzzing and humming and sucking up energy and magic like crazy. It couldn't possibly contain too much more before…

"Um, I don't hear the machine anymore," she said after a pause.

"No, it appears that you did it, Lianne. Your insane idea worked. We generated enough passion to short the thing out before it got to critical overload."

"You mean…we're not going to blow up?"

"Not right now, at least."

It was a lot to take in. She had to think about it for a moment before it dawned on her that Nic's voice was sounding a lot stronger now, too. And he was holding her! He could move again, somehow.

"You're getting your strength back," she noted. "Damn it, Nic, we did it! We're not going to die!"

He gave her a playful squeeze and shook his huge head. "No, I guess we're not. Hell, you saved all of us, Lianne."

"It was a team effort, you'll have to admit. I'm pretty sure I couldn't have done that without you."

"And I know I couldn't have done it without you."

She nuzzled against him. "Well, if you're getting your strength back and we're not about to be tragically vaporized, I have a strong suspicion that it won't be too long before you get to do it with me again."

He laughed at her. "Don't get ahead of yourself. There's still that little matter of your injuries we need to deal with. I've still got to find a way to get you medical help."

"Me? What about you? You've been banged up and beat on just as much as I have. See? Look at those burns on your face, and that tear in your wing, and…hell, Nic, did you know there's a huge cut on your shoulder here? You're bleeding a lot. Let me take a look at it. Does it hurt when I—"

He suddenly thrust her away from him. She staggered back in shock, wondering what she did to offend him this way.

"Don't touch it! Damn it, Lianne, you've got my blood on your hands."

"I was just trying to help you, Nic. I'm sorry if I hurt you, but—"

"My blood is poison to you, Lianne. Hell, why didn't I think about that? I was just so damn glad to have you with me, I didn't even think about how messed up I might be. Hurry, wipe it off on something."

He was moving around quickly now, rousing his huge form and nimbly grabbing her hands to examine them. She was startled by his actions and his words, of course, but clearly he was overreacting. Other than smears of rich, scarlet blood staining her hands, she was fine.

"It's okay, it's only a little bit," she assured him, wiping her hands on her slacks and waving them to show him no harm had been done.

Her slacks, however, immediately began to sizzle. Swatches of fabric fell away where the blood had left a trail. She blinked in amazement, and noticed that other patches of her clothing had mysteriously melted away.

"Um, your blood is dissolving my clothes. Is that normal?"

He watched her carefully. "I think it's dissolving the areas where your own blood had already stained your clothes."

"Your blood is attacking *my* blood?"

"I told you it was toxic."

"But I feel just fine," she said, more than a little perplexed.

He studied her, still careful to keep his distance. "What did the fairies do to you, exactly?"

"I don't know. They threw some sparkly dust in the air and the green guy said it would give me extra strength for a while, the gold-colored one said he was something called a Summer Fairy and he was doing whatever it is that he does to make flowers bloom—isn't that a riot?—and the pink one said she'd grant me a wish."

"And what did you wish for?"

She gave him a sly grin for that one. "I wished for lots of really awesome sex with you for the rest of my life. Hell, if wishing for stuff works, then you're kind of stuck with me for a while, I'm afraid!"

"That kind of wishing does work, I assure you. I'm just really at a loss as for how you can still be alive, though."

She shrugged. "They did their Fairy Dust thing and I came in here with you."

"And you touched me," he said. "You must have gotten my blood all over you."

"I wouldn't know. I was kind of a bloody mess already. Seriously, I must look truly disgusting right now."

"You look beautiful. You look…glowing. And hot."

"And you are a terrible liar. I totally do not look glowing *or* hot right now."

"No, I'm serious. Lianne, look at yourself. Your skin…it's glowing. You're becoming red hot!"

He was right. She glanced down at herself and discovered the pores of her skin seemed to be emitting a strange red glow. She was on fire! Her clothes—what was left of them—suddenly burst into flame and burned entirely off her body. She danced around, desperate to get away from them, but oddly enough nothing hurt.

She looked to Nic, frantic for him to tell her things were all right. She felt itchy and prickly all over, and suddenly the heat rolling off the lava pool started to lose its pungent sting. Despite quite literally combusting a minute ago, she felt suddenly chilled. She met Nic's eyes and wondered why he was shrinking in front of her.

No, wait. He wasn't shrinking—she was growing! Her head was suddenly rising higher off the chamber floor. She felt as if she could stand up halfway to the immeasurably high ceiling. She threw her shoulders back and…holy shit, she had wings!

"Oh my God, Nic. What's happening to me?"

He opened his wide dragon mouth to speak but he could not. He rose up with her, his eyes scanning over her head to toe, and his wings unfurling in wonder. She blinked and let out an amazed breath. A puff of steam blew out of her nose.

"Steam, Nic. I've got steam coming out my nose. What the hell is going on?"

"Well, it appears to me you're turning into a dragon."

"A dragon? I can't turn into a dragon! You can turn into a human, but I absolutely cannot turn into a dragon."

"I believe you just did."

"Well, undo it! How did this happen, Nic?"

"I don't know. It must have been the combination of Fairy Dust, wishes, and the dragon blood you got on yourself. It must have mixed with your blood and the magic just let it co-mingle—probably it had something to do with that flower bloom magic, I would guess."

"You would guess? But what does this mean?"

"It means I'm not toxic to you, Lianne. We've got the same blood now."

She was twisting, thrashing her long neck around to look at her terrifying new body from every angle. No matter how she viewed it, she was a dragon, not as dark and scary looking as Nic, but truly a dragon. She had leathery wings, sharp pointy talons, and a long snakelike tail. Damn, but it was going to take her a while to get used to *that*.

"Do I…do I look okay like this?"

He laughed at her again and she noticed that the heat behind his scales flamed brighter. "Yes. You do. You are one very sexy dragon."

"Don't lie to me, Nic. If I'm some dumpy, awkward-looking dragon, you'd better tell me now."

"You are beautiful, Lianne. I promise. If you'd like, though, I can teach you how to return to your usual form. It won't be easy at first, but you'll get the hang of it."

"So I don't have to always look like this? Well, that's a relief. Not that *you* don't rock the dragon skin, but…damn it, Nic, how the hell did I turn into a dragon?"

"Maybe we'll find those fairies again someday and force them to tell us."

"Do you think we can make them reverse this?"

"Do you want them to?"

She had to pause for a moment at that. Did she want them to? This was quite a lot to take in all at once, sure, but if she let herself think about it for a little bit maybe it wasn't so frightening, after all.

Nic was a dragon. He was one hell of a dragon, actually, and she was crazy for him. He was still running his eyes over her and he didn't look at all freaked out by the dramatic change in her appearance. He liked it, in fact, and she didn't need telepathy to know what the steamy look in his eye and the lazy smoke seeping out of him meant.

But if she was a dragon now, then she would have that telepathy thing. He could teach her to do his mind-control trick! And if she wanted to go shopping for cute shoes, she could still do that once she mastered the knack of changing her form. Most of all, she and Nic could be together wherever he needed to be. She could stay here with him and take care of his clutch.

And there would be lots and lots of ragingly hot sex, that went without saying.

"Yeah. *Lots* of hot sex," he assured her, obviously reading her thoughts.

"I think I'm kind of warming up to this," she said. "I can't really see a downside. This might not be a bad way to spend my last few months."

"Sorry, I have to correct you there," he said, shaking his head.

"What, you think this will alter my life expectancy now?"

"I do. Dragons live for centuries, my dear."

"Dragons like *you* live for centuries, Nic. *I'm* kind of a special case," she reminded him, tapping her head where that damn brain tumor waited to ruin all the fun.

He just smiled at her and puffed out a white smoke ring. "There's one more detail you ought to know, darling."

"Oh? What's that, pookey bear?"

"Dragons don't get cancer."

No cancer? Oh hell, yes. She was totally on board.

"Okay. I'm sold. If you're feeling up to it, buddy, you'd better either teach me how to shift back into my regular body, or tell me where dragons keep their erogenous zones, because you and I are sooooo going to party right now."

Chapter Twenty-Five

Raea made herself comfortable in the tuft of moss in the sheltered cleft of a rock where she and Kyne had decided to rest and wait out the last bits of the storm. They'd used so much of their dust on assisting the woman that they would need to fly home using wind currents rather than magic. It was worth it, though. By all appearances, their efforts worked. She glanced back toward the distant silhouette of the mountain.

"Still no sign of an explosion," she noted.

"But of course," Kyne said with a yawn. "You grant good wishes. I'm sure everything worked out just fine for them. Now settle in here and get some rest. We're out of dust, so it'll be a long journey home."

"Swift said we should have no trouble getting to the land of the Celts," she pointed out. "He says there are plenty of local fairies there to give us some dust for the rest of the way."

"If we think we can trust that. I'm not ready to put Swift on my list of best friends."

"I know he wasn't very nice to us before, but maybe he's changing," she offered.

Kyne grunted in response. She decided to drop the subject. Their green companion had returned to his ship, insisting that he wouldn't mention anything about them or what had really happened inside the mountain. He planned to say that unknown forces had destroyed the equipment and everyone inside the mountain. Clearly that place was too dangerous to return to.

Raea and Kyne had gone to the jobsite where the humans had been staging their research on the mountain and surrounding areas. They used the last bit of their dust to allow seeds of panic to germinate among the group, convincing them all that the mountain was unstable and that cave-ins had taken the lives of all three humans who had gone there. No doubt the project would be canceled and the humans would vacate the area. The clutch of dragon eggs would be safe. Nic and his human would survive their ordeal, and the plot against the dragons would fail.

But now Raea's eyes were heavy and she could hardly keep them open. Kyne was right. She really should get some rest. The sun was already up over the horizon, breaking through the clouds as they swirled and dissipated overhead. Soon it would be fully daylight. They would travel then. It would be warmer, and their auras would not glow so conspicuously when they approached populated areas. She snuggled closer to Kyne and took his hand.

"I hope she'll be okay with him," she mused.

"You saw how they looked at each other," he replied, wrapping his other arm around her. "She'll be fine."

"How do you suppose our magic will work on her? We didn't heal her, you know."

"We bought her some time. Who knows how the human body will react to magic? She was pretty clear in her wish, so at least that much will work in her favor."

Raea nodded. "A human and a dragon. Who would have thought?"

"It seems like the world is full of unlikely pairs."

She studied him, his strong features, the size of his not fully fairylike hands, the beautiful golden glow that surrounded him. She would have never guessed she could love him this much, yet she did. Somehow, against all the odds, they'd found each other.

"We're not so very unlikely," she said. "You and I. Neither of us quite fit the life we tried to belong in, but we fit each other perfectly."

His eyes had been shut but he cracked them open enough to look down at her. He smiled, his fingers trailing over the sensitive skin at her shoulder and collarbone.

"Sometimes we need a little help from Sizing Powder to fit entirely perfectly," he commented.

"I know," she whispered, kissing his ear. "I saved us just a little bit of it."

"By the Skies, I do love you." He pulled her more tightly into his arms and brought her lips up to meet his.

She kissed him with all of her soul. "Now that sounds entirely perfect."

Please turn the page for a preview of the next novella in the Forbidden Realm series,

By the Enchantment of Moonlight.

Available early 2016

Chapter One

It was good to be back in the familiar Fairyrealm. Summer was lush and green here, a far cry from the cold, bleak terrain Swift had encountered in Iceland. As a fairy, Swift had not been negatively affected by the harsh weather in that desolate land, but his recent assignment had been unsettling, to say the least.

Swift had seen far too many disturbing things...*felt* too many disturbing things. He was still not quite sure what to do about them, either. He had devoted his life to serving the Fairy Council and what he had been taught that they stood for. Now not only had his perception of that changed, but his body seemed to have been altered as well.

These new, unusual sensations concerned him. Had his unexpected close proximity to humans on his assignment caused some damage to his system? Perhaps it was only temporary. Perhaps being home, away from corrupting influences, would purge his mind and his body of the unwanted thoughts, the vile urges that had crept over him lately. The last thing he needed was to be a fairy who struggled with the most forbidden of flaws—a fairy who knew passion.

His promotion to full agent within the Department of Restraint and Obedience had been something he'd long worked for. He hadn't questioned the council when his first assignment had seemed somewhat out of the ordinary. He probably should have, though.

By the Skies, what had he discovered? He couldn't make sense of it, but he knew what he had seen: fairies secretly working with humans and strange machinery that affected the very fabric of magic. Even the ancient and illusive dragons had been involved! Yet the council assured him it was all perfectly safe and necessary. If only he could believe them.

But he couldn't. It was nearly impossible to know what he *could* believe anymore. He'd thought it a high calling to serve the council, to track destructive behavior and rogue fairies like Kyne and his sneaky little friend Raea...but nothing was certain now. Swift was unaccustomed to questioning himself or the council. Today, though...

"I can see that you're feeling a sense of inner conflict," Dorn, the Council Leader, was saying as his regal, gray aura emanated around him.

It was an understatement, of course, but Swift dodged the question. "There is no evidence to prove that Pimma helped the fugitive Kyne escape. You've questioned her enough, Dorn. Why has she not been given back her magic?"

"The council is restricting her magical privilege for her own good. We've not taken away her wings, simply her access to Fairy Dust."

"Which she needs to go about her daily life. How is she to protect herself if humans wander into our Realm?"

"The usual safeguards will protect her, as they do all of us."

"And if they don't? You forget, Dorn, that I was made privy to some of the council's concerns."

He was careful not to speak any specifics, but Dorn would know exactly what he meant. Something was happening; magic did not have the strength that it once did. The powerful Veil that kept the human world separate and unaware of their Forbidden Realm was failing. The council had tried to keep it a secret, but with their drastic decision to involve certain humans in an effort to bolster the magic that kept the Veil in place, every day they were in increasing danger.

"The council has decided that Pimma must be considered a suspect. There is simply no other way that renegade Kyne could have broken free from our custody," Dorn said with firm finality.

Swift was careful not to let his disgust show on his face. If anyone in this Realm was innocent of wrongdoing, it was Pimma. The very idea of holding her on suspicion was ludicrous. And very likely illegal.

"Who is her advocate?" he asked.

"She's not been formally charged with anything, Swift."

"Fairy Code specifically states that any fairy who is held under suspicion by council will be allowed an Advocate for the Accused. I believe Pimma is the designated advocate for our Realm, but she can't very well advocate for herself, can she? So who have you assigned to be advocate for her?"

"By the Skies, Swift, these are tenuous times. Exceptions must be made."

Exceptions? All the years Swift had defended the council, danced to their bidding without thought or question, not once had he seen Dorn allow for any exceptions. Now Dorn was calling for the council to be exempted from their own law? No, Swift couldn't go for that. Things had gone too far; he couldn't convince himself the leaders knew best. He'd seen what had come of their secret plans and unquestioned alliances.

It had led to humans playing with magic, veiled creatures battling among themselves, and fairies dallying in passion and desire. No wonder the Veil was shredding around them. Magic was mingling with the mundane, and the Forbidden Realm was falling apart. Clearly, until he knew where things stood here in his own local Fairyrealm, Swift could not allow for exceptions. Of any sort.

"I would like to see her." He met Dorn's eye and waited for an answer.

"You want to see Pimma?" the leader questioned.

"Yes. Now."

Dorn scowled. He clearly did not like having his judgment or his actions

questioned, but he knew Swift well enough to obviously not bother argu-
ing.

"Very well. I'll take you to her."

"No. You'll have her brought to me. You've had more than enough time
to determine that she is not a threat, not a part of Kyne's rogue activities. If
you have cause to pass judgment on her, then you would have assigned her
an advocate and followed procedures."

"But she could be in league with—"

"She isn't, but if she is, I will take full responsibility. Bring her here and
set her free, Dorn. Prove to us all that the Fairy Code still means something
here, that our leaders have not given up on the stability of our Realm."

"Fairyrealm will go on forever. We are the very heart of the Forbidden
Realm."

"Exactly. So what could any of us possibly have to fear from some junior
advocate who was betrayed by one of the first fairies she ever represented?"

"Unless she had a hand in that betrayal," Dorn added.

"Then we will learn that when she tries to contact him. I promise you,
Dorn, if there are things we can learn from her, we won't learn them while
you've got her locked up in some magicless room."

Dorn clearly wasn't fully convinced, but he'd obviously lost the battle.
He cocked his gray head to one side and scowled at Swift. "You will assume
responsibility for her?"

"I will. Now send for her and let's make this right."

* * *

The door to Pimma's subterranean holding cell swung open. She'd been
stretching her wings and wondering if she'd ever actually get the chance to
use them again. The interruption caused her to jump. It wasn't mealtime.
What was going on? The young fairy who served as Dorn's aide peered in
at her and announced that she was being requested.

"What does the Council Leader need with me now?" she asked.

The aide shrugged and simply ordered her to follow him, so she did. He led the way up the narrow, muddy steps into the neat interior of the Council Hall. Pimma blinked when sunlight through the tall, narrow windows met her eyes. Her wings fairly vibrated as warmth and magic slowly seeped back into her body. It felt so good to be aboveground and to feel the familiar tingle of magic and freedom. She wasn't ready to be too optimistic, though.

"Good afternoon, Dorn," she said as the Council Leader met her in the main corridor. "Or good morning, or whatever it is. Sorry, but I haven't exactly been keeping track."

"The sun has not yet reached zenith," Dorn replied. "I'm glad to see you're looking well."

She knew she did not look well at all. Her skin was pale and practically translucent, without a hint of her opalescent sheen. Her wings were sagging and crumpled, and her usual blue glow had faded to practically nothing. Dorn had just added "liar" to the long list of things about him that she'd recently found horribly disappointing.

"Have you brought me up here to finally charge me with something?" she asked, squinting into the brightness and trying to discern the identity of the other fairy in the corridor with them. She could see his colorless silhouette against the glaring light through the high windows above the grand entrance to the hall, but his broad-winged form was unfamiliar to her.

Until he spoke. Then she recognized him immediately.

"You are being released," he informed her.

Swift. He stepped forward and now she could make out his features. Well formed and powerful, he was the pride of the Department of Restraint and Obedience. He looked her over, top to toe, but she would be wasting time if she tried to read any emotion into his expression. He was too careful to give away anything that might be in his thoughts. Likewise, every inch of his solid body was a study in control. His deep, emerald-tipped wings were poised for instant action, yet Swift's movement was smooth and relaxed.

As always, he set her completely off balance.

"I'm being released?" she asked, just to make sure she'd heard correctly.

Dorn replied rather grandly. "Yes. I've determined that you pose no immediate threat. You will be returned to regular duty, so long as you cooperate with us should we have any future questions for you."

"Of course I'll cooperate," she said and probably wasn't quite as successful as keeping her tone perfectly measured as Swift would have been. "I've *been* cooperating, Dorn, even though you've handled me like some sort of criminal."

"We had to be certain you weren't involved in Kyne's escape," Dorn replied, as if that was any sort of explanation for the uncivilized treatment she'd gotten.

"So what finally convinced you?" she asked.

"I did," Swift said. "But until *I'm* totally convinced, you and I will be spending some time together."

Together? Oh no. That would not be good. She didn't like Swift. He annoyed her, with his smug confidence and overly cool attitude about everything. He made her feel...small, incompetent, a little bit silly, even. She hadn't been forced to work with him often in her short tenure here before all this mess, but the time she had spent with him was unsettling. He made her feel something very strange inside; something she didn't know and couldn't understand even a little bit. *Together* was not something she wanted to be with Swift.

"I don't need a babysitter," she informed him.

"I hope that's true," he replied. "It shouldn't take me long to verify everything you've told the council. Then we can all rest easy and get back to our business, right?"

Somehow, she doubted getting back to her business would be so very easy for her. Dorn may have suddenly come to his senses and realized that she knew nothing about how her client, Kyne, escaped confinement here, but it wasn't going to be so simple for Pimma to forget being locked up—without magic—for days on end. Underground, of all places! She hadn't even known the Council Hall had subterranean areas. Now she knew them too well.

"How about if I get my Fairy Dust privileges back, for starters?"

Dorn smiled at her like she was a petulant child begging for another honey drop. "Of course. Swing by distribution and collect what you need for your next assignment."

"And just what is my next assignment?"

"In the city," Dorn replied. "We have a report of unusual Fairy Dust usage and possible detection by humans."

"Not another complaint about that Wish Fairy again," Swift grumbled.

"No, not this time," Dorn replied. "My associate Wain received a report of unusual activity and has gone to investigate."

"Wain? He's not a qualified agent. What's he investigating?"

"I don't have the details, but he's been watching this business for some time. It's a human organization…something called Sandstrom Industries."

Pimma noticed Swift's lip twitch just a bit. Did recognition flash over his face when Dorn mentioned that company? Pimma couldn't be sure. Swift was such a puzzle to her it was impossible to know what he might be thinking. Maybe that dark gleam in his eye was nothing more than excitement at the prospect of heading out to hunt down another wayward fairy.

"Look into this matter with him," Dorn was saying. "If there is a fairy out there acting carelessly, help Wain find him. Bring him—or her—into custody. Pimma, this will be a perfect opportunity for you to prove your loyalty and get back to work. As you know, the council is taking all Forbidden Realm infractions very seriously right now. When we find this offender, the sooner he's assigned an advocate, the sooner we can process him."

Process him? More likely Dorn really meant *convict him.* Obviously their esteemed Council Leader had already decided the guilt of this unnamed fairy he was sending them after. Pimma had a pretty good idea just how Dorn expected her to prove herself, and it would not include assuring her newest client a fair and impartial hearing. What on earth could be going on that Dorn was so willing to ignore proper procedures?

She bit her tongue and listened quietly as Swift got the details on this situation. There weren't many. Dorn's associate Wain seemed to have given him little more than suspicion, yet he was proceeding as if a proper determination had been made. This was all highly unorthodox.

No formal investigation had been made, no report was on file, and Wain was in no way qualified to be hunting fairies out in the human world. Pimma felt more than a little bit awkward taking part in this, but obviously she didn't have much of a choice. To argue with Dorn now could very likely get her stuck in the basement again. Not much of an option either way.

Swift didn't seem to be quite as conflicted over the ethics of the situation as she was. He gathered the information they'd need to go locate their target and didn't even bat a wing when no item of proof could be offered to uphold Wain's supposed suspicions. Apparently he was every bit as willing to ignore rules and procedures as Dorn. That surprised her.

She'd thought better of Swift. All those things that made him off-putting and smug also made him kind of noble. Of anyone she knew, Swift seemed the one she would have most expected to question Dorn's hasty assignment. She'd even respected him for this, just a little bit. Now she didn't very much like him *and* she didn't respect him. How disappointing.

She kept her feelings to herself, though, and wisely pretended to be in complete agreement with Dorn's direction. She even smiled sweetly for Swift and gave her blue wings a little flutter when he held the door of the Council Hall to invite her out into the fresh air and sunshine for the first time in weeks. It was wonderful—almost enough to make her forget all the anger and wariness.

"Don't get any ideas about leaving me," he said firmly, a healthy reminder that the mistrust she felt was a mutual thing.

"I wouldn't dream of it," she replied. "At least, not until after I collect my new Fairy Dust."

"Dorn expects me to keep an eye on you, so that's what I intend to do," Swift warned her. "You'd be smart not to balk at that."

"Would it make any difference if I did?"

"No. For your own good, I'm not letting you out of my sight."

"For my own good, huh?"

They'd been walking silently over the thick moss that carpeted the ground here in their protected little village deep in the undergrowth of a humanless forest. The few little buildings needed for the daily management of fairy life circled the little mossy clearing, tucked up against the roots of ancient trees and hidden by nature as well as by magic. Humans rarely made it this deep into the forest, but if they did, magic would blind their eyes to the tiny village and the glittering creatures who lived there.

At least, fairies were supposed to be glittering. Pimma was sadly dull and lackluster right now, having lost her Fairy Dust and being separated from magic for so long. She didn't care about Swift's warning to stay by his side. If he wanted to keep an eye on her, he'd just have to pick up his pace. She couldn't move fast enough to get to the bark-covered round hut that served as the Dust Distribution Office.

"The best way to get Dorn to leave you alone is to let me assure him you're on his side," Swift said, matching her step easily.

She paused, glaring at him. "On his side? What other side is there? Aren't we all on the same side?"

"No, Pimma. We're not. Soon you'll have to decide where you stand on things."

"You mean, on things like this so-called assignment we're being sent off on? I can't believe you're not questioning the justice of it. Dorn thinks some fairy was a little bit sloppy with his dust and he's treating it like a crime."

"Nobody has said there's been any crime."

"You're an enforcer and I'm an advocate. Since when do we get assigned to anything other than a crime?"

He narrowed his green eyes and studied her. She narrowed her eyes and studied him back. What was really going on here? What had she missed while Dorn was keeping her locked up in the council's basement? Why did Swift suddenly talk Dorn into releasing her today?

"I guess we'll just have to go find out what sort of crime has been committed," Swift said.

"You already sound certain there is one."

"I am," he said but, as usual, what he really meant by his words was impossible for her to discern.

No sense wasting time. She'd never figure Swift out. Maybe once they found their target and had a chance to talk to him, she could at least determine what was going on there. "I guess we'll have to meet up with Dorn's associate to find out anything more. I can't even guess why Wain would be involved in something like this investigation."

"I can."

She waited for Swift to elaborate, but he didn't. He simply nodded toward the distribution hut. She shrugged. By the Skies, it would feel good to have her glitter back.

Chapter Two

They had found a broken window and entered the cavernous factory warehouse that Dorn directed them to. Discolored skylights allowed pale rays from the noon sun to filter in, leaving the area dusty and dim. This seemed an unlikely place to find a fairy, but after some of the strange human and fairy interactions Swift had seen on his last assignment, he realized nothing would surprise him.

He motioned for Pimma to follow him to a shadowy spot atop a tall stack of shipping crates. They could settle in and scan their surroundings from here. The subtle buzz of their wings was the only sound he could detect, so Swift held up his hand to remind Pimma to stay otherwise silent.

Her none-too-subtle eye roll did not go unnoticed. It was more than a little obvious she would have been anywhere else than here right now with him. Or perhaps it was just the "with him" part that she would have rather been without. She wasn't going to be declaring herself his very best friend anytime soon, that much was certain.

And that was fine with him. He wasn't the sort to keep many friends. In his position, friends were often a liability. He needed to keep his judgment clear and his loyalties certain. Right now, he was having more than enough difficulties with both of those. The last thing he needed was a friend.

Especially not an uppity novice like Pimma. She was too young, too naive, and far too…feminine. As a creature of the Forbidden Realm, he wasn't supposed to be aware of those particular attributes. Gender was a human concern, not something for fairies to consider. He was above that. Magic kept him beyond the taint of human lusts. At least, that was the way it was supposed to be.

Lately, he'd been feeling decidedly tainted. Pimma's fluttering, feminine presence had caught his attention in all the wrong ways. He'd never known this sort of awareness, and he shoved the stray thoughts back with all of his might. Fairies were not human. They did not give themselves over to things like that. They did not glance at their partner and notice that the sheer cloth of her iridescent blouse clung so tightly to her form that he could clearly see the perfect form of her breasts, the tempting curve at her tiny waist, and the luscious flare of her hips. By the Skies, a decent fairy would never let his thoughts linger on such things. He wouldn't find himself going hot in sensitive places like this, either.

Something had happened to him. His control was slipping; he was becoming helpless to deny these changes. Unwelcome changes. If he didn't get his wayward thoughts under command right now, though, Pimma might become aware of these unwelcome changes, too.

His groin was on fire and he could feel himself hard as a rock. Desire was burning inside him, and his body craved things he could not have. By the Skies, he had to find a way to make it stop. Now.

"Look, someone's coming," Pimma said, laying a hand on his shoulder and nearly scalding him with her light touch.

He tore his mind from the scorching sensation and glanced in the direction she indicated. Sure enough, there was movement at the far end of the row of shipping crates. Two forms came into view, their footsteps echoing on the concrete floor. One was a generally attractive human female Swift had never seen before, but the other was a fairy he recognized easily. Wain.

"But we can't do anything until we have McGowan," Wain was saying.

He had assumed a large, human-sized form, and he walked beside the human, his wing tips idly brushing the rows of crates as he moved. Dirt particles and cobwebs swirled in lazy, neglected circles around them, glittering like weak Fairy Dust in the pale light. Whatever this warehouse was, it did not see much use. Clearly Wain and his human companion did not intend to encounter anyone here.

"Crandall McGowan has gone off to Iceland," the woman snapped sharply. "You heard what happened there. He went to find out what happened to his daughter. We can only hope he doesn't figure anything out while he's gone."

Swift instantly latched onto the woman's words. She had mentioned Iceland! But who was this McGowan she spoke of? Somehow that name was familiar. Clearly whatever was going on here had something to do with the things Swift had encountered on his previous assignment. There was no way this could be pure coincidence.

"There's no telling how long McGowan will be gone. Should I tell some of my associates to go take care of him?" Wain asked.

The woman merely gave him a scathing look. "If I wanted him dead I'd do that myself. No, we still need him. This will just delay us awhile."

"The council said we don't have room for any more delays. Things are worse than they knew—the Veil is in grave danger. We need the equipment in place and running immediately."

Suddenly the woman's contemptuous expression was gone. She flashed dark, almond eyes and smiled a sultry smile. The effect on Wain was obvious. He stood as if frozen in place while the woman traced one long, elegant finger along the side of his jaw.

"Now, Wain, don't be so impatient. You know I always keep my promises, don't I?"

"Yes, but the council—"

"Stop worrying so much about the council. They don't know everything that's going on, do they?"

Now her fingers trailed over the nervous fairy's chest and down toward his belt. She tugged at the clasp there.

"Miranda…you know we can't do this," he said with obvious strain in his voice.

"Of course we can, just like we could do this the last time we met here, and the time before that," she replied.

"If the council finds out…"

She was practically purring as her eyes and fingers continued their exploration. "Like I said, they don't know everything, and they don't need to. Come on, Wain, you know you can do things to me no one else can. I've been waiting so long to see you again. Don't make me wait any longer."

"I thought we were here to handle some of the equipment issues?"

"How about if I handle *your* equipment?" the woman cooed at him.

She wasn't about to let this be merely a suggestion, either. Swift heard Pimma draw in a shocked gasp as the woman practically threw Wain against the row of crates and rubbed her shapely human body completely against him. His quivering blue-green wings splayed out against the crates and he seemed completely helpless as she forced herself on him.

"We should go help him!" Pimma hissed in a whisper.

Swift wasn't quite sure how to explain to her that it had been fairly obvious—despite Wain's frail protests—that he did not really want any help. At least, not the kind of help Pimma was suggesting. As the woman's hands stole inside Wain's clothing, he groaned in aching pleasure. Swift cursed under his breath as his own traitorous body responded with a fiery need he would have given anything to be able to ignore.

"What is she doing to him?" Pimma murmured.

Swift would have given anything to be able to ignore that, too. Her voice was soft and breathy, and so very close to his ear that he could feel the heat from her lithe body. Her wing brushed his, sending additional unwanted sizzle through him. She had no idea, of course, the effect she was having, what watching the groping forms just a few yards away did to him.

His throat was dry and painfully constricted. That was nothing compared to the ache in his groin. He could not trust himself to give her a quiet, intelligible answer.

"Is she seducing him?" Pimma gulped.

Indeed, she was. This Miranda woman was touching Wain in places that would have sent any human male into sexual frenzy. A fairy, however, should have been unaffected, protected from lust and desire by his magic and his very nature. It was obvious, though, that this fairy was very much affected. Not only was he allowing the woman to pleasure him now, but he had begun to willfully participate. Clearly this was not his first time dabbling in such disgusting human activity.

Wain wrapped the woman in his arms, grasping her fleshy buttocks and grinding himself into her. From their perch high up on the crates, Swift did not actually see what was transpiring where those two bodies pressed tightly together, but he could well imagine. The woman's short skirt rode up higher and higher as her hips began a rhythmic gyration that was hypnotizing to watch.

"Now I believe Wain is seducing *her*," Pimma commented softly.

Swift nodded. That was all he could do. Wain was thumping loudly against the crate behind him as he thrust and thrust again, driving himself into the woman and clutching her tightly against him. Swift clenched and unclenched his own fists as Wain kneaded his woman's tight skin. He tasted blood. By the Skies, but he bit into his own cheek, desperate to maintain control as the sound and the sight of this wanton lovemaking surrounded them and fed his torrid desire.

Finally Wain groaned loudly. His features contorted and he arched against the woman. She sighed loudly, if not a bit overly dramatic.

"You are magical, Wain," she murmured. "I came so hard for you."

Wain was panting. "Did you? Did I take you all the way there, Miranda?"

"Oh, yeah. You're amazing. But—" She paused, pushing herself away from him and pulling her skirt down. "Like you said, we don't want to get caught here. Why don't you go clean yourself up and then we can get back to business. These boxes won't ship themselves, you know."

"Right. Of course." Wain was stammering, putting his clothing back in order and trying to regain his balance. "We've got business here."

He grabbed Miranda and pulled her to him for one quick kiss before she shoved him away.

"Go, hurry up now," she ordered.

He nodded, but wasted a few seconds more just staring at her, shaking his head. "You are so amazing, Miranda. I can't believe you chose me, over everyone else."

"Yeah, only you, Wain. Nobody else does me like you. Now go wipe yourself off."

He shuffled off and she was left alone, patting her still impeccable hair and smiling smugly. Swift was only now beginning to be able to breathe again, so he was just about to suggest to Pimma that they make a hasty exit when the woman turned and glanced up in their direction. Her smile increased as her eyes darkened.

"So, little fairies, did you enjoy the show?"

Please turn the page for an excerpt from the first book in Serena Gilley's Forbidden Realm series,

Kissed by the Wave.

Available now!

Chapter One

Aliya flipped her fins and let the cool water of the lake glide over her. The moonlight glittered like tiny stars in the lapping waves. Her pale hair fanned around her, then fell slick against her naked skin as she pushed up through the surface, scanning the skyline and finding the large, familiar shape.

A boat—a very specific boat. *He* was here again. She knew he would be. After all, she was a mermaid; her mind sensed things like that. When this human was near, she could feel his presence. Her people generally did not reach their minds out to touch the humans who came onto the lake, but something about this man was different. Aliya had felt his thoughts, the burning pain and aching emptiness deep inside him, and it had triggered something inside her. She'd yearned to know more.

For nearly two cycles of the moon now she'd watched him, tracked his movements in the evenings when he would leave the safety of the human shore and venture into her world on his big, gleaming boat. Every time, she'd felt his suffering. She could not explain why this man's emotions should touch her in such a way, but she had come to expect it. He was here now and she had to get closer.

Yes, she could feel him more strongly now. Strange, it was almost as if this human—this man—were reaching out for her, trying to touch her in some way...but of course he could not be. Everyone knew humans did not possess powers like that. She must be imagining it.

To make sure she was not, she stilled herself and opened her mind to let his emotion flood her. Yes, she could feel the familiar ache she always sensed from him, knew the emptiness that filled him. He did touch her, but he clearly had no awareness of it. And his touch reached more than just her mind. Her body felt something, too.

The velvety scales of her lower body tingled...the satin skin of her arms and her breasts pricked with sensation. She went rigid, floating helplessly as her body responded to sensations she could never put into words. They were energizing, delicious...and forbidden. Whatever she felt from this human, whatever he did to her, it was not something she ought to encourage.

She liked it, though. She wanted more. The Great Code of all creatures in the Forbidden Realm dictated she avoid any sort of interaction like this. It was bad enough that she'd come so near this same human on numerous occasions, but to let his mind and emotions touch her in such a way...she knew it was wrong. Still, it drew her like a moth to an inferno.

She was near his vessel now. The crystal surface of the water changed and distorted her view, but she could see him. He was tall and broad, standing alone to gaze out over the water. His shirtless form was solid against the night sky and moonlight glowed off his bronze skin. She broke through the thin surface of the water. He would see her.

The Veil could not protect her tonight, not while the man was so empty and so very lost. Usually she made sure when she needed to approach humans that they were occupied, busy with their mundane concerns that kept the Veil firmly over their eyes. If they caught sight of her they shrugged it off as a shadow, a fish, or a shift in the current. All her life she'd been careful that way; she knew her place.

But tonight...the feelings were too strong. The man needed her and she needed him. She needed to learn what it was that drew her to him, that made her feel hot and shivery all at the same time. She needed to let him see through the Veil and recognize her for what she was.

Her movement caught his attention. Her heart pounded as she felt the cool air on her skin, the damp weight of her pale hair lying against her neck. Unfiltered moonlight glittered off the wet droplets at her eyelashes. She blinked, determined to see clearly when finally his eyes met hers.

And they did. He saw her at last and she gazed steadily at him. It was too dark to know the color of his eyes, but she did not need her telepathy to read the astonishment in them.

"Where in the world did you come from?" he asked.

She was suddenly afraid. No human had ever spoken to her before! Instinct told her to get away from this place as quickly as possible. Humans brought danger and destruction; she was in peril right now. Why was she not filled with panic?

Another instinct—something deeper, ancient, and unfamiliar—told her to stay. She would obey that one. She would remain where she was, allowing the human to gaze at her. And somehow she would find a way to answer in a language he might know. If only she could find her tongue.

"Are you stranded here?" he asked when she made no reply. "Do you need help?"

His astonishment was turning to concern. She liked how that felt, the warmth it conveyed and the tremors of care he sent out around him. He needed to be reassured, though, so he did not worry in vain. Despite how pleasant it was to feel those emotions directed toward her, it was not fair to leave him in such uncertainty.

But her reply was interrupted before it even left her lips. The human was not alone. It appeared he had a companion with him, a partner. A human female moved into view, sliding up beside him as he stood at the railing.

Aliya's mind was only vaguely aware of her. The woman transmitted very minimal vibrations of sensation and emotion. It was obvious enough what she wanted, though. She paid no mind to the water or the mermaid just below her. Instead, her attention was fully on the man as she ran her hands over his body and murmured into his ear.

Aliya could feel the man's reaction, visceral and immediate. His eyes left her and he blinked, as if rousing himself from a sleep. The woman ran her fingers through his wind-tousled hair and he turned to her. The cold emptiness washed over Aliya once again.

"Who are you talking to?" the woman cooed at the man.

He hesitated before answering. "No one. I thought I saw…no, nothing. We're all alone."

The woman murmured some more and the man pulled her tight up against himself. He did not look back over the lake. His pain resonated in the waters around Aliya even as he led the woman out of view, inside the boat's body. It was not difficult to guess what would happen next. Aliya knew the man's pattern.

He came out to the lake to escape whatever it was that plagued him. He brought females with him, women he seemed to know little about and cared little for. He distracted himself with the women, playing at games of human passions that both fascinated and confused Aliya. As the man's emptiness attracted her, the inevitable passion drew her to stay.

Just as she did now. She pushed up next to the boat, touching its smooth polished side and waiting for the sensations from inside the boat to travel out to her. Yes, as expected, there they were. The man and his woman were beginning the strange dance of coupling that humans engaged in.

Aliya shut her eyes, letting vibration surround her, reaching her mind up to connect with the man. She could feel what he felt, the building sense of longing and burning desire. She was rocked by the waves even as the humans rocked up above her.

Slowly she became aware of something else…someone else. Someone was coming! She could feel the magic coming closer. She pulled away from the boat and blinked up into the sky. There, she was just in time to notice the small, nonhuman form that glittered above. A fairy, her pink glow reflecting off the sides of the craft and her tiny wings humming, was hovering.

"Come to visit the human again?" the little creature asked. "Not that I blame you. He is pretty interesting, this one."

Aliya tried to calm her beating heart and hide her nervous tail flicking. She splashed a few droplets of water up toward her friend.

"Raea! You're looking especially sparkly tonight."

"You seem to be glowing a bit yourself. Anything unusual going on?"

"No, of course not. I'm simply patrolling these waters and thought I'd make sure things were going well with this vessel."

The fairy buzzed up to peer in through one of the circular windows on the boat. "Oh, things seem to be going very well for the humans, I'd say."

Aliya shook out her hair and hoped her color was fading back to normal. She hoped the glow Raea mentioned was gone, too, although parts of her still felt a bit tingly.

"And how are things going for you?" Aliya asked, eager to take the focus off what the humans were doing, and how she was apparently affected by it. "You've been called out here to grant wishes, I suppose."

"I'm a Wish Fairy; it's what I do. These humans start wishing, so I sprinkle a little dust and give them what they want."

Aliya didn't need to ask what the human wanted tonight. She could feel it. He wanted to do things with his female—things that made him forget his pain and numbed him by those exotic human sensations. Sensations that would then be transmitted through the waves.

Sensations that a mermaid had no business being curious about.

"It's good to know your Fairy Dust is so reliable," Aliya said. "But he's probably done wishing for the night."

"Him? Maybe not. Seems like he's got extra stamina or something. Not that I'm any kind of expert on this sweaty human recreation."

"He's extra lonely."

"What do you know about that? You have some dealings with this human?"

"No...not at all. It's just that I've seen him out here on the lake before. I can sense how alone he feels, that's all."

"Well, you'd better keep that mermaid telepathy to yourself. The Fairy Council has been cracking down lately on questionable interactions, and I know they're generally in close agreement with the mermaid leadership. You don't want to find yourself being accused of anything, Aliya."

"I haven't done anything! I am careful around humans."

Mostly. There was something so alluring, so out of the ordinary about this human...

"Well, just be careful that you don't...shh, someone's here."

Aliya glanced up in the direction of Raea's quick gaze. A faint red-gold light reflected off the water. It appeared roughly the same size as the Wish Fairy's pink glow and was moving toward them. Another fairy. Great. What could have drawn this one out here?

"It's Kyne," Raea said softly. She didn't seem particularly pleased about it, either.

"A friend of yours?"

"Hardly. He's in league with the Fairy Council, spying on us, keeping tabs on how we do our jobs. You'd better go. As you can see, everything is fine on the boat. No sense getting mixed up with Kyne."

Aliya knew the fairy was right. She'd never been one to pay much attention to Forbidden Realm politics, and she was happy to remain blissfully uninvolved. If this Kyne was some sort of spy for the council, trying to make trouble, she wanted no part of it. As far as anyone needed to know, she'd been simply doing her job, keeping the Veil secure and separating the human's mundane world from their own.

The Veil was a magical force that ensured protection for creatures like fairies and mermaids. Humans had no idea it even existed, and that was the way it had been for millennia. If she were suspected of allowing a human to see through the Veil, to become aware of their Realm...well, that would certainly upset things.

"All right, I'll go," she said to the fairy. "It was good to see you again, Raea. Enjoy the rest of your wishes tonight."

The fairy nodded and shushed her away. Aliya sank into the dark waters. She would leave. It was the right thing to do. She would swim away and pay no more special attention to the man on this boat. She'd go about her duties, keeping things quiet and secure out here in her section of the Great Lake. She would ignore how he reached out to her, would ignore the forbidden things that her body felt when she was near him. She would go and never come near him again.

At least, she would do that after a little while. It certainly wouldn't hurt to stay nearby right now, just in case Raea's wishes were not strong enough to bring the man the relief that he wanted. What if he recalled what he had seen before his woman had pulled him back to the mundane? What if that woman was not proving distraction enough and he started snooping around? It was her duty, of course, to keep track of these things.

Best keep track of things out of view from the fairies, though. She dropped deeper into the water, watching the fairy glow fade above her. The dark silhouette of the boat loomed and she could still feel those sensations emanating from the man on board. Slow and rhythmic, gaining in momentum...she closed her eyes and let the feelings, like a torrent, envelop her.

Chapter Two

Raea watched her mermaid friend disappear. Good. Aliya had not asked why she'd been here, spying on the humans long after the man's carnal wish had been granted and he was well on his way toward the satisfaction he craved. Aliya seemed sweetly unaware of what was transpiring. With Kyne, however, Raea was not likely to be so lucky.

"You've been watching them go at it again, haven't you?" he asked as he came closer.

His accusation made Raea glow even pinker than usual. She spun around, turning her back to the boat. There was no way she could deny what was going on inside of it, though. The steady thumping of those nearby—and naked—humans played loudly against the silence of the lake. The heavy breathing of the couple inside could be heard through the open window, and sounds of passion echoed over the water. Anyone with half a brain could not help but know what the humans were doing. And realize that Raea had been watching.

Great. Of all the fairies in the Forbidden Realm, Kyne *would* be the one to show up now.

"You like watching, don't you?" he asked.

"No, I'm not *watching*," she replied, purposefully snippy. "I was *overseeing*. It is my job, after all."

He gave her a smile that was half sneer, half dazzle. "Funny, but it didn't look like overseeing. It looked like watching."

"Well, it wasn't. I was simply doing my job; granting wishes and making sure the humans are minding their own affairs."

"Yes, it seems like you keep them minding one affair after another. Seems to me you must like it."

Oh, but he irked her. He was always making snide comments like that, not quite accusing her of overstepping her bounds, but still…she felt uncomfortable around Kyne. And she really felt uncomfortable having this conversation right here, right now.

Based on human behavior she'd noted in the past—noted for purely academic purposes, of course—at any moment the sounds of rasping breath and shifting mattress would turn to animal moaning, guttural grunting, and maybe even a cry out to their deity. She recognized the pattern; the intensity of the man's passion, the woman's writhing, then the inevitable climax. Kyne was just in time for the fireworks.

She needed to end this discussion and get away from here. Now.

"What are you doing out here anyway, Kyne?" She huffed, barely remembering to use her Veiled voice to keep hidden from the humans, just one open window away.

"You mean a measly Summer Fairy shouldn't be rubbing elbows with such a grand and respected Wish Fairy?" he drawled, golden eyes flashing under their long lashes.

His wisping, flamelike wings stroked the air lethargically, but Raea knew better than to trust his calm exterior. Kyne was just as fiery on the inside as he appeared on the out—quick to react and burning with ambition. He was not one to ignore a perfect opportunity that might benefit his position. Somehow he'd managed to benefit himself right into a position working directly for the council, along with his usual summer duties, of course. He'd done that even with all the wild rumors that circulated about him.

Rumors that hinted Kyne might just have reason to know much more about humans and their lustful behaviors than normal fairies like Raea could ever dream of knowing.

"You know that's not what I meant," she said. "Did you follow me out here to spy on me for the Fairy Council?"

His wings flamed brighter and he fanned them with purpose. The whip-like tips cracked in the air.

"I'm not their puppet, despite what everyone says."

"Then you have no reason to hang around and pester me, do you?" she asked, happy to turn the focus on him.

He shrugged. "I thought maybe you wanted some pestering."

"What I want is to be left alone to do my job."

"Which is to watch humans have sex, apparently."

"So your job is to assume the worst about everyone?"

"And I'd love nothing better than to be proven wrong."

She doubted that. The council didn't want to be wrong, why would Kyne? He may not be their puppet, exactly, but with all those rumors swirling around about him he needed to keep on their good side. He had too much to lose. Raea knew better than to believe rumors—especially rumors like these—but Kyne didn't make them easy to disregard. His blistering aura and off-putting habit of turning up in unexpected places certainly didn't engender trust.

"I'm sorry if I seem unfriendly," she said, eager to get away from the boat and what was developing inside. "I'm just not used to the council sending lackeys to keep track of me."

"Who said the council sent me out here?"

"I don't see any flowers that need pollinating or dancing sunbeams you need to direct. Why else would a Summer Fairy be out here at night? Besides, I saw you going into the Council Hall again this evening. I know you're working with them."

"And you have some reason to dislike the Fairy Council?" he asked in his unfairylike deep voice.

She didn't bother to answer him. Why should she? It would just encourage him to launch an interrogation about the various wishes she granted. She really did not need that. What she needed was to leave this place, put these humans far away from them before things got…awkward.

"I simply think the Fairy Council needs to back off and give us more freedom."

"More freedom?" he asked, occupying what would be her flight path. "Is that what you really believe?"

Had that been the wrong answer? She made a halfhearted attempt to push him out of the way, but he didn't budge. Those bright, vapor-thin wings of his were stronger than they appeared. He hovered securely in place, blocking her. If she wanted to escape, she'd have to swoop down past the window on the boat—fully in view of the humans inside.

True, she was still in her usual stealth form, no bigger than the palm of one of those human's hands and fluttering in frequency unlikely to be detected by them, but an unsanctioned sighting was the last thing she needed on her record. The paperwork alone would take her forever.

"I need to get back to work now," she insisted.

"What do you mean about freedom? What would you do with more freedom?"

"I would do my job without need of you looking over my shoulder."

"Then you'd be free to find more horny humans so you can watch them go at it."

"I grant wishes that keep humans content," she declared, as if he needed a primer on what Wish Fairies did and why. "I can't help it that they're such raging animals and sex is what they all wish for."

"Only because you make it so easy for them to get it."

"That's what I do! I make sure they get what they wish for so everything stays neatly in balance, the Veil kept strong and secure."

"There must be hundreds of other wishes that could keep the humans safely in their place. Why are you so fixated on granting wishes like these? What these humans do with each other is vulgar and foul. Any true fairy should find it distasteful."

To punctuate his point the couple on the boat chose that very moment to break into the hoarse cries, gasping groans, and loud exclamations of pleasure she'd been afraid of. Raea cringed. Kyne's wings flapped more forcefully and he peered past her to see in through the boat window.

"No wonder you like to watch. By fate, they certainly do go at it. Beasts."

"If it bothers you so much, leave," she said. "Unless maybe it *doesn't* bother you."

"It bothers me. A lot."

"Fine. Then let's get out of here. Sometimes after they couple like that they're a little more open to seeing us, you know. I don't want to have to write up a Viewing Report tonight. My shift's almost done."

She shoved past him and took off. So what if her wings smacked him in the face? Maybe the other fairies thought Kyne and his light amber eyes, deep, dusky voice, and annoying little smirk were good company, but she didn't. Not right now.

He ought to be back over land changing a caterpillar into a butterfly, nurturing bees, or whatever it was those seasonal fairies did. He had no business out here interrupting her while she was working.

Instead he was following her. She stopped and whirled to face him. An angry poof of Fairy Dust escaped her and glittered in the air around them. Fortunately, the boat was a distance away now, so she wasn't overly worried about being spotted. Her wings turned the dust into a sparkling whirl.

"Leave me alone, Kyne. I can't…I can't think straight with you here."

"I'm just flying the same direction. What is it you plan to do out here that my presence makes you so nervous?"

"Nothing. I mean, I plan to do my job. I don't need a babysitter."

"You want me to leave you alone, to let you be free to go about your business?"

"Exactly," she said, relieved that he finally got it. "I'd like a little freedom."

A slow smile moved over his lips. The breeze turned warm and for just a moment Raea felt as if she couldn't quite catch her breath. Kyne's eyes held on to her in a manner she'd not known before, and she couldn't move away.

"What would you do, Raea, if you really were free? If you didn't have to dance to the whims of these humans, if you didn't have to worry about so-called babysitters from the council? How would you be *free* tonight?"

His question rolled over and over in her mind. What was he asking her? His words made no sense, yet something about them touched a place deep inside her. *Freedom.* What did it mean? She could hardly imagine a life where she didn't have to grant wishes, to be at the beck and call of frustrated humans, or under the watchful eye of the council.

What would she do if life wasn't that way? What would she do right now, right here, if she really were *free*?

The heat and the glow coming off Kyne felt like sunlight on her skin, familiar and enticing, as if she could let down her guard and let go of duty and responsibility. For a moment she almost thought about giving in to the feeling, finding out just what it was she *did* feel inside. A fish splashing below brought her back to reality, though, and she was glad for it.

If what Kyne was making her yearn for was freedom, then freedom was terrifying.

"Fairies *are* free," she said sharply. "We've managed the humans this way for centuries. Who are we to say things ought to be changed?"

"I bet you'd change things if you didn't enjoy granting these kinds of wishes so much," he said with a warm, smoky laugh.

Infuriating.

"Leave me alone, Kyne. You've sprouted too many daffodils or something."

"I don't do daffodils. I do *summer* flowers. If you weren't so busy helping humans copulate you might notice the difference."

"I grant wishes. It hardly matters to me whether they're for an hour of sweating and strange noises or for a new pair of shoes."

"I've never seen you peeking through windows to watch shoes, though."

She glared at him, wondering how he could be so beautiful and so annoying all at the same time.

"I grant the wishes they want, Kyne. I follow the Great Code; I keep our laws and protect the Veil. You can go back to the Fairy Council and tell them that. The Forbidden Realm is safe because I keep the humans distracted and content."

"And sex is the only thing that will do that for them? Surely they must have some higher qualities."

She shrugged. "Not that I've noticed. The males seem especially single-minded."

"You sound just like the council," he said, nearly hissing his words. "Humans are base, brutish creatures, they say, and we must dedicate our lives to managing them. Well, I say there's another way. There's got to be some other way."

"They're earth creatures, Kyne," she said gently, hoping to soothe the new fury that radiated off him. "They're not of the air, like us. Since their animal lust doesn't affect us, what does it matter what wishes we grant?"

"Are you sure their lust doesn't affect you?" he asked.

"Of course it doesn't."

He stroked the air for a moment, then pinned her with his eyes.

"Well then, I propose a bet. I say you have exaggerated the importance of this human need for passion. I say you grant the wishes you wish to grant. Humans are more sensible than you give them credit for being.

When not distracted by moonlight and Fairy Dust and your sordid curiosity, they would make a more rational wish."

"What? All right, Kyne, I'll take your bet. Now how shall I prove that you don't know the first thing about human sexuality?"

"A virgin."

"A what?"

"A virgin," he repeated, still smiling. "I take it you don't see too many of those."

"I most certainly do." She smiled back. "They are some of my most ardent wishers!"

"Then this should be a fair test."

"Don't be ridiculous. All it will prove is what I've been saying all along."

"Maybe, and maybe not. As long as you follow the rules. Are you sure you want to do this?"

"Oh, I wouldn't miss it for the world. Tell me your terms."

"It's simple," he said. "If you can find one of these virgins wishing for a partner, offer her this option: you'll grant any three wishes in the world—money, good health, popularity, whatever—or you'll grant her one night of physical coupling with the partner of her choice."

"You want me to be seen by a human? But that's…forbidden!"

"Is that your excuse for backing out?"

"You're just trying to catch me breaking the rules so you can go running to the council."

"Maybe I ought to do that now, since you obviously can't defend your claim that all these disgusting wishes are necessary…"

"They are! It keeps humans out of our Realm. Very well, I'll play your games. I'll give the virgin your option. I suppose you won't turn me in if I use some Forgetful Dust on her afterward? I won't put the Veil in danger of detection just for your stupid bet, Kyne."

"Agreed. Once the experiment is completed, your virgin can't have any memories of magic."

"It's a stupid bet, Kyne. You'll lose for sure."

"No, I wasn't finished with my terms. There's a stipulation. If your virgin takes the other wishes, she gets them free and clear. If she takes the animal passion, all she gets is twenty-four hours. After that, she is wiped from her partner's mind and she goes back to her normal, clueless life, dull and passionless as it was before."

"But…"

He gave a fiery grin and hovered over her.

"No buts, Raea. *This* is my wager, and I'll give you a whole week to accomplish it. Do you still say you've been granting the right wishes all along? Or are you ready to admit your motives are less than pure?"

"I'll take your stupid wager, Kyne. So what do I win when you lose?"

He thought for a moment, smiling that lopsided, sizzling grin that was really starting to bug her. His golden eyes studied her carefully and his skin was taking on a bronze shimmer under the starry sky. Was the night air getting chilly? It must be, although Raea could never remember being affected by weather temperatures before. But something was making her skin prickle.

"If you win, I'll give the Fairy Council a glowing report about you," he said.

"You ought to do that anyway."

"You're pretty sure of yourself."

"I can afford to be," she said, giving him a heated grin of her own.

"And you're not the least bit worried what I'll expect on the off chance I might win?"

"All right, tell me. What would you expect me to do if—by some miracle—you win?"

"Grant a wish, of course."

By the Skies, what was he up to, asking for wishes? Not that it mattered, of course. She was going to win this without half trying. Kyne and his stupid wager were doomed.

She nodded and held up her hand. "All right, the bet's on, Kyne."

He smiled and laced his fingers through hers in the familiar Fairy Covenant. It didn't feel like the usual covenant grip, though. She wasn't sure what it was, but darned if more strange prickly sensations didn't start out in her fingers and travel through her arm. To her surprise, in seconds her whole body was tingling and warm.

Well, so much for blaming it on the cold night air. Parts of her were positively burning. What was wrong with her tonight? She pulled her hand away quickly, throwing off her balance so that she tottered a bit.

"I need to get back to work," she said, fluttering madly to regain equilibrium. "I'll see you later. When I watch you deliver my glowing report to the council."

"Or perhaps when you're granting my wish," he said, searing her with a smoldering leer.

"Enjoy the rest of your night, Kyne," she said as she spun and headed off in whatever direction would take her away from him.

"I've enjoyed it so far," he called back behind her.

She ignored him and shook her head, trying to be rid of the feel of his eyes on her. Was there something off with the moon phases, perhaps? She felt strange.

She waited until she was nearly to shore, then glanced backward to watch Kyne dart off, his form so much more solid and defined beneath his orange glow than she was accustomed to seeing. He was not like other fairies. Maybe that explained why she had such a hard time figuring him out. Kyne was somehow…different.

Not that she was prepared to speculate on what that difference might be. Her mind was just running away from her, that was all. She was not about to let herself wonder if maybe, just maybe, those rumors about him could possibly bear any truth. They were ridiculous, after all. No one could possibly take any of them seriously.

Kyne—it was said—was half human.

About the Author

Serena Gilley grew up reading fantasy and fairy tales, and believing there was a distinct possibility that both of them were real. Somewhere. Even all these years later, Serena's belief in magic and mystery hasn't diminished. In fact, she is living out her own happily-ever-after with a handsome prince in a beautiful castle, taming dragons and granting wishes every day. Okay, so the prince is a regular guy, the dragons are really just teenagers, and the wishes she grants are as spectacular as frozen pizza on Friday night, but it's a fantasy world just the same.

Learn more at:
SerenaGilley.com
Twitter @SerenaGilley13
Facebook.com/SerenaGilleyAuthor